W9-BWZ-826

INSTANT KARMA

INSTANT KARMA

MARISSA MEYER

FEIWEL AND FRIENDS
NEW YORK

A FEIWEL AND FRIENDS BOOK
An imprint of Macmillan Publishing Group, LLC
120 Broadway, New York, NY 10271

INSTANT KARMA. Copyright © 2020 by Rampion Books.
All rights reserved. Printed in the United States of America.

Our books may be purchased in bulk for promotional, educational, or business use.
Please contact your local bookseller or the Macmillan Corporate and Premium Sales
Department at (800) 221-7945 ext. 5442 or by email at
MacmillanSpecialMarkets@macmillan.com.

Library of Congress Control Number: 2020908578
ISBN 978-1-250-61881-8 (hardcover) / ISBN 978-1-250-80135-7 (special edition)
978-1-250-78657-9 (special edition) / ISBN 978-1-250-61882-5 (ebook)

Book design by Rich Deas and Michelle McMillian
Feiwel and Friends logo designed by Filomena Tuosto

First edition, 2020
fiercereads.com
1 3 5 7 9 10 8 6 4 2

For Dad,
who always filled our home with music

INSTANT KARMA

ONE

Quint Erickson is late.

Again.

I shouldn't be surprised. I'm not surprised. I'd be more surprised if he was actually on time for once. But really? Today? Of *all the days*?

I'm simmering in my seat, my fingers drumming against the presentation board that's folded up on our lab table. My attention is divided between watching the clock over the classroom door and silently repeating the words I've been memorizing all week.

Our beaches and coastal waters are home to some remarkable species. Fish and mammals and sea turtles and—

"Sharks," says Maya Livingstone from the front of the room, "have been severely mistreated by Hollywood over the decades. They are not the monsters that humans have made them out to be!"

"Plus," adds her lab partner, Ezra Kent, "who's eating who here? I mean, did you guys know people actually *eat* shark?"

Maya glances at him, frowning. "Mostly just their fins. To be clear."

"Right! They make soup out of them," says Ezra. "Shark fin soup is, like, a super delicacy, because they're, like, chewy and crunchy *at the same time*. Wrap your head around that! But I mean, I would totally try it."

Some of our peers pretend to gag in disgust, even though it's obvious Ezra is trying to get this exact reaction. Most people call him EZ, which I used to think might be a reference to numerous sexual escapades, but now I think it's just because he has a reputation for being a jokester. Teachers at our school have learned not to seat him and Quint together.

"Anyway," says Maya, trying to bring their talk back on point. She goes on about the horrible methods by which hunters catch the sharks and cut off their fins, then release them back to the water. Without their fins, they sink to the bottom of the ocean and either suffocate or get eaten alive by other predators.

The whole class grimaces.

"And then they turn them into soup!" Ezra adds, just in case anyone missed that part before.

Another minute goes by. I bite down on the inside of my cheek, trying to calm the nerves twisting inside of me. The same frustrated rant begins to repeat in my head, for the eight millionth time this year.

Quint. Erickson. Is. The. Worst.

I even reminded him yesterday. Remember, Quint, big presentation tomorrow. You're bringing the report. You're supposed to help me with the introduction. So, please, for the love of all things good and righteous in this world, this one time, don't be late.

His response?

A shrug.

I'm a busy guy, Prudence. But I'll do my best.

Right. Because he has so much to do before 8:30 a.m. on a Tuesday.

I know I can handle the introduction on my own. I've been rehearsing without him, after all. But he's supposed to bring our papers. The papers that the rest of the class can then stare at while we talk. The papers that will keep their bored, disinterested eyes off *me*.

The class starts to applaud half-heartedly and I snap back to attention. I bring my hands together for one, two claps, before dropping them to the table. Maya and Ezra gather up their presentation board. I glance at Jude, in the first row, and though I can only see the back of his head, I know his gaze hasn't left Maya since she stood up, and won't leave her until she's sitting back down and he has no choice but to either look away or risk drawing attention to the staring. I love my brother dearly, but his crush on Maya Livingstone has been

2

well-documented since the fifth grade, and—if I'm being honest—has started to seem a little bit hopeless.

He has my sympathy. He really does. She is *Maya Livingstone*, after all. Pretty much the whole sophomore class has a crush on her. But I also know my brother. He will never have the guts to actually ask her out.

Hence, hopeless.

Poor guy.

But, back to poor *me*. Maya and Ezra are dropping into their seats and there's still no sign of Quint. No sign of the papers that he was supposed to bring with him.

In an act of desperation, I fish my red lipstick from my bag and quickly apply a new layer, just in case it's started to wear off since I put it on before class. I don't like to wear a lot of makeup, but a bold lipstick is an instant boost to my confidence. It's my armor. My weapon.

You can do this, I tell myself. *You don't need Quint.*

My heart has started to warble inside my chest. My breaths are quickening. I tuck the tube back into my bag and snatch up my index cards. I don't think I'll need them. I've practiced so many times, I talk about habitats and environmentalism in my sleep. But having them with me will help calm my jittery nerves.

At least, I think they will. I hope they will.

Until I have the sudden fear that my sweating palms might make the ink bleed, rendering it unreadable, and my nerves kick up into high gear again.

"That brings us to our last presentation of the year," says Mr. Chavez, giving me a look that's almost sympathetic. "Sorry, Prudence. We've delayed as long as we can. Maybe Quint will join us before you've finished."

I force a smile. "It's fine. I planned on doing most of the talking anyway."

It is so not fine. But nothing can be done about it now.

I stand up slowly, tuck the notes into my pocket, and pick up the presentation board and the tote bag I brought full of bonus materials. My hands are shaking. I pause just long enough to fully exhale, to squeeze my eyes tight, to repeat the refrain that I always tell myself when I have to speak or perform in front of people.

It's just ten minutes of your life, Prudence, and then it will be over and you can move on. Just ten minutes. You can do this.

Opening my eyes, I square my shoulders and make my way to the front of the class.

It's not that I'm terrible at public speaking. I actually think I'm quite good at it, once I get started. I know how to project my voice so everyone can hear me. I always practice ad nauseum beforehand so I don't trip over my words, and I work hard to be lively and entertaining.

It's just the moments before I begin that are dreadful. I'm always convinced that something will go wrong. My mind will go blank and I'll forget everything. I'll start to sweat. I'll turn bright red. I'll pass out.

But once I get started I'm usually okay. I just have to start . . . and then, before I know it, the whole thing is over. And I'll hear what I always hear: *Wow, Prudence. You seem so natural up there. You're such a great presenter. Nicely done.*

Words to soothe my frantic soul.

At least, my teachers usually say stuff like that. The rest of my fellow students rarely bother to pay much attention.

Which is perfectly fine with me.

It takes me a few seconds to get set up, balancing the presentation board on the whiteboard tray and tucking my surprise bag of goodies off to the side. Then I pull over the small rolling table with the model I brought in before class started, still draped with a blue sheet.

With my index cards in one hand, I grab the stick that Mr. Chavez uses to point out details on his PowerPoint slides with the other.

I smile at my peers.

I try to catch Jude's eye, but he's doodling in his sketchbook and not open to incoming messages.

Gee whiz, Bro. Thanks for the support.

The rest of the class stares back at me, practically comatose with boredom.

My stomach twists.

Just begin.

It's only ten minutes.

You're going to be okay.

I take in a breath.

"I was going to have supplementary materials for you guys to look at," I start. My voice pitches high and I pause to clear my throat before continuing, "So you could follow along with the presentation. But Quint was supposed to bring them and . . . he's not here." My teeth grind. I want to call out the unfairness of this. Everyone else's partner showed up! But mine simply couldn't be bothered.

"Oh well," I continue, swiping the stick dramatically through the air. "Here we go anyway."

I pace in front of the presentation board and exhale a clipped breath.

Just begin.

Beaming, I launch into my prepared introduction.

"One thing we've learned in regard to marine biology, thanks to the exceptional tutelage of Mr. Chavez"—I pause to point enthusiastically at our teacher. He points back at me, with markedly less emotion—"is that we are so lucky here in Fortuna Beach to have access to such thriving marine life. Our beaches and coastal waters are home to many remarkable species. Fish and mammals and sea turtles and sharks—"

"Sharks *are* fish," Maya says.

I tense and shoot her a glare. Nothing can throw off a well-rehearsed presentation like an unnecessary interruption.

Interruptions are the enemy.

I reaffix my smile. I'm tempted to start over, but I force myself to get back on track. *Fish and mammals and sea turtles and sharks* . . . "Straight down to the rich ecosystems of plankton and plant life found in Orange Bay. These resources are a gift, and it is our responsibility not only to enjoy them, but to protect them. Which is why, for our semester project, Quint and I decided to focus our efforts on"—I pause for dramatic effect—"marine conservation by way of ecotourism!"

With a flourish, I take hold of the blue fabric and whisk it off the display, revealing my handcrafted model of Main Street, Fortuna Beach's tourism hot spot that runs parallel to the beach and boardwalk.

I can't resist glancing around to see my classmates' reactions. A few in the front rows are craning their heads to see the model, but a fair number are staring blankly out the sun-streaming windows or trying to discreetly text with their phones hidden beneath the lab tables.

Mr. Chavez, at least, looks intrigued as he studies the model. And Jude has looked up, knowing firsthand the long, tireless hours I've put into crafting this presentation. He catches my eye and gives a subtle yet encouraging thumbs-up.

I move behind the table so I can stand over the diorama and point out the most notable features. My adrenaline has kicked in and I no longer feel like I'm going to crumple into a ball of panic. Now I'm energized. "Our new central tourism hub will be the Orange Bay Resort and Spa, which will cater to high-end clientele. Visitors who appreciate luxury, yearn for adventure, but—gosh darn it!"—I cheekily snap my fingers—"also care about protecting our environment." I tap the stick against the high-rise building. "Featuring recycled building materials and numerous water-conservation and energy-saving features, this resort will be the talk of the town. But our tourists don't just come here to sleep. They come here to explore. Which is why Fortuna Beach needs new electric bike rental stations positioned at both ends of the boardwalk"—I thunk the stick down on the little bike stands—"and electric boat rentals that jet off right from the resort's private dock." *Thunk.* "But what's really going to draw in the clientele, what's really going to set Fortuna Beach apart as a must-see destination for our eco-conscious travelers—"

The classroom door swings open, banging hard against the wall.

I jump.

"Sorry, Mr. C!" comes a voice that makes the hair prickle on the back of my neck. My surprise vanishes, replaced with barely restrained rage.

My knuckles clench around the pointer as I slide my gaze toward Quint Erickson. He strolls between the tables and accepts a high five from Ezra, their usual daily greeting.

Part of me wishes he would have stopped by the front first and offered *me* a high five in greeting. It would have been a perfect opportunity to smack him with the stick.

I grit my teeth, scowling at the back of his head as he reaches our shared lab table in the back row and drops his backpack on top of it. The zipper is as loud as a jet engine. He starts to whistle—*whistle*—as he digs through the chaos of papers and books and pens and nine months of accumulated junk he keeps in that thing.

I wait. Someone in the class coughs. From the corner of my eye, I can see Jude beginning to fidget, uncomfortable on my behalf. Except, for some reason, I'm not uncomfortable. Normally, an interruption as enormous as this would turn me into a flustered mess, but right now I'm too busy strangling the pointer stick and pretending it's Quint's neck instead. I could stand here all day, awkward silence or not, waiting for Quint to realize what a disruption he's caused.

But, to my endless frustration, Quint seems blissfully unaware. Of my annoyance. Of stopping me right in the middle of *our* report. Of the awkward silence. I'm not sure he even knows what *awkward* means.

"Aha!" he announces victoriously, pulling a neon-green folder from the bag. Even from here I can see that one corner is bent. He opens it and starts taking out the reports. I can't tell how many pages. Three or four, probably double-sided, because who wastes paper on a report about environmentalism?

At least, he'd better have made it double-sided.

Quint hands out the reports—stapled pages for our classmates, and a three-ring binder for Mr. Chavez. He doesn't do the efficient take-one-and-pass-it-on method that I would have done, possibly because he is the most inefficient human being on the planet. No, he walks up and down the aisles, handing them out one by one. Grinning. Being grinned at. He could be a politician, wooing the masses with that casual saunter, that laid-back smile. One of the girls even flutters her lashes at him as she takes the report, mumbling a flirtatious *Thanks, Quint.*

My knuckles have gone white around the stick. I imagine Quint stubbing his toe on one of the table legs or slipping on spilled lab chemicals and twisting an ankle. Or no—even better—I imagine that in his tardiness and haste, he grabbed the wrong folder and has just passed out thirty-two copies of an impassioned love letter he wrote to our principal, Mrs. Jenkins. Even *he* couldn't be immune to that sort of embarrassment, could he?

None of this happens, of course. My dreams of cosmic justice never do come true. But my nerves have calmed somewhat by the time Quint makes his way to the front of the classroom and finally deigns to look at me. The change is instant, the defensiveness that comes over him, the lifting of his chin, the darkening of his eyes as we prepare for battle. Something tells me he's been bracing himself for this moment since he entered the room. No wonder he took his sweet time handing out the papers.

I try to smile, but it feels more like a snarl. "So glad you could join us."

His jaw twitches. "Wouldn't miss it. Partner." His eyes swoop toward the model and, for a moment, there's a hint of surprise on his face. He might even be impressed.

As he well should be. Impressed, and also ashamed that this is the first time he's seeing it.

"Nice model," he mutters, taking his place on the opposite side of my miniature Main Street. "I see you've left out the rehabilitation center I suggested, but—"

"Maybe if I'd had more help, I could have catered to gratuitous requests."

He lets out a low groan. "Caring for the animals who get injured as a result of tourism and consumerism isn't—"

Mr. Chavez loudly coughs into his fist, interrupting the spat. He gives us both a weary look. "Two more days, guys. You have to suffer each other's company literally for just two more days. Can we please get through this presentation without any bloodshed?"

"Of course, Mr. Chavez," I say, in unison with Quint's "Sorry, Mr. C."

I glance at him. "Shall I continue, or do you have something to contribute?"

Quint feigns a bow, flourishing one hand in my direction. "The stage is yours," he says, before adding under his breath, "Not that you'd share it anyway."

A few of our classmates in the front row hear him and snicker. Oh yes, he's hysterical. Next time, *you* try working with him and see how funny he is.

I bare my teeth again.

But when I turn back to the presentation board, my mind goes blank.

Where was I?

Oh no. *Oh no.*

This is it. My worst nightmare. I knew this would happen. I knew I would forget.

And I know it's all Quint's fault.

Panic floods my system as I pull out the notecards and fumble with them single-handed. *Resort and spa . . . electric bike rentals . . .* A few cards slip to the floor. My face is suddenly as hot as a stove top burner.

Quint stoops down and picks up the dropped cards. I grab them away from him, my heart racing. I can feel the class's eyes boring into me.

I hate Quint. His complete disregard for anyone but himself. His refusal to ever show up on time. His inability to do anything useful.

"I could also say something?" says Quint.

"I've got this!" I snap back at him.

"All right, fine." He lifts his hands protectively. "Just saying. This is my presentation, too, you know."

Right. Because he did *so* much to help us prepare for it.

"What's really going to set Fortuna Beach apart?" Jude whispers. I go still and look at him, as grateful for him as I am irritated with Quint. Jude flashes me another thumbs-up, and maybe our twin telepathy is working today, because I'm sure I can hear his encouraging words. *You've got this, Pru. Just relax.*

My anxiety ebbs. For the millionth time I wonder why Mr. Chavez had to torture us with assigned lab partners when Jude and I would have been such an awesome team. Sophomore year would have been a walk in the park if it hadn't been for marine biology and Quint Erickson.

TWO

hanks, I mouth back to Jude, setting down my notes. All I needed was that reminder, and the words come flooding back to me. I continue with my speech, trying my best to ignore Quint's presence. At least some of our peers have turned their attention to the papers he passed out, so not *everyone* is still staring. "As I was saying, what's really going to draw in a whole new variety of enthusiastic eco-conscious travelers is our phenomenal array of events and adventures. Visitors can go to the bottom of the ocean aboard private-party submarines. There will be kayaking tours to Adelai Island where you can help tag, track, and even name your own seal. And, my personal favorite, we'll host weekly raging beach parties."

Some of the glassy-eyed stares of my classmates come into focus at this. Ezra even lets out a hoot. He *would,* of course.

Bolstered, I forge ahead. "That's right. Fortuna Beach will soon be famous for its regular beachy shindigs, where you can dine on sustainably sourced seafood and all-organic hors d'oeuvres while hobnobbing with other eco-conscious individuals like yourself. The best part? Everyone at the party receives a garbage bag and a grabber upon arrival, and at the end of the evening, after they've filled that bag with litter they've collected off our beaches, they can trade it in for a reusable tote overflowing with hand-selected gifts. Things like . . ." I set down the stick and reach for the bag on the floor. "A BPA-free aluminum water bottle!" I take out the bottle and toss it into the crowd. Joseph barely catches it, startled. "Take-them-anywhere bamboo utensils! A journal made from recycled materials! Shampoo bars with plastic-free packaging!" I throw each of the gifts out. My peers are definitely paying attention now.

Once all the gifts are gone, I ball up the tote bag and launch it toward Mr. Chavez, but it only makes it halfway. Ezra plucks it from the air instead. People are starting to notice that each of the gift items has been branded with the new logo and slogan I came up with.

FORTUNA BEACH: FRIENDLY ENVIRONMENT, ENVIRONMENTALLY FRIENDLY!

"These ideas and many more are outlined in detail in our report," I say, gesturing at one of the stapled papers on the nearest lab table. "At least, I'm assuming they are. I haven't actually seen it, as something tells me it was finished about ten minutes before class this morning." I smile sweetly at Quint.

His expression is tight. Annoyed, but also a little smug. "I guess you'll never know."

This comment sends a jolt of uncertainty down my spine, which I'm sure is exactly what he intended. The paper has my name on it, too, after all. He knows it'll be driving me bonkers to know what's in it, and if it's any good.

"Before we finish," I say, turning back to the class, "we want to take a moment to say thank you to Mr. Chavez for teaching us so much about this amazing corner of the world we live in, and all the incredible sea life and eco-systems right in our backyard. I don't know about the rest of you, but I know *I* want to be a part of the solution, to ensure that we protect and maintain our oceans for our children and grandchildren. And luckily for us, as I think we've managed to prove today: By *going green,* Fortuna Beach can *bring in the green!*" I rub my fingers together, pretending to be holding a handful of cash. I'd told Quint about how I was going to conclude my speech. He's supposed to say it with me, but of course, he doesn't. He can't even be bothered to hold up the imaginary money. "Thank you for listening."

The class begins to clap, but Quint steps forward and holds up a hand. "If I could add one thing."

I wilt. "Do you have to?"

He flashes me a smirk, before turning his back on me. "Sustainability and tourism don't usually go hand-in-hand. Airplanes create a lot of pollution, and people tend to produce a lot more garbage when they travel as opposed to when they stay at home. That said, tourism is good for the local economy and, well, it's not going anywhere. We want Fortuna Beach to have a reputation for taking care of its visitors, sure, but also its wildlife."

I sigh. Didn't I basically say all this already?

"If you read the report in front of you," Quint continues, "which I'm sure none of you will, except Mr. Chavez, you'll see that one of our major initiatives would be to establish the Fortuna Beach Sea Animal Rescue Center as a top tourist destination."

It takes all my willpower not to roll my eyes. He's been harping on this rehabilitation center idea all year. But who wants to spend their vacation looking at malnourished dolphins in sad little pools, when they can go swimming with dolphins in the actual bay?

"For people to understand the effect their actions have on the environment, they need to see firsthand the consequences of those actions, which is why we . . ." He pauses. "Why *I* believe that any ecotourism plans should focus on education and volunteerism. The report will explain all that in more detail. Thank you."

He glances at me. We share a look of mutual disdain.

But—that's it. It's over. This awful, soul-sucking project is finally finished. I'm free.

"Thank you, Mr. Erickson, Miss Barnett." Mr. Chavez is flipping through Quint's report and I can't help but wonder if he's included *any* of my ideas. The resort, the bikes, the beach parties? "I think it's fairly obvious, but just for clarification, could you each tell me your contributions to this project?"

"I made the model," I say, "and the presentation board, and designed and ordered the eco-friendly merchandise. I would also say that I was the project manager throughout."

Quint snorts.

Mr. Chavez raises an eyebrow. "You disagree, Mr. Erickson?"

"Oh no," he says with a vehement head shake. "She definitely managed. Soooo much management."

I stiffen. I can feel the outburst on my tongue. *Someone had to! It's not like you were going to step up and get any of this done!* But before it comes out, Mr. Chavez asks, "And you wrote the report?"

"Yes, sir," says Quint. "And provided the photographs."

Our teacher makes a sound like this is interesting information, but my lip curls in dismay. Provided the photographs? I'm sorry, but a second grader can cut photos out of *National Geographic* magazine and glue them to a poster board.

"Great. Thank you both."

We start to head to our lab table, each of us taking a different aisle to get there, but Mr. Chavez stops me.

"Prudence? Let's leave the pointer stick at the front, shall we? Would hate for Mr. Erickson to be impaled when we are so very close to the end of the year."

The class laughs as I walk the stick back to the front and set it on the whiteboard tray, trying not to feel sheepish. With my hands free, I pick up the model and carry it back to the table with me.

Quint has his face cupped in one hand, covering his mouth, watching me as I approach. Or, watching the model. I wish I could read him. I wish I could see guilt there, knowing that he did nothing to help with this part of the project. Or at least shame for being late, on the most important day of the year, leaving me to fend for myself.

I'd even love to see embarrassment as he realizes that my part of the project totally smoked his. Or perhaps some show of appreciation for my carrying our so-called partnership this whole year.

I set down the model and take my seat. Our stools are both shoved to the far ends of the table, an instinct to keep as much space between us as possible. My right thigh has been bruised for months from being smashed up against the table leg.

Quint tears his gaze away from the model. "I thought we decided not to do the boat tours to Adelai, since they could be disruptive to the elephant seal population."

I keep my attention glued to Mr. Chavez as he takes his place at the front of the room. "You want people to care about elephant seals, then you have to show them elephant seals. And not half-dead ones being bottle-fed on a medical table."

He opens his mouth and I can feel his response brewing. I ready myself to shoot down whatever inane comment he's about to make. My fury is building again. I want to scream. *You couldn't be here? Just. This. Once?*

But Quint stops himself and gives his head a shake, so I keep my anger bottled in, too.

We fall silent, the model resting between us, one of the closed and stapled reports within reach of my hand, though I refuse to take it. I can see the cover, though. At least he kept the title we agreed on: "Conservation through Eco-tourism in Fortuna Beach," a report by Prudence Barnett and Quint Erickson. Marine Biology, Mr. Chavez. Underneath our names is a gut-wrenchingly sad photograph of a sea animal, maybe an otter or a sea lion or even a seal, I can never tell them apart. It's wrapped in fishing line, tangled up like a mummy, with lacerations cut deep into its throat and flippers. Its black eyes are looking at the camera with the most tragic expression I think I've ever seen.

I swallow. It's effective for stirring up emotions, I'll give him that.

"I see you put my name first," I say. I'm not sure what makes me say it. I'm not sure what makes me say half the things I do around Quint. There's something about him that makes it physically impossible for me to keep my mouth shut. It's like there's always one more bullet in my ammunition, and I can't help but take every shot.

"Believe it or not, I know how to put things in alphabetical order," he mutters back. "I did pass kindergarten, after all."

"Shockingly," I fire back.

He sighs.

Mr. Chavez finishes making notes on his clipboard and smiles at the class. "Thank you all for a fantastic group of presentations. I'm impressed with the hard work and creativity I've seen this year. I'll have your grades handed out tomorrow. Please go ahead and pass your final lab reports up to the front."

Chairs scrape and papers shuffle as my classmates start digging through their backpacks. I look expectantly at Quint.

He looks back at me, confused.

I raise an eyebrow.

His eyes widen. "Oh!" He pulls his backpack closer and starts rifling through the chaos inside. "I forgot all about it."

Friggin' figures.

"You forgot to bring it?" I say. "Or you forgot to *do* it?"

He pauses with a grimace. "Both?"

I roll my eyes and he lifts a hand, his momentary embarrassment already evaporating. "You don't need to say it."

"Say what?" I respond, even as a flurry of words like *incompetent* and *lazy* and *helpless* are circling through my thoughts.

"I'll talk to Mr. Chavez," he says. "I'll tell him it's my mistake and that I can email him the report tonight—"

"Don't bother." I open my biology folder, where the final completed lab report rests right on top, neatly typed and featuring a bonus environmental toxicology pie chart. I lean over the table and pass it up the aisle.

When I look back, Quint looks . . . angry?

"What?" I ask.

He gestures toward the paper, which has disappeared into the stack of assignments. "You didn't trust me to do it?"

I turn to face him. "And I was right not to."

"What happened to being a team? Maybe instead of doing it yourself, you could have reminded me. I would have done it."

"It is not my job to remind you to do your homework. Or to get to class on time, for that matter."

"I was—"

I cut him off, throwing my hands up in exasperation. "Whatever. It doesn't matter. Let's just be grateful this *partnership* is finally over."

He makes a noise in the back of his throat, and though I think he's agreeing with me, it still makes me flush with annoyance. I've carried this team all year long, doing far more than my share of the work. As far as I'm concerned, I'm the best thing that could have happened to him.

Mr. Chavez takes the last of the papers as they're passed to the front. "Now, I know tomorrow is your very last day of sophomore year, and you're all eager to get on with your vacation, but tonight is still a school night, which means, here's your homework assignment." The class releases a unanimous groan as he uncaps a green marker and starts scrawling across the whiteboard. "I know, I know. But just think. This could be the last chance I get to impart you with my superior wisdom. Give me my moment, would you?"

I take out a pen and begin copying the assignment down into my notebook. Quint doesn't.

When the bell rings, he's the first one out the door.

THREE

I'm not opposed to homework, generally speaking," says Jude, idly flipping through the pages of his marine biology textbook. "But homework on the second-to-last day of school? That's the mark of a tyrannical overlord."

"Oh, stop whining," says Ari from behind her menu. She spends a great deal of time studying the menu each time we come in, even though we always end up ordering the same things. "At least you get a summer break. Our teachers gave us detailed reading lists and assignment plans to 'keep us busy' over vacation. July is Greek mythology month. Hooray."

Jude and I both give her dismayed looks. The three of us are sitting in a corner booth at Encanto, our favorite spot on Main Street. The restaurant is a bit of a tourist trap, right off the main thoroughfare—you can even see traces of the beach through the front windows—but it only ever gets crowded on the weekends, making it the ideal quiet hangout after school. In part because the fusion of Mexican and Puerto Rican food is mind-blowingly good. And in part because Carlos, the owner, gives us free sodas and as much chips and salsa as we can eat without ever complaining about us taking up valuable booth space. To be honest, I think he likes having us around, even if we only ever order food between three and six o'clock so we can get the half-off appetizer specials.

"What?" Ari asks, finally noticing the looks Jude and I are giving her.

"I would study Greek mythology over plankton any day of the week," says Jude, gesturing at an illustration in the textbook.

Ari huffs in that signature you-guys-don't-get-it way. Which, admittedly, we don't. The three of us have been arguing about which is worse—attending the prestigious St. Agnes Prep or navigating our Fortuna Beach High—ever since we met nearly four years ago. It's a typical grass-is-greener situation. Jude and I are forever jealous of the seemingly obscure topics and lesson plans that Ari complains about. Things like "How the Transcontinental Spice Trade Changed History," or "The Influence of Paganism on Modern Religious Traditions." Whereas Ari yearns for the teen-movie normalcy that comes with low-quality cafeteria lunches and not having to wear a uniform every day.

Which, I mean, fair enough.

One thing Ari can't argue, though, is that St. Agnes has a music program that is far superior to anything she'd find in the public schools. If it wasn't for their dedicated classes on music theory and composition, I suspect Ari would have begged her parents to let her transfer.

Jude and I go back to our papers while Ari turns her attention to two women who are sharing a dessert at the next table. Ari has her notebook in front of her and is wearing her trying-to-come-up-with-a-rhyme-to-make-this-song-lyric-work face. I imagine a ballad about coconut pudding and early love. Pretty much all of Ari's songs are about early love. That, or they're about the tumultuous angst of love-gone-wrong. Never anything in between. Though I guess that could be said for almost every song.

I read the assignment again, thinking that maybe it will inspire an idea. "Two hundred fifty words on what sort of underwater adaptation would be useful in our aboveground environment." It's not a hard assignment. I should have been done an hour ago. But after the last few nights spent finishing the ecotourism project, my brain feels like it's been put through a meat grinder.

"That's it! Basking shark!" says Jude, thumping a finger down on his book. The image shows a positively horrific shark, its enormous mouth gaping open, revealing not huge, sharp teeth, but what appears to be its skeleton or rib cage or something extending back into its body. It reminds me of the scene when Pinocchio gets swallowed by the whale. "It swims through the water, scooping up whatever bits of food come its way."

"And that would be useful to you, how?" I ask.

"Efficiency. Whatever food I passed by could just get swept down my throat. I'd never have to chew or stop to eat." He pauses, a thoughtful look coming into his eye. "Actually, that would make a great dungeon monster."

"That would make a disgusting monster," I say.

He shrugs and jots down a note in the sketchbook that is always at his elbow. "You're the one who's obsessed with time management."

He does have a point. I grunt and flip through my textbook for the sixth time while Jude takes our shared laptop and pulls it toward himself. Rather than opening a new document, he merely deletes my name at the top and replaces it with his before he starts to type.

"Here we go, little worker bees," says Carlos, arriving with a basket of tortilla chips, guacamole, and two kinds of salsa. A sweet guava-based salsa for me and Jude, and an extra-fiery pseudo-masochistic why-would-anyone-do-this-to-themselves? spicy one for Ari. "Your school isn't out yet?"

"Tomorrow's our last day," says Jude. "Ari's got out last week."

"Does that mean I'll be seeing more of you, or less?"

"More," Ari answers, beaming at him. "We're pretty much going to live here this summer, if that's okay with you." Ari has had a schoolgirl crush on Carlos since we started coming here. Which might seem a little weird, given that he's got to be close to forty, except he looks an awful lot like a young Antonio Banderas. That, plus the Puerto Rican accent, plus the man can cook. Who can blame a girl for being a little smitten?

"You three are always welcome," he says. "But try not to take too much advantage of my free-refill policy, yeah?"

We thank him for the chips as he saunters off to tend to another table.

Jude sits back and dusts off his hands. "Done."

I look up from a photo of an anglerfish. "What? Already?"

"It's only two hundred and fifty words. And this assignment isn't going to count for anything. Trust me, Pru, this is just the tyrannical overlord's way of testing our loyalty. Don't overthink it."

I scowl. He and I both know it's impossible for me not to overthink.

"That's a good one," says Ari, gesturing with her chip toward the book. A speck of salsa lands on the corner of the page. "Oops, sorry."

I wipe off the splotch with my napkin. "I do not want to be an anglerfish."

"The assignment isn't to say what you would *be*," says Jude, "just what sort of adaptation could be useful."

"You'd have a built-in flashlight," adds Ari. "That would come in handy."

I hum thoughtfully. It's not terrible. I could work in something about being a shining light in dark times, which may be a bit poetic for a science paper, but still. "Okay, fine," I say, pulling the laptop back in front of me. I save Jude's document before starting my own.

I've just finished my first paragraph when there's a commotion at the front of the restaurant. I glance over to see a woman wheeling in a handcart stacked with speakers, electronic equipment, a small television, a stack of thick three-ring binders, and bundles of cords.

"You made it!" says Carlos from behind the bar, loud enough that suddenly everyone is looking at the woman. She pauses, blinking into the dim light, letting her eyes adjust from the bright afternoon sun. Carlos rushes over to her and takes the cart. "I'll take that. I thought we'd set up right over here."

"Oh, thank you," she says, pushing back a long fringe of hair that's been dyed candy-apple red. Other than the bangs that nearly cover her eyes, her hair is tied into a hasty topknot, showing her natural blond growing out at the roots. She's wearing clothes that demand attention: worn and faded cowboy boots; dark jeans that are as much shredded holes as they are denim; a burgundy velvet tank top; enough jewelry to sink a small boat. It's a far cry from the flip-flops and surf shorts that usually populate Main Street this time of year.

She's also beautiful. Stunning, actually. But it's kind of hard to tell given the coating of black eyeliner and smudged purple lipstick. If she's local, then we would definitely have noticed her around, but I'm sure I've never seen her before.

"How's this?" says Carlos, ignoring the fact that most of his customers are staring at the two of them.

"Perfect. Lovely," says the woman with a bit of a southern accent. Carlos often hosts live music on the weekends, and they're standing on the little platform where the bands perform. She takes a second to inspect the area before pointing at the wall. "Is that the only outlet?"

"There's another behind here." Carlos pulls a busing station away from the corner.

"Excellent." The woman spends some time turning in a circle, inspecting the TVs that hang throughout the restaurant, almost always showing sports. "Yeah, great. This will work. Nice place you've got."

"Thanks. You want help setting up, or . . . ?"

"Naw, I've got it. Not my first time at the rodeo." She shoos him away.

"All right, fine." Carlos takes a step back. "Can I get you a drink?"

"Oh. Uh . . ." She thinks about it for a few seconds. "Shirley Temple?"

Carlos laughs. "Sure thing."

He returns to the bar, and the woman starts moving tables around and setting up the equipment she brought. After a few minutes, she grabs the stack of binders and approaches the nearest table. *Our* table.

"Well, don't you all just look like some upstanding Fortuna Beach youth?" she says, taking in our textbooks and computers.

"What's going on?" says Ari, nodding toward all the stuff she brought.

"Weekly karaoke night!" says the woman. "Well, this is actually the first, but we're hoping it'll become a weekly thing."

Karaoke? I'm immediately overcome with visions of crooning old people and squawking middle-aged ladies and a whole lot of drunks who can't carry a tune and . . . oh no. So much for our quiet study session. At least the school year is pretty much over.

"I'm Trish Roxby and I'll be your host," she continues. Noticing our less-than-enthused expressions, she juts her thumb toward the bar. "Y'all didn't notice the signs? Carlos told me he's been advertising for a couple weeks now."

I glance toward the bar. It takes a minute, but then I notice. On the chalkboard by the door, above the listing of daily specials, in messy handwriting, someone has scrawled the words: JOIN US FOR WEEKLY KARAOKE, EVERY TUESDAY AT 6:00, STARTING IN JUNE.

"So, think you'll be joining in tonight?" asks Trish.

"No," Jude and I say in unison.

Ari just bites her lower lip, eyeing the binder.

Trish laughs. "It's not as scary as it sounds. I promise, it can be a whole lotta fun. Besides, girls like to be serenaded, you know."

Realizing she's speaking to *him,* Jude immediately starts to squirm. "Uh. No. This is my twin sister." He tilts his head toward me, then gestures between himself and Ari. "And we're not . . ." He trails off.

"Really? Twin sister?" says Trish, ignoring whatever he and Ari aren't. She looks between me and Jude for a moment, before slowly nodding. "Yeah, okay. I can see it now."

She's lying. No one ever believes that Jude and I are related, much less twins. We look nothing alike. He's six foot one and skinny like our dad. I'm five five and curvy like Mom. (Our grandma loves to joke that I took all of Jude's "baby fat" when we were in the womb and kept it for myself. I never found that joke particularly funny when we were kids, and it has not improved with age. Insert eye-roll emoji here.)

Jude is blond and super pale. Like, vampirical pale. His skin burns within thirty seconds of stepping into the sunlight, which makes living in Southern California not completely ideal. I, on the other hand, am brunette and will be sporting a halfway-decent tan by the end of June. Jude has cheekbones. I've got dimples. Jude has full-on mood lips that make him look a bit like an Abercrombie model, though he *hates* when I say that. And me? Well, at least I have my lipstick.

Trish clears her throat awkwardly. "So, you ever done karaoke before?"

"No," Ari answers. "Though I've thought about it."

Jude and I exchange looks because, actually, we have done karaoke before. Lots of times. Growing up, our parents used to take us to this gastropub that had family-friendly karaoke on the first Sunday of each month. We'd belt out Beatles song after Beatles song, and my dad would always end "his set," as he called it, with "Dear Prudence," then call us all up together for "Hey Jude." By the end of it, the entire restaurant would be singing—*Naaaa na na . . . nananana!* Even Penny would join in, even though she was only two or three years old and probably had no idea what was going on. It was sort of magical.

A little nostalgic part of me lights up to think of Dad's slightly off-key rendition of "Penny Lane" or Mom's over-the-top attempts at "Hey Bulldog."

But then there was one time, when I couldn't have been more than ten or eleven years old, when some drunk in the audience shouted—*Maybe that kid should spend less time singing and more time doing sit-ups!*

We all knew who he was talking about. And, well, the magic was pretty much ruined after that.

Come to think of it, that might have been the start of my public-speaking anxiety, and that all-encompassing fear that everyone will be watching me, criticizing me, waiting for me to embarrass myself.

"Well, you kids just think it over," says Trish, setting the binder down next to the chips. She takes a pen and some slips of paper from a pocket and sets them down, too. "If you find a song you wanna sing, just write it down here and pass it up to me, all right? And if the song you want isn't in the book, you let me know. Sometimes I can find it online." She winks at us, then wanders off to the next table.

We all spend a few seconds staring at the binder like it's a poisonous snake.

"Yeah," Jude mutters, and starts tossing his things into his backpack. "That's not going to happen."

I feel exactly the same way. You couldn't pay me to get up and sing in front of a bunch of strangers. Or non-strangers, for that matter. Fortuna Beach isn't a big town, and it's impossible to go anywhere without running into someone you sort of know. Even now, glancing around, I notice my mom's hairstylist at the bar, and a manager from the corner grocery store at one of the small tables.

Ari, however, is still staring at the binder. Her eyes spark with yearning.

I've heard Ari sing. She isn't bad. At least, I know she can stay in key. Besides that, she wants to be a songwriter. Has dreamed of being a songwriter since she was a kid. And we all know that to have any sort of success at all, there will be times when she's probably going to have to sing.

"You should give it a try," I say, nudging the binder toward her.

She flinches. "I don't know. What would I even sing?"

"Like, any song recorded in the past hundred years?" says Jude.

She gives him a look, even though it's clear his comment pleases her. Ari loves music. All music. She's a walking Wikipedia of everything from 1930s jazz to eighties punk to modern indie. In fact, we probably never would have met if it wasn't for her obsession. My parents own a record store a block from Main Street, Ventures Vinyl, named after a popular surf-rock band from the sixties. Ari started shopping there when we were in middle school. The allowance her parents gave her was way more than I ever got, and every month she would bring in the money she'd saved and buy as many records as she could afford.

My parents adore Ari. They joke that she's their sixth child. They like to say that Ari has single-handedly kept them in business these past few years, which would be charming if I wasn't afraid that it might actually be close to the truth.

"We could duet?" says Ari, looking at me hopefully.

I bite back the instinctual and impassioned *no*, and instead gesture hopelessly at my textbook. "Sorry. I'm still trying to finish this paper."

She frowns. "Jude wrote his in ten minutes. Come on. Maybe a Beatles song?" I'm not sure if she suggests this because of how much I love the Beatles, or because they're the only band for which I could be trusted to know most of the words. Growing up around the record store, my siblings and I have been inundated with a variety of music over the years, but no one, in my parents' eyes, will ever compete with the Beatles. They even named each of their five kids after a Beatles song—"Hey Jude," "Dear Prudence," "Lucy in the Sky with Diamonds," "Penny Lane," and "Eleanor Rigby."

Realizing that Ari is still waiting for a response, I sigh. "Maybe. I don't know. I need to finish this." As she continues flipping through the songbook, I try to return my focus to the paper.

"A Shirley Temple sounds pretty good," says Jude. "Anyone else want one?"

"A little girly, don't you think?" I tease.

He shrugs, sliding out of the booth. "I'm comfortable enough in my masculinity."

"I want your cherry!" Ari calls after him.

"Hey, that's my brother you're hitting on."

Jude pauses, looks at me, then Ari, then proceeds to blush bright red.

She and I both burst into laughter. Jude shakes his head and walks toward the bar. I cup my hands over my mouth to shout after him, "Yes, get some for us, too!"

He waves without looking to let me know he heard me.

We're not supposed to cross the rail that divides the twenty-one-and-over area from the rest of the restaurant, so Jude stops at the invisible barrier to give the bartender our order.

I'm one more paragraph into the paper when Jude returns, carrying three tall glasses filled with fizzing pink soda and extra cherries in each one. Without asking, Ari takes a spoon and scoops out the cherries from both mine and Jude's and plops them into her own glass.

"Hello, everyone, and welcome to our very first weekly karaoke night!" says Carlos, speaking into a microphone that Trish brought with her. "I'm Carlos and I run this joint. I really appreciate your business and hope you all have a fun time tonight. Don't be shy. We're all friends here, so come on up and give it your best! With that, I'm pleased to introduce our karaoke host, Trish Roxby."

There's a smattering of applause as Trish takes the mic and Carlos starts to head back to the kitchen.

"Whoa, whoa, aren't you gonna sing?" Trish says.

Carlos turns around, eyes wide with horror. He chuckles lightly. "Maybe next week?"

"I'll hold you to that," says Trish.

"I said *maybe*," says Carlos, retreating some more.

Trish grins at the restaurant patrons. "Hello, folks, I'm so excited to be here tonight. I know nobody ever likes to go first, so I'll get this party started. Please do bring up those slips of paper and let me know what *you* wanna sing tonight, otherwise you'll be stuck listening to me for the next three hours."

She punches something into her machine and a guitar riff blares through the speakers—Joan Jett's "I Love Rock and Roll."

I try not to groan, but . . . come on. How am I supposed to focus on finishing this paper with *that* playing in the background? This is a restaurant, not a rock concert.

"So, uh, this is unexpected," says Jude.

"I know," says Ari, nodding appreciatively. "She's really good."

"Not that," says Jude, elbowing me in the side. "Pru, look. It's *Quint*."

FOUR

y head bolts up. For a second I'm sure Jude is playing a practical joke on me. But no—there he is. Quint Erickson, loitering next to the SEAT YOURSELF sign just inside the doorway. He's with a girl I don't recognize—Asian, petite, with her hair tied in two messy buns behind her ears. She's wearing denim shorts and a faded T-shirt that has a picture of Bigfoot on it with the words HIDE-AND-SEEK WORLD CHAMPION printed underneath.

Unlike Quint, who is watching Trish sing her heart out, the girl is engrossed by something on her phone.

"Whoa," says Ari, leaning over the table and lowering her voice, even though there's no way anyone can hear us over Trish Roxby's guttural demand to put another coin in the jukebox, baby. "That's Quint? *The* Quint?"

I frown. "What do you mean, *the* Quint?"

"What? He's all you've talked about this year."

A laugh escapes me, harsh and humorless. "He is not!"

"He kind of is," says Jude. "I don't know which of us is more excited for summer to start. You, so you won't have to deal with him anymore, or me, so I don't have to listen to you complain about him."

"He's cuter than I imagined," says Ari.

"Oh yeah, he's a stud," says Jude. "Everyone loves Quint."

"Only because his ridiculousness appeals to the lowest common denominator of society."

Jude snorts.

"Besides"—I lower my voice—"he's not that attractive. Those eyebrows."

"What do you have against his eyebrows?" says Ari, looking at me as if maybe I should be ashamed for suggesting such a thing.

"Please. They're huge," I say. "Plus, his head is a weird shape. It's, like . . . square."

"Biased much?" mutters Ari, shooting me a teasing look that crawls straight beneath my skin.

"I'm just saying."

I won't relent on this point. It's true that Quint is not *un*attractive. I know this. Anyone with eyes knows this. But there's no elegance to his features. He has boring, nondescript, basic brown eyes, and while I'm sure he must have eyelashes, they've never once caught my attention. And with his perpetual suntan, short wavy hair, and that idiotic grin of his, he pretty much looks like every other surfboard-loving boy in town. Which is to say, completely forgettable.

I put my fingers back on the keyboard, refusing to let Quint or karaoke or anything else derail my focus. This is the last homework assignment of sophomore year. I can do this.

"Hey, Quint!" yells Jude, his hand shooting up into the air in greeting.

My jaw falls. "You traitor!"

Jude turns to me, grimacing. "Sorry, Sis. He caught my eye. I panicked."

I take in a slow breath through my nostrils and dare to glance toward the front of the restaurant. Sure enough, Quint and his friend are making their way toward us. Quint is grinning, as per usual. He's like one of those dopey puppies that are incapable of realizing when they're surrounded by cat people. They just assume that everyone is happy to see them, all the time.

"Jude, what's up?" says Quint. His attention swoops to me and he takes in my textbook and computer, his smile hardening just a tiny bit. "Prudence. Hard at work, as always."

"Quality work doesn't just appear out of thin air," I say.

He snaps his fingers. "You know, I used to think that, but after a year of working with you, I'm beginning to wonder."

My eyes narrow. "Sure was nice running into you." My sarcasm is so thick

I almost choke on it. I look back down at the screen. It takes me a second to remember what the assignment was.

"Quint," says Jude, "this is our friend Araceli. Araceli, Quint."

"Hey," says Quint. I look up through my lashes as they bump fists. With Quint initiating, it seems like the smoothest, most natural greeting in the world, even though I don't think I've ever seen Ari fist-bump anyone before. "Nice to meet you, Araceli. Cool name. You don't go to our school, do you?"

"No. I go to St. Agnes," she answers. "And you can just call me Ari."

I make a face, but my head is still lowered so nobody can see it.

"And, oh, this is Morgan. She goes to the community college in Turtle Cove." Quint gestures to the girl, who has lingered a few steps away and is watching the stage with something akin to dismay. When Quint says her name, her focus swivels to us and she produces an uncomfortable smile.

"Nice to meet you," she says, polite but lukewarm.

There's a round of awkward *heys* and *hellos*, but Morgan's attention has already returned to the stage, where someone is singing a country song, crooning about cold beer and fried chicken.

"Morgan says the food here is great," says Quint. "She wants me to try . . . what are they again? Ton . . . Tol . . ." He looks questioningly at Morgan.

"Tostones," she says, returning her attention to her phone. She looks angry as she punches the screen with her thumbs, and I have a vision of some nasty text war happening between her and a boyfriend.

"They're really good," says Jude.

Quint gestures at the karaoke setup. "I wasn't expecting dinner to come with free entertainment."

"Neither were we," I mutter.

"It's a new thing the restaurant is trying." Ari pushes the song binder toward the edge of the table. "Think you'll sing?"

Quint laughs, sounding almost self-deprecating. "Naw. I'll have mercy on the poor people of the boardwalk. Would hate to scare away the tourists so early in the season."

"Everyone thinks they're terrible at singing," says Ari, "but very few people are really as bad as they think they are."

Quint cocks his head to one side and looks from Ari to me. "I'm sorry. You're friends with *her*?"

"Excuse me?" I say. "What does that mean?"

He shrugs. "I'm just so used to your criticism, it's strange to have someone give me the benefit of the doubt."

"Hey, look!" yells Jude. "It's Carlos! Just in time to prevent a painfully awkward moment."

Carlos passes by, carrying a tray of empty glasses. "Just checking on my favorite table. Are you guys joining them? Can I get you some drinks?"

"Uh . . ." Quint glances at Morgan. "Sure. A drink sounds good. What are these?" He gestures to our matching reddish beverages.

"Shirley Temples," says Ari.

Quint looks confused. "That's an actress, right?"

Ari perks up. "Have you never had one? I mean, yes, she was an actress, a kid star. But the drink . . . You should try one. Think joy in a glass."

"Think diabetes and a severe lack of dignity," mutters Morgan, still engrossed in her texting rant.

Quint casts her a look that's almost amused, tinged with something like pity. It annoys me that I recognize this look. That it's been directed at me almost every day since the start of the school year.

"I just realized how much you and Prudence would probably get along," he says.

Morgan glances up, confused, and I know she's wondering who *Prudence* is, but instead of asking, she says, "Why did that sound like an insult?"

Quint shakes his head. "Long story." He nods at Carlos. "We'll take two Shirley Temples."

"No. Pass," says Morgan. "I'll have an iced coffee with coconut milk."

"Sure thing," says Carlos. "You'll be joining my regulars here?"

Quint eyes our booth. It's a big booth—could probably fit up to eight people if they wanted to feel cozy. We could definitely fit two more.

But his gaze lands on me and the icy glare I'm sending his way and he miraculously gets the hint. "Naw, we're actually going to . . ." He turns. The restaurant is filling fast, but there's a two-top table right by the stage that's just been abandoned, half a basket of tortilla chips and some crumpled napkins left behind. "Is that table free?"

"Sure is. I'll get it bused for you." Carlos gestures at the songbook. "Don't be shy, kids. We need more singers. Get those songs put up, all right? I'm looking at you, Pru."

Quint makes a sound in his throat, something between disbelief and amusement. It makes my skin prickle. "Funny," he says as Carlos heads toward the bar.

"What's funny?" I ask.

"The idea of you singing karaoke."

"I can sing," I say defensively, before feeling compelled to add, "Sort of."

"I'm sure you can," Quint says, smiling—because when is he not smiling? "It's just hard to imagine you loosening up enough to do it."

Loosening up.

He doesn't know it—or maybe he does—but Quint has just dug his thumb into a very sore spot. Maybe it comes with being a perfectionist. Maybe it's because I'm a rule follower, an overachiever, the sort of person who would rather host a study group than go to a kegger. Maybe it's because my parents gave me the unfortunate name of *Prudence.*

I do not like being told to loosen up.

I can relax. I can have fun. Quint Erickson doesn't know me.

Jude, though, knows me all too well. He's watching me, his expression dark with concern. Then he turns to Quint and says, maybe too loudly, "Actually, Pru and I used to do karaoke all the time when we were kids. She used to do a brilliant rendition of 'Yellow Submarine.'"

"Really?" says Quint, surprised. He's looking at Jude, but then his gaze slides to me, and I can tell he has no idea how much my blood is boiling right now. "I'd pay money to see that."

"How much?" I spit.

He pauses, like he's not sure whether I'm joking or not.

A waitress appears and gestures to the small table, now cleared of old dishes, sporting two glasses of ice water. "Your table is ready."

"Thanks," says Quint. He seems relieved to have an escape from this conversation. I'm ecstatic. "Good to see you, Jude. Nice to meet you . . . Ari, right?" His focus returns to me. "Guess I'll see you in class."

"Don't forget." I thump the textbook. "Two hundred and fifty words on your preferred aquatic adaptation."

"Right. Thanks for the reminder. See? Was that so hard?"

"Just seems so pointless," I say sweetly, "since we both know you'll still be writing it five minutes before class starts. If you write it at all."

His smile stays firmly affixed, but I can see it's becoming weary. "Always a pleasure, Prudence." He gives me a one-fingered salute before he and Morgan head off to their table.

"Ugh," I groan. "You know he's going to forget. And the worst part? Mr. Chavez will give him a pass, like he always does. It's—"

"Infuriating," Ari and Jude parrot together.

I huff. "Well, it is." I wake up the laptop. It takes me a minute to remember what I was writing about.

"Don't kill me for saying this," says Ari, "but he didn't seem all that bad?"

"He's not," says Jude. "Terrible lab partner, maybe, but still a nice guy."

"Terrible is the understatement of the year. I honestly don't know what I did to deserve such karmic punishment."

"Oh!" Ari's eyes brighten. "That gives me an idea." She pulls the songbook toward her and begins flipping pages.

Jude and I look at each other, but don't ask what song she's looking for. Jude grabs his drink and finishes it off in one long swig. "I need to get going. I'm supposed to meet the guys at seven to start planning our next campaign." His brow furrows as he looks at Ari. "Do you really think you'll sing? Because I could probably stay, if you need moral support."

She waves a hand at him. "I'll be fine. Go explore your goblin-infested dungeons or whatever it is."

"Kobold-infested, actually," says Jude, sliding from the booth. "And I've got some great ideas for booby traps in this campaign, too. Plus, you know, there will probably be a dragon."

"Can never have too many dragons," says Ari, still scanning the songbook.

I consider asking what a kobold is, but I'm not sure I have the brain space for one of Jude's over-enthused explanations, so I just smile. "It's not called Dungeons and Dragons for nothing."

"They have it!" says Ari, swiveling the book around and pointing. "I know you know this song."

I'm expecting her to have picked something by the Beatles, but instead she's pointing at the title of a song from John Lennon's solo career: "Instant Karma! (We All Shine On)."

"Oh yeah, that's a good one," says Jude, leaning over the table to see. "You could pull it off, Pru."

"I'm not singing."

Ari and Jude both raise their eyebrows at me.

"What?"

Ari shrugs and pulls the book away again. "I just thought maybe you'd want to prove Quint wrong."

I lift an angry finger. "I have nothing to prove to him."

"Of course you don't," says Jude, slinging his backpack over one shoulder. "But there's nothing wrong with showing people that you can do more than get straight As. That you can actually, you know"—he takes a step back, maybe worried that I'm going to smack him, and whispers—"have fun."

I glare at him. "I do know how to have fun."

"*I* know that," says Jude. "But even you have to admit that it's a pretty well-guarded secret."

FIVE

Jude leaves, and I try to focus on my paper. I only have a few more sentences to wrap it up, but it's slow-going. Jude's words are in my head and, to my endless annoyance, so are Quint's. *Loosen up. Have fun.*

I can feel Ari giving me the occasional uncertain look. She's the most empathetic person I've ever known and can always tell when someone is upset. But she also knows that I'll talk when I'm ready, and to nudge won't usually get her anywhere. So we work in silence—me finishing up the paper, and her jotting words down in her notebook. Well, *silence* is a relative term, given the various levels of singing prowess that continue to assail our ears. Some of the singers are actually pretty good. One guy performs the newest Bruno Mars single, then one of the women from the next table does a jaw-dropping Cher impersonation. But other performers are less than stellar. There's a lot of mumbling and discomfort and staring awkwardly at the screen projecting the words.

I have a theory about karaoke, one I developed way back during our family karaoke nights. No one in the audience is expecting the next Beyoncé to show up onstage, but if you're going to get up there, you have to at least try to be entertaining. If you have a great singing voice, awesome. Belt it out. But if you don't, then you have to make up for it somehow. Dance. Smile. Make eye contact with the audience. Look like you're having fun, even if you're terrified, and it will carry your performance a lot further than you'd think.

"There," I say, shutting the computer. "Last assignment of the year. Check." I take a swig of my Shirley Temple, which I've been neglecting. It tastes a little watered down, but the rush of syrupy cherry deliciousness feels like a well-deserved reward.

I've barely been paying attention to Ari, but I can tell she's gotten some new ideas. I'm about to ask her if she's working on something new, or perfecting something old, when I hear her name being called.

"Next up: Araceli Escalante!"

We both look up, startled. Trish Roxby is looking at us, holding the microphone. "With a name like that, I think we've got our next superstar coming to the stage. Come on up, Araceli!"

Ari gives me a nervous look.

"When did you put your name up there?" I ask.

"When you were working," she answers. "Here I go."

She slides out of the booth and approaches the small stage, her movements stiff and robotic. She hasn't even taken the mic yet and I'm already cringing for her. Now I'm wishing I'd told her about my karaoke theory.

Most of the singers have chosen to stand during their song, though there is a stool by the monitor for those who want it. Ari takes the stool, pushing it closer to the mic stand. I think it's the wrong choice—you have more energy when you stand, more movement—but I know it's a comfort and right now she's probably just wanting to get through this without her knees buckling under her.

Her song pops up on the television screen attached to the back wall: "A Kiss to Build a Dream On" by Louis Armstrong. It's not a song I'm familiar with, though that's not saying much.

Ari closes her eyes as a jazzy piano melody rings out. She keeps them closed as she begins to sing. Her voice is sweet, almost fragile, and the song is so very *her*. Romantic. Dreamy. Hopeful. I can feel Ari's emotions coming through as she sings, and it's clear she loves this song. The words, the melody, they affect her, and she's holding her feelings in a bubble, precariously close to bursting.

It's lovely, listening to her, and I'm proud of her for having the courage to go up there, and to sing not for a reaction from the audience, but with her actual heart.

For some reason, my eyes dart to Quint. He's turned away from me, watching Ari, while his friend is still scrolling through her phone. I notice that Quint's hair is messy in the back, like he hasn't bothered to comb it today.

Then Quint turns his head. His expression is sour. For a second I think he's turning to look at me, like maybe he could feel me staring, *judging*. But no, he's watching the booth next to ours. I crane my neck to see two college-age guys, one downing the last dregs of a pint of beer. The other cups his hands around his mouth and calls out, "Quit it with the boring jazz crap!"

My jaw drops. *Excuse me?*

His friends laugh, and the one with the beer raises his empty glass into the air. "Come on over here. I'll give you a kiss to dream about."

The other guy adds, "Maybe then we can play some real music!"

No way. They're *heckling* her. What is wrong with people?

I return my attention to Ari. She's still singing, but her eyes are open now and her voice has taken on an uncertain waver. Her cheeks are flaming red.

I think of how much this moment probably means to her, and my fist clenches under the table at how those jerks just tainted it.

I look back at the boys' smug expressions. I imagine one of them choking on a tortilla chip. The other spilling salsa down his Tommy Bahama shirt. Honestly, universe, if you've ever—

Something small flies toward the booth, smacking the first guy in the eye. He yelps and clamps a palm over his face. "What the hell?" he roars. He reaches for a napkin, but doesn't realize the edge of his own beer glass is on top of it. He pulls. The glass tips and falls, sending beer flowing over the table's edge and into both of their laps. There's a flurry of curses as they try to move away from the growing puddle on their seats.

Ari lets out a barking laugh. The chords of the song continue to float around her, but she's stopped singing. Her mortification is gone, replaced with gratitude, and for a second I think it was me. *Did I just . . . ?*

But then Ari looks at Quint, and I see his shoulders trembling with restrained laughter. He's swirling a spoon around his glass, the ice clinking against the sides.

The boys in the next booth are still looking around, vainly rubbing their drenched pants with the shoddy paper napkins. One of them finds the projectile and holds it up. A cherry.

Carlos bustles over to them, trying to act the part of the concerned restaurant owner, though there's a coldness in his expression that makes me think he probably heard their heckling earlier. He gives them a tight apology and slaps a stack of napkins on the table.

He does not offer to replace the lost beer.

Ari finishes the song and scurries from the stage like it's on fire. She plops back into our booth with a sigh of relief. "Was it really terrible?"

"No, of course not!" I say, and I mean it. "You were great. Ignore those buffoons."

She scoots closer to me in the booth. "Did you see Quint throw that cherry at them?"

I nod. As much as I don't want to, I have no choice but to admit, "That was pretty awesome." I roll my eyes dramatically. "I suppose he might have some redeeming qualities. But trust me. They are few and far between."

We stay to listen for a couple more acts. It's a lot of contemporary music that I know I've heard, but couldn't tell you who the artist is. Ariana Grande? Taylor Swift? Then someone gets up and does a Queen song, so at least I know who they are.

"Next up, for your listening pleasure," says Trish, checking something on the karaoke machine, "please welcome to the stage . . . Prudence!"

Ari and I both swivel our attention to her, but I just as quickly turn back to Ari. "Did you put my name up there?"

"No!" she says vehemently, lifting her hands. "I wouldn't! Not without your permission, I swear."

I growl, but not at Ari. I believe her. It's not something she would do.

Could there be another Prudence in the bar? What are the chances of that? I have yet to meet another person with my name, and no one is going up onstage.

"Jude must have sneaked it in before he left," I say.

"You don't have to," says Ari. "Tell her you changed your mind. Or that someone put your name up there without asking."

My eye catches on Quint's. He's looking over his shoulder, surprised. Curious.

My pulse is starting to race. Ari is right. I don't have to go up there. I didn't put my name in. I didn't agree to this.

My palms become slick. I haven't even left the booth yet and already it feels like people's eyes are on me. Waiting. Judging. It's probably just my imagination, but knowing that doesn't keep my throat from tightening.

"Prudence?" Trish asks, searching the audience. "You out there?"

"Do you want me to tell her you've changed your mind?" asks Ari.

I shake my head. "No. No, it's fine. It's just a song. I'll do it." I exhale sharply and slide out of the booth.

"Wait!"

I look back at Ari. She leans forward and reaches her thumb for the corner of my mouth, rubbing hard for a second. "Your lipstick was smeared," she says, settling back into the booth. She gives me an encouraging nod. "All better. You look great."

"Thanks, Ari."

I clear my throat and approach the stage, making a point not to make eye contact with the goons in the booth. Or Quint, for that matter. I tell myself that I'm not nervous. That I'm not positively terrified.

It's only four minutes of your life. You can do this.

But please let Jude have picked a decent song . . .

Trish sets the microphone stand in front of me and I look at the monitor, displaying the song choice. *Whew.* Okay. Not bad. Jude took Ari's suggestion and has signed me up to sing the John Lennon song, one I love and definitely know by heart.

I lick my lips and shake out my shoulders, trying to get into a performance mindset. I'm no great singer, I know that. But what I lack in natural-born talent, I can make up for with stage presence. I am Prudence Barnett. I don't believe in mediocrity or lame attempts, and that includes belting out a karaoke song in a dimly lit tourist trap off Main Street. I will smile. I will work the crowd. I might even dance. I figure, my singing may not win me any awards, but that doesn't mean I can't have fun.

Loosen up. Right, Quint? Let's see you get on this stage and loosen up.

The first chords of "Instant Karma!" blare from the speakers. I don't need the monitor feeding me the lyrics. I flip my hair and start to sing. *"Instant karma's gonna get you!"*

Ari whoops encouragingly. I wink at her and can feel myself getting into the song. My hips sway. My heart races, with adrenaline as much as nerves. My fingers spread out like fireworks. Jazz hands. The music builds and I do my best to channel John Lennon and the passion he brought to his music. My free arm stretches to the sky, then drops toward the crowd, my finger pointing, search-ing. *"Who on earth do you think you are? A superstar? Right—you are!"* I'm trying to give a shout-out to Carlos, but I can't find him, and soon I find myself pointing at Quint instead. I'm startled to find him watching me with marked attention. He's smiling, but it's in a stunned, almost bewildered way.

Pulse skittering, I swivel my attention back to Ari, who is dancing inside the booth, swaying her arms in the air.

I take imaginary drumsticks into my hand and hit the cymbals in time with the drum solo that launches me into the chorus. I'm feeling almost giddy as I sing. *"Well, we all shine on, like the moon . . . and the stars . . . and the sun!"*

The song blurs into familiar chords and beloved lyrics. I roll my shoulders. Stretch my fingers to the sky. Belt my way through to the end. I don't dare look at Quint again, but I can feel his gaze on me, and despite my determination not to let his presence unnerve me, I am unnerved. Which just serves to make me even *more* determined to appear *un*nerved. Because it would have been one thing if he'd been outright ignoring me, or cringing with embarrassment on my behalf.

But no. In that split second when I caught his eyes, there'd been something unexpected there. I don't think it was simple amusement, or even sheer surprise, though I definitely think I surprised him. There was something more than that. Something almost . . . mesmerized.

I'm overthinking it. I need to stop thinking at all and focus on the song, but I'm on autopilot as the lyrics repeat and start to fade. *Like the moon and the stars and the sun . . .*

As the song comes to an end, I take an elaborate bow, flourishing my hand toward Quint like how he fake bowed to me in biology class that morning.

And yet, Quint's whooping cheer is the loudest in the bar. "Killed it, Pru!"

Heat climbs up my neck, burning across my cheeks. Not embarrassment, exactly. More like a rush, a glow, from his unwanted, unsolicited, totally unnecessary approval.

As I step away from the microphone, I can't keep from glancing at him. I'm still energized from the song, a smile stretched across my lips. He meets my eyes and for a moment—just a moment—I think, okay, maybe he's halfway decent. Maybe we could be friends, even. As long as we never have to work together again.

To my surprise, Quint lifts his glass, as if toasting me. Which is when I realize I'm staring.

The moment ends. The weird connection snaps. I pry my attention away from him as I head back to the booth.

Ari claps enthusiastically. "You were so good!" she says, with, I can't help but notice, a hearty sense of disbelief. "The whole place was mesmerized!"

Her words remind me of the look Quint was giving me during the song and I flush deeper. "I actually enjoyed that more than I thought I would."

She raises her hand for a high five. I'm still a few feet away, passing by the booth where the hecklers had been sitting, though they've since left.

I move to accept the high five.

I've forgotten about the spilled drink.

My heel slips forward. I gasp, throwing my weight to try to regain balance. Too late. My arms flail out to the sides. My feet kick out from underneath me.

I go down hard.

SIX

rince is playing over the speakers, but no one is singing. The back of my head feels like it was just hit with a two-by-four. The pounding inside my skull is in perfect rhythm with the drumbeat of "Raspberry Beret."

It takes three separate tries to pry my eyes open, only to have them accosted by neon tequila advertisements and a TV on the wall showing one of those weird karaoke videos from the eighties that don't have anything to do with the song. I flinch and squeeze my eyes shut again. Ari is saying something about calling an ambulance. Carlos is talking, too, sounding confident and calm, but I can't understand what he's saying.

"It's all right, Pru," says another voice, a deeper voice. One that sounds an awful lot like . . . Quint?

But Quint's never called me *Pru* before.

A hand slides under the back of my head. Fingers in my hair. My eyes squint open again and the light is less intense this time.

Quint Erickson is kneeling beside me, watching my face with an expression that is weirdly intense, especially with those dark eyebrows stooped over his gaze. It's so different from his usual goofy grin that it startles a painful laugh from me.

He blinks. "Prudence? Are you okay?"

The pounding in my head gets worse. I stop laughing. "Fine. I'm fine. Just . . . this song . . ."

He glances up at the monitor, as if he'd forgotten there was music playing at all.

"Doesn't make sense," I continue. "I've never found a raspberry beret at a secondhand store. Have you?" I grit my teeth at another onslaught of head-throbbing. I should probably stop talking.

Quint's frown has deepened. "You might have a concussion."

"No." I groan. "Maybe. Ow."

He helps me sit up.

Ari is on my other side. Trish Roxby is nearby, too, biting her thumbnail, along with a waitress who is holding a glass of water that I think is probably meant for me. Even Quint's friend, Morgan, has finally put down her cell phone and is looking at me like she halfway cares.

"I'm fine," I say. The words don't slur. At least, I don't think they do. It gives me confidence, and I repeat them, more emphatically: "I'm *fine*."

Ari holds two fingers in front of my face. "How many fingers am I holding up?"

I scowl at her. "Twelve," I deadpan. The throbbing in the back of my head is starting to subside, which is when I realize that Quint is still holding me, his fingers tangled in my hair.

Alarm surges through me and I shove his arm away. "I'm fine."

Quint looks startled, but not particularly hurt.

"Your friend is right," says Carlos. "You might have a concussion. We should—"

"He's not my friend," I say. It's a bit of a reflex. I've started now, so I keep going, lifting an explanatory finger. "Plus, I've seen the way he handles lab results. Forgive me if I don't have a whole lot of confidence in Dr. Erickson's diagnosis."

"Well, she sounds okay," says Ari.

I reach for the ledge of a table and use it to pull myself up. As soon as I'm on my feet, a wave of dizziness passes over me. I steady myself on the table, squeezing my eyes shut.

My free hand feels around the back of my head. There's a lump, but at least I'm not bleeding.

"Prudence," says Quint, still hovering too close. "This could be serious."

I round on him so fast that stars flicker in and out of my vision, cutting off my hasty response. "Oh, *now* you decide to take something seriously?" I say as the stars begin to dissipate.

He takes a step back, deflates, then rubs the bridge of his nose. "Why do I bother?"

"Why *do* you bother? I don't need your help."

His expression hardens and he lifts his hands in surrender. "Clearly," he says. Rather than turn away, though, he reaches past me, suddenly so close that I press my hip against the edge of the table with a rush of panic. Quint grabs the stack of napkins left behind by those jerks and turns away without acknowledging, or perhaps even noticing, my reaction. He throws the napkins onto the spilled drink that I slipped on and starts sopping it up, pushing the soggy paper around with the toe of his sneaker.

"Pru?" Ari touches my elbow. "Really, should we call for an ambulance? Or I could drive you to the hospital?"

I sigh. "Please, don't. I'm not discombobulated or anything. My head hurts a little, but that's all. I just need a Tylenol."

"If she can correctly use words like *discombobulated*, she's probably okay," says Trish, and I can tell she's trying to be helpful. "You thirsty, sweetheart?"

She holds the water toward me, but I shake my head. "No. Thanks. I think I'm going to head home, though." I turn to Ari. "My bike is outside, but . . ."

"I'll give you a ride," she says, without letting me finish. She ducks back into our booth, gathering our things.

"Thanks," I murmur. I feel like I should say something, do something. Carlos and Trish, Quint and Morgan, are all still standing there, watching me. Well, Quint is throwing the wet napkins in a wastebasket and avoiding meeting my eye, but the rest of them are staring, expectant. Am I supposed to give them hugs or something?

Carlos saves me by dropping a hand onto my shoulder. "Will you call me tomorrow, or drop by after school or something? Let me know you're all right?"

"Yeah, of course," I say. "Um . . . the karaoke thing . . ." I look past him to Trish. "It's actually kind of a cool idea. I hope you keep doing it."

"Every Tuesday at six," says Trish. "That's the plan, at least."

I follow Ari toward the back door. I make a point of keeping my eyes away from Quint, but I sense him there all the same. The twinge in my stomach feels something like guilt. He'd just been trying to help. I probably shouldn't have snapped at him.

But he had all year to help. Too little, too late.

Ari pushes open the back door, landing us in the gravel parking lot behind Encanto. The sun has just set and there's a refreshing breeze coming in off the ocean, full of salt and familiarity. I feel instantly revived, despite the dull ache at the back of my skull.

Ari drives a turquoise-blue station wagon from the sixties—a beast of a car that was a gift from her parents on her sixteenth birthday. She tries not to make a big deal out of it, but her family has money. Her mom is one of the most successful realtors in the county and has made a small fortune selling fancy vacation homes to very wealthy people. So when Ari starts swooning over something like a completely impractical vintage car, it's not a huge surprise that one shows up in their driveway. Which might be enough to make some teenagers act entitled, but her abuela, who lives with them, seems to keep tight reins on that. She'd be the first to knock Ari off her pedestal if she ever started acting spoiled, though with Ari, I don't think there's any cause for concern. She's pretty much the kindest, most generous person I know.

I try to help Ari load my bike into the back of the car, but she urges me to get in and take it easy. The headache has started to get bad again, so I don't argue. I slump into the passenger seat and lean back against the headrest.

Sometimes I think Ari is intentionally trying to live her life like she's in a period documentary film. She wears mostly vintage clothes, like the mustard-yellow romper she's wearing now, drives a vintage car, and even plays a vintage guitar. Though she knows way more about contemporary music than I do, her true passion lies with the singer-songwriter heyday of the 1970s.

With my bike secured, Ari drops into the driver's seat. I buckle my seat belt while she goes through the carefully orchestrated procedure of checking her mirrors, even though they couldn't possibly have moved from when she drove it here a few hours ago.

She's still getting used to driving a stick shift, and she only kills the engine once before pulling out onto the main thoroughfare. It's a vast improvement from when she first got the car and popped the clutch about fifty times in a row before she could get it to move. "Are you sure you're okay? I could take you to the hospital? Call your parents? Call Jude?"

"No, I just want to go home."

She bites her lower lip. "I was so worried, Pru. You actually passed out."

"Just for a second, right?"

"Yeah, but . . ."

I put my hand on hers and say, solemnly, "I'm okay. I promise."

Her face relents before her words do. After a second, she nods. I sigh and stare out the window. We pass by ice cream parlors and boutique shops that are as familiar as my own bedroom. I hadn't realized how late it was. The sun has just dipped below the horizon, and Main Street is lit up like a movie set, the palm trees wrapped with small white lights, the pastel-painted businesses glowing under the old-fashioned streetlamps. In another week, this town will be full of tourists on vacation, bringing something akin to a nightlife with them. But for now, the street feels almost abandoned.

We turn away from Main Street, into the suburbs. The first couple of blocks are the mansions—mostly second homes for people who can afford almost-but-not-quite beachfront property. But soon it's just another neighborhood. A hodgepodge of Mission style and French Colonial. Tiled roofs, stucco walls, brightly painted shutters, window boxes overflowing with petunias and geraniums.

"So, don't be mad," Ari says, and I immediately bristle with the expectation of being mad, "but I thought Quint seemed okay."

I relax, realizing that for some reason I'd been bracing for an insult. But Ari is too sweet to criticize anyone. Even, evidently, Quint Erickson. I snort. "*Everyone* thinks Quint seems okay, until they have to work with him." I pause, considering. "It's not that I think he's a bad guy. He's not a jerk or a bully or anything like that. But he's just so . . . so . . ." I flex my fingers, grasping for the right word.

"Cute?"

I cast her an icy stare. "You can do better."

She laughs. "*I'm* not interested."

There's something in the way she says it, like she's leaving something unsaid. *She's* not interested, but . . .

The words linger in the air between us. Is she implying that I am?

Gross.

I fold my arms tightly over my chest. "I was going to say inept. And selfish. He's late for class all the time, like whatever he's doing is so much more important than what we're doing. Like his time is more valuable, and it's okay for him to stroll in ten minutes into the lecture, disrupting Mr. Chavez, making us all pause while he gets settled, and he cracks some stupid joke about it like . . ." I drop my voice in imitation. "*Aw, man, that Fortuna traffic, right?* When we all know that there is no Fortuna traffic."

"So he's not punctual. There are worse things."

I sigh. "You don't get it. Nobody does. Having him as a lab partner has been downright painful."

Ari gasps suddenly. The car swerves. I grip my seat belt and turn my head as headlights blaze through the rear window. I don't know when the sports car showed up behind us, but they're riding the bumper, dangerously close. I lean forward to look in the side mirror.

"There was a stop sign back there!" Ari yells.

The sports car starts swerving back and forth, its engine revving.

"What does he want?" Ari cries, already on the verge of hysteria. Though she has her license, her confidence behind the wheel still has a way to go. But something tells me having an erratic car on your tail would freak out even most experienced drivers.

"I think he wants to pass us?"

"We're not on a freeway!"

We're on a narrow residential street, made narrower by rows of vehicles parallel parked on both sides. The speed limit is only twenty-five, which I'm sure Ari had been following precisely. Now, in her anxiety, her speed has dropped to twenty. I suspect this is only further irritating the driver behind us.

They lay on the horn—extra rude.

"What's their problem?" I shout.

"I'm pulling over," says Ari. "Maybe . . . maybe there's a woman giving birth in the passenger seat or something?"

I look at her in disbelief. Leave it to Ari to excuse this inexcusable behavior. "The hospital's that way," I say, jerking my thumb in the other direction.

Ari eases toward the side of the road. She finds a spot between two parked cars and does her best to angle her way in—no easy task with how long the station wagon is. Still, it leaves enough room for the other car to pass.

The engine revs again and the sports car shoots past. I catch a glimpse of a woman hanging out the passenger window with a lit cigarette. She flips Ari the bird as they speed by.

Fury washes over me.

My fists clench, nails digging into my palms. I imagine karmic justice striking them. A blown tire that would send them spinning off the road, crashing into a telephone pole, and—

BANG!

Ari and I both yelp. For a second I think it was a gunshot. But then we see the car, nearly a block ahead, spinning out of control.

It blew a tire.

I press a hand to my mouth. It feels like watching a video in slow motion. The car turns a hundred eighty degrees, miraculously missing the other vehicles parked on the side of the road. It wheels onto the sidewalk, stopping only when the front bumper smashes into—not a telephone pole—a giant palm tree. The hood crumples like an aluminum can.

For a moment, Ari and I are frozen, gaping at the wreck. Then Ari is scrambling to unbuckle her seat belt and kick open her door. She's running toward the wreck before I can think to move, and once I finally do, it's only to unclench my fists.

My fingers are tingling, on the verge of numbness. I look down at them, my skin tinted orange from the streetlamp.

Coincidence.

Just some freaky coincidence.

I somehow find the wherewithal to dig out my phone and call the police, and by the time I've given the operator the information, my hand has stopped shaking and Ari is making her way toward me. "Everyone's okay," she says, breathless. "The airbags went off."

"I called the police. They'll be here soon."

She nods.

"Are *you* okay?" I ask.

Ari sinks into her seat. "I think so. Just scared the heck out of me."

"Me too." I reach over and squeeze her hand.

Her expression is pained when she looks at me. "This is terrible, but when it happened—like, that first split second after they crashed, my first thought was . . ." She trails off.

"Serves them right," I finish for her.

Her face pinches guiltily.

"Ari, they were being jerks. And driving really erratically. I hate to say it, but . . . it *does* serve them right."

"You don't mean that."

Rather than respond—because I'm pretty sure I *do* mean that—I withdraw my hand from hers. "I'm glad no one is seriously hurt," I say. "Including us." Reaching up, I rub the back of my head, where the lump seems to be going down. "I don't think my head could handle another collision tonight."

SEVEN

My headache is mostly gone the next morning, but there's a lingering grogginess that clouds the inside of my skull as I print out the anglerfish paper, along with Jude's piece on the basking shark, and get dressed.

"Last day," I whisper to my reflection in the bathroom mirror. The words are a bit like a mantra, motivating me as I brush my teeth and untangle the same knots from my hair that I work to untangle every morning. *Last day. Last day. Last day.*

I've slept in almost an hour past the time I normally like to get up, and I can hear my family's chaos already in full swing downstairs. Dad has a Kinks record playing and it's one of their lively, upbeat tunes, "Come Dancing." Dad has this theory that starting out the morning with music that makes you feel good will automatically turn the day into an awesome day. I mean, I think there's something to that, and I believe in starting out on the right foot as often as possible, but sometimes his chipper morning tunes are more grating than inspiring. Everyone in the family has tried to tell him this on different occasions, but he brushes off the criticism. I think he might have the morning playlist for the entire summer already picked out.

Over the music, Ellie—four years old and full of Big Emotions—is screaming about who-knows-what. There are days when I feel like Ellie's life is just one big tantrum. *No, I won't take a bath. No, I don't want to put on socks. No, I hate Goldfish crackers. Hey, Lucy is eating my Goldfish crackers, it's not faaaaaiiiir.*

I hear a loud thump and something crashes downstairs, immediately followed by my mom's shrill scream. "Lucy! I said, not in the house!"

"Sorry!" comes Lucy's not-really-that-sorry-sounding apology. A second later, I hear the back screen door squeal on its hinges.

Lucy, thirteen years old and embittered to be going into freshman year after the summer, where she'll officially be back on the bottom of the social pecking order, was probably switched at birth with our actual sibling. At least, that's what Jude and I have theorized. Lucy is popular, for starters. Like, weirdly popular. And not that cliché teen-movie type of popular. She doesn't wear high heels to school, she doesn't spend all her free time at the mall, and she is neither ditzy nor mean. People just like her. All sorts of people. From what I can tell, in my limited knowledge of Fortuna Beach Middle School's current social circles, she has a connection to pretty much all of them. She plays nearly every sport. She has a functional knowledge of pep rallies and fundraisers and other school events that Jude and I have habitually avoided. It can be unsettling to watch.

The only group she doesn't seem to have much connection to is us. She has no interest whatsoever in music—she hardly listens to it on the radio and often puts in her headphones so she can listen to the latest true crime podcasts rather than Dad's record of the day. She's the only one in our family who's never even tried to learn an instrument. (Whereas I took piano for two years, and Jude gave the guitar a real shot. Neither of us ever got any good and we both gave up by the end of middle school. The poor keyboard my parents picked up for me at the local pawnshop has been collecting dust in a corner of our living room ever since.)

And then there's nine-year-old Penny, who loves music, but not the kind my parents have done their best to brainwash us into loving. Instead, she likes pop and R & B and some alternative, the kind of Top 40 hits that don't usually show up in a record store. She's the only reason I have any knowledge of contemporary music at all, and to be honest, my familiarity is still pretty sparse. In fact, if my parents hadn't dragged us to see *Yesterday*, a movie inspired by the Beatles, I probably still wouldn't know who Ed Sheeran is.

Ironically, Penny is also the only one of the Barnett kids who plays an instrument. Sort of. She's three years into learning the violin. One would think that, even being a kid, she would have made some progress in three years, but the sounds she squeaks out of those strings are just as ear-bleeding now as they were the day she started. I can hear her practicing in the bedroom she shares with Lucy as I put on the most vivid red lipstick I have. I need the energy today. I'm not sure if she's trying to play along to the Kinks or cramming for a lesson. Either way, it's bringing back my headache. I huff in irritation and start to close the bathroom door.

A foot appears from the hallway, stopping the door in its path. It bounces back at me.

"Hey," says Jude, leaning against the door frame. "Can you taste the freedom in the air?"

I smack my lips thoughtfully. "Funny. It tastes just like Crest extra whitening." I cap my lipstick and drop it into my makeup bag. Squeezing past him, I duck into my bedroom. "Did you make all your plans to lay siege to Goblin Cavern or whatever?"

"The Isle of Gwendahayr, if you really must know. I'm designing it to include a series of ancient ruins that all hold clues for a really powerful spell, but if you try to chant the spell in the wrong order, or you haven't gotten to them all yet, then something really awful is going to happen. Not sure what yet." He hesitates before adding, "Maybe it will open up a cavern full of goblins." He's followed me, but lingers in my doorway. It's an unspoken rule in our house—never enter a bedroom without a verbal invitation. In general, our family tends to be lacking in firm boundaries, so this is one Jude and I protect at all costs. The house we live in isn't equipped for all seven of us. There are only three official bedrooms— the master for my parents, Lucy and Penny in bunk beds, and me in the third bedroom, with Jude down in the converted basement. But with "baby" Ellie still sleeping on a toddler bed in my parents' room, and outgrowing it quick, there's been talk lately of having to do some rearranging. I'm terrified that means I'm going to be losing my private sanctuary. Luckily, my parents have been too busy with the record store to bother with rearranging and redecorating, so the status quo continues. For now.

"So how was the rest of karaoke?"

I frown at him. "Kind of you to ask, as *someone* put my name up to sing 'Instant Karma!' and didn't bother to tell me."

50

His brow creases. "Really?"

I raspberry my lips. "Please. It's fine. I'm not mad. It was actually"—I bob my head to the sides—"kind of fun. But still. Next time, give me some warning, okay?"

"What? *I* didn't put your name in."

I pause from braiding my hair and look at him. Really look.

He seems legitimately baffled.

But then, so did Ari.

"You didn't?"

"No. I wouldn't do that. Not without your okay."

I wrap a band around the end of the braid, securing it in place. "But if you didn't, and Ari didn't . . ."

We're quiet for a moment, before Jude says hesitantly, "Quint?"

"No." I'd been thinking the same thing, but I have to dismiss it. Quint couldn't have heard us talking about that song. And Carlos wasn't around, either. "Maybe the woman who was running the karaoke? Think she heard us and thought I needed the extra push?"

"Wouldn't be very professional."

"No. It wouldn't." I grab my backpack from where I hung it on my chair last night. "Anyway, I guess it doesn't really matter. I sang. I danced. I was halfway decent, if I do say so myself."

"I'm sorry I missed it."

"I bet you are. I printed out your paper for you, by the way." I hand him the one-page report.

"Thanks. So, hey." He raps his knuckles against the door frame. "I was thinking of going to the end-of-year bonfire tonight."

"What? You?" The annual Fortuna Beach High's bonfire party is as much Jude's scene as it is mine. We didn't go last year, even though lots of freshmen did. I even remember some of our peers going when we were still in middle school. "Why?"

"Just thought I should see what it's all about. Don't knock it till you try it sort of thing. Think you and Ari want to go?"

My gut reaction is *No way, we're good, thanks.* But I'm still trying to figure out Jude's motives. I squint at him. He seems casual. Too casual.

"Ooooh," I say, sitting on the edge of my bed as I pull on my socks. "It's because Maya will be there, isn't it?"

He shoots me an unimpressed look. "Believe it or not, I don't live my life by Maya Livingstone's schedule."

My eyebrows rise. I'm unconvinced.

"Whatever," he grumbles. "I've got nothing better to do tonight, and without any homework to keep you busy, I know you don't, either. Come on. Let's go check it out."

I picture it. Me, Jude, and Ari, swigging sodas by a huge bonfire, sand in our shoes, sun in our eyes, watching as the seniors get drunk on cheap beer and wrestle one another in the waves.

My utter disinterest must show on my face, because Jude starts to laugh. "I'm going to bring a book," he says. "Just in case it's awful. Worst-case scenario, we stake out a place near the food and read all evening. And I'll tell Ari to bring her guitar."

My interpretation of the night changes, and I see the three of us lounging around, books in one hand, s'mores in the other, while Ari strums her newest tune. Now that actually sounds like a delightful evening.

"Fine, I'll go," I say, grabbing my backpack. "But I'm not getting in the water."

"Wasn't even going to ask," says Jude. He knows that I find the ocean terrifying, mostly because *sharks*. I would also be lying if I didn't say that the thought of putting on a swimsuit in front of half the students at our school didn't fill me with an abundance of unmitigated horror.

We head downstairs. Dad has just put on a new record, and the upbeat harmonies of the Beach Boys start to fill up the living room. I glance through the doorway and see Dad swaying around the coffee table. He tries to get Penny to dance with him, but she's lying on the floor, playing a video game on Dad's tablet, doing a superb job of ignoring him.

I generally try to avoid the living room, because over the years it's become a bit of a junkyard. Cleaning and organizing hasn't taken priority in my parents' lives in a while, and all the random things we don't know what to do with tend to get piled up in the living room corners. Not just my old keyboard, but also boxes of abandoned craft projects and stacks of unread magazines. Plus, there are the records. So many vinyl records, spilling across every surface, piling up on the ancient carpet. It stresses me out just looking at it.

Jude and I turn the other way, into the kitchen. Ellie's tantrum seems to be over, thank heavens, and she's sitting in the breakfast nook, wearing her favorite dress with the sequined monkey on the front and mindlessly shoveling cereal into her mouth. She has a magazine spread out in front of her. She can't read yet, but she likes looking at the photos of animals in *National Geographic Kids.* Through the window I spy Lucy in the backyard, kicking a soccer ball against the back of the house.

The elementary and middle school terms ended yesterday, making this Penny's and Lucy's first official day of summer vacation. Eleanor's preschool got out last week. One glance at Mom, sitting across from Ellie with a glass of tomato juice, her laptop, and a couple piles of receipts spread around her, suggests she's already feeling frazzled by the change.

"I wanted to make pancakes for your last day," she says when Jude and I enter, before giving us a helpless shrug. "But I don't think it's going to happen. Maybe this weekend?"

"No worries," says Jude, grabbing a bowl from the cabinet. He would gladly survive on cereal alone if our parents allowed it.

I plug in the blender on the counter to make my usual morning smoothie. I pull out the milk and peanut butter, then turn to reach for the fruit bowl. I freeze.

"Where'd all the bananas go?"

No one answers.

"Uh, Mom? You bought two bunches of bananas, like, two days ago?"

She barely glances up from her screen. "I don't know, honey. There are five growing kids in this family."

As she's talking, a movement catches my eye. Ellie has lifted her magazine, holding it up in front of her face.

"Ellie?" I say warningly, crossing the room and snatching the magazine from her hand, at the same time that she shoves the last few bites of a banana into her mouth. Her cheeks bulge and she struggles to chew. The peel is still in her hand. A second banana peel lies next to her empty cereal bowl. "Eleanor! Seriously? That's so rude! Mom!"

Mom looks up, glaring—at me, of course. "She's four, and it's a *banana*."

I start to groan but bite my tongue. It isn't because it's a banana. It's the principle of the thing. She heard me saying I wanted it, which is the only reason she stuffed it into her mouth. If it had been Jude, she would have passed it to him on a silver platter.

I toss the magazine back onto the table. "Fine," I mutter. "I'll find something else."

But I'm still simmering as I start rummaging through the freezer, hoping for a bag of frozen berries. When I come up empty, I step back, balling my hands into fists. I cast a withering look at Ellie over my shoulder, just as she swallows the banana. Ugh. That selfish little—

A soccer ball comes sailing into view. It strikes Mom's glass, knocking it to the table. Mom yelps as tomato juice floods over the surface. She snatches up the nearest piles of receipts, while Ellie sits frozen, wide-eyed, doing nothing as a river of deep red juice spills over the edge of the table and straight into her lap.

I blink, having flashbacks to the drunk hecklers at Encanto last night. The cherry. The spilled beer. The déjà vu is bizarre.

"Lucy!" Mom shrieks.

Lucy is standing in the back door, her hands still extended as if there were an invisible soccer ball in them. She looks bewildered. "I didn't do it!"

Mom makes a disgusted sound. "Oh, right. I'm sure the universe just plucked it out of your hands and threw it at the table!"

"But—"

"Don't just stand there! Get a towel!"

I know she means Lucy, but Jude is a step ahead of everyone, bringing a wad of paper towels over to help sop up the mess.

"Mom!" Ellie's voice warbles. "It's my favorite dress!"

"I know, sweetie," says Mom, though I can tell she's barely listening as she checks the underside of her computer to see if there's any juice on it. "Pru, could you help your sister get changed?"

Hearing my name shakes me from my daze. It's just a spilled glass. It's just a soccer ball. It's just coincidence.

But it's also so *weird*.

My fingers tingle as I release my fists and stretch them out. I go around the table and Ellie compliantly lifts her arms for me to pull the sticky wet dress off her.

"It's my favorite," she says, pouting. "Can it be saved?"

The way she says it is beyond melodramatic, but I can't help feel a tug of guilt. Even though this isn't *my* fault. I was nowhere near that glass of juice, or the soccer ball for that matter. Lucy really does need to learn to be more careful.

"I'll put some Spray 'n Wash on it and we'll hope for the best," I say. "Go pick out something else to wear for today."

She casts a feisty scowl at Lucy, though it goes ignored as Lucy helps Mom and Jude clean up. Ellie harrumphs and storms upstairs.

"Jude, I'm going to go throw this in the wash, then we should get going," I say. "Last day. Shouldn't be late."

He nods and throws the red-tinged paper towels in the trash. "Want a bagel for the road?"

"Sure, thanks." I head into the laundry room, grab the stain remover from the plastic tote beside the washing machine, then spread out the damp fabric. The stain runs the whole length of the dress, from just above the ear of the sparkly monkey's head, all the way down to the bottom of the skirt.

It's probably just my imagination, but I swear the stain is in the exact shape of a banana.

EIGHT

I've barely stepped through the classroom door when Mr. Chavez barks at me—"Papers on the table, please, then pick up your graded final project over there." He points the capped end of a dry-erase marker at a pile of papers on the front table.

I pull out my report on the anglerfish and set it down on the stack with the others. As I make my way between the tables, I'm startled to see that my lab table isn't empty. Quint is already there. Early. Earlier than *me*.

I freeze. I honestly hadn't expected Quint to be here today at all, even if he had mentioned it last night. Being the last day before summer vacation, I'd assumed he'd be MIA, along with half the sophomore class and nearly all the juniors and seniors.

But there he is, flipping through a three-ring binder full of clear sheet protectors. It's the report he turned in yesterday. Our report.

I eye him warily as I make my way to Mr. Chavez's desk and pick up the diorama of Main Street. I scan it for some indication of my grade, but don't see anything.

Quint glances up at me as I approach our shared table and set the model down on the corner.

"How are you feeling?" he asks.

The back of my head throbs, just barely, in response to his question. It's hardly bothered me all morning, but being reminded of my fall has me instinctively feeling for the lump on my skull. It's almost nonexistent now.

"That depends," I say, dropping into my seat. "How did we do?"

He shrugs and peels a large blue sticky note off the front cover of the report. He presses the paper onto the table between us.

My stomach drops as I read the words.

Prudence: B-
Quint: B+
Overall: C

"What?" I say, practically yelling. "Is this a joke?"

"I thought you might not be thrilled," says Quint. "Tell me, is it the C that's most upsetting or that my individual grade is higher than yours?"

"Both!" I slump forward, reading the words that Mr. Chavez has written beneath the grades. *Prudence: exemplary work, but little applied science. Quint: strong concepts, but messy execution and unfocused writing. Project displays an overall lack of cohesiveness and follow-through on key ideas. Both grades would have benefited greatly with improved communication and teamwork.*

"What?" I say again, followed by a dismayed growl in the back of my throat. I shake my head. "I knew I should have just written it myself."

Quint laughs. It's a hearty laugh, one that draws more than a few stares. "Of course that's what you take from those comments. Clearly my involvement was the problem, even though . . ." He leans forward and taps his B+.

I stare at him. "That has to be a mistake."

"Naturally."

My heartbeat is drumming in my chest. My breaths become short. How is this possible? I've never gotten a C before, not on anything. And my model! My gorgeous model, that I worked so hard on, all those hours, the details . . . That only got me a B-?

Something's wrong. Mr. Chavez got confused over who had done what. He had decision fatigue from reviewing too many papers by the time he got to ours.

This cannot be right.

"Okay, but seriously, grades aside," says Quint, picking up the sticky note and placing it back on the front of the report, "how's your head?"

I know it's a legitimate question. I know he probably doesn't mean anything cruel by it. But still, it sounds almost accusatory, like I'm overreacting to something he deems insignificant.

"My head is fine," I seethe.

I shove my stool away from the table and snatch up the three-ring binder. Then I'm stomping toward the front of the class. The few students who haven't decided to skip today are still filtering in, and Claudia all but lunges out of my way as I bulldoze down the aisle.

Mr. Chavez sees me coming and I see the change in his stance, his shoulders, his expression. A bracing, an expectation, a total lack of surprise.

"I think there's been a mistake," I say, holding up the binder so he can see his own inept sticky note. "This can't be right."

He sighs. "I had a feeling I'd be hearing from you, Miss Barnett." He folds his fingers together. "Your work is strong. You're an exceptional presenter, your ideas are solid, the model was gorgeous. If this were a business class, it would have been A-plus work for sure." He pauses, his expression sympathetic. "But this isn't a business class. This is a biology class, and your assignment was to present on a topic related to the subjects we've covered this year." He shrugs. "Now, ecotourism and biology certainly have plenty areas of overlap, but you didn't address any of those. Instead you talked about profit potential and marketing campaigns. Now . . . if I believed that you had been involved with *anything* that's in that report, that would have boosted both your individual and combined grades significantly. But you and Quint made it pretty clear that this was not treated as a team assignment." He lifts his eyebrows. "True?"

I stare at him. I can't argue, and he knows it. Of course this wasn't a team assignment. In my opinion, it's a miracle Quint submitted this report at all. But it isn't my fault I was paired with him!

I sense the sudden burn of tears behind my eyes, born of frustration as much as anything else. "But I worked so hard on this," I say, struggling—and failing—to keep my voice even. "I've been researching since November. I interviewed community leaders, compared the efforts of similar markets, I—"

"I know," said Mr. Chavez, nodding. He looks sad and tired, which some-how makes it worse. "And I'm very sorry, but you simply did not meet the scope of the assignment. This was a science project, Prudence. Not a marketing campaign."

"I know it's a science project!" I look down at the binder in my arms. That photograph is staring up at me, the one of the seal or sea lion or whatever, entangled in fishing line. Its sorrowful eyes speaking more than words ever could. Shaking my head, I hold it up again for Mr. Chavez to see. "And you gave Quint a better grade than me? All he did was take my ideas and type them up, and according to your note here, he didn't even do *that* very well!"

Mr. Chavez frowns and rocks back on his heels. He's staring at me like I've suddenly started speaking a different language.

That's when I realize that the class has gone silent. Everyone is listening to us.

And I'm not standing up here alone anymore. Mr. Chavez's eyes dart to the side. I follow the look and see Quint standing beside me, his arms crossed. I can't read his expression, but it's almost like he's saying to our teacher, *See? This is what I've had to put up with.*

I straighten my spine and sniff so hard it makes the back of my sinuses throb, but at least it keeps the tears from falling. "Please," I say. "You told us this project is worth thirty percent of our grade, and I cannot have it pulling my average down. There must be some way to fix this. Can I do it over?"

"Miss Barnett," Mr. Chavez says, sounding cautious, "have you even read your report?"

I blink. "My report?"

He flicks his fingers against the cover. "Quint's name isn't the only one on there. Now, clearly, you two have struggled to work together. You've probably struggled more than any other team I've ever had in this class. But surely you at least read the report. Didn't you?"

I don't move. I don't speak.

Mr. Chavez's gaze slips to Quint, full of disbelief, then back to me. He chuckles and rubs the bridge of his nose. "Well. That explains some things."

I look down at the report in my hands, for the first time curious as to what's in it.

"If I allow you a do-over," our teacher says, "then I need to offer the same chance to everyone."

"So?" I swoop my hand back toward the class, which is still half empty. "None of them will take it."

He frowns, even though we both know it's true. Then he heaves another sigh, longer this time, and looks at Quint. "How about you, Mr. Erickson? Are you interested in resubmitting your project?"

"No!" I yell, at the same time Quint starts laughing as if this were the funniest thing he's ever heard. I glance at him, aghast, and try to turn my shoulder to him as I face Mr. Chavez again. "I didn't mean . . . I'd like to do the report again. Just me this time."

Our teacher starts to shake his head, when Quint catches his breath and adds, "Yeah, nope. I'm good. Perfectly happy with the C, thank you."

I gesture at him. "See?"

Mr. Chavez shrugs hopelessly. "Then, no. I'm sorry."

His words crash into me, and now I feel like I'm the one having difficulty translating. "No? But you were just going to—"

"Offer you both the chance to resubmit it, if you would like to. And"—he raises his voice, looking around at the class—"anyone else who feels they didn't complete the assignment to the best of their abilities and would like one more chance. But . . . this is a team project. Either the whole team works to improve their score, or it doesn't count."

"But that's not fair!" I say. The whining in my voice makes me cringe. I sound like Ellie. But I can't help it. Quint says he won't do it. I shouldn't have to rely on *him,* one of the laziest people I've ever met, just to bring up my own grade!

Behind me, Quint snickers, and I turn blazing eyes to him. He quickly falls silent, then turns on his heel and saunters back to our table.

Mr. Chavez starts to scribble something onto the whiteboard. I lower my voice as I step closer. "I want a different teammate, then," I say. "I'll do it with Jude."

He shakes his head. "I'm sorry, Prudence. Like it or not, Quint is your teammate."

"But I didn't choose him. I shouldn't be punished for his lack of motivation.

And you've seen how he's always late. He certainly doesn't care about this class or marine biology or this project!"

Mr. Chavez stops writing and faces me. I want to believe that he's reconsidering his position, but something tells me that's not it. When he speaks, my irritation only continues to rise with every word.

"In life," he says, speaking slowly, "we rarely get to choose the people we work with. Our bosses, our peers, our students, our teammates. Heck, we don't even get to choose our families, other than our spouses." He shrugs. "But you have to make do. This project was as much about figuring out a way to work together as it was about marine biology. And I'm sorry, but you and Quint didn't do that." He raises his voice, speaking to the class again. "Anyone wanting to resubmit their project can email their revised papers to me by August fifteenth, and must include a summary of how the work was divided."

My teeth clench. I realize I'm gripping the binder, squeezing it against my chest.

Mr. Chavez's attention finds me again and he glances down at the binder, no doubt noticing my whitened knuckles. "A word of advice, Prudence?"

I swallow. I don't want to hear what he has to say, but what choice do I have?

"This is biology. Maybe spend some time learning about the animals and habitats your plan strives so hard to protect and you'll be able to tell people why they should care. Why the *tourists* should care. And . . ." He swirls the marker toward the binder. "Maybe take the time to read what your partner wrote? I'm sure this will surprise you, but he actually has some pretty good ideas."

He gives me a look that borders on chastising, then turns back to the board.

Clearly dismissed, I plod back to the table, where Quint is tipped back on the hind legs of his stool, his fingers laced behind his head. I imagine kicking the seat out from under him, but refrain.

"How about that?" Quint says jovially as I slump into the seat beside him. "I actually have some pretty good ideas. Who knew?"

I don't respond. My pulse is pounding in my ears.

This. Is. So. Unfair.

Maybe I can talk to the principal? Surely this can't be allowed?

I stare daggers at Mr. Chavez as he goes over the final grades with a few other students. I've never felt so betrayed by a teacher. Under the desk, I tighten my hands into two balled fists. I picture Mr. Chavez's pen leaking and getting dark blue ink all over his shirt. Or coffee spilling across his computer keyboard. Or—

"Morning, Mr. C!" bellows Ezra, slapping Mr. Chavez hard on the back as he strolls over to a wastebasket.

"Ow!" Mr. Chavez yelps, lifting a hand to his mouth. "Ezra, tone it down. You made me bite my tongue." His fingers come away and though it's too far to tell for sure, I think there might be a little bit of blood there.

Huh.

I hadn't been hoping for physical harm, necessarily, but you know what? I'll take it.

"Sorry, man. Forgot you're old and frail." Ezra cackles as he heads to his table, where Maya is looking over their paper.

I settle back in my seat. I feel a tiny bit mollified, but I'm still stewing over the botched grade.

Ezra whoops loudly and offers Maya a fist bump. "B-plus! Nailed it!"

My jaw drops. "Even Ezra got a better grade than us? All he did was talk about the palatability of shark fin soup!"

No. This cannot stand.

Meanwhile, Quint has pulled out his phone and is scrolling through his photos, as relaxed as can be.

My mind is spinning, and I consider what Mr. Chavez said about my model, my presentation. I can't fathom what I would change about it. More science? More biology? More talk of local habitats? I did all that.

Didn't I?

Still, right or wrong, there's a C watching me from that sticky note, and a B- next to my name. I exhale sharply through my nostrils.

"Quint?" I say. Quietly. Slowly. Staring at that hateful sticky note.

"Yep?" he responds, infuriatingly chipper.

I swallow. Under the table, I dig my fingers into my thighs. A precaution. To keep from throttling him.

"Will you"—I clear my throat—"*please* redo this project with me?"

For a moment, we're both still. Statue-still. I can see him from the corner of my eye. He waits until the screen on his phone goes black, and still, there's silence.

My focus slips along the edge of the table. To his hands, and the phone gripped in them. I'm forced to turn my head. Just enough. Just until I can meet his eye.

He's staring at me. Utterly without expression.

I hold my breath.

Finally, he drawls, his voice etched with sarcasm, "Tempting offer. But . . . no."

"Oh, come on," I say, swiveling to face him fully. "You have to!"

"I most certainly do not have to."

"But you heard what Mr. Chavez said! It has to be teamwork."

He guffaws. "Oh, and *now* I'm supposed to believe that we'll be a team?" He shakes his head. "I'm not a masochist. I'll pass."

"All right, class," says Mr. Chavez, clapping his hands to get our attention. "Consider this a free period while I grade these papers."

The class explodes with joy to know he isn't going to give some last-minute pop quiz.

Quint's hand shoots into the air, but he doesn't wait to be called on. "Can we switch seats?"

Mr. Chavez's attention darts toward our table, landing ever so briefly on me. "That's fine, just keep it quiet, okay? I've got work to do."

Quint's stool scrapes across the linoleum floor. He doesn't even look at me as he gathers up his stuff. "See you next year," he says, before going to sit with Ezra.

I snarl as the two of them high-five each other over their project grades.

This can't be happening. Quint can't be in charge of my grade, my success, my future!

"Pru? You okay?" says Jude, sliding into Quint's empty seat.

I turn to him. My insides feel like a thundercloud. "What did you and Caleb get on your report?"

Jude hesitates, before pulling a paper from his school binder. There's another blue sticky note. Straight As across the board.

I groan with annoyance. Then, realizing how that sounds, I give Jude a begrudging look. "I mean, good for you."

"Real convincing, Sis." He glances at the back of Quint's head. "You really want to try to redo it?"

"Yeah, but Quint refuses. I'll think of something, though. He can't keep me from resubmitting *my* portion of the project, can he?"

"Quint or Mr. Chavez?"

"Both." I cross my arms, scowling. "Evidently, I didn't include enough *science*. So right now, my plan is to science the heck out of this report. I will dream up a Fortuna Beach tourism sector so mired in science, the residents will be given master's degrees by default."

"Excellent. That will save me a lot of money on tuition payments."

Jude pulls out his sketchbook and starts drawing a group of bloodied, war-torn elves. He has no problem relaxing, as he well shouldn't, with his sticky note full of As.

By the end of the period, Mr. Chavez passes back our papers. Our last, inconsequential homework assignment. For opting to take on the adaptations of an anglerfish, I get an A+. It does nothing to subdue my rage.

As soon as the bell rings, I leave Jude behind as he starts to put away his sketchbook. Quint and Ezra are already halfway out the door. I chase after them. "Wait!" I say, grabbing Quint's arm.

His . . . bicep?

Holy cow.

Quint spins back to me. For a moment he's startled, but his expression quickly cools. "Now you're just acting desperate."

I barely hear him. What is under this shirt?

"Prudence?"

Snapping back to reality, I withdraw my hand. Heat rushes into my cheeks.

Quint's eyes narrow suspiciously.

"Please," I sputter. "I can't have a C on my record."

His lips quirk to one side, like my little problems are hilarious to him. "You make it sound like you're going to jail. It's just sophomore biology. You'll survive."

"I heard that!" calls Mr. Chavez, who is tidying his desk.

"Mr. Chavez, please!" I say. "Tell him he has to do this with me, or . . . or say I can do it on my own!"

Mr. Chavez looks up and shrugs.

Gah.

"Look," I say, turning back to Quint. "I know it's not the end of the world, but I've never gotten a C before. And I worked really hard on that model! You have no idea how much work I've put into this project." My eyes start to water, catching me off-guard. I squeeze them shut, trying to reel back my emotions before I give Quint even more ammunition to attack Workaholic Prudence.

"You're right," he says.

I open my eyes, startled.

"I don't have any idea how hard you worked on that project." He takes a step back, shrugging. "Because I wasn't trusted enough to help."

You weren't trusted? I want to scream. *You didn't even try!*

"Besides," he adds, "I have more important things to do with my summer."

I snort. "Like what? Play video games? Go surfing?"

"Yeah," he says with an ireful laugh. "You know me so well." He pivots and starts to walk away.

I feel like I've run out of options. Helplessness sweeps through me, further igniting my anger. I do not like feeling helpless.

As I stare at Quint's retreating back, I ball my fists and picture the earth opening up beneath him and swallowing him whole.

"Oh, wait, Mr. Erickson?" calls our teacher.

Quint pauses.

"Almost forgot." Mr. Chavez riffles through his papers and grabs a folder. "Here's that extra-credit assignment. Great work here. The photos are really impressive."

Quint's face softens and he takes the folder with a smile. "Thanks, Mr. C. Have a good summer."

I gape, stunned, as Quint leaves the room.

What was that?

I spin on Mr. Chavez. "Hold on. You let him do an extra-credit assignment? But I can't do something to bring up *my* grade?"

Mr. Chavez sighs. "He had extenuating circumstances, Prudence."

"*What* extenuating circumstances?"

He opens his mouth, but hesitates. Then he shrugs. "Maybe you should try asking your lab partner about it."

I let out an infuriated roar, then stomp back to the table to gather my things. Jude is watching me, worried, both thumbs locked behind the straps of his backpack. We're the only students left in the classroom.

"That was a valiant effort," he says.

"Don't talk to me," I mutter back.

Ever accommodating, Jude doesn't say anything else, just waits while I shove the binder into my bag and grab the street model.

It feels like the universe is playing a practical joke on me.

NINE

The rest of the school day is uneventful. It's clear that the teachers are as eager for summer vacation as we are, and most of them are phoning in these last obligatory hours. In Spanish class, we spend the whole period watching some cheesy telenovela. In history, we play what Mr. Gruener calls "semi-educational" board games—Risk, Battleship, Settlers of Catan. In English, Ms. Whitefield reads us a bunch of bawdy Shakespearean quotes. There's a lot of insults and sexual humor, which she has to translate out of the old-fashioned English for us, but by the time the hour is over, my classmates are all cracking up and calling one another things like "thou embossed carbuncle!" and "ye cream-faced loon!"

It's actually a really fun day. I even manage to forget about the biology debacle for a while.

As we're leaving our final class, Mrs. Dunn sends us off with goody bags full of gummy bears and fish crackers, like we're six-year-olds heading out on a picnic. I guess it's our prize for bothering to come in on the last day.

"Sayonara! Farewell! Adieu!" she sings as she passes the bags out at her door. "Make good choices!"

I find Jude waiting on the front steps of the school. Students are drifting out in waves, electrified with their sudden freedom. The weeks stretch in front of us, full of potential. Sunny beaches, lazy days and Netflix marathons, pool parties and loitering on the boardwalk.

Jude, who had Mrs. Dunn earlier in the day, is munching his way through the plastic baggie of Goldfish. I sit beside him and automatically hand over my snacks, neither of which I find remotely appealing. We sit in companionable silence. It's one of the things I love most about being a twin. Jude and I can sit together for hours, not speaking a single word, and I can come away from it feeling like we just had the most profound conversation. We don't do small talk. We don't need to amuse each other. We can just be.

"Feeling better?" he asks. And since this is the first time I've seen him since biology class, I know immediately what he's talking about.

"Not even a little bit," I answer.

He nods. "Figured as much." Finishing his snacks, he balls up the plastic baggie and tosses it at the nearest trash can. It falls short by at least four feet. Grumbling, he walks over and scoops it up.

I hear Ari's car coming before I see it. A few seconds later, the blue station wagon swings into the parking lot, never straying above the five-miles-per-hour limit posted on the signs. She pulls up to the bottom of the steps and leans out her open window, a party horn in her mouth. She blows once, unraveling the silver-striped coil with a screechy, celebratory blare.

"You're free!" she squeals.

"Free of the overlords!" Jude responds. "We shall toil away at their menial drudgework no longer!"

We get into the car, Jude and his long legs in front, me in the back. We've had this afternoon planned for weeks, determined to start the summer out right. As we pull out of the parking lot, I vow to forget about Quint and our miserable presentation for the rest of the day. I figure I can have one day to revel in summer vacation before I set my mind to solving this problem. I'll figure something out tomorrow.

Ari drives us straight to the boardwalk, where we can binge on sundaes from the Salty Cow, an upscale ice cream parlor known for mixing unusual flavors like "lavender mint" and "turmeric poppy seed." When we get there, though, there's a line all the way out the door, and the impatient looks on some of the patrons' faces make me think it hasn't moved in a while.

I trade glances with Ari and Jude.

"I'll go pop my head in and see what's going on," I say as the two of them get in line. I squeeze through the door. "Sorry, not trying to cut, just want to see what's happening."

A man standing with three young kids looks about ready to explode. "*That's happening*," he says, gesturing angrily toward the cashier.

A woman is arguing—no, *screaming* at the poor girl behind the counter, who looks like she's barely older than I am. The girl is on the verge of crying, but the woman is relentless. *How incompetent can you be? It's just ice cream, not rocket science! I put in this order a month ago!*

"I'm sorry," the girl pleads, red-faced. "I didn't take the order. I don't know what happened. There isn't any record . . ."

She's not the only one on the verge of tears. A little girl with pigtails stands with her hands on the glass ice cream case, looking between the angry woman and her parents. "Why is it taking so long?" she whimpers.

"I want to speak to your manager!" yells the woman.

"He isn't here," says the girl behind the counter. "There's nothing I can do. I'm sorry!"

I don't know why the woman is so furious, and I'm not sure it matters. Like she said, it's just ice cream, and clearly the poor cashier is doing her best. She could at least be civil. Not to mention that she's keeping these poor kids—and *me*—from getting our ice cream.

I take in a deep breath and prepare to storm up to the woman. Maybe if we can be rational, we can get the manager's phone number and he can come down and deal with this.

I clench my hands at my sides.

I take two steps forward.

"What's going on here?" bellows a stern voice.

I pause. The people in line shuffle out of the way as a police officer strolls into the ice cream parlor.

Or . . . I could let him deal with it?

The woman at the counter opens her mouth, clearly about to start yelling again, but she's cut off by all the waiting customers. The presence of the police officer encourages them, and suddenly they're all willing to speak up on behalf of the cashier. *This woman is being a nuisance. She's being rude and ridiculous. She needs to leave!*

For her part, the woman seems genuinely shocked when no one, especially those closest in line who have heard the whole story, comes to her defense.

"I'm sorry, ma'am, but it sounds like I should escort you out," says the officer.

She looks mortified. And stunned. And still angry. With a snarl, she grabs a business card off the counter and sneers at the girl who is wiping tears from her cheeks. "I will be calling your manager about this," she says, before storming out of the parlor to a huge roar of approval.

I make my way back to Jude and Ari, shaking out my hands. My fingers have that weird pins-and-needles feeling in them again for some reason. I explain what happened, and soon the line starts moving again.

After we've finished our ice cream, we overpay for a surrey from the rental kiosk and spend an hour pedaling along the boardwalk under its lemon-yellow awning, Ari snapping too many photos of us making kooky faces, and Jude and me yelling at her to stop slacking off and start moving her legs.

Until we come across a group of tourists who are taking up the whole width of the boardwalk and meandering at a turtle's pace.

We slow down the surrey so we don't crash into them. Ari honks the little bike horn.

One of the tourists looks back, notices us, and then goes right back to their conversation. Ignoring us entirely.

"Excuse us!" says Jude. "Could we get by?"

They don't respond.

Ari honks the horn again. And *again*. They still don't get out of the way.

What the heck? Do they think they own this boardwalk or something? Move!

My knuckles whiten on the steering wheel.

"Coming through! Can't stop! Get out of the way!" someone yells, charging toward us from the other direction.

The tourists yelp in surprise and scatter as five teens on skateboards come barreling toward them. One of the women loses her sandal and it gets squashed beneath one of the skateboard's wheels. A man hauls himself backward so fast he loses his balance and falls off the edge of the boardwalk, landing on his behind in the sand below. They all start yelling at the inconsiderate teenage hooligans, while Jude and Ari and I look at one another and shrug.

We pedal quickly past the tourists before they can regroup.

After returning the surrey, we order a gigantic basket of garlic fries from the fish-and-chips stand and sit out on the sidewalk, kicking sand at the greedy seagulls who come too close, trying to snap up our fries. When one of them comes so close it sends Ari squealing and ducking around a picnic table, Jude tosses some of the burnt bits from the bottom of the basket for the birds to fight over.

A second later, one of the stand's employees sees him doing it and starts yelling because "every idiot knows better than to feed the wildlife!" Jude gets a guilt-ridden look on his face. He doesn't do well with chastisement.

As soon as the employee turns away, I shake my fist at his back. I'm just lowering my arm when a seagull swoops down and snatches the paper hat off the employee's head. He cries out and ducks in surprise as the bird soars away.

I watch as the bird and the hat disappear into the sunset.

Okay.

Is it just me, or . . . ?

I glance down at my hand.

No. That's ridiculous.

As the sun begins to sink toward the horizon, we finally make our way to the cove where the bonfire party is held each year, a stretch of shore about a mile north of downtown. I don't know how long the bonfire tradition has been going on. How many classes have danced drunkenly around the flames, how many seniors have splashed fully dressed into the surf, how many make-out sessions have taken place in the rocky alcoves where people go to, well, make out. Supposedly. I wouldn't know firsthand, but you hear stories.

We're not the first ones to arrive, but we're still on the early side. A couple of seniors are unloading coolers from the back of a pickup truck. A boy I recognize from math class is arranging kindling for the fire. The first arrivals are already staking out their spots, spreading blankets and towels on the beach, producing volleyballs and beer cans from large woven tote bags.

We pick a spot not far from the bonfire, unrolling the blanket that Ari brought with her and setting out a few low-slung beach chairs. Within minutes, Jude gets hailed by a few of our classmates and goes over to chat.

Ari turns to me. "I already know the answer to this, but just to be sure. Do you want to go in the water?"

I curl my nose in distaste.

"That's what I thought." Standing, she surprises me by pulling her paisley printed sundress over her head, revealing a pale pink bathing suit underneath. She's clearly been wearing it all day, and it startles me a little bit to realize that I had no idea.

"Wait, you're going swimming?" I ask.

"Not *swimming*," she says. "But it's a beach party. I figured I should at least get my feet wet. Sure you don't want to join me?"

"Positive. Thanks."

"Okay. Watch my guitar?"

She doesn't wait for me to respond, because of course I will. Ari marches off down the shore. She doesn't say hi to anyone, and I notice a few people giving her curious looks, wondering whether they should recognize her. Jude says she didn't hesitate when he invited her to come to this party, even though she won't know anyone. I wonder if she's hoping to meet some more Fortuna Beach youth while we're here, make some new friends. I should probably introduce her to some people when she comes back, but . . .

I look around, frowning. Honestly, I don't know many people here, either. It's almost entirely seniors and juniors so far. And the few sophomores I recognize, like Maya and her crew, I'm not exactly friends with.

Jude, though, will know lots of people. Even though he's sort of a nerd, who watches old seasons of *Star Trek* and has a whole shelf of *Lord of the Rings* Funko dolls, people like Jude. He has his own sort of charm. He has a soothing, easy-to-be-with presence.

Just one more reason no one ever believes it when we say we're related.

So, if Ari is interested in making friends, he's more equipped to help out.

Reaching over, I take a hold of Ari's guitar case and pull it closer to my side.

"Not going in the water, Prude?"

I look up to see Jackson Stult smirking at me. Now that he has my attention, he laughs and makes a show of smacking his own forehead. "Never mind, that was a stupid question. I mean, you're pretty much allergic to fun, aren't you?"

"Nope, I'm just allergic to morons," I say, before adding in a deadpan voice, "Achoo."

He snickers and waves as if this has been a delightful interaction before wandering over to join some of his equally obnoxious friends down the beach.

His words sting, even though I know they shouldn't. After all, this is pretty much everything I know about Jackson Stult: One, he cares more about his designer jeans and fancy brand-name shirts than anyone else I've ever met; and two, he will do anything for a laugh, even if it comes at someone else's expense. Which it often does.

I would be more offended if he actually liked me.

But still.

Still.

The sting is there.

But if ruining my night was Jackson's plan, then I refuse to allow it. I lie back on the blanket, staring up at the orange-glowing clouds that drift by overhead. I try to immerse myself in the good things about this moment. Laughter pealing over the beach. The steady crashing of the waves. The taste of salt and the smell of smoke as the fire gets started. I'm too far away to feel the heat of the flames, but the blanket and sand are warm from baking under the sun's rays all afternoon.

I am relaxed.

I am content.

I won't think about biology projects.

I won't think about spineless bullies.

I won't even think about Quint Erickson.

I let out a long, slow exhale. I read somewhere that regular meditation can help hone your focus, making you more efficient and productive over time. I've been trying to practice meditation ever since. It seems like it would be so easy. Breathe in. Breathe out. Keep your focus trained on your breaths.

But there are always thoughts that invade the serenity. There are always distractions.

Like right now, and that terrified screech suddenly cutting across the beach.

I sit up on my elbows. Jackson is carrying Serena McGinney toward the water. He's laughing, his head tipped back almost maniacally, while Serena thrashes and struggles against him.

I sit up more fully now, my brow tensing. Everyone knows Serena is afraid of the water. It became common knowledge when she refused to participate in mandatory swim class in ninth grade, even going so far as to bring a note from her parents excusing her from any pool activities. She doesn't just have a slight aversion, like I do. It's an outright phobia.

Her screams intensify as Jackson reaches the water's edge. He's carrying her damsel style, and until now she's been flailing her arms and legs, trying to get away. But now she turns and clutches her arms around his neck, yelling—
Don't you dare, don't you dare!

My eyes narrow. I hear one of his friends call out, "Dunk her! Do it!"

I swallow. I don't think he'll do it, but I don't know for sure.

"Come on, it's barely ankle deep!" Jackson says. Playing to his audience.

It's clear that Serena does not think it's funny. She's gone drastically pale, and though I know she must be hating Jackson right now, her arms are gripping his neck like a vise. "Jackson Stult, you jerk! Put me down!"

"Put you down?" he says. "Are you *sure?*"

His friends are rooting for him now. A sick chant. *Do. It. Do. It. Do. It.*

I scramble to my feet and cup my hands around my mouth. "Leave her alone, Jackson!"

His eyes meet mine, and I know I've made a mistake. It's a challenge now. Will he or won't he?

I plant my hands on my hips and try to convey through osmosis that if he has any dignity at all, he will leave her alone.

He laughs again, an almost cruel sound. Then, in one fluid motion, he releases Serena's legs and uses his hand to reach back and unhook her arms from his neck. While she's still scrambling to wrap her knees around him, he hurls her as far as he can out into the waves.

Her scream pierces my ears. His friends cheer.

It's not that deep, but when she lands on her backside with a splash, the water comes nearly to her neck. She scrambles to her feet and bolts from the water, her dress coated in sand and clinging to her thighs. "You asshole!" she shrieks, shoving Jackson in the stomach as she rushes past him.

He barely moves, other than to reach down and brush away the smear of sand she left on his shirt. "Hey now, this is dry-clean only," he says, his voice rich with amusement.

Serena storms away, trying to tug the damp skirt away from her hips. As she passes me, I see furious tears building in her eyes.

My teeth are clenched as I turn back to Jackson. His arms are raised victoriously. Not far away, still knee-deep in the water, Ari is watching him with evident confusion.

"Dude," says Sonia Calizo, disgusted, but loud enough that almost the whole beach can hear, "she almost *drowned* when she was a kid."

Jackson sneers. "She's not gonna drown. Jesus. It's barely two feet deep."

"Couldn't you tell how scared she was?" says Ari. I'm surprised. It isn't like Ari to confront anyone, much less a total stranger. But she also has a keen sense of justice, so maybe it shouldn't seem surprising at all.

Either way, Jackson ignores her. His expression is still gloating, lacking any remorse.

I exhale and as Jackson takes a step toward the shore, I imagine him tripping and falling face-first in the sand. I imagine those pretty, expensive clothes of his coated in salt water and muck.

I squeeze my fist.

Jackson takes another step and I hold my breath, waiting.

Nothing happens. He does not trip. He does not fall.

My shoulders sink. I feel silly for having hoped, even for a second, that the coincidences of the past twenty-four hours could have been caused by me. How? By some cosmic retribution gifted to me by the universe?

Yeah, right.

Still, disappointment crashes over me like a wave.

Like . . . like *that* wave.

The laughter from Jackson's friends halts as they notice it, too. A wave, one of the biggest I've ever seen, rears up behind Jackson, framing him beneath its frothy crown.

Seeing his friends' expressions, he turns. Too late. The wave strikes him, bowling him over. It doesn't stop there. The water storms up the beach, dousing his friends' legs and rushing over their towels and chairs, sweeping cans of beer into its current.

The wave keeps coming. Heading straight toward me.

My jaw is slack. It doesn't even cross my mind to move as I watch the wave break. The foam curls up into itself. The last vestiges of the wave's power start to slow, from a rush of water to a steady crawl.

The edge of the water, kissed with white foam, comes to within an inch of my toes and the edge of Ari's guitar case. It pauses, seeming to hesitate for the briefest moment, before sweeping back out to sea again.

I follow its course, stunned. When I look up, I catch Ari's eye. She looks just as bewildered—maybe even more so. Because the strangest thing isn't that the water came so very close to me yet left me untouched. The strangest thing is that Ari was standing so very close to Jackson, but the wave passed her by entirely.

In fact, despite the wave's enormous size, the only people it touched were Jackson and his friends.

TEN

It takes a minute for my brain to catch up with what just happened. For the disbelief to slowly crumble and fade and then rebuild itself into something, well, almost believable.

My hand unclenches and I flex my fingers, sensing each joint. My palm is hot. My knuckles feel strained, like they've been clenched for hours, rather than just a few seconds.

All around me, people are hollering with laughter. It's hysterical, watching Jackson pick himself up out of the surf. He's drenched from head to foot. His clothes stick to him like a second skin, plastered with muddy sand. A string of seaweed hangs over his shoulder. His hair is matted to his brow.

His face is priceless.

"Ha!" a girl yells. "Karma's a bitch!"

I blink and turn my head. It's Serena. Her own clothes are still wet, but all signs of tears have vanished. She's beaming. The color has returned to her cheeks.

Karma.

Instant karma.

"Holy mothballs," I breathe as something starts to make sense. Sort of. Does it make sense? Can this be real?

I consider the evidence.

The car crash.

The spilled tomato juice.

Mr. Chavez biting his lip.

The ice cream parlor. The tourists on the boardwalk. The rude employee at the fish-and-chips stand . . .

And now this. A wave that came from nowhere, smashing only into Jackson and his jerk friends, even on this very crowded beach.

Surely it can't be coincidence. Not all of it, anyway.

But if it isn't coincidence, what is it?

John Lennon's lyrics echo through my head. I mutter them quietly under my breath. *Instant karma's gonna get you, gonna knock you right on the head . . .*

I reach for the back of my head, where I can still feel a small, sore lump from my fall. I go over the events of the evening before. Seeing Quint and his friend. Those guys heckling Ari while she sang. Our conversation about karma. My name being called, though no one has admitted to putting it up there. Singing the song. Dancing. Quint giving me that look of bewilderment. Slipping on the spilled beer. Hitting my head . . .

If it's not coincidence, then that means that somehow, for some reason . . . it's been me. I've been causing these things. I've been . . . exacting instant karma on people.

"Pru? Are you okay?"

My attention darts up to see Ari strolling back through the sand. She grabs a towel off the back of one of the beach chairs and wraps it around her waist. She's still mostly dry, though sand is clinging to her ankles.

"Yeah," I say, my stomach fluttering. "That was weird, right?"

She laughs. "So weird. But so perfect. Is he always like that?"

"Pretty much. Jackson's always been a bully. It's nice to see him get what's coming to him, for once." I lean toward her, lowering my voice. "I bet you anything that shirt cost a couple hundred dollars. He'll try to play it cool, but believe me, this is killing him."

Ari flops onto the towel and pulls a soda from the small cooler we brought. She pops the tab, then holds the can up toward the water, as if in a toast. "Nice work, ocean." Then she glances around. "I just hope that girl's okay."

I don't respond. I'm distracted, looking around at the beach towels and blankets and chairs that have taken over the shore. I'm distracted by Jackson, using the corner of a towel to get water out of his ears.

"I'll be right back." I turn and hike up the sandy beach, seeking solitude along the rocky cliff side. It's too early for the infamous make-out sessions to have begun, and it's easy for me to find an empty alcove among the towering rocks. I lean against a boulder and press my hand to my chest. My heart races underneath my skin.

"This is just wishful thinking," I whisper. "A fairy tale. Brought on by end-of-year stress, and all those fantasies of wanting to punish people when they deserve it, and . . . maybe a slight concussion."

Despite my rational words, my brain shoots back a number of counter-arguments. The song. The car accident. The wave.

But every time I start to think—maybe it *was* me—I chastise myself. Am I really considering the possibility that I sang a karaoke song, and now I have . . . what? Magic powers? Some sort of cosmic gift? The completely preposterous ability to bestow the justice of the universe?

"Coincidences," I repeat, beginning to pace. Sand gets into my sandals and I kick them off. I march back and forth between the rocks. "That's all this is. A bunch of bizarre coincidences."

But—

I pause.

Too many coincidences have to mean something.

I push my hair back from my face with both hands. I need to be sure. I need proof.

I need to see if I can do it again, on purpose this time.

Gnawing on my lower lip, I peek out through a gap in the rocks, surveying the crowded beach. I'm not sure what I'm looking for. Inspiration, I guess. Someone here must be deserving of punishment for *something*.

My gaze lands on none other than Quint. He's helping a few of our peers set up a volleyball net.

Ha. Perfect. If anyone deserves cosmic retribution for their behavior this year, it is definitely Quint Erickson.

I think of all the times he was late. All the times he slacked off. How he left me to fend for myself on presentation day.

How he absolutely refuses to help me redo our semester project.

I squeeze my fist tight.

And wait.

"Hey, Quint," says a girl from our class, striding over to him. I perk up. What is she going to do? Slap him for some mysterious melodrama I'm not aware of?

"How's it going?" says Quint, returning her smile.

"Good. I brought some homemade cookies. Want one?" She holds out a tin.

"Heck yeah, I want one," he says, taking a cookie. "Thanks."

"Of course." She beams at him before walking away.

I'm dumbfounded.

I mean, I guess the cookie could be poisoned? But I highly doubt it.

Quint devours the cookie, then finishes staking down the net.

I keep watching for another minute, utterly confused. Soon it becomes clear that nothing horrible is about to befall Quint. In fact, once the volleyball game starts, he scores the first point for his team, receiving a round of whoops and high fives.

Pouting, I finally relax my fist.

"Well. There's that," I mutter. The disappointment is hard to swallow, but I'm not sure if I'm more disappointed in the universe, or myself, for almost believing something so absurd.

I roll my shoulders. Enough of that. I'm going to spend the rest of the evening reading the book I brought, eating s'mores, listening to Ari as she tries to piece together the right chord progression for her newest song. I am going to relax.

I grab my shoes and start to slip them back on.

"Please. He's such a nerd. You know he plays Dungeons and Dragons, right?"

I freeze. I don't have to look to know it's Janine Ewing, her voice carrying easily into this little alcove. I can't see her, or who she's talking to, but there are only a few boys she could be talking about. Jude and his friends—Matt and César, also sophomores, or Russell, a freshman who joined their group a few months ago.

"Seriously?" says another female voice. Katie? "That weird role-playing game from the eighties? That those kids play in *Stranger Things*?"

"That's the one," says Janine. "It's like—really? You don't have anything better to do with your time?"

I peer through the gap in the rocks to see Janine and Katie just a few feet away from the cliff side, lounging on an assortment of vivid beach towels in bikinis and sunglasses. And . . . oh. Maya is with them, too. Together, they look like a sunscreen advertisement, and not in a bad way. Maya especially looks like a Hollywood starlet. She's the sort of girl who could have just stepped out of a makeup commercial. Dark skin warmed by the setting sun, thick black hair left natural and curly, framing her face, and a smattering of freckles that are so stinking charming they could inspire whole sonnets.

Unsurprisingly, Jude isn't the only guy at school with a schoolboy crush on her.

"Isn't Demons and Dragons some kind of devil-worship game?" asks Katie.

I roll my eyes, and to Maya's credit, she slides her sunglasses down her nose and gives Katie a look that suggests she agrees with me on just how unnecessary this comment was. "*Dungeons* and Dragons," she says. "And I'm pretty sure that's a rumor started by the same people who thought Harry Potter was evil."

And I have to admit, while I often question Jude's mindless devotion to her, Maya does have her moments.

She nudges her glasses back into place. "Anyway. Lay off. I like Jude."

My eyes widen. Pause. Rewind. She *likes* Jude?

Does she mean that she *like* likes him?

I become giddy. I strain my ears to catch every word they're saying. If I could go back to Jude with empirical evidence that his feelings aren't unrequited after all, I would be a shoo-in for the Best Sister of the Year Award.

"Of course you like him," says Janine. "Who doesn't? He's so nice."

"So nice," Katie agrees emphatically. So emphatic it almost sounds like an insult.

"But he's also . . ." Janine trails off. It takes her a long moment to find the words to elaborate. "Just, like, *so* into you. It's kind of creepy."

I make a sound of derision. Jude is not creepy!

I duck back behind the rock before they look back and see me, but their conversation doesn't falter.

"He does sort of stare at me sometimes," Maya concedes. "I used to think it was flattering, but . . . I don't know. I don't want to be mean, but you'd think he'd get the hint that I'm not interested, right?"

I flinch.

So much for that plan.

"It does come off as sort of obsessive," adds Katie. "But in a sweet way?"

I peer through the rocks again, scowling. Jude is not obsessed!

At least, not *that* obsessed.

He just has a crush on her. It's not a crime! She should be over the moon to have caught the attention of someone as kind and wonderful as Jude!

"Again, I like Jude," says Maya. "But it makes me feel a little guilty, to know how he feels when . . . well, it's just never going to happen."

"You have nothing to feel guilty about!" says Janine. "You didn't do anything."

"Yeah, I know. I guess it isn't my fault I'm not interested in him."

Katie shushes her suddenly, but it's with an almost-cruel giggle. "Shh, Maya, god. He's right over there. He'll hear you."

"Oh!" says Maya, clapping a hand over her mouth. "I didn't know."

But Janine just nudges her with an elbow. "Oh well. Maybe he'll take the hint."

I glance around and spot Jude walking past. I barely catch a glimpse of his expression as he turns away to head back toward our spot on the beach, and I can't tell whether he's heard them or not. I can't tell if the darkness crossing his face is embarrassment, hurt . . . or just the shadows as the sun sinks into the horizon.

It doesn't really matter. It was a mean thing to say. This whole conversation feels born out of cruelty, an unnecessary dialogue intended to mock Jude, for no other reason than to boost Maya Livingstone's inflated ego.

And for her to be mean to *Jude,* of all people. Patient, thoughtful Jude, who is beloved by all. Who has no enemies. Who can slip into any conversation, sit at any lunch table, attend any party.

And yeah, maybe he plays D&D on the weekends, and reads books with dragons on the covers, and was legitimately excited to go to his first Renaissance Faire last summer. He even wore a tunic and, in my opinion, he looked downright chivalrous in it, too. But I hate to think what Maya or her friends would say if they ever saw the photos.

I stare daggers at the top of Maya's head. How dare she hurt him like that? My fist tightens.

This time, I feel it. The tiniest, almost imperceptible jolt in the base of my stomach. Like the flip of your insides when you do an underwater somersault, but more subtle.

Except, still, nothing happens.

I wait. And I wait.

The sun disappears, casting the sky in shades of violet. The first stars begin to blink and shimmer. The cliffs are lit in flickers of gleaming orange from the bonfire.

Maya sits up and reaches for the long sweater beside her towel. I watch her thread her arms through the sleeves. I feel bitter, and more than a little annoyed. At her. At myself. At the universe.

I sigh and finally leave the safety of my haven. Enough of this. I haven't inherited some magical power for restoring balance to the universe. For punishing the wicked and the unworthy.

Time to move on.

Jude and Ari are on our shared blankets. Ari is playing something on her guitar and a handful of people have even stopped to listen, a few of them dropping into the sand in a little half circle around her. But Jude is looking off toward the waves, his posture sullen. I don't have to see his face to know he's brooding. He must have heard Maya after all.

It makes me angry all over again.

I start to move toward them, when I hear a gasp. A horrible, startled sound.

"No! No, no, no. You can't be serious."

I slowly turn around. Maya is on her hands and knees, frantically digging around in the sand.

"What?" says Katie, backing away as Maya flips up the edge of her towel. "What is it?"

"My earring," says Maya. "I've lost an earring! Stop staring and help me look!"

Her friends still look a little baffled, but they don't argue. All three of them are soon rooting through the sand. Every now and then Maya pauses to feel her ear, then pat down her sweater and check her hair. It soon becomes obvious that her search is in vain.

A smile stretches across my lips, and I think I understand something.

Instant karma.

Maybe it has to be instant. An immediate retribution for a wrongdoing. Nothing happened to Quint because our fight was hours ago.

But Maya was being mean *now.*

Her expression is pained, even bordering on tears, by the time she gives up searching, but I don't feel the tiniest bit sorry. Her earring might have been fancy and expensive. I can see its match dangling from her other ear. It's a drop earring, with a single stone in the center of its design that I think might be a diamond. Maybe they belong to her mom, who will be so mad that one was lost. Or maybe it was some piece of memorabilia to commemorate one of Maya's many achievements—"Student of the Week" or "I gave blood!" or something. It doesn't matter to me. She hurt my brother, and she deserves to pay the price.

Pivoting on my heels, I start to head back to my friends. There's a new bounce in my step. My fingers are tingling, as if this unexpected cosmic power is swirling in my veins.

I'm so distracted that I almost don't notice the volleyball soaring toward me. Instinct takes over and I duck, screaming.

A figure emerges in my periphery, smacking the ball and sending it back toward the net.

I look up, blinking, my arms still held protectively over my head.

Quint's lips are pinched, his eyes dancing. It's clear he's doing all he can to not laugh at me. "What did you think it was, a shark?"

I drop my arms to my sides. I attempt to reclaim my dignity the best way I know how—with palpable disdain. "I was distracted," I say, glaring at him. "It startled me."

He lets a small chuckle escape. "We need another player. Don't suppose you'd be interested?"

I guffaw. If there's a sport I'm naturally gifted at, I have yet to figure out what it is. Definitely nothing they make us play in gym class. "Not even a tiny bit. But thanks for . . . that."

"Rescuing you?" he says, loud enough that anyone nearby might hear. He looks almost gleeful. "Could you say that again, but louder this time?" He leans toward me, cupping a hand around his ear.

My glare deepens.

"Go on," he prods. "I believe the exact words you're looking for are, *Thank you for saving my life, Quint. You're the best!*"

I scoff. Then an idea strikes me and I grin, taking a step toward him. He must see something troubling in my face, because he immediately takes a step back. His look of amusement changes to mistrust.

"I'll say thanks after you agree to redo that biology project with me."

He groans.

Behind him, a junior girls yells, "Quint, come on! You're still playing, right?"

"Yeah, yeah," he says, waving a dismissive hand toward her. I glance over at the girl. She's watching me, her mouth puckered to one side.

Don't worry, I want to tell her. *He's all yours.*

Quint starts to walk backward toward the net. He lifts a finger, pointing directly at me. "The answer is still no," he says. "But I appreciate your persistence." He turns and jogs back to the game.

I exhale sharply. It was worth a shot.

"Yo, Prudence," calls a voice.

It takes me a second to realize it's Ezra Kent, who's standing on the other side of the volleyball net, waiting for the game to resume. Once he has my attention, he tips his chin at something behind me. "Who's the hot girl with the guitar?"

Blinking, I look around. For a second I've forgotten what I'm doing, where I was going. Then I see Ari sitting cross-legged on our blanket, the guitar settled on her lap, but she's not playing. She's talking to some people from school— one girl I know is in jazz band and a couple seniors I've never spoken to. Jude is there, too, but he's sitting slightly apart from the group, still sulking. His bare feet are buried into the sand.

I spin back around and glare warningly at Ezra. "Someone who's out of your league."

He exaggeratedly rubs his hands together. "I like a challenge."

I flash a saccharine smile. "And she likes integrity, so don't waste your time."

He cackles. "Aw, man. I am going to miss you this summer."

"That makes one of us," I mutter, rolling my eyes. I'm about to walk away when a thought hits me.

I hesitate, turning back just as Quint is getting ready to serve.

"Hey, Quint?"

He pauses and glances at me. I walk closer so I can keep my voice down and one of his enormous eyebrows shoots upward, as if my mere presence were cause for suspicion. "You know, Jude is halfway decent at volleyball. If you're still wanting another player?"

This might be a lie. But it might not be. My brother and I haven't had gym class together since sixth grade, so I honestly have no idea how good he is at volleyball.

Quint glances past me, spying my brother. "Yeah, cool. Hey, Jude! You in for a game?"

I walk away, doing my best to look casual so Jude won't know I instigated this invitation. But it works. A couple seconds later, Jude is jogging across the beach. He nods at me, maybe realizing that this is the first time we've seen each other since we got here.

"Doing all right, Sis?" he asks as he passes by. I know the undercurrent of the question. The true meaning. I didn't want to come to this party in the first place. He basically dragged me and Ari along.

But I think of the wave that crashed over Jackson and Maya's panicky voice as she looked for her missing earring and the small crowd of people who have stopped to listen to Ari and her guitar, and suddenly I'm smiling. A real smile. A ridiculous, delighted, absolutely over-the-moon grin.

"Honestly? I'm having a great time." I tilt my head toward the volleyball game. "Gonna play?"

"Yeah, I'll give it a try. Try not to make a fool of myself."

"You've got this." I give him an encouraging punch in the shoulder and we go our separate ways.

The sand beneath my steps has turned to clouds as I stroll back toward Ari, feeling like all the power in the universe is at my fingertips.

ELEVEN

I wake up early the next morning, the smell of woodsmoke clinging to my hair, proof that the bonfire party was real. That I didn't dream it all up. There's a logical voice in my brain still insisting that this whole karmic justice thing is only wishful thinking, but I do my best to shush that voice.

I lie in bed thinking of all the times I've been frustrated at the unfairness of life. At the students who slack off and still somehow manage to earn the teacher's approval. The bullies who never seem to get caught. The jerks who rise to the top of the social ladder.

Well, not anymore. At least not in Fortuna Beach.

There's a new judge in town.

I'm giddy as I get up and move through my usual routine of making my bed, brushing my teeth, getting dressed. The day feels full of potential. My *life* feels full of potential.

I check the clock: 6:55 a.m. on the first full day of summer vacation. I'm dressed and ready, lipstick and everything, and still, the rest of the house continues to sleep. I know I should be exhausted, since Jude and I didn't come home until after midnight, but I'm wide-awake.

I sit on the edge of my bed and drum my fingers against my knees. I usually love this time of day, when I'm the only one in my family awake. The serenity and solitude feel like a rare gift to be cherished. Whenever possible during the school year, I try to get up so I can get some things accomplished without being pestered by my parents or sisters, but now I feel like I'm in limbo.

No homework. No projects. Nothing to do.

I glance over at my bookshelf, thinking maybe I'll read for a while, but I know I won't be able to focus.

My eyes land on the stack of folders and notebooks I emptied from my backpack the night before, all sitting neatly at the corner of my desk.

Quint's binder sits at the very top, that forlorn seal peering up from the cover.

I pick it up. That hateful sticky note greets me and I make a face. I don't want to open it. A huge part of me wants to tear this report into tiny pieces and toss it out the window, but that would be littering, so I don't. Nevertheless, I'm confronted with something almost like fear as I carry the report back to my bed and settle into my pillows.

Fear of what, though? That I might have been wrong all this time? That Quint, in a shocking twist to all, might actually have done good work? That the words in these pages will be well-written, thoroughly researched, and altogether brilliant? That maybe *I* was the weak link in our partnership?

I read Mr. Chavez's words again, but this time I focus on his critique of Quint. *Messy execution. Unfocused writing.* So, okay. There's that. I know it isn't some great piece of literature. I know there are flaws.

And yet, his grade is above mine, above *ours*.

Steeling myself, I open the binder.

At first, as I peruse Quint's report, I'm surprised, even a little impressed. First impressions go a long way and, well, the first impression of his paper is not at all what I expected. Rather than the typical twelve-point, double-spaced, Times New Roman affair that's standard in all our coursework, Quint has designed the report to appear like a magazine article with two justified columns interspersed with images of wildlife and marine habitats. Each section is divided by a bold aquamarine title, and the captions beneath the photos are tidy and stylized. He even included a subtle beige footer along the bottom of each page: *Marine Conservation by Way of Ecotourism | Prudence Barnett and Quint Erickson*.

The overall effect is nice. Classy. Even professional. It's not at all what I expected and I feel a tinge of regret. How was he capable of this quality of work all this time and I had no idea?

And then there are the pictures. Every page has at least one photograph and they are as breathtaking as they are horrifying. Seabirds drenched in black oil. Seals with deep gashes along their sides. Sea lions with dozens of fishhooks caught in their skin. I've never given a lot of credence to the idea that a picture is worth a thousand words, but I have to admit, these illustrations are very effective. My gut twists as I return to the first page.

I start to read the text, and . . . my opinions begin to plummet.

Typos. Misspellings. Run-on sentences. Rambling, almost incoherent statements.

Criminy. How did this guy pass ninth-grade English?

The parts I can read without cringing and wishing I had a red pencil in hand are passionate, though, and surprisingly full of relevant facts and statistics. He spends a great deal of time outlining how human behavior has negatively affected our local ecosystems. He goes into explicit detail on the declining populations of a number of marine species and how they're being impacted by waste, pollution, and overfishing practices. It's all way more than I would have done. After all, the report is on ecotourism, not environmental decline. But I have to hand it to him, there is a lot of science. I even learn a few things while I read, things that make me want to check his sources and see if they're real, including a number of statistics that suggest that ecotourism itself, if not carefully monitored, can be more detrimental than beneficial to the very environments visitors are hoping to conserve.

My estimation of Quint and his work is beginning to climb again, when I *finally* reach the part of the paper on our suggestions for creating a vibrant ecotourism industry in Fortuna Beach. I expect the next couple of pages to be familiar. After all, this is what we discussed, on the few occasions Mr. Chavez gave us time in class to work on the project together. I'm looking forward to reading the text version of my well-thought-out plan. The resort. The sea adventures. The beach parties. All the things that will have tourists flocking to Fortuna Beach in the name of fun, exploration, and a hearty dose of philanthropy.

Except . . . there's none of that. He doesn't talk about the resort. He leaves out my brilliant array of boating and snorkeling tours. There's not even a word about the spa with all-natural, organic treatments!

Instead, according to Quint, tourists will come to Fortuna Beach in order to . . . volunteer at an animal rescue center.

I groan loudly and thump my head back against my headboard. My skull still smarts, a reminder of my fall the other night.

Seriously? In all our conversations, Quint was insistent that we should focus on the Fortuna Beach Sea Animal Rescue Center. He thought people who truly cared about helping our oceans would love to come to the center, help care for the animals, learn about what goes into rehabilitation, and discover beneficial lifestyle changes they can make going forward.

I rolled my eyes every time he brought it up, just like I'm rolling my eyes now. Why would our community put the money into building an animal rehab center when we can have a *spa*? We want to attract millionaires, not hippies!

I'm fuming as I skim the last few paragraphs and turn to the final page. At least he bothered to include a bibliography, though I notice he hasn't credited the sources where he got the photography, which is schoolwork blasphemy in my opinion.

My eye catches on one of the sources and I go still. Unlike the other listings, which are mostly websites with a couple of magazines and books thrown in for good measure, Quint has included an interview subject.

Rosa Erickson, founder and owner of the Fortuna Beach Sea Animal Rescue Center. Interview conducted by Quint Erickson.

"Hold the phone," I mutter, sitting up straighter. "The rescue center is a real place?"

I grab my phone off the charger on my nightstand and do a quick search. And there it is—no official website, but a business listing with an address a couple miles north of downtown. A bit more digging and that name pops up, too. Rosa Erickson.

"You jerk!" Dropping the phone onto the blankets, I launch out of bed and begin to pace. I don't know if Rosa is Quint's mom or aunt or grandma or what, but they must be related. How could he have neglected to mention that this rescue center he was so set on including is an actual, existing place? And that he has a personal connection to it? If I'd known that, I would have completely reworked my plan for the project. We could have focused on the impact of rescue centers in a community or done some cool hands-on demonstration of the sort of work the center does. We could have invited this Rosa person to come and talk to the class, or maybe even gotten permission to take our classmates on an awesome field trip.

We could have knocked this project out of the park!

How could Quint have kept this a secret? And, maybe more important, *why*? Why didn't he tell me?

I stop pacing and stare ice-daggers at the report. I'd flipped it back to the front when I jumped up from the bed, and there's that sticky note again. That C, mocking me.

I can understand Mr. Chavez's note better, at least. There's almost nothing between my street model and Quint's paper that suggests we were a team, working together on one cohesive project. But that's not *my* fault, and I refuse to let my GPA fall because Quint couldn't deign to fill me in on this hugely relevant piece of information.

I grab my phone and check the address of the rescue center again.

I don't care about Mr. Chavez and his rules. I'm going to redo this project and I'm going to make it so brilliant, he'll have no choice but to award me the grade I truly deserve.

TWELVE

Dad is in the kitchen, sitting at the table by himself with a cup of coffee and the newest issue of *Rolling Stone* magazine.

He glances up when I come in, then checks the time on the stove. "Up before eight o'clock! Aren't you on summer vacation?"

"Dad, when have you ever known me to sleep in past eight, vacation or otherwise?" I slide a slice of bread into the toaster. There's a new bunch of bananas on the counter, but I don't feel like mucking around with the blender this morning. "I've got things to do, you know."

"Do you?" Dad says, with a slight chuckle. "Not too much, I hope. Your mom and I actually have a few ideas for how you can spend your time this summer."

I frown at him, instantly on edge. "Like what?"

"Well . . ." He uses one of those subscription cards to mark his place and closes the magazine. "We were going to wait and discuss this with you at dinner, but since you asked. We thought it might be time for you and Jude to start helping out at the store."

I stare at him. Helping out at the store?

The *record* store?

The next three months flash through my mind, full of clueless tourists who think that an old-school vinyl store is *wow, such a novelty,* versus the obnoxious music "aficionado" who likes to rant on and on about how digital music *has no soul, man,* versus the people who come in trying to sell their grandfather's collection and can't comprehend why we'll only pay them fifty cents for a beat-up copy of *Hotel California.*

I stare at my dad and I know that laughing out loud is the wrong tactic, so instead I say simply, "Huh."

That's it. That's all I can think to say. *Huh.*

My dad, sensing my utter disinterest, swiftly morphs from jolly and hopeful to chastising. "It's a family business, you know. And you are a part of this family."

"Yeah, no, I know," I say quickly. "It's just . . ." I stall, searching for an excuse. Any excuse. Any excuse other than *I have zero desire to spend my summer stuck behind the counter of your dingy record store, smelling like mothballs and telling the regulars that, no, sorry, we haven't gotten in any new hair metal since last week.*

"It's just . . . I was . . . thinking of volunteering," I hear myself say.

Wait. What?

My dad lifts an eyebrow and says sardonically, "Volunteering? Where, the boardwalk?"

Indignation flares inside my chest. It can't be *that* surprising that I would volunteer my time to a worthy cause. All through middle school I tutored a couple of kindergarteners and first graders after school, twice a week, which mostly just meant I would sit and read picture books to them, but still. I believe in good deeds and charity. I may not have had much time lately, but the idea that I would do something philanthropic shouldn't garner suspicion.

"No, not the boardwalk," I say, mocking his dismay. "It's this place called, um, the Fortuna Beach Rescue Center. They take in distressed animals. Sea lions and stuff. And help them get better." At least, I assume this is what they do. I skimmed most of those pages in Quint's paper and still only have a vague notion of this rescue center's purpose.

"Oh," says Dad. I know this *oh.* I can hear pages of confusion written into that *oh.*

Oh, I didn't realize you liked animals. *Oh,* it's been so long since you talked about any sort of volunteering. *Oh,* I thought you were planning to spend your entire summer vacation with Ari, eating ice cream and counting the days until it becomes socially acceptable to start obsessing over college applications.

(Not before the start of junior year, evidently, though I do have a checklist started for when the day comes.)

But Dad doesn't say any of this. Instead, he says, "I've never heard of it."

"No, I hadn't, either. A friend told me about it." I visibly shiver at the idea that Quint is a *friend,* but I turn back to my toast, which has just popped, and focus on slathering it with peanut butter.

"Is this for school?"

I hesitate. "Sort of? And also, just . . . you know. I thought it'd be good to do something for the community, and our local . . . marine . . . habitats." I drop the knife into the sink. "I thought I'd go there today and see if they could use my help." I hesitate, smiling uncertainly, before asking, "Is that okay?"

His brows pucker in the middle. "Well," he drawls slowly, uncertainly. I can see the wheels whirring in his head as he tries to determine the best parental approach. Insist that your child help with the family business in order to build personal responsibility and a strong work ethic, or encourage this unexpected interest in altruism and animal welfare? Finally, he clears his throat. "I tell you what. You go talk to them today and see if it seems like a good fit for you, and I'll talk to your mother about it, and we'll reconvene at dinner tonight." He finishes this statement with a pleased nod. I can practically see him congratulating himself on another parenting dilemma, conquered. Or, at least, postponed until Mom can give her input. "Do you need me to drive you there?"

"No, thanks. I'll take my bike. It's only a couple miles away."

He nods again, but then seems to reconsider something. "You know, Pru, I was teasing before, about spending your time at the boardwalk. You've worked hard this year. You deserve to relax during your vacation. So . . . volunteer at this rescue place or come hang at the store with me or whatever works out. But don't forget to get out and enjoy the sunshine sometimes, too, all right?"

I stare at him. He says it so innocently, but I can't help but feel like there's a tiny, hidden attack in his words. *Don't work so hard that you forget to have fun.*

Why is everyone so concerned that I don't know how to have fun? To relax? Yes, I work hard. Yes, I believe in practicality and efficiency and excelling at the things I do. What's so wrong with that?

I don't say any of this, though. Instead, I give Dad a tight smile. "Thanks for the advice. I'll take it under consideration."

He sighs at me. "You do that." He turns his attention back to his coffee and his magazine, enjoying his last moments of peace before the rest of my siblings begin to stir.

I grab my toast and head out the door. I haven't quite decided how I feel about my little white lie by the time I'm strapping on my bike helmet and cramming the last bite of toast into my mouth. Under no circumstances had I considered volunteering my summer hours at some nonprofit organization—at least, I'm assuming the center is nonprofit, though even that is unclear. Either way, if I had intended to volunteer somewhere, I would have chosen something like writing newsletters for our local YMCA or starting a Little Free Library on Main Street or organizing bake sales in order to send some kid in an impoverished third-world country to school or . . . something. But sea turtles and otters or whatever it is they work with at this place? I mean, I have nothing against sea animals. And I do need to fix our project for Mr. Chavez, and this seems like a sure way to do it.

But still. It's not exactly the cause of my heart.

Maybe, if things don't go well today, I can come up with a plan B. Find some other organization to volunteer my time at—something a little more fitting to my interests—and tell my parents there's been a change of plans.

Curating a Little Free Library *would* be fun . . .

I pause, frowning at this thought. Something tells me very few people would agree with this sentiment. Is it possible that *my* idea of fun, relaxing, enjoyable activities is really so far afield from everyone else's?

But does that mean something is wrong with me, or them?

I shake my head. Whatever I decide about volunteering, at least it will look great on college applications. A summer spent at a sea animal rescue center may not have been the original plan, but I can see how it will have long-term benefits. I'm envisioning all the heartwarming application essays I'll be able to write explaining how I managed to make the world a better place through my selfless dedication. My future résumé will be a step above other candidates' for having spent a portion of my time in such impressive service.

This is good, I tell myself repeatedly, as my legs pump against the bike pedals.

This is for the best.

It certainly beats out a summer spent at the record store, anyway.

The salty wind is refreshing against my cheeks, blowing through my hair. The morning is warm but pleasant. I pass loads of people walking their dogs, and even some kids splashing through the sprinklers on their front lawn. I pass an old man mowing his grass and a bunch of house painters setting up scaffolding. I pass more people on bikes—some in suits, some in swim trunks. We give each other neighborly smiles.

I stop outside a convenience store, waiting for the traffic light to change. The car beside me has the windows down and I smile when "Good Day Sunshine" comes on over their speakers. I tap my fingers against the handlebars, humming along. I even picture myself singing this song at karaoke night—if we go back for karaoke night.

Hecklers and spilled drinks aside, it was kind of fun.

I'm still distracted, thinking that maybe I would consider doing a duet with Ari, when the light for crossing traffic turns yellow. I adjust the pedals, getting ready to go, when I glance toward the convenience store parking lot. A shiny SUV is pulling into a parking spot.

My eyes narrow like laser beams.

It's the disabled-persons parking spot. But there's no wheelchaired stick figure on the car's license plate, no tag hanging from the rearview mirror.

I swivel the front wheel of my bike up onto the curb. I examine the car more thoroughly as I get closer, looking for any sign that they might deserve this coveted spot right by the entrance. This spot that's supposed to be used only by those who truly need it.

The driver's-side door opens and I watch as a middle-aged man climbs out and hurries into the store. As far as I can tell, he doesn't have a disability. Not even a limp.

And there's no passenger.

I shake my head in disgust. Who does he think he is? Someone who actually needs that spot could show up at any minute! Is he going to make some poor elderly grandmother struggle across the parking lot with her walker or cane?

I wriggle my fingers first, feeling the blood pumping into them. There's a moment when I think—you're kidding yourself, Prudence—this isn't going to work.

But I ignore the doubt and squeeze my hand tight.

The instant I do it, a seagull flies overhead and drops a perfect white blotch of excrement onto the SUV's windshield, right smack in the driver's view.

A surprised bark of a laugh escapes me, and I clap my hand over my mouth. *Bull's-eye.*

The man darts from the store a second later, carrying nothing but an energy drink. He takes one look at his car and curses.

I swivel my bike around and soar back onto the street, my whole body tingling with satisfaction.

The ride grows more interesting after that. I'm like a radar, seeking out injustices in the world. My newfound power is twitching at the ends of my fingers, ready to be released. I'm hungry for another chance to see it in action, and the opportunities are suddenly everywhere.

I pass a couple of middle-school-aged boys as they're abusing the vending machine outside Ike's Grocery.

I squeeze my fist and their stolen sodas explode in their faces.

I notice a little girl throwing pebbles at a squirrel. A second later she stubs her toe and runs off wailing to her mother.

I see a man at a bus stop making inappropriate catcalls as a woman jogs by. She ignores him, steely-faced. When he leans forward to admire her backside, I gift his jeans with a split seam down his *own* rear end.

I am on fire. I am shaking with glee. I'm on a total power trip and I know it, but it's not like I asked for this gift, so I figure I must have done something to deserve it.

I'm only a few blocks away from the rescue center when I pass a billboard that I've probably passed by a hundred times without really paying it much attention. Except now there's a ladder leaned against it, and a person standing on the platform, dressed in a baggy sweatshirt and a green beanie cap, holding a can of spray paint.

I stop my bicycle, a little stunned to think that someone would be bold enough to vandalize a billboard in broad daylight like this.

The billboard is an advertisement for Blue's Burgers, a joint that's been a staple in our community since the 1960s. On the right side of the humongous image is a close-up of one of their cheeseburgers, overflowing with pickles and lettuce and creamy special sauce. In the background is a green pasture, with two black-and-white-spotted cows, contentedly grazing. Blue's slogan is printed in speech bubbles over their heads: WE'RE HAPPY COWS, SO YOU'LL BE HAPPY DINERS!

But the vandal has sprayed an X over that message and is starting to scrawl something over the picture of the cows.

Indignation flares inside of me. That's a locally owned business. That's public property. And now someone is going to have to clean this up or pay to have it replaced.

I huff and clench my fist.

The vandal reaches down for a different color of spray paint—and slips.

The ladder jolts. I hear a scream and am surprised to realize it's a girl.

Then she's falling.

It happens in slow motion. Her hands scrabbling for the ladder and finding nothing. Her body plummeting at least ten feet to the ground below. There's a patch of grass and weeds, not asphalt, but still—I hear the snap.

My gut twists, bile rising in my mouth at that terrible noise, followed by her cry of pain.

Her cap has fallen off. She has shiny black hair pulled into two tight buns behind her ears.

My heart stutters. It's *Morgan*, Quint's friend from the other night.

I drop my bike against a tree and prepare to race across the road to help her, but a car has pulled up to the curb and a woman is already running, cell phone in hand. *Oh my god, are you okay? I'll call an ambulance!*

I swallow and take a step back. I still feel sick to my stomach. Cold sweat has beaded on the back of my neck and my bike helmet feels too heavy, too confining. I ignore the sensation and slide my leg over my bike seat.

I turn and pedal as fast as I can the other way.

THIRTEEN

I ride to a nearby park and drop my bike before collapsing onto a wooden bench. Ripping off my helmet, I press my forehead into my hands. I keep seeing it again and again—that moment when her foot slipped. When she lost purchase. When she cried out and fell.

I did that. *I* did that.

I could have killed her.

It takes a long time to calm myself down. A long time before my heart stops palpitating and I can think rationally about what just happened.

It's an even longer time before I convince myself that, no, of course *I* didn't do that.

The punishments I've been doling out have not come from me. I may have thought that something should happen to all those people, but the universe has been deciding what those punishments should be. *I* never would have made someone fall off a ladder, whether they were breaking the law or not. That was all the universe's doing.

Besides, if anyone's to blame, it's Morgan herself. She put herself in danger by climbing up there. She probably didn't think to secure it. Or maybe she's naturally clumsy.

Besides, she must have deserved it. She was harming someone else through her actions. The livelihood of a local business owner. The beauty of our quaint coastal town. Plus, she was so snotty when we met at Encanto, the way she wouldn't stop staring at her phone, even when people were performing.

The universe knows what it's doing. It has to. It's *the universe*.

Gradually, my hands stop shaking.

I know I'm trying to justify what happened, but what else can I do? I have to believe the universe has my back in this.

Finally, after a few mindful breaths in which I try to exhale all my negative energy, I climb back on my bike.

I'm closer to the rescue center than I realized, and the rest of the ride is merely coasting down a two-lane street lined with cypress trees and over-grown blackberry bushes. Not only do I not see anyone behaving badly, I don't see anyone at all. This is a quiet road, one I don't think I've ever been on. Far enough from Main Street and the beach to not attract tourists. I can see evidence of a handful of houses tucked back among the trees—farmsteads with chickens and goats and acreage.

I almost ride right past the center. At the last minute I squeeze the hand-brake and drop my feet onto the pavement.

I don't know what I'd been expecting until the building fails to meet those expectations. It's suddenly clear why Quint didn't bother to include any pictures of this real-world animal-saving "tourist" destination in the report. I guess I'd been picturing an aquarium. Something sleek and modern, with copious amounts of parking that could cater to busloads of kids arriving for school field trips. I was picturing an educational center, with plaques expounding on the delicate ecosystems in our oceans and how humans can help by drinking less bottled water and choosing to eat sustainably caught fish. I've been picturing great glass tanks full of tropical fish and the occasional chortling sea lion, or maybe even gigantic enclosures for whales and dolphins. And also a petting pool where you could slide your knuckle down the rough backs of starfish or let the urchins wrap their spiny needles around your finger.

I realize then, as I turn into the gravel parking lot, that I've been picturing the conservation center in Pixar's *Finding Dory*. High-tech. Fancy. With educational messages from Sigourney Weaver piped through the speakers every couple of minutes.

Which might have been an unrealistic expectation. After all, if Fortuna Beach had an institution like that, I would have known about it before today.

But the reality of the Fortuna Beach Sea Animal Rescue Center is that . . . it's small. And, on the outside at least, entirely unremarkable.

The stench of dead fish hits me before I've stopped pedaling. There's no bike rack, so I set it against a stair rail near the entrance. I take off my helmet, hang it on the handlebar, and scan the small two-story building. It's long but narrow, with a flat roof and concrete walls. Very industrial. Very utilitarian. Very unwelcoming. At least someone has made an attempt to brighten the facade with a coat of coral-colored paint.

Two white vans in the gravel parking lot have the name and phone number of the center printed on the side, encouraging people to call if they see a stranded or hurt animal. There's a stack of crates against the fence, alongside a row of kennels, like something you'd see at the dog pound. A couple of temporary plastic storage sheds stand nearby, their doors padlocked shut. I can hear barking, and it takes me a moment to remember I'm not at a dog pound at all. It must be seals making the noise, or maybe sea lions.

For a moment, I wonder what I'm doing here. I have to write a report—a *better* report, something that will win over Mr. Chavez and his inane rules—and this morning I was convinced that this place was my ticket to doing just that. I would figure out Quint's tie to the center and redo my portion of the presentation to align with the paper he wrote. If I play my cards right, I may even be able to submit the revised project without Mr. Chavez knowing that Quint wasn't involved. Because . . . he *is* involved. In a roundabout way.

I think I can make it work.

I study the building again, my nose wrinkling as a new waft of spoiled seafood overtakes the first rush of salt and fish.

But I haven't committed to anything yet. I'll just go in and check it out, talk to them, figure out who Rosa Erickson is, and who she is to Quint, and glean whatever I can to use in my revised project. Then I'll be out of here, nothing to it. As for what I'll tell my parents about my new volunteer position . . . well, I'll cross that bridge when I come to it.

I swipe on a coat of lipstick, smooth the creases from my shirt, and make my way to the entrance—a faded yellow door with a mail slot near the bottom. I hesitate, wondering whether I should knock. It's a place of business, but as far as I can tell, it isn't open for the public to visit.

I go ahead and rap my knuckles against the door. I wait, but all I hear are the continued yelpings from whatever sea animal is making all that racket.

After a few seconds, I check the knob. It opens and I peek my head into a small room, which I suppose might pass for a lobby, though it's smaller than my bedroom at home. A collection of houseflies are buzzing around a single wooden desk that is overflowing with paperwork. One wall is covered in fake wood paneling, almost identical to the stuff in our basement that was remodeled in the seventies. There's a collection of framed photographs showing men and women holding hoses and push broom and grinning at the camera, or linked arm in arm on the beach, or examining a sea turtle on a metal table.

On the opposite wall is an open door that leads to a long, narrow hallway. A quick glance makes me think of a horse stable, with a series of low walls divided into sections—separate rooms for the animals. But instead of hay, this stable has linoleum-tiled flooring, and it reeks of fish instead of fertilizer.

Next to the door is a framed movie poster—the iconic *Jaws* poster, of all things.

But no, on closer inspection I see that it's a spoof. The giant shark head looming up from the depths is actually a gray speedboat seen from above, and the swimming girl has been replaced with a harmless-looking shark. The title, *Laws*, has a caption: HUMANS KILL 11,400 SHARKS PER HOUR. SHARKS KILL 12 HUMANS PER YEAR. PETITION TO CHANGE SHARK-CULLING LAWS.

"Per hour?" I mutter. Can that statistic possibly be real?

I also can't help but shudder at the second number. The idea of being snagged in the ocean by a great white has literally kept me up at night, and I've never even seen *Jaws*.

A single sheet of white office paper catches my eye. Someone has printed another *Jaws* spoof poster and taped it next to the poster. This time, the title reads *Straws*, the swimming girl has been replaced by a sea turtle, and the "monster" coming out of the deep to devour it is nothing but a bunch of plastic straws in the shape of a shark's head.

I chuckle. That's actually pretty clever.

The barking of sea animals suddenly increases and I turn toward a screened-in back door. Beyond it is a large courtyard full of chain-link fences and blue plastic pools and . . . well, I've found the noisemakers.

I inch my way around the desk, careful not to bump any of the teetering paper stacks, and approach the screen door.

The courtyard has no fancy tanks. No giant aquariums. But a heck of a lot of seals. Or maybe sea lions. Or otters? I don't know, but they're shiny and relatively cute and taking turns splashing through the plastic pools or chasing one another around the concrete that shines with puddles of water everywhere.

I notice that, while some of the pools are small plastic kiddie pools like I'd buy at the variety store on Main Street, there are other larger pools built into the ground along the far side of the courtyard. An array of awnings and pop-up tents and tarps tied to the tops of the chain-link fences offer mottled shade as the sun tops the side of the building. A tangle of hoses wind their way from platform to platform, and there is equipment piled up in every corner: coolers and pool nets and scrubbing brushes and more plastic buckets than you'd see at the local hardware store.

A door bangs off to my right, making me jump. Two women, wearing identical yellow T-shirts, emerge from the far end of the building. They approach one of the kiddie pools, which is housing a solitary animal. It watches the women approach, its whiskers twitching around its nose.

"Excuse me?" I say, pushing open the screen door. It screams on its hinges.

The women spin toward me. One of them looks to be about my mom's age, with wispy black hair pulled back into a messy braid. The other is older and stockier—seventies, maybe—with white hair curled in a bob and a strand of pearls around her neck that don't go with the basic T-shirt at all.

"Hello?" says the younger woman. "Can I help you?"

"Yes, maybe. My name is Prudence Barnett, and I'm doing a project on local ecotourism. I was hoping to learn more about this center. What you do here and how it benefits the local wildlife, and also the community. Maybe I could even . . . help out? Like, on a volunteer basis? For a few hours . . . or ask you some questions, if you're not too busy?"

The older woman laughs and tucks a clipboard under one arm. "Oh, sweetie pie. We're always busy." She sighs and looks at the other woman. "I'll see if I can dig up those pamphlets from last year to give to her."

But the dark-haired woman ignores her. Her eyes are on me, her brow taut. "Did you say *Prudence*?"

"Yes, ma'am." I dare to take a few steps away from the door. I glance at the nearest pool, which is behind one of the fence enclosures. The animals there don't seem to notice that there's a stranger in their midst. That, or they simply don't care. "I won't take up too much of your—"

"You go to Fortuna High?" she interrupts.

I pause. "Yes."

"Huh." The woman's gaze slips over me, head to toes, but I can't tell what she's trying to assess. "I think you might know my son. Quint."

I freeze. My expression remains neutral, professional, but inside I'm shocked. This is Quint's mom? And also . . . he's mentioned me? To his *mom*?

Drat. I can only imagine all the horrible accusations he's cast my way. If he rants about me half as much as I've ranted about him, then it's going to be a long uphill battle to get on this woman's good side.

I briefly consider apologizing and excusing myself and scurrying away, but I hold my ground. My smile brightens, and I try to forget that Quint and I have been mortal enemies for the past nine months. Maybe, just *maybe,* all he told his mom was that we were lab partners, tasked with doing our semester project together.

"That's right," I say, giving an extra bubble to my voice. "We were lab partners this year in biology. You must be Rosa?"

"Yes." She draws out the word. She seems more than a little confused. "This is our office manager, Shauna."

Shauna smiles at me, her round face dimpling. "So lovely to meet a friend of Quint's. I've been wondering when he'd start bringing girls around. Thought it was only a matter of time."

I laugh awkwardly. Oh, if she only knew. "It's nice to meet you both."

"Are you taking summer classes or something?" asks Rosa.

"Oh, no. I just . . ." I pause. How much to tell her? "I'm just doing a bit of extra-credit work. Everyone says I should stop being such an overachiever, but I can't help it! And . . . well, Mr. Chavez's class really gave me a new appreciation for our local sea life. I'm dying to learn more about it."

For the first time, my answer seems to have pleased Quint's mom.

"You do know we aren't a public facility?" says Shauna. She unclips a pen from the clipboard, thumping it against the pages. "But I can surely help you schedule an appointment. Rosa, I'll go check your calendar for the week." She heads into the building, humming to herself.

"I'm sorry," I say to Rosa. "I didn't mean to intrude. If I could just ask a few questions about, say, local marine habitats, and maybe how tourism impacts the lives of these gorgeous animals?"

Rosa chuckles, but it lacks humor. "Well, I could give you loads of information about that," she says dryly. "But Shauna is right. This isn't a good day. I'm sorry. One of my volunteers didn't show up, and we just recovered a sea lion this morning—it's the second time she's been brought in, which is . . ." The groan she makes is full of disappointment. But then she waves her hand at me, brushing her frustration aside. "Never mind. It's a sad story. Maybe we can schedule a phone call? Or here, I'll give you my card and maybe you could just email your questions?"

"Yeah," I say as Rosa walks past me into the lobby. She starts riffling through a desk drawer. "That would work. That'd be great, actually."

She finds a card and hands it to me, then stands back, two fingers pressed to her lips. Her apprehensive frown has returned. "You know," she says uncertainly, "Quint could probably tell you as much about this place as I could. Maybe you could talk to him?"

I laugh. I can't help it. If she's making this suggestion, then she must not know the details of our less-than-stellar partnership after all.

"No," I say, wishing I could snatch back the laughter as soon as it's out. "I mean, I'm sure he's . . . I just really think it will look better for my project if I can talk to the . . ." I glance down at the card. "Owner and director. Not, you know. Her son."

"Well, be that as it may, I know your biology teacher was very supportive of Quint's time here. If you do decide to come back, maybe we can talk a bit about those volunteer opportunities you mentioned. Honestly, it's been a long time since we brought in new help, so I'm not entirely sure what I'd do with you. But with some training, it might actually be nice to have another set of hands."

"Right," I say, tucking the card into my pocket. "Volunteering. Yeah. I'm really sorry no one is around to . . . train me? I'm sure that really takes a lot of time and effort. You know, I should probably just let you get back to work. But I'll email you some questions for sure. Thank you."

Her eyes wrinkle around the edges when she smiles, and it's odd how she can look simultaneously too young and too old. I find myself searching for a resemblance to her son. Her hair and skin are darker, and her eyebrows are reasonably tamed . . . though I suppose that could be maintenance as much as genetics. She's a beautiful woman, and I can see vestiges of her youth. I think she might have looked more like Quint at one point. But she also seems tired, stressed. Like there's a weight on her shoulders that hasn't been lifted for a long time. Whereas Quint exudes a carefree confidence, like there isn't a thing in this world that could worry him.

"Thanks for stopping by," she says.

"Of course." I tip my head gratefully, backing toward the door. "I'll just let you—"

My back smacks into something and I stumble. A hand grabs my arm to steady me.

I glance over my shoulder and freeze.

So does *he,* his hand still gripping my arm.

"Oh. Quint," I say, daring to smile. "Wow. What a small world!"

FOURTEEN

P-Prudence?" Quint stammers.

He's wearing a yellow T-shirt, too, and now I can see the logo printed on the chest. The words FORTUNA BEACH SEA ANIMAL RESCUE CENTER surrounded by a ring of turtles and seals and dolphins.

"What are you doing here?" I say, even though I'm staring right at the answer.

He works here.

But that means that Quint Erickson has a job. Or, at least, a volunteer job. I wonder if his mom pays him to be here. Somehow, that idea seems easier to digest. Either way, though, the utter lack of responsibility he showed all year long makes it impossible to imagine him staying in anyone's employ for long.

Maybe his mom just hasn't had the heart to fire him.

Quint lifts an eyebrow and his hand falls away. He walks around me, into the lobby, which is suddenly cramped with the three of us standing there. "I work here," he says. Then his eyes narrow, first skeptically, and then into something almost smug. "You read the paper, didn't you?"

I cross my arms. "Maybe."

I wish his mom weren't here so I could immediately start yelling at him. All my annoyances from the morning come storming back. How he went completely rogue on our project, without even bothering to inform me of the particularly relevant and might-have-been-helpful information that *his mom runs an animal rescue center.*

"So, what? You came here to critique my spelling?"

"That wouldn't be my first comment, but since you're bringing it up . . . you do know that *Fortuna* is spelled with an *a,* not an *e,* right?"

His jaw tightens. "Autocorrect," he deadpans.

"Proofreading," I counter.

"Okay!" he practically shouts. "This was a fun encounter. Thanks for stopping by."

His mom clears her throat, drawing both of our gazes toward her. She looks expectantly at Quint.

His shoulders shrink into something almost like a pout, and he lazily gestures from me to his mom and back. "Mom, this is Prudence. Prudence, my mom. I think I've maybe mentioned her . . . a time. Or two."

"Yes, we actually met a few minutes ago," says Rosa. She smiles at me. "Quint has told me that you're exceptionally dedicated to your schoolwork."

Quint looks almost uncomfortable at this statement. We both know *dedicated* is not the word he used to describe me. Bossy, maybe. Or controlling. Or *impossible to please.* If he's comfortable cursing around his mom, he might even have said worse.

I'm sure that whatever he's told her, it definitely wasn't something as generous as *dedicated.*

"Oh!" says Rosa, her eyes suddenly brightening. "That's it! You can train her!"

My focus snaps back to her. "What now?"

"It's perfect. You already know each other, you've worked together . . . I don't know why it didn't occur to me before." She sighs and tucks a loose strand from her braid behind her ear. "My brain is so scattered these days."

"Whoa, whoa," says Quint, looking from her to me and back. "What are you talking about?"

"Prudence," she says, gesturing at me, "came by today because she's doing some extra-credit work for your science class, and she wanted to get some hands-on information, maybe even spend some time doing volunteer work for us."

Quint shoots me a look. I smile sheepishly back.

"And I don't have time to train anyone new, but it *would* be nice to have an extra hand over the summer. And then you show up and . . . I don't know. It seems a little serendipitous."

Quint raises an eyebrow. "Extra credit, huh?"

I shrug. "I need to bring up that grade somehow."

"Oh, and Quint . . ." Rosa sets a hand on his shoulder and her expression is suddenly disheartened. "I was going to send you a text when I got a second, but . . . well, Luna was brought back today. She was found up at Devon's Beach, horribly dehydrated."

It's clear this news is upsetting to Quint. I suspect Luna is the sea lion she mentioned earlier, but I'm surprised at Quint's reaction. He doesn't even try to disguise his horror.

"Is she . . . ?"

"Opal is with her now. It's touch and go so far. You know how these first hours are so critical . . ."

Quint swallows, then nods. "She'll fight. She did last time."

Rosa, though, doesn't look as confident. "It seems like she's still having problems feeding herself. I'm worried . . ." She makes a sound in her throat, hopeless and distraught. "It's possible we may not be able to rehabilitate her. If she pulls through this, we might need to consider other options. I don't know. Let's wait and see what Opal finds out."

Quint drags a hand through his hair, making the front stick up oddly above his brow.

A sorrowful silence falls between them.

I inch forward. "Um. Who's Luna?"

Quint shuts his eyes, like he forgot that I was there, or maybe he was just hoping that I'd magically vanished. "No one."

But Rosa answers, "She's a sea lion that was found washed up on the beach last year. We had her for five months and thought she was ready to go back, so we released her a few weeks ago. But . . ." She shakes her head. "She was brought in again this morning."

"How do you know it's her?"

"We tag all our animals, so we can keep track of them even after they're returned to the ocean," says Rosa. "And . . . she was always one of Quint's favorites. I'd recognize her even without the tag."

Quint frowns at her, then turns his irritation on me. "You should probably leave," he says. "We have things to do here, and I'm sure you don't actually intend to volunteer."

I straighten. "You don't know that."

"Please. You? Working with sea animals?"

"Quint——" says Rosa warningly, but he cuts her off.

"It's a terrible idea, Mom. Trust me. Morgan and I can handle the feeding and washing just fine, especially now that I'm on break."

"Morgan isn't coming in today," Rosa says. "She had an accident this morning and had to go to the hospital."

"Hospital?" says Quint.

"I guess she broke her leg and will be out for a few weeks, at least."

"Broke her leg? How?"

Rosa shrugs. "She said she was doing some painting and fell off a ladder."

My heart skips.

Hold on. *Morgan.*

Oh, criminy.

"Okay, okay." Quint waves his hands at his mom. "I'll handle it. You go take care of the pools. I'll start in on the food."

"And . . . ?" Rosa tilts her head toward me.

Quint's voice darkens. "We'll see."

His mom must know this is all she's going to get from him right now. And she also must sense the animosity between us. She flashes Quint a grateful smile and heads back out the door. I spot Shauna still outside, standing over one of the pools and jotting notes on a clipboard.

"Well," says Quint, the second his mom out of earshot. "I have a lot to do. See you around, Prudence." He turns to head down the long corridor.

"Hold on!" I say, following him. "I am redoing that project whether you like it or not, and I'm not leaving here until I have enough science-based information that I can go back and outline the best plan for ecotourism the state of California has ever seen."

He spins back so fast I nearly crash into him for the second time that day. His thick eyebrows are drawn tight, making his features look almost severe. I'm startled to realize he's angry. Not irritated. Not mildly annoyed. This is actual anger.

Quint Erickson doesn't get angry.

I take a step back, though I'm not proud about it.

"Do you ever listen to anything anyone else says?"

I blink at him.

"In case you weren't paying attention, we took in a new rescue today, which means Mom and the vet already have enough to deal with, and we're suddenly short-staffed, which leaves me to clean two dozen pools and feed almost a hundred animals, and you and I both know that you didn't come here today so you could slop around buckets of fish guts."

I grimace.

"On top of that, Mr. Chavez made it very clear that he would only accept revisions if they're a team effort, and there is no power in the universe that could get me to spend another minute working with *you*."

I gape at him, speechless. His breathing is ragged, his cheeks red. It's a side of Quint I've never seen before, and it takes me a second to realize . . . he's not just mad, though clearly I've done something to upset him. No. He's *stressed*.

Laid-back, not-a-care-in-the-world Quint Erickson actually takes this job seriously.

When I don't say anything, he turns and walks away. His words echo around me. *No power in the universe . . .*

I try to dig up my own anger. He can't just walk away. He has to help me with this project. He has to at least let me try.

I squeeze my fist, trying to summon that very power, because he's wrong. Maybe the universe could persuade him to do this project with me. Or it could at least punish him for being such a jerk about it.

I stand there, shoulders tense, fist clenched, and wait.

Until—

Something hard clobbers me on the head.

"Ow!" I yelp, spinning around. The push broom that had been hanging from a couple of wall pegs a second before clatters to the floor. I rub the side of my head where it hit me.

"What?" says Quint. I turn back to see that he's stopped walking and is scowling at me, like he thinks I might have just hit myself with the broom in order to get his attention.

As if.

"That broom just attacked me," I say.

He snorts. It's a mocking sound, and one I find patently unfair. After all, it *did* attack me. And it hurt!

Except, I know that it wasn't really the broom. It was something much bigger.

What's the big idea, Universe?

"Should I call the doctor?" Quint says.

I glower as I pick up the broom and hang it back on the pegs, checking that it's secure before I hastily step away. When the broom doesn't make any more sudden movements, I face Quint again. "Look. I know this last year was miserable. I don't want to redo this project any more than you do. But I cannot get a C!"

"Not my problem." He starts to turn again.

"I'll make you a deal!" I'm practically shouting now.

Quint stops walking. He massages his brow. "I'm not interested—"

"You help me with this report. Not a lot, just enough to show that we did it together. You know, tell me more about the center, and maybe we can spend just a few minutes brainstorming ideas about how we could tie it into the local tourism?"

He rolls his eyes skyward. "Great. A brainstorming session. My favorite."

"In return," I say, my heartbeat quickening, "I'll work here for . . . for a week. Every day. You don't even have to pay me."

He looks at me askance. "Yeah, because . . . volunteers generally don't get paid. You know that, right?"

I flinch. "Of course I know that. I'm just saying . . . you're shorthanded, you're overwhelmed—"

"I'm not overwhelmed."

"Your mom certainly seems to be."

To this, he doesn't argue.

I press a hand to my sternum. "I'm here. I can work. You know I have a strong work ethic. I can"—I brace myself—"schlep fish guts, or whatever you need."

He watches me, and for the first time I can tell I'm making progress.

I attempt a smile. I'm getting dangerously close to begging, but all that matters is that he says yes.

But he doesn't say yes. Instead, he says, "Four weeks."

I sneer. "Four weeks? Every day? Um, no. I think there might be child labor laws—"

"Not every day." He considers. "Four days a week."

"Two."

"That's only eight days, which is only one day more than your original offer."

I shrug.

"Four days a week," he repeats. "That's how much Morgan worked. Hopefully by the end of your sentence, she'll be back."

I twist my lips to the side. Four weeks. With Quint.

It sounds dreadful. But I have to keep my eyes on the prize.

"And in return?" I ask.

Quint sighs. "We can redo the stupid project."

A smile spreads across my lips and I'm two seconds away from an actual squeal when he takes one giant step toward me and lifts a finger between us. "But this time, we are going to actually work together."

Oh, *please,* I want to say. He's going to lecture me on teamwork? The guy who couldn't be bothered to show up half the time?

But I'm so close, so I decide it's best not to bring this up. We'll see how involved he really intends to be once we get started. All I need is for him to sign off on the final product, but now is not the time to discuss details.

"All right," I say, clapping my hands together. "Train away. Let's do this."

He looks at me for what feels like ages, before something shifts in his expression. His lips quirk, just a little. His eyes darken into something that seems almost cruel.

He gestures for me to follow him. "Come on, then. We'd better get you an apron."

FIFTEEN

ood prep. Quint tells me we'll be starting with food prep.

I want to believe that means we'll be making cheese sandwiches for the staff, but something tells me I won't be that lucky. We make our way down the long corridor and pass another half-dozen workers in matching yellow shirts. I was beginning to think it was just me, Quint, Rosa, and Shauna. Oh, and that Opal person that was mentioned, who I think might be the vet. I wonder if the other people here are volunteers or paid staff. They seem busy, whatever they are, tending to the animals inside the little cubicles that reminded me of horse stalls. A few of them give smiles and nods to Quint, and curious glances to me, but for the most part they're focused on their tasks.

I take in as much of the center as I can, trying to figure out what might be useful, but this is about as far from a tourist destination as I can imagine. Some of the walls have shower heads, and all the floors have drains. Some even have tiny plastic kiddie pools. There are crates full of blankets and towels scattered throughout the hall, and metal carts loaded with cleaning supplies and scissors and boxes of latex gloves and plastic tubes and measuring cups and harnesses and a whole lot of tools and bizarre medical equipment.

The wall beside each enclosure has a piece of paper tucked into a plastic sleeve with the name of the animal inside, along with notes on their care. I try to read a couple, seeing things like feeding schedule and medications listed there, but Quint whisks me quickly to the end of the hallway.

We turn into a small room, not much bigger than a closet, with three large utility sinks. Quint grabs a canvas apron off a peg on the wall and hands it to me. I slip it over my neck and tie the cord around my waist. The heavy-duty material is covered in brownish-rust-toned stains that I do *not* want to think about.

Then Quint opens a giant refrigerator and the reek of fish increases tenfold.

I stumble back, my stomach heaving. I'm staring at buckets of dead fish, their black eyes dull and bulging.

I clamp a hand over my mouth and nose. "Oh, gross."

"Having second thoughts?" Quint says, pulling on a pair of latex gloves. Without waiting for a response, he grabs a bucket and thumps it on a nearby counter. "So, a lot of the animals that end up here haven't learned to feed themselves."

"Seems like a flaw of evolution," I mutter, thinking back to ninth-grade science and all that talk of *survival of the fittest*. I don't say it out loud, and I don't think Quint picks up on my subtext. *Let the smart ones that figured out how to devour fish the right way live, and the rest can become shark food. Circle of life, right?*

He grabs a stainless-steel bowl and sets it on an electric scale beside the bucket. "Well, sometimes it's because they got separated from their mom too early, before she could teach them to properly hunt for themselves."

I bite my tongue, hating that he had a perfectly reasonable and depressing explanation.

"They need to eat the fish headfirst," he goes on, "because if they eat them tail-first, the scales will scratch up their throats." He's working as he talks, pulling dead fish from the bucket, inspecting each one before tossing it into the bowl. "We also check each fish to make sure there aren't any cuts on its body, which could introduce harmful bacteria to the animals. Then sort them by size. This bowl is going to Joy in pen four, who is pretty young still, so she gets small to medium fish, and the bigger fish will go to the more mature animals out in the yard." He points to a label on the bowl, which does indeed read, *Joy—Pen 4—5 lb.*

"Seems easy enough," I mutter.

Once the scale hits five pounds, Quint turns on the faucet and starts running each fish beneath the spray, using his gloved hands to clean off . . . whatever it is he's cleaning off. Salt? Sand? *Scales?*

"Lastly, we rinse off the scales," he says, and I cringe. I'd been hoping that wasn't it. "Mostly just so they don't clog the drains and dirty up the water. And that's it. On to the next." He sets Joy's bowl down on the counter and reaches for another, this one labeled for Ladybug in pen five. "They get fed three to four times a day depending on their needs. You and I will prep the food for this morning, and the afternoon volunteers will handle the next batch."

Once Ladybug's bowl is ready, he pauses and looks at me. "You're not going to throw up, are you?"

"No," I say defiantly, though I suspect my face has taken on a greenish tinge.

"Then what are you waiting for? You said you wanted to help."

"Yeah, but can't *helping* be, like . . . I don't know. Training some cute little seal to balance a ball on its nose or something?"

The look he gives me is so full of derision, I wilt a little.

"This isn't a circus. We rescue animals that are half-dead, do our best to treat them, and then release them back to the wild. That's what we do here. You do know that, right?"

"Yes?" I say, though I had only gotten a vague idea of all of this.

"So what use, exactly, would it serve to teach them circus tricks?"

"Relax, Quint. It was a joke." I'm suddenly defensive. I hate how he's talking to me, looking at me. Like I'm some prissy snob who is clearly only here to get a good quote for my paper and then I'll be on my way. Like I'm the sort of person who doesn't care about things.

I do care about things. I care about lots of things.

I've just never particularly cared about sea animals before.

But he does back off a little, and for a second I think he might even look a little guilty. He exhales sharply through his nose, then shakes his head. He closes his eyes and the tautness in his expression fades. "Wow," he says, opening his eyes again. "Never thought *you* would be telling *me* to relax."

"Yeah, well, you're being kind of intense. They are just animals, you know."

He cuts a look to me, and I can't tell what he's thinking. Whatever it is, it seems to pass. He gestures at the bucket. "Are you gonna help or not?"

I gulp. "Do I get gloves?"

He reaches into a box tacked to the wall and pulls out another pair of latex gloves. I take them greedily and pull them over my hands. It's the first time I've ever worn latex gloves and I hate the way they cling to me, but when I go to reach into the bucket for my first dead fish, I'm beyond grateful to have them. Even so, I imagine I can feel the sliminess, the slick scales. I can't ignore the bulbous dead eyes or the pudgy, lifeless fish lips. I can't keep the disgust from my face, even when I feel Quint watching me, judging me, laughing at me.

"Amazing you don't come to school smelling like fish every day," I say, after we've gotten through the first bucket.

"Honestly, sometimes I worry about that," he says, "so I'll take it as a compliment. You'll definitely want to take a shower after working here for a few hours. The smell will stay with you."

"Do you ever get used to it?"

"Yeah, sort of," he says. "But if I don't come in for a few days, it hits me all over again when I come back."

While we're working, another volunteer comes and stacks the prepped bowls on a metal cart before wheeling it away down the hall. I watch, dismayed, as our hard work disappears.

"Hold on. We don't get to feed them?"

"We're on food prep duty, not feeding duty."

I turn to him, aghast. "But how do I get to be that volunteer? The one that gets to see their cute little faces, all excited over food?"

"For starters, you volunteer for more than twenty minutes," says Quint. "If you really stick this out for four weeks, you'll get to feed them eventually."

I frown. It's clear he thinks this is a passing phase, and I can't blame him. Despite our deal, I'm not sure I can imagine coming back to this place day after day. I feel like I've already seen enough to rope the center and its mission into my ecotourism plan. I can't exactly expect tourists to pay for the pleasure of sorting stinky dead fish, but *feeding* the animals seems like it would hold some appeal.

But how would I get Quint to sign off on it?

"So," I say, trying to act interested, "how many more buckets do we need to clean?"

"All of them."

I freeze, one hand gripping a cold, slippery body. "All of them? You mean everything in . . . in there?" I use the fish to gesture at the refrigerator.

"That's right," he says. The cruel glint in his eyes is back. "We go through tons of fish every week. We get it delivered by the crate load."

I look at the refrigerator. The bucket. The fish in my hand. "Yippee."

Quint chuckles. "Not the glamorous life of a volunteer you had in mind? Maybe you'd be more suited to"—he thinks for a second—"leading a Girl Scout troop or something."

"Unfortunately, I don't think that would get me far with Mr. Chavez."

He grunts. "Tell me, do you even like animals?"

I open my mouth, but hesitate. I don't *dislike* them, but I know that isn't the same thing. Finally, I confess, "We had a gerbil when I was a kid. I liked him well enough."

For a moment, Quint doesn't move. He just holds my gaze, as if waiting for something more.

Then he throws his head back and laughs. "Awesome," he says. "You're a shoo-in."

I bristle, but there's not much more to say, so we both get back to work. Now that I know we're expected to get through all those buckets, I force myself to move faster. No matter how disgusted I am, I will not give Quint any reason to call me lazy. After all, that's my line.

"So," he says, once we've finished our fifth bucket, "the healthier animals get the whole fish—those are the ones that have been here awhile and have more or less figured out the eating thing. But when they first get here, they're usually so weak and dehydrated, they need some added assistance. Which means, step two: fish smoothies."

I blanch. "Tell me that's not what it sounds like."

He grins and points to an industrial-size blender. "It's exactly what it sounds like."

It's *revolting* is what it is. Quint and I spend the next forty minutes chopping the heads and tails off yet more fish, tossing them into a blender along with some corn syrup and Pedialyte, and watching it all turn into a goop of guts and scales and sharp little bones. The smell, impossibly, gets even worse. By the time we're passing the last batch off to another volunteer, who will feed it to the recent rescues, I'm once again rethinking my conviction. This cannot be worth a good grade. Not an entire summer of this.

I'll tell Dad it didn't work out. I'll find another way to research animal habitats and our sensitive ecosystems.

Quint wipes down the counter, giving me odd, knowing looks from the corner of his eye. "Ready for your lunch break?"

My stomach lurches at the thought of food. My distaste must be evident because he starts chuckling again as he throws the towel into a bin. I can tell he's enjoying this, the torture he gets to inflict on me. "I actually can't believe you're still here."

"I said I'd help, didn't I?" It's annoying, to think he can see right through me. How I'm dying to bolt for the exit the first chance I get. But I haven't yet. Maybe to prove something to myself or my parents or even Mr. Chavez, though I can't help but suspect that part of it might be wanting to prove something to Quint, too.

He's still eyeing me, not trying to hide that he's suspicious. Staring me down. Waiting for me to cave and admit that this is absolutely not what I signed up for. That I'll be saying goodbye now, thanks.

I plant one hand on my hip, daring him to test my resolve.

"Well?" I say, breaking the silence. "What next? Do we bake them octopus pies? Maybe a crab cake?"

His cheek twitches. "Crab is too expensive. But they do like squid."

I gag quietly. "Yum."

"What, you've never had calamari? It's delicious."

"Everything is delicious when you deep-fry it."

"Come on. If you haven't been scared off yet, I suppose I should give you the grand tour."

I have the feeling that this all might have been a test and, somewhat shockingly, I seem to have passed. We step out into the hallway, and Quint starts explaining the various rooms and workstations. This is where the animals are first inspected—vitals taken, blood drawn, checked for wounds. This is the surgery room. Laundry. Dishes. This is where the animals that are in critical condition are kept, the ones that need constant monitoring. Storage and admin offices upstairs, along with a break room and small kitchenette because, according to Quint, my appetite will return eventually. I'm not sure I believe him, but fine.

It's all a little disconcerting given how civil he's being. How civil *I'm* being. And then it hits me.

We actually accomplished something together.

Sure, that accomplishment was nothing more than pureeing up a bunch of fish guts, but still, the fact that I only sometimes wanted to strangle him seems kind of huge.

All signs of Angry Quint have gone. He's back to his old casual self. But—no. Not exactly like his old self, the Quint Erickson who's driven me absolutely bonkers all year. It's more like being with a Quint clone. I never, in a million years, would have pictured him working someplace like this. The beach, yes. On a surfboard, sure. Playing video games in his mom's basement until he's forty, oh, most definitely. But this is a side of Quint I didn't know existed, that I never even considered a possibility.

But his confidence here, his knowledge, his ability to actually do what needs to be done. It's unsettling.

And maddening.

Why couldn't *this* guy have been my lab partner?

"Ready to meet some of the patients?" Quint asks, oblivious to my silent stewing.

I smile tightly. "Been waiting all day."

We return to the long corridor. Most of the enclosures have three or four animals inside them, with the names of the patients written on a small white-board beside each gate, but Quint doesn't need to look at them as we pass by. "We can get up to two hundred animals in a single season," he says, "and it can be tough coming up with new names for them all, so we tend to put them in groups. Lately we've been on a superhero kick, so here we've got Peter Parker, Lois Lane, and Iron Man. Avenger and Hulk are out in the yard."

"Does your mom come up with the names?"

"Naw, usually we let the rescue crew name them, or sometimes whoever found them and called us. People get really excited when they get to name the animal they found, and that can inspire a whole new slew of names. This year someone named an elephant seal Vin Diesel, which inspired an entire action-flick group—Bruce Willis, Lara Croft, James Bond . . . We also have a huge Harry Potter group going on right now, because one of the volunteers is a megafan. So far, we've got . . ." He inhales deeply and his eyes rise to the ceiling as he tries to count them all off. "Harry, Hagrid, Percy, George, Fred, Krum, Draco, McGonagall, Dumbledore, Tom Riddle"—he pauses to give me a secretive look and whispers—"he was always bullying the others. And . . ." He perks up and crouches down in front of one of the gates. A sad-looking animal is resting on its side, staring up at us with unblinking eyes. "Luna Lovegood." He shakes his head. "You weren't supposed to come back here. What happened?" He shakes his head. "Poor girl. You look terrible."

I stare at the animal. I don't think she looks that terrible. Just tired. And definitely skinnier than a lot of the others we've passed.

"She's lost a lot of weight since we released her," he says, as if reading my mind. He sighs. "Back to step one."

"Will you try to release her again? After she gets better?"

"I don't know." He stands up. "Our goal is always to return them to the ocean, but if she can't survive on her own . . ." He shrugs. "I guess we'll see what Opal thinks."

"Opal's the vet?"

He nods. "Sorry, I guess I should introduce you to more people." His expression is hesitant and I know he's thinking it would be a waste of time. I know he still doesn't expect me to come back.

But for the first time all day, I realize I'm actually not eager to escape. Fish guts aside, it's actually been kind of interesting.

"So, the animals here, they all . . . what? Washed up on the beach? And someone called you?"

"Usually, yeah. People can tell something's wrong. A lot of times it's obvious stuff, like they have wounds from a shark bite or something, or maybe they've got a bunch of fishing line tangled around them." Quint's expression darkens. "One time we rescued a sea lion that had nineteen fishhooks caught in his skin."

I shudder, remembering the photo in his report.

"That's awful. Was he okay?"

"He made it. We released him a couple years ago. We named him Captain Hook."

I laugh. "Was there also a Peter Pan?"

"No," Quint says, in a tone that suggests this is a ridiculous thing to ask. But then he grins. "But we did have a Mr. Smee and a Tinker Bell."

I fold my arms on top of the short wall that separates the enclosure from the walkway and peer down at Luna. "What are those markings on her side?"

"That's how we tell them apart. It's like a code. There's a chart in the office that explains it, but pretty much every mark is a different number. We shave the fur, but it's easier to make straight lines than curves, so they get a little V instead of the number five, and two dashes instead of a nine, that sort of thing."

Luna's markings are two arrows, each pointing toward her head.

"How many volunteers are there?" I ask. "As opposed to staff."

"There are only three people on staff. Mom, Shauna, and Opal—Dr. Jindal. Then we have . . ." He pauses, and I can tell he's counting in his head. "Sixteen volunteers, including me and Morgan. My mom would love to hire more people, but money is . . ." He trails off. "I mean, we're pretty reliant on government grants, which barely makes enough to keep the animals fed, much less pay a bunch of employees. But the volunteers are great. It's kind of like a family, and everyone really cares about what we're doing." He pauses and looks at me, and I can see the hint of accusation there again: the *what are* you *doing here?* But it passes quickly. "I mean, look at those eyes. You can't help but fall in love, right?"

I startle. My heart skips, and it takes me a second to realize he's gesturing at Luna. Except, when I glance down, her eyes are closed. I think she might be sleeping.

"All right," says Quint. "I need to get to work. I'm setting you free."

"My, how generous," I say, but I'm frowning. "But why not let me help you?"

He shakes his head. "I can do it faster on my own. We'll continue your training tomorrow." He gives me a sideways look as we start walking back toward the lobby. "That is, if you're still planning on coming back. Because if this isn't for you . . ."

"I'll be here," I say. Firmly. "And by the end of summer, we will submit one killer report to Mr. Chavez. That's the deal, right?"

Quint's jaw seems to tighten, but then he holds out his hand.

I swallow, but my hesitation is brief. I take his hand and we share a determined shake.

SIXTEEN

It's so gross!" I say, flopping onto the sofa in Ari's den. "It's literally fish puree. Plus, I had to chop off fish heads! Ugh, I feel sick just thinking about it. And *then,* you can't just feed it to the animals, right? Oh no. You have to give it to them through a tube." I shudder.

Ari makes a sound like she's trying to care about my complaints, but I know she's mostly ignoring me. She's sitting cross-legged on the floor, her guitar in her lap, leaning forward to study something on her phone.

I sigh and stare at the ceiling.

"But I have to go back," I say, as much to myself as to Ari. "If I want to redo that project, I have to go back. For four whole weeks."

Ari plucks a few strings, then frowns and shakes her head. She finally looks up at me. "Why can't you just settle for the C?"

I give her a withering look.

She shrugs. "Just saying. It's what almost anyone else would do."

"Well, it's not what I would do. A *C.* It will haunt me the rest of my life if I don't get it fixed."

"Will it, though?" says Ari sweetly. "It's not like you're going to need science credits when you apply to business school. Literally no one but you cares about this project or the grade you got."

"Exactly. *I care,* which is the most important thing."

She considers this. "I suppose that's true. So you're officially volunteering at an animal rescue center for the next month. How very selfless of you, dear Prudence."

"Hey, I can be selfless," I say, noting the dryness in her tone.

She laughs. "I know you can, but don't you see the irony? You're only doing this for the grade."

"So?" I sit up, suddenly defensive. "Actions make a person good, not motives."

"I'm not sure I agree with that," she says wistfully. "But it'd make a good theme for a song. Good or bad, right or wrong . . . do the means justify the ends and vice versa . . ." She goes into her dazed songwriting look, but it passes quickly. She bends over the phone again, long wisps of dark brown hair falling over her face like a curtain. She pulls them back with one hand, twisting her hair once at the nape of her neck, before letting it drape across her shoulder. The wisps will return in a few minutes, and I consider offering her my hairband, but she never uses them so I don't bother.

Ari's brow furrows and she plucks the same strings over again. She harrumphs, frustrated. "Other than fish smoothies, how was it working with Quint?"

I snarl. "It feels like I'm being punished for something." My brow crinkles upon further consideration. "Although I guess it wasn't as terrible as it could have been."

Her eyebrow lifts, and I grab a pillow to throw at her. She hunkers forward, protecting the guitar. "Stop it. I am not interested in him. I'm just saying, evidently, he can be a halfway-decent human being when he's doing something he cares about." Because I could tell he does care about the center, a lot. "That still does not excuse all the stress he put me through this year. And I guarantee that when it comes time for us to finish this project, *again,* it's going to require just as much prodding and tooth-pulling as it did the first time. Ideal scenario: I do it myself and we just use Quint's email address to submit it, so our teacher thinks he was involved."

"I thought you said part of the reason you got a bad grade was lack of teamwork?"

I sneer. "Again—not my fault. *You* try working with him."

Ari giggles. "And yet, you've signed up to do just that."

"I know." I groan and stretch out on my side.

Ari tries the strings again, playing the same melody over and over until she lets out a frustrated groan. "Okay, this is clearly not right. Whoever wrote this arrangement had no idea what they were doing."

She stands up and goes to her shelves of vinyl records. She scans the spines for a second before pulling a record from its paper sleeve and setting it onto the ancient turntable that has lived in this room since the day I met her. Probably it's lived in this room since the day her family moved into this house. Ari's record collection is something else—an entire wall of built-in shelves, floor to ceiling, each one packed full. There's an order to the system, but it's lost on me. Genre? Era? I know there's a section of Mexican music somewhere, because Ari introduced me to an eighties rock band called La Maldita a while back, and they turned out to be pretty awesome, but I couldn't say where their records live in all of this.

I do know where to find the Beatles, though.

That's not what Ari is putting on now.

A beautiful melody begins to play, but it takes me a minute to place it. "Elton John?"

Ari shushes me. "Just listen. Oh, I love this intro. A flute! Who thinks of that? I never would have thought of that. But it's so perfect!"

I make a face. *Whatever you say, Ari.* But she's not paying attention to me.

On the record, Elton John starts singing about someone named Daniel, who's traveling to Spain.

"Oh, hey, that reminds me," I say. "Did Jude talk to you about working at the record sto—"

"Yes! Prudence. Stop talking."

I press my lips together. Ari picks up her guitar again, but she doesn't play. Her face is set with single-minded focus as she listens to the song.

My mind drifts back to the center and all the photos in Quint's report. Fishhooks. Fishing line. Shark bites. Sad, tragic eyes.

I think about Quint, how angry he looked at first.

But then the way he lit up when he was telling me about the different animal patients they've had this year.

For some reason, I find myself thinking of his smile. His eager, ever-present smile. It seemed different today somehow. More energized.

Oh, come on, Brain. Are we really wasting valuable space toward analyzing Quint's smiles? Knock it off.

My memories circle back to how Quint and the other volunteers seemed so busy, and Rosa so stressed. And why they don't just hire more staff.

The song ends, and Ari hops up to stop the record before it can move on to the next song. She grabs her guitar, and I realize she's trying to figure out how to play the intro, the part that the flute plays on the album.

"I think they might be in trouble," I say.

Ari stops playing. "What? Who?"

"The center. Quint's mom seemed super tense, and maybe it's just because they were shorthanded today, but I don't know. I just have a feeling, like, things aren't going so well there. Most of their money comes from grants and it sounds like that's barely enough to keep them afloat." I massage my forehead. "I can only imagine what they spend on *fish,* much less everything else it takes to keep the place running."

"Do they do any fundraising?" Ari asks.

"I don't know." I mull this over. There was all that paperwork in the lobby. Financial reports? Donor information? Grant applications? But if they are fundraising, they seem to be doing a terrible job at it.

"Araceli!" yells her dad from the kitchen. "Is Prudence staying for dinner?"

Ari glances at me.

"Is Abuela cooking?"

"I don't think so."

I pout, but it's still the best offer I've had. "Yeah, fine. As long as it's not fish."

Ari sets down her guitar and darts upstairs. When she comes back, she gives me an affirmative nod. "He's ordering pizza. No seafood involved."

I give her a thumbs-up. "So, are you excited to work at the record store?"

She gives a small squeal. "Are you kidding? It's my dream job! Well, my dream summer job, anyway. I start next week."

"Better you than me."

She lifts the needle on the record player. "Speaking of dream jobs, did you know that Elton John didn't write his own lyrics? He did the music, but the words were almost entirely written by a guy named Bernie Taupin. Can you imagine? I want to be him *so bad.*"

She starts the song again, but she doesn't pick up her guitar this time. Instead, she lies down on the floor and shuts her eyes, her face tense with concentration. The flute introduction plays and is soon joined by a keyboard and Elton's sorrowful voice.

"Listen to this," says Ari, her fingers dancing through the air. *I can see the red taillights heading for Spain . . .* She throws her hand upward, mirroring the rise in the music, then brings her hand back down in a giddy fist. "There! Did you hear that E-seven? A non-diatonic dominant chord, but then it resolves straight to the A minor. Brilliant. Honestly, piano players write the best chords." She presses both palms against her forehead and sighs heavily.

I have literally zero idea what she's talking about.

"Maybe I should take up the piano," she says.

"I have a keyboard you could have."

She turns her head to look at me. "Really?"

"Sure. It's in our living room, abandoned and unloved. You can totally have it. I mean, it's not super-high quality. Probably your mom could buy you something way nicer, but if you want it . . ."

Ari grimaces. She hates it when anyone mentions her family's affluence, which I guess I can sort of understand. She doesn't want to be judged for having money any more than I want to be judged for *not* having it.

"I would love to have it. Thank you," she says. "And I promise to take very good care of it. Now, shush, listen. This part—"

Elton sings about the scars that won't heal, about the eyes that have died. Ari looks positively euphoric as both hands shoot upward again, pointing at the ceiling. *Daniel, you're a star . . .*

"Oh," she croons wistfully. "Listen to that high note! He's hitting the tonic note over a modal interchange chord. So simple, yet so brilliant. It's just . . ." She sighs, dropping her hands down to her heart. She starts to sing along, but I can barely hear her over the album.

Honestly, I find these music-theory riffs of hers brilliant, but she seems like she's speaking another language entirely. One I definitely do not speak. Her music descriptions are even harder to understand than the rapid Spanish she speaks with her family, because with music, she expects me to sort of understand what she's talking about. At least I have *some* rudimentary knowledge of Spanish, having taken it for three years in school, but all I remember from piano lessons is how to play "Twinkle, Twinkle, Little Star." (With feeling.)

As Elton drones on, my mind wanders again. To ecotourism. To the rescue center.

To Quint Erickson and his mom and how they need more staff and how dingy the building was.

What the center needs to do is stop acting like a nonprofit focused on helping poor stranded animals, and start acting like a business. It needs someone with vision. Someone who can help them be profitable. Well, profitable for a nonprofit, at least. If that makes sense. I don't know, it doesn't matter, because my wheels are turning, and it seems suddenly clear that . . .

What the center needs is someone like *me*.

"That's it!" I sit up suddenly and look at Ari. "Ecotourism! I can . . . I . . ." I frown. "Are you crying?"

Ari, embarrassed at being found out, swipes the tears from her cheeks. "No," she says. Then sniffs. Then, "Yes! I can't help it! It's just so *sad*."

I listen to the song as the final verse plays.

Oh God, it looks like Daniel. Must be the clouds in my eyes.

I shrug. "Who the heck is Daniel?"

Ari starts to laugh. "I have no idea!"

I groan and stand up to shut off the record player, just as the last melody plays on the flute. "So, the whole time Quint and I were working on that project for biology, he kept talking about this animal rescue center. Well, I think he maybe had a point. What if the center could become a huge draw for tourists? They might even be able to make some money! I mean, they'd still be a non-profit, but some nonprofit CEOs are, like, millionaires. Not that this is about money. But I'm just saying. I could take what I learned doing that stupid report and . . . and what if I *rescued* the rescue center?"

Ari sits up and blinks at me. Her cheeks are tinted pink, but the rush of emotions brought on by the song seem to be fading. "I'm sorry. What are you doing?"

"I'm going to come up with a business plan! For the rescue center!"

Ari still looks confused. "You know I admire your ambition, but you've been there for exactly one day."

"Which gives me the perfect outsider point of view. I'm not mired in the day-to-day business and caretaking. What they need is an injection of new ideas, something to bring new life to the organization and their mission. Something that will make them . . . you know . . . valuable."

"You don't think saving the lives of animals is valuable?"

I roll my eyes. "You sound like Quint. That's not what I mean. They need a way to make money, and it turns out seals and turtles don't have deep pockets." I stand up and start to pace, rubbing my hands together in a way that might be construed as a little maniacal. My brain is firing on a dozen different levels, the possibilities exploding before me. "It's perfect. This can be a real-world example of how ecotourism benefits the tourists, the community, the local economy, *and* the environment. The paper practically writes itself, and if I succeed—if *I* bring a nonprofit organization back from the brink of bankruptcy—just imagine how good that will look on my college applications! I'll get to pick any business school I want to."

"Do you know that they're on the brink of bankruptcy, or are you just speculating?"

"It's an educated guess," I say. "And stop trying to burst my bubble. This is genius. Wow, I'm actually kind of excited to tell Quint about this." I frown. "But don't tell him I said that."

"Your secret is safe."

I start to pace again. I can't help but feel like the universe has nudged me toward this somehow. All the signs have been pointing in this direction, all the dominoes lined up just right. Being partners with Quint, the poor grade, Morgan's fall off the ladder, right down to Rosa's suggestion that Quint train me as a volunteer. I might have been resistant at first, but now it makes sense, especially given that it's all happening so soon after the discovery of my brand-new cosmic power. It has to mean something. Something bigger than me, bigger than Quint.

Maybe this is a sign that I've been put on a path toward my destiny.

Now I just have to follow along and see where it leads.

SEVENTEEN

I arrive at the rescue center bright and early, as instructed, but this time I have a folder tucked under my arm. I hardly slept last night. My mind was awash with ideas, and I stayed up far too late making plans and researching nonprofits and fundraising methods. I have ideas. So many ideas. They're carrying me along now, buoyed like a barrel in the water. I'm not tired at all as I step into the lobby. I'm electrified. I'm ready to make a difference.

But my feet halt as soon as I step through the door. Quint and his mom are both standing by a desk, along with Shauna and another woman wearing a white lab coat—Dr. Jindal? Two other volunteers hover nearby, too. They're all looking sullen, arms crossed over their matching yellow shirts.

Quint blinks when he sees me. "You came back," he says, clearly surprised.

I bristle and push my sunglasses up to the top of my head. "Of course I came back." I make a show of checking my watch, which Ari gave me for a birthday present last year. "And you're not late for once?"

He almost smiles. "I guess miracles happen."

"Thank you, Opal," says Rosa, handing a piece of paper to the vet. "I'll start putting calls out to institutions today." She shrugs sadly at the waiting volunteers. "Time to break out the toys, I guess. Been a while. Hope all those beach balls haven't deflated."

I frown, motionless, as the volunteers and Dr. Jindal walk away. "What's going on?"

"Luna has a cognitive disorder," says Quint. "She'll never be able to feed herself, which means we can't send her back out into the ocean."

"Oh." I don't bother trying to hide my confusion. It takes everything in me not to ask, *What's so wrong with that?* When clearly this is a big deal to everyone else. "So she'll go to an aquarium or a zoo or something?"

"When she's ready," says Rosa. "It will be a few months. I'm so happy we found her, and that she'll survive. It's just . . . we always hope they'll be released to their natural habitat in the end."

"There is a silver lining," says Quint. "When our animals do end up at zoos and aquariums, they can teach people about wildlife and conservation. They become advocates, sort of, for other animals and for the center."

I still feel like I'm missing something. To me, the idea of going to a lovely zoo where I'm hand-fed fish all day and get to frolic in the water while adorable children coo and clap sounds like a much better life than trying to hunt for my dinner and risk getting tangled up in fishing line. But I know I'm probably the only person here who feels that way, so I bite my tongue.

"We'll find a nice place," says Shauna, squeezing Rosa's shoulder. "The nicest place that will take her. It's going to be fine."

Shauna is wearing some intense jewelry today, having traded in the strand of pearls for hoop earrings that are almost the size of baseballs and a rhinestone brooch shaped like a butterfly that she's pinned to her T-shirt. I suppose when your job comes with a uniform as awful as those yellow shirts, it's natural to want to display your personal sense of style. For me, it's lipstick. For Shauna, evidently, it's blingy costume jewelry. At least her accessories kind of fit with the cute grandma vibe she has going on.

"So, this might be bad timing?" I say, stepping closer to the desk. "But I had some ideas to share with you."

Rosa looks at me. "What sort of ideas?"

"Yeah," says Quint, sounding wary. "What sort of ideas?"

"Just some things that occurred to me. About the business here and how things are run . . ."

Quint snorts and casts his eyes skyward, as if pleading for patience. "Of course you did," he mutters.

I'm not sure what he means by that.

"Mostly just fundraising ideas," I continue, ignoring him. "And some community outreach. Things that I think will help bring more attention to the center, raise awareness for the animals . . . hopefully even increase revenue. It sounded like money has been tight."

Rosa lets out a weary groan. "Understatement." She opens her palms, waving her hands over the stacks of teetering piles on the desk. "We've tried fundraising over the years. It's hit or miss." She looks despondent. Like this is merely a fact of the nonprofit world. And maybe it is. But I'm convinced it doesn't have to be. At least, not for this center. "Thankfully we've had much more consistent success with grants."

"Right," I say. "I heard that, too. But, well, you know Quint and I did this project for biology this year." For some reason, I find myself avoiding Quint's gaze as I say this. I can feel him watching me, frowning, and it's making me nervous. In part because I have no idea what he has to be upset about. "And I think I can use my research to help the center, which in turn will help with my extra-credit assignment. I'm thinking of this as a symbiotic relationship. Like sharks and those little suckerfish that help them clean off the parasites."

I grin, proud of myself for remembering that lesson from class, and I can't help casting a look at Quint. He looks radically unimpressed. His voice is flat when he says, "In this scenario, are you the shark or the suckerfish or the parasite?"

His words hit hard and I gape at him, even as Rosa chastises, "Quint!"

But I don't need her to defend me. I take a step toward him. "I'm sorry, but what is your problem? I did everything you asked yesterday, I showed up today, *on time,* even though you clearly didn't expect me to. So what is this about?"

His eyes are blazing and he opens his mouth to speak, but then hesitates. He glances at his mom and his expression darkens. Crossing his arms over his chest, he gives his head a shake. "Nothing. I'm just dying to hear these ideas of yours."

"Quint," Rosa says again. "You're being rude. And heaven knows any sort of financial boost would go a long way around here."

"Thank you," I say. I hold Quint's eye a second longer before turning to Rosa. I tighten my grip on the folder and launch into the speech I practiced a dozen times in front of my mirror last night. "Consider me your new business consultant. First, I want to start with a community event, something we can use to really get the locals involved. I've lived in Fortuna Beach my whole life, and I just learned about this place, so it's clear that we're lacking visibility in the community, and that needs to be remedied. Plus, people want to be a part of something. They like to think they can make a difference through their actions. It's not just about clicking the donate button on Kickstarter, right? But once they see what great work is happening here, I know more people will want to contribute financially, too."

Rosa stops me with a laugh. "Well, Quint didn't exaggerate. You are certainly dedicated. Prudence, I do appreciate your optimism." She scratches the back of her neck. "But I have to stop you there, because, to be honest, I feel like we've tried *everything,* and nothing seems to stick. We have fundraisers every year, but the money seems to evaporate as fast as it comes in. We've tried hosting events, and we had that Facebook page at one time, although it's probably been a while since it got updated." She shakes herself, as if realizing how cynical she sounds. "The thing is, no one here has time for any of that. Including me. Especially me." She sighs and stands. "I don't want to discourage you. Maybe we can talk more in the next couple of days? But right now, I need to check on Luna and some of our other patients. And I know you both have a lot of work to get through today, too. I'm sorry, Prudence. I hate to leave you hanging, but . . ." Despite her words, the look she gives me is the definition of *discouraged.* "We'll talk more about this later, all right?"

I don't think she means it. I don't think she's trying to dissuade me from coming up with ideas, but she looks exhausted as she walks away, and her day has only begun. Maybe she's just so overwhelmed with the day-to-day trials of keeping this place going, she simply can't process the idea of adding anything else to the mix.

Which means, if this is going to work, my plans can't revolve around Rosa, at least not beyond getting her approval.

I'm far from discouraged. In fact, this will work out even better. I didn't really want her looking over my shoulder anyway as I'm doing my best to breathe new life into this place.

As Rosa heads into the corridor—what they call the critical care wing—I feel a hand on my shoulder. I startle and turn to see Shauna smiling at me, the wrinkles pronounced around her eyes.

"She's just under a lot of stress. It's been a tough season," she says. "For one, I think some new fundraising campaigns could help a lot. I hope you give it a try."

I nod. "Thanks."

Shauna departs, too, then, heading up the stairs to the second floor.

I thump the edge of the folder in my palm and turn to Quint. His eyes are dark, his lips pressed tight.

"What?" I snap. "Why are you looking at me like that?" My cheeks have already reddened and we're not even arguing, *yet,* but I can feel his animosity and it's making me defensive, though I have no idea what we're fighting about.

"No reason," he says, in the most blatant lie of all time. "I have work to do." He turns and shoves open the screen door.

I follow him, still clutching my folder. Quint snatches a pool brush that was leaning against the wall and starts in on one of the kiddie pools. It had sea lions in it yesterday, but it's since been emptied out. I wonder how often the pools have to be cleaned. How much time is spent shuffling animals around. I mean, can that possibly be necessary? Their natural habitat is gross, sludgy seawater, after all.

"What is your problem?" I say. A couple of volunteers are feeding fish to the animals in the next pool. They turn to me and Quint, startled, but we both ignore them. "And give me a real answer. I thought you'd be excited about this!"

"Oh yeah, it's thrilling." Quint squirts some dish soap directly into the empty pool. "Good thinking, partner. So glad we have you on the team." He takes the brush and starts scrubbing furiously.

I throw my free hand into the air. "You haven't even heard my ideas yet! Don't you *want* this place to make more money? To be successful?"

He stops scrubbing, both hands gripping the brush handle like he's resisting flinging it at me. "You've been here for one day, Prudence. One. Day. Do you even know how to tell the difference between harbor seals and sea lions yet?"

I blink at him, bewildered, then glance to the nearest pool. At the plump, shiny-bodied creatures diving in and out of the water. "Seals," I say, waving the folder at them.

"Wrong."

Shoot.

"Sea lions are the ones with flaps over their ears, among other things."

What? What flaps?

I look again.

Oh. They do have funny little ear things. Who knew?

"Do you know what a pinniped is?"

My nose curls in irritation. "No. But I bet I can spell it better than you can!"

He glowers at me and, yeah, I know, it was a cheap shot. But I don't understand why he's acting like this!

"A pinniped is a mammal that's evolved to have fins instead of feet. Like, for example . . . seals! And sea lions!"

I plant one hand on my hip. "So I don't know the terminology. What does that matter?"

"How about what kind of fish we worked with yesterday? You never even asked."

"It's fish! It was gross. They eat it. Who cares?"

"It matters because *you don't care.* All you care about is whether or not you can swoop in and take over another project so you can prove to everyone how"—he waves his hand toward me—"brilliant you are, or whatever. But you don't know anything about these animals or what we're doing here. Whereas my mom has been running this place for almost twenty years. What makes you think that you know better than her? Than me? Than the volunteers who have been putting their hearts and souls into this place for years? Oh, wait!" He smacks his hand to his forehead. "You think we should make more *money*? Wow, Prudence, you're a genius. Why didn't we think of that?"

He rolls his eyes. I've never been attacked with such utter derision before, and for a moment I'm left speechless, though the blood is running hot beneath my skin. Quint goes back to scrubbing the pool. The muscles in his shoulders are knotted. The volunteers in the next enclosure have emptied the bucket of fish but I can see them lingering, unsure if they need to interject themselves into our argument or are just too nosy to walk away.

"Fine. Maybe you're right," I say, lowering my voice. Quint keeps scrubbing. I sense that this will be the most squeaky-clean pool these animals have ever experienced by the time he's done with it. "I don't know a whole lot about this place. Until yesterday, I didn't even know it existed. But I just spent the last six months researching exactly this sort of thing—how organizations that care about animals and the environment can actually be profitable. It's a booming industry right now, and from what I've seen—in, admittedly, just a day—this center isn't taking advantage of this opportunity at all. You don't even update your Facebook page! Quint, this is exactly what our paper was about. The idea that people will pay money to be a part of something good. Something important. But first we need people to know that the center even exists. We need them to care."

His eyes flicker toward me. There is no sign of relenting. "We?"

I frown at the implication that I am clearly not a part of this team, this *family*. "You. Your mom. These volunteers. My point is, I can help."

"Right. Because you wrote a report on ecotourism." He tilts his head. "Tell me, what grade did you get again?"

I snarl. It's a low blow, and I sense he's getting back at me for the spelling comment earlier.

"I didn't get a bad grade because I don't know what I'm talking about," I say through clenched teeth. "I got a bad grade because . . ." My attention darts toward the cluster of sea lions again. They're all in the pool, but as soon as I glance over, one of them leaps out, and within seconds the rest have all charged up after him onto the pool deck. Like the world's cutest game of follow-the-leader.

I swallow. "Because I didn't know why it mattered," I hear myself saying. "I know how our community can make money by focusing on ecotourism, I just . . . didn't express why it's important. Why these animals and their habitats are important."

"And *do* you think they're important?" He flattens the brush on the bottom of the pool and leans on the handle. "Truly. Do you think saving these animals is a worthwhile cause? Or is this just one more box for you to check on your list of accomplishments? A nice addition to the résumé of Prudence Barnett."

I let out a frustrated groan. "Look. I'm not going to lie and say I don't want that, but in this case, if I succeed, then so do you. So does your mom. Can't you at least let me try?"

"I'm sure I couldn't stop you if I wanted to."

"Why would you want to?" My voice is rising again. I don't want to yell, but—*gah*—can't he at least give me a chance? I'm tempted to take that brush out of his hand and smack him over the head with it.

He exhales noisily through his nostrils and ignores my question. Pushing the brush to the side, he grabs a hose and starts rinsing out the small pool.

Eons pass. He rinses it out *three times* before shutting off the hose and daring to look at me again. I'm still simmering, fingers digging into my hip. But he, at least, seems to be calming down.

I almost don't dare to hope that maybe I've won him over. And only when I realize that do I begin to question why I'm bothering to win him over at all. This is his mom's organization. She's the one whose opinion matters.

But I can't be fighting Quint every step of the way. I may not need him, but it sure will be easier if he's on board.

"All right," he finally says. His voice is rough, and I sense that this isn't an easy concession for him to make. But I don't care. Relief is already welling up in me. "I'll hear you out," he continues. "But not today. We're swamped as it is."

"Fine, no problem. I'll go put on an apron and then I can help . . . clean. Or something."

His cheek twitches.

"And maybe we can talk about this"—I hold up the folder—"tomorrow? I mean, the sooner we can get started, the better. Right?"

He sighs. A heavy sound, halfway to melodramatic. "Yeah, awesome," he says. "I can't wait."

EIGHTEEN

ncanto has what Carlos generously refers to as a "patio" along the front of the restaurant. It's actually just three small café tables in a little roped-off section of the sidewalk, but it can be a nice place to sit and people-watch. This is where I sit down to wait for Quint. I have my folder, plus a bunch of new material, mostly online pamphlets and statistics and reports from other nonprofits that I found online. I discovered one cancer research charity that brought in nearly a billion dollars in a single year. Their CEO's salary was $2.4 million! Not that I think I'm going to be anywhere near that, especially not over just one summer, but it's nice to know that it can be done. I guess it's kind of refreshing to know how generous people can be with their money and how it can really add up to make a huge difference.

Well, not that we've cured cancer yet. But I have to assume that charity has done *something* worthwhile with all that dough.

Once I'm all set up for my meeting with Quint, my papers neatly organized and a bulleted list of talking points at my elbow, I check my watch. We're meeting at noon. I'm five minutes early.

A waiter comes out to check on me and I order a sparkling water and some tostones, which is a Puerto Rican specialty and Carlos's signature appetizer. It's basically plantains, which are kind of like firm bananas, that have been squished, fried, and salted, and they are mouth-wateringly delicious. Crisp on the outside, tender on the inside. Plus, he serves them with both a chimichurri and a chipotle-mayo dipping sauce and my mouth waters just thinking about it. Jude and I usually order separate plates because they're too good to share.

I consider ordering something for Quint, but that might be weird, so I don't. The waiter disappears back inside. I take off my sunglasses and use the skirt of my dress to polish off a smudge. Slipping them back on, I relax into my seat, waiting.

Tourist season hasn't fully kicked off yet, but already the town is feeling more lively than it did just a couple of weeks ago. Shopkeepers are dusting off their wares and washing their windows and putting out big CLEARANCE racks full of last year's goods to entice all the new customers that are starting to arrive.

I grab my phone and check a few social media feeds, but no one I care about has posted anything new so I soon grow bored.

The waiter brings out my water and I drink nearly half the glass in one gulp. My nose tickles from the carbonation. I check my watch again. It feels like I've been waiting a long time, but it's only 12:03.

I try to keep my mind occupied by seeking out people on the street who may be in need of a karmic confrontation. I'm catching on that once I start looking for wrongdoing, it seems to be everywhere—the girl who sticks her chewing gum on the underside of the next table. The man who doesn't clean up after his dog.

A smirk and a tightening of my fingers, and next thing you know, the girl has dripped salsa down the front of her dress, and the man, distracted, puts his own shoe right into the pile of excrement.

It becomes a game, looking for reprehensible behavior. And there is plenty to see. I wonder if this strange power is somehow attracting abhorrent people, pulling them into my path so they can feel the wrath of the universe, or if there are truly that many inconsiderate people in this world.

Speaking of inconsiderate . . .

I check my watch. 12:39!

My teeth clench. I've been so distracted by doling out punishments to those around me, I've barely touched the plate of tostones that was brought a while back. I grab one now and shove it into my mouth. I've been sitting here long enough that they've started to get cold.

In my mind, this, too, is Quint's fault.

I swallow, a little painfully.

For a second, I try to use Ari's tactic and give him the benefit of the doubt. Could he be stuck in traffic?

Um, no. Unless there's some festival or something going on, traffic in Fortuna Beach is pretty much nonexistent.

Maybe he forgot the time? Or forgot that we were supposed to meet at all? This seems likely, but it hardly makes it okay.

Maybe he's sick?

Please. I would be so lucky.

Honestly, after seeing him at 8:00 a.m. at the center yesterday, I'd begun to think maybe I'd been mistaken about him. Maybe there is some part of him that can be responsible. That takes his obligations seriously. Maybe he's not a total delinquent.

As soon as my watch ticks over to 1:00, making him an entire hour late, I feel my annoyance boiling over. It's one thing to be late to class. Yes, it would have been nice to have a reliable lab partner, but whatever, I did the work myself. But to stand me up like this? On my day off? When I've put in all this work to help *his* mom and *her* center.

It's inexcusable!

This rant continues in my head another ten . . . fifteen . . . *twenty-two minutes,* until I'm about ready to scream at the infuriating seagulls that are squawking around, searching for dropped food.

And then—*then*—I see him.

He's strolling up the sidewalk, his eyes hidden by sunglasses and the afternoon light glinting off his dark hair. He's wearing flip-flops, swim trunks, and a white T-shirt with a picture of a surfboarding octopus. He is not hurrying. He in no way looks anxious or apologetic. He looks relaxed. Too relaxed.

How is it that *I* can have such high expectations, for myself and those around me, while Quint can be so . . . so *Quint.* I've even spent the last year lowering my expectations for him, bit by bit, and still he manages to disappoint. I've truly asked so little of him. Just show up on time so I don't have to explain the assignment to you every single day. Just read the chapter from our textbook beforehand so you have a clue what we're talking about. Just take a few notes or take accurate measurements or do something useful rather than putting it all on my shoulders.

Somehow, he failed. Again and again and again. And now this. To not only be late, but to be so casual about it.

I'm positively fuming when Quint spots me and smiles in greeting.

Smiles.

That! Jerk!

My hand clenches under the table, squeezing until I can feel the pulse of my own blood in my knuckles.

Quint pauses, his eye catching on something. Please, oh please, let a seagull swoop by and drop a big one right on his head.

Or let some kid plant a half-devoured chocolate ice cream cone right into that Hawaiian-printed butt of his. (Not that I'm thinking about his butt. Oh, gross, stop it, Brain!)

Or . . . or . . . *gah*, I don't care, just something horrible!

As I watch, my hand aching and images of vengeance swirling through my head, Quint stoops down and picks something off the sidewalk. I squint, trying to see what it is.

Paper? Green paper?

Hold on. Did he just find *money*?

Quint walks up to a nearby shopkeeper who's sweeping his front stoop and shows him the paper. The man shakes his head. Quint steps away, looks up and down the sidewalk, but there's no one else to ask. No one to talk to. He gives the facial equivalent of a shrug, then starts heading toward me again.

My fist slowly relaxes. What is going on here?

"Look," he says, sliding into the chair opposite me. "I just found twenty bucks."

I gawk at the bill in his hand. *What?*

He holds it toward me. "We'll call it our first anonymous donation." He grins. "See? We're making a good team already."

My brain feels like it's shutting down. I can't process what just happened. I feel like the universe betrayed me. I take the twenty, a little dazed, and stare at it. Maybe it's counterfeit, and he'll get arrested if he uses it?

But, no. I know it's real. I know that, for whatever reason, he just got rewarded, after being nearly an hour and a half late to our meeting. Was that the universe's doing, or just coincidence?

That would be an easy explanation, except I'm reaching a point where I'm not sure I believe in coincidences anymore.

I set the money down on the table between us.

"Wow," I say, a little numbly. "Cool. I'll . . . start a ledger."

"Yeah. Or it can just pay for lunch. I'm starving." He takes a tostone without asking, dips it in the chipotle sauce, and tosses it into his mouth. "Mm, so good," he says. He doesn't seem to notice that they're cold. You know, because they've been sitting out for *more than an hour.*

"So," I start, as my anger once again begins to boil. "You do know how to tell time, right? Like, you didn't sleep through those lessons in elementary school?"

He lifts an eyebrow at me. Takes his time chewing. Finally swallows. He leans over the table. "Or," he says, "you could try starting this conversation with something like, 'Wow, Quint, you sure are late today. Did something happen?'"

My jaw tightens and I lean forward. "Or *you* could start with an apology. I've been here for an hour and a half. You think I didn't have anything better to do with my time than wait for you? You couldn't text, or—"

"I don't have your number."

I point toward the windows beside us. "You knew where we were meeting. You could have called the restaurant."

This seems to give him pause. He pulls back slightly, his mouth open. It takes a couple of seconds before he says, "I didn't think of that."

I huff righteously and cross my arms over my chest.

"Okay. I'm sorry."

"Sure, whatever. I just hope you were having a good time, beating your high score on . . . on Pac-Man, or whatever it is you were doing."

His eyes narrow, a cross between amused and irritated. "Pac-Man?"

I wave my hand at him. "Ari has an old . . . never mind."

He shakes his head. "Well, yeah. I totally destroyed my Pac-Man record. You know, right after I helped our rescue crew untangle a sea otter from a fishing net. Are you done with these?" He doesn't wait for a response before gobbling down two more tostones.

Which is good, because I'm actually speechless.

I want to believe he's making that up, but . . . I don't think he is.

The waiter returns and Quint orders a root beer.

"She's going to be fine," Quint says once our server has gone again. "The otter. In case you're wondering."

I clear my throat, refusing to feel sheepish. "For the record, there was absolutely no way for me to know about that."

"Yeah, I know." Quint shrugs. "But just once, it'd be nice if you didn't assume I'm an asshole."

"I don't think you're an asshole. I just think you're . . ."

He smiles expectantly. "Go on. You won't hurt my feelings."

"Irresponsible," I say.

He hums thoughtfully and polishes off the last of the tostones. "Is that all?"

It feels almost like he's mocking me, but . . . come *on*. I'm the one who had to put up with his immature antics all year.

"It's enough," I say. "A person can only be late to class so many times before their priorities become pretty obvious."

He takes his time licking salt from his fingers. Our server delivers the root beer and Quint orders a plate of nachos topped with pernil asado.

As soon as we're alone again, Quint gives me a smile that seems almost like . . . like he feels bad for me. "For the record," he says, and again I can hear the mocking in his tone, repeating my words from earlier, "I work most mornings at the center. Even during the school year. That's why I'm late so much, especially in the spring, because that's when a lot of the animals separate from their moms and have to survive on their own, which just doesn't go too well for everyone, so we get a slew of new patients all at once. It'll be slower in the fall. Not that you care."

I stare at him.

"Mr. Chavez knows this," says Quint. "He understands that I have *responsibilities*"—drawing out the word like it's the first time he's ever said it—"and so he gives me a pass for when I'm late. In return, every two weeks my mom signs a form stating what I did at the center that justifies my absence at school, and Mr. Chavez gives me credit for it. It's a—what was that fancy word you used yesterday? Ah—a *symbiotic* relationship." He

lowers his voice conspiratorially. "Between you and me, I think I'm probably the suckerfish."

I raise my hand. "Hold on. You're telling me that all this time you just let
me believe you were sleeping in and . . . slacking off at the arcade or something, when you've actually been scrubbing pools and making fish puree?"

"Don't forget the rescuing of baby sea otters," he says.

I shake my head. "You did not say it was a baby."

He shrugs. "It wasn't. This time."

I throw my hands up. "Why didn't you tell me?"

"I tried to."

"When?"

"Last fall, after maybe the third or fourth time I was late. I could tell you
were mad, so I started to explain, but you just"—he waves his hand in mimicry
of the queen of England—"waved me off. You didn't want to hear it. In fact, I
believe your exact words were 'I don't want to hear it.'"

"But . . . ! But that doesn't mean I didn't want to hear it!"

He chuckles. "You do know how language works, right?"

"Oh, shut up." I kick him under the table.

His chuckle turns into an outright laugh. "All right, all right. Maybe I
should have tried harder. But you were . . . I mean, come on. You pissed me
off, too. I thought, if you won't bother to give me a chance, why should I try?"

"Because we were supposed to be partners!"

His smile vanishes and he gives me a look that's like a silent reality check.
"Prudence Barnett. You and I were never partners, and you know it."

I want to argue with this statement. I do.

But . . . I can't.

We were never partners. It's the truth.

But that's as much his fault as mine. I clench my teeth, thinking back to
those horrible moments when I realized he wasn't going to be there for our
presentation. That he had ditched me, on that most vital of days.

"You couldn't even be bothered to show up for our presentation," I say
darkly. "After I . . . I practically begged you to be on time. And you couldn't
even do that."

"The center was shorthanded that day. My mom needed me to help out."

But I needed you, too, I want to say. But I can't, not to him. Instead, I bite the inside of my cheek and look away, staring down the sidewalk. The memory of that morning brings back the same anger, the same dread, and Quint must be able to tell that this argument is different, because when he speaks again, his voice has a tinge of concern behind it.

"Look, I knew you'd be fine. You're . . ." He trails off, then gestures at me. One hand circling in the air.

I return a cool gaze to him. "I'm what?"

"You're good!" he says with an uncomfortable laugh. "You're, like, the best presenter in class. You didn't need me."

"But I did!" I yell.

Startled, he leans back in his seat.

I exhale harshly through my nostrils. My hands have started to shake. I need him to understand. All the other times he was late? Fine. Whatever. I can deal with it. But that day. *That day.* It was a betrayal. Doesn't he get that?

"I hate speaking in front of people," I start, but then I pause. I shut my eyes tight and give my head a quick shake. "No, that's not . . . Once I'm up there, it's fine. But beforehand? Thinking of how everyone will be watching me? It's terrifying. The only reason I can do it is because I practice and practice and practice, and remember? I'd told you that we should get together and practice the speech beforehand, and you said you were too busy, even though you obviously just didn't want to spend any more of your precious time on it, or maybe you just didn't want to spend any more time with me. Which is—I get it, whatever." I wave my hands through the air. "But I can't just wing it like you can! So I had to do it all myself. I had to plan the speech without you, I had to rehearse without you, but at least . . . at least I thought you'd be there when the time came. I thought you'd bring our papers and then people wouldn't be staring at me, and also, you could . . . you know. Do the thing you do." It's my turn to gesture vaguely at him. "Make people laugh. Put them at ease. Then I could give our presentation, and it would be great. Except you weren't there! And realizing that you weren't going to be there? It was awful!"

I finish.

I'm not really finished. I could go on. The way he interrupted the speech.

The way he took his sweet time handing out the papers. But my eyes are starting to prickle and I don't dare keep talking.

I can't look at him, so I stare at the table instead, scratching my temple with the pen.

Only when Quint laughs, which is as infuriating as it is unexpected, do I realize I've used the ink end and just scribbled on my face. I grimace and rub at it with my fingers.

"I meant to do that," I mutter.

"Trendsetter," he mutters back. Then he grabs a napkin, dunks it into a glass of ice water, and leans across the table. "Here," he says, scrubbing the ink from my skin.

When he's finished, he drops the crumpled napkin onto the table. Our eyes meet. I can't read his expression, but I can tell he's mulling something over. Something big.

The table is small. He could probably lean across and—

"I'm sorry," he says, startling me from the so-not-okay direction my thoughts were heading. "I didn't know. I thought . . . You always seem so confident in front of the class. I had no idea."

He does look legitimately sorry.

He inhales and goes on, "You know the other night when they were having karaoke here?"

I nod. I've barely thought about karaoke these past few days, but now the memories come surging back. The first powerful chords of "Instant Karma!" The way the restaurant faded away as I sang. All except Quint, for that one moment, his eyes glued to me, his half-astonished smile . . .

I look down at the table, suddenly flustered, and . . . oh good heavens, I'm *blushing*.

What the heck?

"I was watching some of those people get up to sing," says Quint, and I snap my attention back to him. "And I thought, I literally cannot imagine anything more painful than to sing in front of a crowd like that. I would rather have a root canal." He gives an exaggerated shudder. "So, I get it. In a way. Stage fright, or whatever. And you're right. I should have been there. You did ask me to." He pauses. "I'm really sorry."

We sit in silence for a while, tourists and beachgoers passing by on the sidewalk. Birds squawking nearby, hoping we'll leave behind some crumbs of food.

"I have a trick," I say quietly.

Quint's eyebrows go up.

"When I have to perform in front of people, I tell myself, this is only five minutes of my life. Or ten, or twenty, or whatever it is. In the grand scheme of things, five minutes is nothing, right? And that's all I have to get through, and then it will be over."

His mouth quirks. "If I ever decide to do karaoke, which is highly unlikely, I'll keep that in mind."

"Most songs are under four minutes long."

He nods, and now he's smiling. His smile is familiar, but it's not very often that I've been the recipient of it.

I swallow.

"Look, Prudence. I don't want this summer to be as miserable as biology class was all year. Do you think maybe we can try something different?"

I don't look away as the threat of tears starts to fade. "Well," I say, "that does seem better than the alternative."

NINETEEN

The waiter arrives, swapping out the empty appetizer plate with a giant platter of nachos, piled high with roasted pork, gooey cheese, and all the fixings. Quint thanks him, and as soon as the waiter walks away, Quint nudges the plate toward me, pushing it on top of some of my papers. "You can have some if you want."

"Thanks," I mutter. "Given that you did eat my food."

He smirks. He knows as well as I do that if I were going to finish the tostones, they would have been long gone before he arrived.

I huff and take a chip.

Quint groans in approval as he takes his first bite, and washes it down with a swig of his soda. "So much better than rice and beans."

"Rice and beans? That's a weird comparison."

He chuckles. "There are only, like, three things on this menu that Morgan can eat. She pretty much just comes here for the tostones, and they are amazing, but a guy sometimes needs a bit more. So we had rice and beans, but the Puerto Rican kind? What's it called?"

"Pigeon pea rice."

He snaps his fingers. "Right. Except even that is usually made with ham or bacon or something, so she ordered the vegetarian option. It wasn't bad, but this?" He sweeps his hand toward the nachos. "Oh my god. So good."

"She's vegetarian?"

"Vegan. And, I mean, she always *says* that she's fine with people eating meat and dairy in front of her, but . . ." He gives me a knowing look. "Believe me, she is judging. She is judging hard. So I've found it's easier to just get whatever she gets."

"Huh. I guess that explains the billboard," I say, picturing the cows in their green pasture, and the big X drawn over their happy thoughts. It still doesn't make what she did okay, but if she's opposed to meat, then of course she's opposed to the local burger joint.

"What billboard?"

I blink, realizing that Quint probably doesn't know about the graffiti. "Oh. I was just thinking about this billboard I saw, advertising Blue's Burgers? Someone had vandalized it, and I was just thinking how, you know, to me, eating a cheeseburger isn't exactly a question of morality. But Morgan would probably disagree."

"Oh, she would disagree with all the raging fires of hell," says Quint. Then he shrugs. "I mean, she's cool. I like Morgan a lot. She's really smart and super fun to work with. But when it comes to the meat industry and the humane treatment of animals, she is"—he takes a second to search for the right word before settling on—"passionate."

Something tells me he's using *passionate* to describe Morgan the same way he used *dedicated* to describe me.

"I guess that's good to know," I say. "Honestly, she mostly just seemed rude the other night."

He grimaces. "She did, didn't she? I know I shouldn't apologize for other people or anything, but she's not usually so disconnected. I guess there was, like, this big online petition thing going around, trying to get the government to shut down some local factory farms that have been caught using inhumane practices. So she was writing emails to all our local politicians and trying to blow it up on social media."

Factory farms? Is this connected to the billboard incident, too?

But Blue's Burgers gets their meat from cows that graze happily on fresh green grass all day. That's what all their advertising has been telling us for years. They don't have anything to do with some shady factory farms.

And even if they did, Morgan was still committing a crime. The universe still punished her for it.

Quint goes on, looking a tiny bit embarrassed when he adds, "Not that she couldn't have stopped for two seconds to give your friend her attention or some applause or something. And you too, for that matter."

I shrug, feeling suddenly self-conscious. Again, I think about his gaze on me, the way he'd toasted me with his Shirley Temple as I left the stage.

"You were really good, by the way."

It takes a moment for Quint's words to register.

"I don't think I said that yet," he continues. "But you were." He's suddenly intent on his nachos, like choosing a chip with the perfect amount of cheese-to-pork-to-jalapeño ratio is a life-or-death situation.

I blush again, but this time it spreads all the way down my throat and across my chest.

"Thanks," I say quietly. I have to clear my throat. "But I know I don't have a great singing voice. You don't have to——"

"No, I know. That's not . . ." He hesitates. "I mean, your voice is fine."

"Fine," I say with an erratic laugh, "is barely a step above tolerable."

"That's not what I meant. You were . . ." He trails off.

"I'm flattered," I deadpan.

He shakes his head. "I'm just trying to say, you were . . ." He flicks his wrist through the air, trying to summon a word or maybe trying to convey his meaning through a flourished gesture, but the message isn't translating.

I should probably appreciate the twin telepathy I have with Jude more than I do. Clearly, communication is hard.

"I was?"

His fingers stall, then clench briefly, before swooping down and grabbing a chip off the pile. "Never mind."

My knee starts to bounce anxiously under the table. I find myself staring at him, even as he turns his head and fixes his attention resolutely on the sliver of beach that can be seen beyond the buildings on the other side of the street.

His cheeks. They look redder than before, too.

Which I am *obviously* imagining. Or maybe he forgot to put on sunblock—an amateur mistake here in Fortuna Beach.

That must be what it is.

"You just seemed really confident up there," he says, speaking a little too fast all of a sudden.

"I'm a pretty confident person in general."

"Believe me, I've noticed. But it was more that . . . you looked like you were having a lot of fun. That's all."

Oh. There it is. The f-word. The note of surprise. The implication—Wow! Prudence Barnett knows how to have *fun*? Who knew?

"Right. Because all I know how to do is work hard and get good grades and study."

He glares at me, and just like that, we're all bristled up again. "Honestly? I've wondered."

It's terrible, the way this comment burns. There's no way for Quint to know how he's just jabbed a stick straight into one of my weakest places. I know I can be a bit of a control nut. I know I take things too seriously some- times. I know I'm not a jokester or the life of the party or one of those breezy "cool girls" that are portrayed in the films like the fantasy of every red-blooded boy out there.

I know the words someone like Quint uses to describe someone like me. Buzzkill. Uptight. *Prude.*

But he's wrong.

"I can have fun," I say. "I *do* have fun. And for your information, I have friends who like hanging out with me. People who legitimately enjoy my com- pany. Maybe I don't go surfing or . . . or do kegstands or whatever—"

"Whoa, whoa, whoa," says Quint. "That's not what I—just never mind, okay? Let's just forget I said anything."

I inhale sharply through my nostrils. My pulse is running hot, but I force my anger back down from whence it came. I admit to myself that maybe, just maybe, that was a slight overreaction. Though I'd never give him the satisfac- tion of knowing that.

"Fine," I mutter. "It's forgotten."

"Great."

"Okay."

"Fine."

Aaaaand . . . suddenly, things are weird. Uncomfortable. Like there's been something left unsaid but neither of us is quite willing to say it, and—to be honest—I have no idea what that thing is. But it's looming over our heads, daring us to take notice.

"Okay!" I say again, so loud and sudden that Quint jumps a little. "So. Let's talk fundraising strategies, shall we? I have so many ideas. I'm bursting with ideas. Here. I made a list, organized in order from lowest to highest start cost, but then on this side I've noted what I think the potential income could be." I flip around the top piece of paper and hold it toward Quint. He scans it as he eats a few more nachos. I take my pen and tap the top item—bake sale. "Obviously, a bake sale would be incredibly cheap and easy, but how much money can we really expect to make selling brownies?"

"I don't know. People really like brownies."

"True. And I also have this page of supplementary ideas, and under bake sale I did think we could make themed goods? Like, cookies shaped like dolphins, that sort of thing. But, anyway, I think we can do better than a bake sale." I tap a few more items on the list. "Other cost-effective options are creating a mailing list and working on our educational outreach with local schools, and we definitely need to step things up on social media. The only cost there is our time. On the other end of the spectrum, down here, we have things like—"

"Gifts with donations?" says Quint.

"Yes! Like in our project. Remember? Reusable tote bags and water bottles, all branded with the center's logo. Just a little incentive, based on various donation amounts. But we would have to pay to produce those items, and it's better to order that stuff in bulk so that the price-per-item goes way down."

"Field trips?"

"Right! I thought, if we can get kids excited about the center, then they'll go home and tell their parents. We can invite classes to come and see the animals, watch us feed them, maybe do a fun craft project, like I found these sea turtle suncatchers on Pinterest that are made out of tissue paper and super cute, and then—"

"Prudence. Pause."

My words halt.

"Before we can do any of this, we need to figure out our message. Our mission. I mean, I know why my mom started the center, and why so many of the volunteers donate their time there, but we need to be able to convey it to people who've never heard of us. Who maybe have no idea that these animals are in danger. Because no one is going to give us money if they don't know why it's important."

"Of course it's important," I say, more than a little confused.

Quint laughs. "*You* don't think it is."

"That's not true. I'm here, aren't I?"

"You're here because you want a better grade on that project."

My hackles rise and I'm about to argue, when Quint lifts both hands. "Just stick with me here. We rescue and rehabilitate sea animals. Why?"

"Because . . ." My mouth stays open, but nothing else comes out. "Because . . . because people think they're cute?"

He rolls his eyes. "People. But not you?"

"I don't know. They're not bad."

"Have you ever seen a baby sea otter?"

I roll my eyes. "No, but I'm sure they're great. I'm just saying. They're sea animals. They're not puppies."

"Ah. So you're a dog person."

I make a face. "Ick. No."

Quint laughs, tipping back in his chair and balancing on the back legs. I'm tempted to kick it out from under him. His teeth, I notice for the first time, are weirdly perfect. Like, toothpaste-model teeth.

"Oh, stop it," I hiss. "I'm not a monster. I can see that puppies are adorable, and I'm sure baby sea otters are, too. But . . . I like people. I like kids."

He looks surprised at this. "You do?"

"Well, sure. I mean, when they're not related to me. I used to tutor kinder-gartners in reading and they were the best."

He stares. "Huh."

"Don't *huh* me," I say, pointing a finger at his face. "I do more than study, you know."

He cocks his head to the side, and I can see that this is new information to him. But I can also see him struggling not to say that. "You said you like kids when they're not related to you. Jude isn't your only sibling?"

"I wish. We have three younger sisters. Lucy is thirteen, Penny is nine, and Ellie is four."

"Ellie," he says, curious. "Short for Eleanor?"

I nod.

"Wow. Your parents were really committed to the Beatles thing, weren't they?"

My eyes widen. He picked up on that *really* fast. "You know Beatles music?"

"Of course. They were pretty much all my dad listened to when I was growing up."

His dad? This is the first I've heard of Quint's dad. I don't recall seeing a wedding ring on Rosa, but then, I wasn't looking for one, either. And with her line of work, it's possible she would take it off anyway.

Then I catch the subtext of Quint's words. That's all his dad listened to *when he was growing up.*

But not now?

Did he pass away?

Curiosity floods through me, but I know I shouldn't ask. Instead, I shrug, trying to act nonchalant. "Yeah, well, I'm just glad my parents kept having girls, because there aren't a lot of guy-friendly names in Beatles songs. I mean, there's Maxwell, who murders people with a hammer. Or Rocky, who gets shot in a saloon . . . It's really slim pickings."

Quint chuckles again, but at least this time he doesn't seem to be laughing *at* me, which is a nice change. "I love it. I always wanted a little brother or sister."

"Everyone says that, because they have no idea what a pain they are."

He shrugs. "I think I'd be a pretty kickass big brother."

I want to argue, to shoot a hole or two in that theory, but . . . maybe he's right. I mean, Jude is a great big brother. He's way more patient with our sisters than I am and more willing to play with them or help with homework or babysit. Not that it's a competition, but we both know who the better older sibling is.

"Do you have any older siblings?" I ask.

"Nope. Just me and my mom." He pauses before adding, "And because I know you're dying to ask—my dad is alive. They divorced when I was nine."

"Oh," I say, trying not to let on that I'd definitely been picturing a great childhood tragedy in which his dad died in some sudden and horrible way. Something like relief surges through me, even though I know that divorce can be really hard on a kid, too.

"He lives in San Francisco with his new wife," Quint adds. "I spend two weeks with him every summer and some major holidays. I'm not sad. I'm not traumatized. It's fine."

I press my lips together. It's tempting to tease him for this speech, which he's clearly given a time or two in the past, but I resist the urge. For three whole seconds. "And you've spent how many years in therapy trying to get to this point of well-rounded acceptance?"

The look he gives me is withering, but in a good-natured way. It occurs to me, somewhat bewilderingly, that this conversation has actually turned into something kind of . . . friendly.

"Funny," he says. "So, do you like your name? I've always wondered."

I shrug. "I don't dislike it. There have been times when I hated it, especially with a twin named Jude, because the jokes pretty much write themselves. Prudence the Prude and her weird brother, Jude . . . Heard that one a lot in middle school."

Quint grimaces. "Your parents didn't think that one through?"

"I'm not sure how they could have missed it. But 'Dear Prudence' is a beautiful song, one of my favorites, in fact. So . . . whatever. People are jerks. I'm used to it."

"It kind of fits you, doesn't it?"

I stiffen, the words striking me between my rib cage. My eyes narrow. "Because I'm *such* a prude?"

He looks startled. "No, that isn't . . . Why do you keep doing that?"

I roll my eyes. "Please. I know what people think about me. I get it. I don't goof off. I take things too seriously. But I'm not a total killjoy, either." I swallow, finding it suddenly impossible to hold his gaze. I don't say it out loud, but this is actually one of my biggest fears. That, in reality, I *am* a total killjoy. And these arguments sound defensive even in my own head, and I realize I'm biting the inside of my cheek to keep from blurting something rude right back at him. *Maybe if you'd ever showed up on time to class you could have taken five seconds to get* to know me, rather than just asking what you missed and copying off my notes. "I know I can be intense. I know I'm not . . . silly or flirtatious or whatever, but—"

"Okay, stop!" Quint leans over the table. "You just put, like, a zillion words in my mouth that I didn't say. I'm sorry. I didn't realize I was a hitting a nerve here."

"You did not hit a nerve."

"Prudence." He looks bewildered. "Ten minutes ago you almost took off my head for suggesting you were having fun while singing karaoke. Here. Just, give me a second." He takes out his cell phone and types something into it. "'*Prudent*. Adjective. Acting with or showing care and thought for the future.'" He turns the phone so I can see the definition from dictionary.com. "You care about stuff. Yeah, you take things seriously. That's not necessarily a bad thing."

I swallow, feeling simultaneously embarrassed and . . . strangely flattered.

"Anyway," he says, putting away the phone. "It's better than being named for a surly old sea captain."

"Sea captain?"

"Yeah. Quint." He eyes me speculatively. "Captain Quint?"

I shake my head.

"The shark hunter from *Jaws?*"

I shrug.

"Hold on. You've never seen *Jaws?*"

"Hold on. Your marine-animal-loving mom named you after a shark hunter?"

"My question first."

I give him an exasperated look, then swing my arm in the direction of the boardwalk. "No, I've never seen *Jaws*. We live on the beach. I'm already afraid of sharks. Why would I make it worse?"

He drags a hand through his hair. "Exactly! We live on the beach! It's like the best beach-town movie of all time!"

"No, thank you. I'm good."

"I do not accept that. It's a classic. You have to see it."

"I do not have to see it. My life is perfectly satisfactory as it is." I thump my palm on the stack of papers. "Also, are we going to get back to this discussion sometime today, or did you just lure me here for the nachos?"

"Speaking of." Quint points at the plate, of which he's devoured at least two-thirds. "Are you buying? Because if not, I might need that twenty dollars back."

I make an annoyed sound, but Quint immediately starts laughing again. "I'm joking. I've got this. I'll get your banana things, too."

"How generous. Of course, you did eat most of them."

His eyes twinkle. "Okay. Where did we leave off?"

I try to think back to our conversation. We covered bake sales and social media . . .

Quint snaps his fingers. "Have you ever been snorkeling?"

I stare at him. Clearly he's just trying to irritate me at this point. "Snorkeling?"

"Yeah. You know, with the tube and the goggles—"

"I know what snorkeling is. And no, I haven't. What does that have to—"

"That's what I figured. Let's go. Today. You probably don't have a swimsuit with you?"

His eyes travel down the top of my dress—not in a creepy way, but still, he does seem to realize the implication and quickly snaps his focus back up to where it belongs.

"No, I don't have a swimsuit with me, and no, I am not going snorkeling. Did I not just tell you that I'm afraid of sharks?"

He snorts. "You know what the chances are of getting attacked by a shark?"

"Twelve people die every year!" I spout, recalling the statistic from that poster at the center.

"Out of how many billion people on the planet?"

I point toward the beach. "Yeah, but how much do your odds increase when you actually go swimming in water with *sharks in it?*"

"Prudence, I will protect you from the sharks."

A bellow of a laugh escapes me. "Thank you. I was, in fact, hoping for a show of chauvinism."

His eyebrows shoot upward. "I prefer chivalry, but go on."

"Is this because you were named after a shark hunter?"

"You're changing the subject. I'm serious. How far away do you live? We can meet back here in . . . an hour?"

"No!" I'm practically shouting. "*Gah*. This is like biology all over again." I pick up one of the folders and shake it at him, barely resisting the temptation to throw it in his face. "We have things to do and all you ever want is to goof off, and before long, I'm doing all the work! Please tell me this whole afternoon hasn't just been a colossal waste of my time."

In response, Quint reaches over and snags the folder out of my hand. "For god's sake, Prudence, just *once*, could you not argue with me? Could you just trust that maybe my idea is relevant?"

"Your idea. To go snorkeling."

"Yes! If you're going to help the center, you need to understand what the center is all about. That means understanding the water here, the animals. And not just seals and sea lions, but all of it. It all works together. You need to see it firsthand."

"I have seen it firsthand. At the aquarium!"

"Prudence." He stretches his free hand across the table and settles it onto my wrist. I jolt with the unexpected touch. His palms are surprisingly warm, and surprisingly rough with calluses. "You might know business, but I know the center. And remember, this time, we're supposed to be a team."

I swallow. I wish he would stop throwing that back at me.

His hand doesn't leave me the whole time I'm considering, and I try not to be unnerved by it, or the teensy little part of me that wonders how it would feel to turn my palm up and lace our fingers together. But that would be super weird. Even weirder than this moment, which is stretching on and on and . . .

"Fine," I mutter.

He starts to smile. Him and his perfect teeth.

"But if I get eaten by a shark, I swear to you on my dad's first issue of *The White Album* that my bloody, half-devoured corpse will haunt you until the end of time."

TWENTY

Though I have lived next to the ocean my entire life, I have never understood people's obsession with the water. Even when we were kids and our parents brought me and Jude and Lucy to the beach, I would get my toes wet, splash a few times, then spend the rest of our trip collecting shells and building sandcastles from the security of my *Tangled*-themed beach towel. I hated how the sand got into my bathing suit, itching all my unmentionable parts. I didn't like how the water would push and tug at me if I went out too far. I didn't like how everyone joked about sharks, even though every year there were real-life news stories about real-life shark attacks.

I'm sure people—people like Quint—think I've missed out on some of the most wonderful things about living here. Surfing. Bodyboarding. Diving. And, yes, snorkeling. But I figure, the water just isn't my thing. There's nothing wrong with that.

So I'm mystified to find myself pulling on my swimsuit, still practically brand-new even though I bought it more than two years ago, in order to go snorkeling with Quint Erickson. It feels a little bit like I've been tricked.

Looking in my bedroom mirror, I'm struck by a wave of doubt. I don't give much thought to my body in general, and when I do it's with indifference. I know that I don't look like a cover model, and I'm okay with that. I think of my curves in lukewarm terms. They are squishy and soft and they are mine. I never think *sexy,* I never think *voluptuous,* but neither do I think *fat* or *gross,* like I've heard other girls talk about themselves in the locker room after gym class.

Suddenly, though, I feel self-conscious. It's been a long time since I've worn a bathing suit in front of any of my peers, and the only time I ever go swimming is when I'm over at Ari's house, since she has a pool and, again, the ocean and I just haven't gotten along. Historically speaking.

And now I'm going snorkeling? With Quint? It's just so weird.

As my hand traces the paneled side of my swimsuit, I find myself wondering whether *his* feelings toward curves are as lukewarm as mine.

The question leaves me just as quickly, replaced with mortification that I would care, that I would even hesitate to don a swimsuit now when this whole thing was his idea. What does it matter? It's *Quint.*

I pull a fluttery blue dress over the suit and slip on my sandals. I grab my lipstick, through habit as much as anything, but hesitate. Is it weird to put on lipstick to go snorkeling?

Grumbling, I toss it back into my bag and leave before I can second-guess myself.

Quint is waiting at the beach, right where we agreed to meet. He's taken off his T-shirt, but I can see now that he was wearing a gray surfing shirt underneath, and there's a disturbing flutter of disappointment when it occurs to me that he is not going to be shirtless during this excursion.

What the heck, Prudence?

"I was beginning to think you might ditch me," he says.

I cast a withering smile. "I did consider making you wait for an hour and a half."

"Why didn't you?" he asks, handing me some snorkel gear.

"Oh, you know. I value little things like punctuality. Besides, someone else already rescued all the baby otters, so I didn't have anything better to do."

He snorts. "You know, you're actually kind of funny."

I pause from inspecting the mask and mouth tube to glare at him.

Realizing he's tiptoed too close to that nerve again, Quint takes a defensive step back. "Which is completely expected and unsurprising in every way."

I'm still frowning, but I let it slide. "Have these been sanitized?"

He laughs, as if I were joking. "I'm glad you came. This is going to be fun."

I can't tell whether he's joking or not, but I can tell that he's completely avoided answering my question. I want to press. After all, I don't know where these things have been. But his reaction makes me feel like it's a ridiculous thing to be concerned about and I'm already feeling awkward enough.

"You promised this would be educational," I say instead. "Don't make me regret this."

"Fun *and* educational," he confirms. "I'll show you how to use those when we get in the water. You know how to swim, right?"

"Of course I know how to swim."

"I had to ask. You'd be amazed how many people don't." His eyes sweep down my dress and I feel a little kick in the base of my stomach. *Is he checking me out?* He looks like he's about to say something, but then seems to think better of it as he turns away. "Come on, there's a great place a little farther up."

I follow him in silence, our sandals flipping up the sand. It isn't until I see the two neatly folded beach towels stacked on a rock that I realize I forgot to bring mine. Quint, who probably notices this, too, doesn't say anything as he kicks off his sandals and heads toward the water.

I slide my sandals off my feet and tuck them beside the towels. My heart has started to thump erratically. I realize how much I haven't thought this through.

I'm going to be in my swimsuit. In the ocean. With Quint Erickson.

Alone.

Why is this starting to feel like a date?

It's *isn't* a date. Obviously. He hasn't said or done anything to imply this is a romantic excursion, and . . . I mean, it's pretty clear how much he dislikes me. He's only here because I've basically coerced him into helping me with our project, and in turn, helping the center.

And that's for the best, because I'm so not into him. Not in that way. Not in any way.

My mind is rambling. I struggle to shut it off.

Quint walks out into the surf until he's shin-deep, then looks back at me, confused. "You okay?" he yells.

"Yeah," I yell back. For good measure, I give him a thumbs-up.

"What are you waiting for?"

I tighten my grip on the snorkel gear, like I'm holding a weapon. My breezy dress feels suddenly like a shield. I don't want to take it off. I don't want to be here. I don't want to do this.

What was I thinking?

Brow creasing, Quint starts walking back toward me. He looks legitimately concerned. "Okay, I shouldn't have teased you about the sharks. But I checked, and there's *never* been a shark sighting along this stretch of beach. You're going to be fine."

"It's not . . ." I shake my head.

He cocks his head to one side, considering. "Are you afraid of the water?"

"No," I say, perhaps a little too defensively, only afterward realizing that to say yes would have been a perfect way to get out of this.

"Prudence, it's okay if you are. But you should say—"

"I'm not afraid of the water!"

He holds up his hands, his snorkel gear dangling from his fingers. "Okay, okay. So what's the holdup?"

I open my mouth, but what can I say? That I'm too shy to take my dress off? That I don't want him to see me in my swimsuit, when half the people in our town practically *live* in their swimsuits this time of year?

"I just . . ." I shake my head again. "Nothing. Whatever." I set down the mask and turn away from him, because that's as close to seeking privacy as I can get out here on the open beach. I suck in a deep breath and before I can talk myself out of it, before I can make it any weirder than it already is, I pull my dress up over my head and drape it over the rock beside our towels. I grab the snorkel gear and pass by Quint without meeting his gaze.

I have no idea if he bothers to look at me. To *look* look.

And I don't want to know.

I've never gotten into the water so quickly.

The sand shifts under my bare feet. The waves push at my legs and hips, and soon the foam is swirling around my waist.

"Keep the tube out of the water," says Quint, and I jump. I didn't realize he was so close to me, and now his hand is beneath mine, lifting the gear away from the gentle waves. "Nothing like a mouth full of seawater to ruin the experience."

He smiles, his eyes catching the light that's reflected off the water, and they are not boring, nondescript, basic brown eyes at all. They are rich and captivating.

My mouth dries.

Goodness gracious, what is *happening* to me? Why is this starting to feel like . . . like . . .

Like the start of a crush.

Ha! No! Absolutely not. A storm of silent laughter surges through my thoughts. That is absurd.

This is Quint Erickson. He is so not my type. He is the polar opposite of my type.

Okay, I'm not entirely sure what my type is, but I do know it is not *him*.

"Ready?" Quint pulls on his goggles, and I'm grateful that my internal hysteria is brought to a screeching halt. I must look confused, because he takes my goggles away from me and adjusts the mouth tube attachment. "Like this," he says, pulling the strap on over my head, stretching the band so that it fits under my ponytail. I hold my breath until his hands fall away and I'm left to adjust the goggles so they fit snug, forming a seal around my eyes. "Then this part goes in your mouth—not over it, but inside your lips, okay? Then all you need to do is keep this end out of the water. And that's it." He grins again, before sliding the mouthpiece between his lips, making them puff out. Making him look ridiculous.

He tips forward and pushes off into the water, floating at the surface, the tube puncturing the air beside his ear.

"Get it together, Prudence," I whisper, before stuffing the piece into my mouth. It feels awkward, the plastic pushing uncomfortably against my gums.

Okay. I just have to get this over with and move on with my day. Quint will be satisfied, he won't have to yell at me about being "a team" anymore, and we can get started on the real work.

I walk out until the waves are up to my chest before leaning over and putting my face in the water.

It takes some mental coaching to persuade my body to inhale, and I keep checking that the other end of the tube is still out of the water. But after the first few breaths, it gets easier, despite every instinct reminding me that breathing underwater is not natural.

I peer into the depths.

I see . . . me.

My legs, looking ghastly pale and tinged sea-foam green.

My swimsuit—solid black.

My bright-pink-polished toes being covered up with drifts of sand.

I turn in a circle, noticing a handful of shells scattered across the seabed.

It's . . . pretty. Serene. I like how the light filtering through the water casts swirls around the—

Oh holy shish kebab!

I spit out my mouth piece and scream, back-paddling my arms. My head pops out of the water.

"Quint!"

He's at least thirty feet away. His head snaps up and he tugs out his mouthpiece. "Yeah?"

"Come here! Fast!"

He doesn't ask questions, just starts swimming toward me with perfect front-crawl arm strokes, as opposed to the awkward doggy paddle I consider to be my specialty.

"Look, look, look!" I say, latching on to his arm and pointing. Still wearing the goggles, he ducks his head into the water. I pop my mouthpiece back in and join him, clutching his arm, because as excited as I am, I'm also a little scared.

He sees it, too.

A sea turtle, hunkered down on the ocean floor. It's *enormous*. At least four feet wide, unless that's a trick of the water and the light. If it knows we're here, it's ignoring us.

Quint meets my eye under the water and we share a mutual, awed grin. At least, I'm in awe. His smile is something more akin to *told you so*.

I'm not sure what he thinks he told me, though.

Quint lifts his head up out of the water. I follow suit, only then realizing that he didn't have his mouthpiece in. He takes a minute to catch his breath, but he's beaming.

"Amazing, right?"

I spit out the snorkel gear. "How crazy is that? It's, like . . . right there!"

He nods. "I see them out here all the time."

I gape at him, almost as stunned by the sighting of the sea turtle as I am to realize that, to some people, that's a common occurrence.

I'm still holding on to him, like he's a life raft keeping me afloat. I'm surprised that he hasn't shaken me off.

Licking the salt from my lips, I uncurl my hands and lower my feet back into the sand below. The current has pulled us out farther and the surface is nearly to my sternum now. We're just two goggled heads smiling at each other like loons.

"It still blows my mind," says Quint. "When you're looking at the water from up here, you'd never know." I look down, and he's right. The water is clear—at least I always thought of it as clear—but I can only see the vague murky shapes of our bodies. There's none of the clarity and brilliance that was so striking underneath.

We duck our heads under again. The sea turtle has moved a few feet away, but it's still there, loitering on the ocean floor. I see Quint pull something from a pocket in his swim trunks, like a phone, but bigger. Chunkier. A phone wearing battle armor.

I watch as he dives deeper, getting so close to the turtle I actually become a little worried for him. He swims around a few times and I realize he's taking pictures. The turtle ignores him. I'm beginning to think that Quint will pass out if he holds his breath any longer, when the turtle turns, shockingly quick and graceful, and swims straight for me. I startle and lift up my legs, giving it a wide berth. It passes underneath me and continues on its way toward the shallows.

Quint and I both pop up again. He's panting, his hair plastered to his face. It takes him a few seconds to drain the seawater from his snorkel tube, but he's grinning the whole time.

"Is that a camera?" I ask.

"Naw, just my phone," he answers, holding it up. It looks like a swanky gadget out of one of Jude's favorite sci-fi movies. "My mom got me a waterproof case for my birthday. I'm saving up for a wider lens that'll work with it, but it's good enough for now. So? What did you think of your first real wildlife sighting?"

I consider this. I've seen sea turtles at the zoo, but seeing one here, so close to me, was exhilarating.

"Is there more?" I ask.

He laughs. "Let's find out."

I had expected our snorkeling experiment to last fifteen, maybe twenty minutes, but Quint and I end up being in the water for more than two hours. By the time we finally come ashore, my fingers have pruned, I have a cut on my ankle from a vicious rock, and I feel like I've just journeyed to an alien planet and returned to tell the tale.

Quint knew all the best places to go. He took me to some rocky outcrops and pointed out underground gardens of seaweed and kelp. We saw so many fish, my mind is dizzy trying to remember them all. A kaleidoscope of colors, darting in and out of the rocks, swooping around my knees, shimmering like gemstones. For a grand finale, which I suspect Quint had been planning all along, we swam farther up-shore, to a cropping of large rocks that couldn't be seen from any public beaches. The rocks were crowded with harbor seals, whooping and barking and lazing in the afternoon sun.

I have lived here my whole life. How did I not know this was here, only a few miles from my house?

I've forgotten all about my previous self-consciousness as Quint and I make the trek back up the beach. The tide has gone out and the walk to our towels feels endless. Sand clings to the soles of my feet. Quint keeps glancing over at me, grinning, almost secretive.

"So?" he says as I wrap one of the beach towels around my body.

"That was . . ." I struggle for words. I'm suddenly dying of thirst, and I can feel a sunburn on my back, but it all pales beside the afternoon I've had.

"I know," says Quint, saving me from having to find adequate descriptors. "But here comes the million-dollar question." The way he says it, I feel like this whole afternoon has been a buildup to his next words.

Instantly guarded, I meet his gaze. There are deep red lines around his eyes, a perfect silhouette of his goggles. I probably look just as silly. My hair is frizzing around my face as it starts to dry out. But after the day we've had, none of that seems to matter.

Quint gives me a knowing look, bordering on smug. "Is it worth saving?"

I go still.

Suddenly, it makes sense.

Because no one is going to give us money if they don't know why it's important.

I remember him saying that, but it didn't really sink in until now. I feel a stronger connection to our little stretch of ocean now than I ever have in my life. The magical schools of fish, the shells that shimmer along the ocean floor, the sea turtles. I swam with flipping sea turtles!

And suddenly, I care.

Is it worth saving? Is it worth protecting?

Abso-friggin-lutely.

"Point made," I mutter.

He beams. We spend some time drying off our legs, brushing sand from our feet. I hastily pull on my dress while he's turned away. Quint takes my towel and the snorkel gear, cramming them into a bag, and we start back up the beach, heading toward the boardwalk.

"Are you hungry?" he asks.

"Starving," I answer automatically.

"Cool. Maybe we can get some tacos while we go over the rest of your ideas?"

He's a couple steps ahead of me, his focus turned toward the horizon. I wish I could see his face, because that old uncertainty rears up again, every bit as unbelievable now as it was earlier.

This isn't supposed to be a romantic thing. I mean, there's just no way.

Is there?

"I . . . uh . . . left the folder at home."

"Is it far?" He glances back at me.

"No," I say, perhaps too slowly. "We live over on Sunset."

"Okay. I'll walk with you. Or I can go get us a table somewhere?"

He's being so casual. Which is perhaps the only reason I notice how flustered I've become.

"Actually, I'm kind of exhausted. Maybe we can talk about it tomorrow? At the center?"

If he's disappointed, he hides it well beneath a shrug, utterly devoid of emotion. "Sounds good."

We pause at the boardwalk. The beach is more crowded here and chances are good that we'll see someone we know from school, but if Quint is at all wary about being seen with me—clearly *with* me, given our matching wet hair and goggle impressions—it doesn't show. When it becomes clear that he's heading one way and I'm going the other, we both hesitate, standing awkwardly.

"Okay, well. Tomorrow, then." I start to turn away.

"Hey, could I just hear you say it?" he asks. I glance back. There's a glint in his eye. "Just once?"

"Say what?"

"I just want you to admit that this"—he gestures toward the ocean— "wasn't a waste of time. That *I* actually had a good idea." He taps his chest.

I cross my arms and say in a robotic voice, "This was not a waste of time. You had a good idea."

"And you're glad you came."

I sigh and drop the robotic tone. Honestly, I confess, "And I'm glad I came."

"And you'll never doubt me or argue with me ever again."

I point my finger at his nose. "Too far."

His teeth flash. "Had to try. Hey, I almost forgot. I have something for you."

He starts digging through the bag, shoving aside damp towels and goggles. His hand emerges clutching a yellow T-shirt, printed with the logo of the Fortuna Beach Sea Animal Rescue Center.

I take it from him, surprised, but not sure if I should be flattered to be receiving it or annoyed it wasn't given to me on my first day. After a second of inspecting the shirt, I say, "I'm not really sure yellow is my color."

"I'm not sure it's anybody's color, but it was the printer's cheapest option." Still grinning, he adds, "Besides, you might be selling yourself short. I'll see you Monday, Prudence."

I smile and wave goodbye.

Despite these volunteer shirts being really ugly, I cradle the dumb thing to my chest the whole walk home.

TWENTY-ONE

I'm on a roll, outlining a new section for our revised biology project: educational snorkeling classes for tourists! Guests would go out snorkeling with a trained professional who could tell them what fish and animals they were looking at, and explain the delicate balance of our shallow water ecosystems. The guide would discuss things like—

A screech of a violin invades my ears. I cry out in surprise and cover my ears with both hands.

"Penny!" I yell to the next bedroom.

"Sorry!" she yells back, though her apology is quickly followed by another squeal from the strings.

Sighing, I get up and close my bedroom door. Returning to my bed, I pull my computer back on my lap, doing my best to ignore the painful sounds from the next room. Why on earth are my parents still paying for her to take lessons? Clearly they're not doing any good, and I'm sure they have better things to spend their limited funds on.

Okay. Where was I?

The guide would discuss things like . . . right. The natural food chain and the importance of biodiversity. How predators like sea otters help keep the sea urchin population under control, which prevents the sea urchins from overfeeding on kelp, which then can provide food and shelter for many other species. There are larger environmental factors to—

My bedroom door swings open, admitting not just the earsplitting squeaks of Penny's violin, but also Eleanor, dressed in her favorite llama pajamas.

"Ellie, you're supposed to knock!"

"Will you come play with me?"

"No. I'm busy. Shut the door."

Her lower lip juts out. "But no one will play with me. Penny is practicing her violin and Lucy is on the phone and Mom is watching that dumb baking show again."

"None of this is my problem. Go talk to Jude."

"He went with Dad to get dinner."

I groan and get out of bed. Ellie's face lights up, but she deflates as soon as I grab her by the shoulder and steer her back out the door. "Self-sufficiency is an important skill that you need to start developing."

She makes a frustrated sound and stomps her foot. "What does that even mean?"

"It means, go play with your dolls."

"Jude always says yes, and you always say no!"

"Well, I guess Jude is just a nicer person than I am."

I shut the door. She yells from the other side, "Yes he is!"

I mime strangling her, then throw my hands into the air. I consider taping a DO NOT DISTURB sign to it, but . . . whatever. She can't read yet.

I go back to the report and scan over the last paragraph. Not bad. Moving on.

I vaguely remember Mr. Chavez saying something about how marine plants like kelp and seaweed are more effective at cleaning our air pollution than all the rain forests of the world. But I don't remember the specifics, or how it works.

I open up the internet and start to type in a search query.

Angry footsteps storm down the hallway, then Lucy yells from right outside my door. "MOM! Would you make Ellie go downstairs? I'm trying to have a conversation and she won't stop bothering me!"

"I'm folding clothes and watching my show!" Mom yells back. "Just let her play with your makeup or something!"

"What? No! She makes a mess!"

I flop down on my back and pull a pillow over my head.

Quint was so wrong. Siblings are the worst. My life would be infinitely better if it were just me and Jude.

Outside my door, the violin continues to screech. Lucy is still yelling. Ellie has started to cry—one of her fake tantrum cries that grate on every nerve.

My fingers twitch. I could punish the whole lot of them. For being so rude, so inconsiderate, so *loud*.

But just before my fingers close into a fist, I pause and force myself to stretch my hand out wide instead. What if, by trying to punish my whole family at once for their barbarity, the universe decides to burn our house down or something?

Grumbling, I climb out of bed and go searching for my noise-canceling headphones. I check my desk, the drawers, my book bag. They're not in any of the places I usually put them.

I huff, knowing exactly who has them.

The hallway has been deserted. I shut the door to Penny and Lucy's shared bedroom just as another squeak peals from the violin. I pass the bathroom, where Eleanor is sitting on the bath mat, starting to paw through *my* makeup bag.

"No," I say, snatching it away.

She screams. "Lucy said I could!"

I reach over her head and grab Lucy's makeup kit off the counter and hand it to her. She lights up. With the exception of my vivid lipsticks, Lucy's makeup, with its sparkles and an actual eyelash curler, is definitely preferable to mine or even Mom's. At least according to the four-year-old of the family.

With her own bedroom being used as the ear-torture station, Lucy has set up shop in our parents' room. I open the door and find her sprawled out on the bed, her cell phone to her ear.

"Where are my headphones?"

"Hold on," she says into the phone, before holding it against her chest. She shoots me a hateful look. "What?"

"My headphones. Where are they?"

"How should I know? Go away."

"This isn't your bedroom."

"Mom doesn't care."

Anger is boiling under my skin now. Is it so hard for her to answer a simple question?

"Lucy, you always take them without asking. So where are they?"

"I don't know!" she yells. "Check my backpack!"

I spin on my heels. I've barely stepped back into the hallway when I hear Lucy griping to her friend, "Seriously, my sisters are such pains."

And yeah, maybe it's hypocritical, given that I did just complain about this exact same thing only a few minutes ago, but at least I had the decency to keep the thoughts to myself. Either way, I've reached my limitation on goodwill.

I pause just outside the door and squeeze my fist shut.

"Hello? Jamie? *Hello?*" says Lucy, her voice rising. Then she lets out an exasperated groan. "Great. And now my battery is dead. Thanks, family!"

I poke my head back into the room with a serene smile. "That must mean you have time to look for my headphones."

She finds them in her backpack and hands them over with an icicle glare.

I've just returned to my bedroom and gotten settled into my bed when I hear the front door open downstairs.

"We're back!" Dad yells. "And we come bearing gifts of food!"

Mom follows this up with her own shout, as if Dad had needed a translator. "Girls, it's dinnertime!"

Ellie squeals and dashes down the stairs, which must mean that Dad and Jude were going out to get something good, because usually it's nothing but griping when she gets called to the dinner table. Penny, Lucy, and I follow with less enthusiasm. Lucy is still scowling.

Penny seems oblivious that there's been any conflict at all. "Ooh, Blue's Burgers!" she says when we reach the kitchen. "Yes!"

Mom and Dad are at the counter, gathering napkins and pouring drinks. Jude is pulling baskets of french fries and cheeseburgers from a collection of white paper bags and setting them out on the table. "Wow, Ellie," he says, with a genuine Jude smile. "You look like a movie star."

She beams, showing off the streaks of sparkly purple eyeshadow around her eyes and cheeks. She actually looks like she's been in a bar fight with a fairy godmother, but she seems so pleased with herself I can't bring myself to say so.

"Thought we should do our part to support one of our community staples," says Dad, sitting down and taking one of the burgers from Jude. "They sure have been getting a lot of bad press lately, with all those billboards getting tagged."

My eyebrows rise as I take my seat. "More than one?"

Dad nods. "Five or six, I think. Someone wrote *Lies* on a bunch of them and drew sad faces on the cows. I guess there've been rumors going around that Blue's is getting their meat from some awful farms where the cows are all crammed together and fed slop or what have you. All I know is that Blue's Burgers has been around since the sixties, and they are just as delicious now as when I was a kid. Don't know why anyone would go after them, of all places. It's hard enough for a little family-owned place to stay in business without people trying to tear them down."

"Honestly. What's wrong with some people?" Mom asks as she hands out paper towels.

I unwrap my burger, overflowing with tomato and pickles and Blue's mind-blowing secret sauce. My mouth is already watering. But something gives me pause. I think about what Quint said, how Morgan was petitioning to have the government look into a factory farm, something about inhumane treatment of the animals. But that can't have anything to do with Blue's Burgers. Their cattle come from organic, grass-fed . . . something-something . . . I don't know, whatever their ads say.

Don't they?

And even if they don't, does it really matter to me? I'm not vegetarian. It's never even crossed my mind to be anything other than a content omnivore. I figure, humans are at the top of the food chain for a reason. And it isn't like my parents can afford the expensive meat out of the butcher case, so probably lots of the meat I've consumed over the years has come from those farms that feed them slop or what have you, as Dad so succinctly suggested.

This isn't a cause that means anything to me. They're just cows.

They're just food.

But Morgan. Regardless of how I feel, this cause clearly means something to *her*. So much that she was willing to climb to the top of a rickety ladder to tell people about it.

A choice she's paid the price for.

"Everything okay, Pru?" asks Mom.

I blink up at her. Smile. "Yeah, yeah." I try to shake the thoughts from my head. My family is staring at me. I clear my throat. "I was just thinking about . . . um . . . this project I've been working on. Did you know that sea otters play a vital role in balancing the health of kelp forests?"

"What's a kelp forest?" asks Penny.

I sigh. "It's a forest. Of kelp. Underwater."

Ellie's eyes go wide. "There are forests underwater?"

"Yeah, sort of," I say.

Mom dips a fry into her ketchup. "Did you learn that at your new volunteer job?"

"Um. Yeah," I say, because I'm not about to bring up how I spent the afternoon snorkeling with Quint Erickson. Jude is already giving me a suspicious look.

"I must say, I was pretty bummed when you decided not to come work at the record store," says Dad. "But it sounds like things at this rescue center are going well so far?"

I shrug. "It hasn't been so bad."

"And Ari has been great, hasn't she?" says Mom. "I've heard nothing but good things."

"Oh yeah. That girl!" says Dad, picking up a pickle that's fallen out of his burger. "I think she might know more about music than I do! And, of course, I'm happy to have Jude there."

Jude smiles, but his mouth is full, so he doesn't say anything.

"That reminds me," I say, setting down the burger, unbitten, and wiping my hands on a paper towel. "I told Ari I'd give her my old keyboard. You don't mind, do you?"

Mom and Dad both stop chewing and exchange looks.

"What?" I ask. "We're not using it. No one here even knows how to play."

"Maybe Ellie would want to learn to play," suggests Lucy, which feels like a suggestion made just to thwart me. I frown at her, then glance at Ellie.

"Ellie, do you want to learn to play the piano?"

Eleanor twists up her mouth in deep, thoughtful concentration. She takes a sip of her milk, still thinking. When she sets the cup down, she finally answers, "I want to play the drums."

"Good choice!" says Dad ecstatically, while the rest of us grimace. That's all we need to go along with Penny's violin lessons.

"Either way," I continue, "if Ellie or anyone did decide they wanted it, I'm sure Ari would give it back. But for now, I guarantee she'd get more use out of it than we are."

"Here's the thing," says Mom, dabbing her own paper towel around her mouth. "We would have loved for Ari to have it, if we knew, but . . . well. We don't have the keyboard anymore."

I blink at her. "What?"

Then I shove my seat back from the table.

Ellie, who we are constantly having to scold into staying at the table during dinnertime, immediately points at me and shouts, "No leaving the table!"

I ignore her and cross the floor to peek into the living room.

Sure enough, the keyboard is gone, leaving a gaping hole amid the clutter where it used to sit.

I spin back. "Where did it go?"

"We sold it," says Mom, lifting her hands in something almost like an apology, though not a very convincing one. "You weren't using it. I didn't think you'd even notice."

And she's right. I never would have noticed, if I hadn't wanted to give it to Ari.

I slump back into my seat. "You could have asked."

"And you could have practiced more when you were taking lessons," says Dad, even though I'm not convinced this argument is at all relevant to the conversation.

"I hope Ari can find herself a nice keyboard," says Mom. "She really is such a sweet girl, and we do appreciate her helping out at the store."

I narrow my eyes. "You are paying her, right?"

"Of course!" says Dad, sounding offended. But it had to be asked. I'm fairly sure Ari would work there for free, but I'm not about to tell them that. She deserves to get paid for her time.

"And how is the store doing?" asks Lucy. "Financially, I mean."

Her question surprises me. The directness of it. We all feel the question immediately sending us out onto thin ice. I have to admit, I sort of admire Lucy for being the one to bring it up, when even Jude and I would rather go on pretending that everything is fine.

Again, Mom and Dad look at each other. Even Penny seems to tense. Only Ellie ignores the topic, too busy trying to make a tower of french fries on the table.

"Fine," says Dad. "Slow. But it always is this time of year. Tourist season is coming. It'll pick up."

He says it with confidence, but what else is he going to say? The record store is doomed and we should all start panicking?

Then Mom smiles and changes the subject, asking Lucy how softball practice went earlier that day.

I pick up my burger again and take a bite. I'm sure it's delicious, as it always is, but for some reason, I hardly taste a thing.

TWENTY-TWO

U gh. I can't say it. Not again. Please don't make me."

Quint leans against the short wall. I can sense his smug grin, feel him watching me. But I only have eyes for the creature in the little pen. "Come on, Prudence. You can do this. Here, I'll get you started. Repeat after me. *Quint, you were* . . ."

I cover my eyes with my hands and give my head a vicious shake. But it doesn't last long. I have to open my fingers. I have to peek.

Oh heavens. That fuzzy face, the twitching nose, the sweet little paws curled together over his tummy as he rolls around on the floor . . .

I groan, and feel myself caving. "Fine. Quint. You were"—I grimace, biting back the word for as long as I can—"right."

He makes a victorious fist, pumping his elbow.

"Sea otters are flipping *adorable*. But you cheated! You said it wasn't a baby."

"It's not a baby. He's, like . . . I dunno, our age, probably. But in otter years. Their babies aren't *super* small, but they're smaller than that." He leans toward me conspiratorially. "A couple years ago we were caring for a pregnant sea otter when she gave birth. The pup was like the size of a basketball. A fuzzy, ridiculously cute basketball."

"Stop it."

"I got to bottle-feed it a couple times."

"I hate you."

"I know."

I cut a look at him. He's watching the sea otter, but there's a smile tugging at his lips.

I swallow and look away. I study the little otter as he flops onto his tummy and curls up on top of a blue towel that's been left in the corner for him. His wounds are almost unnoticeable—a few lacerations along his back and side, one cut on his back paw. I never would have seen them if Quint hadn't pointed them out. "Is he going to be okay?"

"Oh yeah, he'll be out in the yard in no time, and then back out to sea."

We finally move away from the newest patient. We have the second shift today, and the time it took to prepare the feedings went a lot faster than before. Quint and I spend a little more than an hour cleaning the kitchen and doing dishes, then sorting the newest delivery of fish for tomorrow's meal prep.

"So what's Jude up to while you're here slaving away?" Quint asks as I dry a collection of bottles and arrange them in one of the cabinets.

"He's working at the record store this summer."

Quint looks at me, surprised. "Ventures?"

"Yep."

"Really? Seems a little . . . hipstery. For Jude."

I laugh, in part because the idea of my parents' store being "hipstery" strikes me as faintly hilarious. "Oh yeah, Jude doesn't fit in there at all. But our parents own the store. You didn't know that?"

He looks at me, surprised. "No. That's cool. It's been years since I've gone in."

"You and ninety-eight percent of the town's population." I sigh, thinking about my dad's die-hard optimism, his certainty that business will start to pick up now that it's almost tourist season. But I'm beginning to see some cracks in his cool exterior. "You know there's been this revival of vinyl records over the past decade? They're suddenly cool again, and diehards will rant for hours about the superior sound quality and collectability and how digital music has"—I curl my fingers dramatically—"*sucked the life out of the music.*"

He snickers.

"But unfortunately, the rise in vinyl sales has happened at the same time as the fastest-rising property values in Fortuna Beach history. My parents don't really talk about that stuff with us, but I overhear them talking about it sometimes, and I can tell they're worried. The store has been in that location for seventeen years. It may not be the most popular place in town, but they do decent business, and it's kind of a landmark, right? But if rent goes up again . . ." I shake my head and give Quint an apologetic look. "Sorry. I didn't mean to ramble."

But he's nodding sympathetically. "It's ironic, right? The economy is great, but it's always a struggle for the little guy."

He sounds almost wise when he says this, and I wonder if these are words his mom has spoken in the past. After all, more wealth in the community should benefit everyone. But if that wealth isn't being distributed . . .

It makes my head spin. I cannot *wait* to take economics in college so that all this might actually start to make sense.

"Anyway, I don't want to give my parents a complete pass. They had the chance to buy the building a long time ago, but my mom had just gotten pregnant again and they didn't think they could make ends meet. But if they'd made different choices, they'd be sitting on a real estate gold mine right now rather than stressing out about next month's payment."

Quint shrugs. "Decisions like that look a lot different in hindsight. Besides, they wanted kids. Can't fault them for that."

I make a face. "They already had twins. Did they really need to make three more babies?"

"Remember, I'm the one who's jealous that you have siblings. You won't get any pity from me."

I put the last of the bottles in the cabinet and shut the door before giving him an appraising look. "You want one? I'll give you a great deal on Lucy."

"Is she the little one?"

"No, that's Ellie. Lucy is thirteen."

He flinches. "Oy. I don't think my big brother skills are ready for a teen-ager."

"No one ever is. You know. Unless that teenager is me. I'm a model daughter."

"I so badly want to make fun of you for that statement," says Quint as we hang up our aprons, "but something tells me it's probably true."

We head up the stairs to the staff break room, which is mostly filled with a long narrow table and mismatched chairs. My backpack hangs on a peg on the wall and I take it down and dig out the same folders and papers I'd had with me for yesterday's meeting, though I was up for two hours last night making changes.

Quint settles into one of the chairs. Someone brought in a box of doughnuts, and he spends a few moments inspecting his options before picking up one coated in cinnamon and sugar. "So once you're done here, will you turn your business knowledge toward helping your parents? You could have a community campaign—Save Ventures Vinyl!"

I hand Quint some of the papers and sit down across from him. "I don't know. I mean . . . I guess I could. I've just always sort of seen it as their problem to fix."

"The center wasn't your problem, either."

"Yeah, but . . ." I trail off.

"Ah. Right. You're just here for the extra credit."

"That's not true." I pause. "Anymore."

A smile flashes over his face, but he quickly tucks it behind one of the papers as he begins to read over my notes. I'm still thinking about the record store, wondering whether I *could* make a difference. Not by working as a minimum-wage employee, but by applying the same sort of tools that I want to use to help the center. Marketing. Publicity. Social media. I know there are record stores that are doing really well, that don't struggle to pay their bills every month.

Why *couldn't* Ventures Vinyl be one of them?

"Prudence?"

My attention snaps back to Quint. "Sorry. Was just distracted."

One thing at a time, I tell myself. I've already dedicated my summer to the Fortuna Beach Sea Animal Rescue Center. My parents' store has lasted this long; it will survive a few more months.

"This looks familiar," says Quint. He's looking at the list of fundraising ideas I compiled a couple of days ago while he polishes off the doughnut.

"Yeah, but we didn't really get around to discussing any of these options."

"A gala?" he says, reading off the paper. "What is it with girls and galas?"

"Galas are how you get fancy people to give you a lot of money. You offer wine and appetizers and have an auction and there's so much peer pressure to look generous that rich people go nuts outbidding one another."

He licks the sugar from his fingertips. "And how much money would it cost for us to host this fancy gala?"

I consider. "Five, ten thousand dollars?"

He fixes a look on me.

"Okay, maybe not a gala." I take the duplicate list that I've saved for myself and scratch it off. "What about opening the center up to the public? Say, one day a week people can come in and see the animals, and we could have volunteers tell them about environmental issues and how they can get involved. You could charge admission . . ." I trail off. Quint is shaking his head at me.

"We used to do that," he says, lacing his hands behind his head and tilting so far back in the chair that it's only in pure defiance of gravity that he doesn't go toppling over. "We were open to the public on Saturdays and Sundays. But you need a lot of volunteers to make it work, and our staff got bitter because they didn't have enough time to do their actual jobs."

"We'll get more volunteers."

"How?"

"We'll advertise for them."

"With what money?"

I throw up my hands. "Okay, I see what's happening. This is a self-fulfilling prophecy. No one knows about the center, so they can't support it. And if no one supports it, the center doesn't make any money. And if the center doesn't make any money, you can't host events or advertise or do things that will inform even more people about the center!"

"Exactly." Quint gestures at my notepad. "Luckily, we have Prudence Barnett on the case. You're the ideas person. What are your ideas?"

"I've been trying to tell you about them for three days now, but every time I do, I either get shot down or coerced into water sports."

Quint wrinkles his nose. "Snorkeling isn't exactly a sport."

I sigh. "You're not being very much help." I tap the end of my pen against my mouth, staring at all the ideas on the list. I won't give him the satisfaction of saying it *again*, but Quint might be right. Or, he at least makes a valid point, one that I've been warring with since the idea of raising money for the center first entered my mind. If there was money to spare, we'd have a lot more options.

I'm really beginning to understand the adage: You need money to make money.

Realizing that Quint has gone abnormally quiet, I glance up.

His gaze is fixated on . . . my lips? Is my lipstick smeared? I move a hand to my mouth, at the exact moment Quint realizes I'm looking at him and immediately turns his attention back down to the box of doughnuts. He picks out another—berry filling, powdered sugar—but cuts it in half this time rather than taking the whole thing. He takes a big bite, still not looking at me. A dusting of sugar sprinkles onto his yellow shirt.

I self-consciously lower my hand and tighten my grip on the pen. "Your . . . um . . . your mom said you've done fundraisers in the past. Do you know if they kept records for those? Maybe we can take a look, see what worked and what didn't?"

He thinks about this while he chews.

"Shauna probably has something we can look at," he says. "From what I remember, fundraisers *do* make money, just . . . never enough. And we do have some long-term donors, people who write us big checks every year. But again . . ."

"It's never enough," I finish. "What do you do to cultivate those relationships?"

"What do you mean?"

"Like, does your mom send handwritten thank-you notes to those people? Invite them for special tours of the center? Maybe we could let *them* name some of the animals?"

Quint stares at me. "But those people are already giving us money."

"Yeah, for *now*. But those few things would barely cost any money to do, and it might keep you from losing a major source of income. There are a billion different charities out there. If something else snags their attention and they start to think their donations could make more of a difference elsewhere . . ."

Comprehension dawns in Quint's eye. He grabs a pen and starts scribbling something in the corner of the paper. "I'll mention it to Mom," he says. "But it doesn't really help with drumming up more money."

"No, but it's good to know that people who do become invested in the center tend to stick around. Having repeat donors means you won't be starting at square one every year. So . . . how do we get people to donate in the first place, and how do we get them to care enough that they'll want to keep helping?"

Quint says nothing. He finishes the doughnut and wipes his hand on a napkin.

"I really think we need to work the local angle," I say. "I mean, if someone in Milwaukee wants to save sea animals, they'll give their money to the World Wildlife Fund or something. They're not going to bother with tiny little Fortuna Beach's rescue center. But people who live here and visit here . . . they care. Or, they should. We need to establish the center as a part of the community."

Quint crumples the napkin and tosses it into the trash can in the room's far corner. He doesn't say anything, and I have the distinct feeling he's waiting for me to reveal some big, brilliant strategy. Which, I guess, is what I promised him. But while I've had lots of ideas, none of them seem like they're enough. Like they have the potential to bring in enough donations that would make the time or money expense worthwhile.

My attention catches on a line of framed photos on the wall behind Quint. I'd noticed them before, but hadn't really taken the time to look. My eyes narrow in thought.

Pushing my chair back, I stand and walk over to them. I feel Quint's eyes on me as I study the first photo. My stomach lurches, but I force myself not to look away. The image shows a sea lion lying in a plastic kiddie pool, perhaps one of the ones I've seen down in the yard, with a blanket draped over its back. The flesh around its mouth is punctured through with so many fishhooks, it looks like it's just been to a body-piercing convention. "That's awful," I whisper.

"That's Captain Hook," says Quint.

I move to the next photo. This one depicts an elephant seal on the beach, with fishing line entangled around his throat and one of his fins, cutting so deeply that it's left a row of gashes. I'm a little proud of myself for being able to tell this one's a male, even though with elephant seals it's really obvious, as only the males have the strange trunk-like snout that gives them their name. In my opinion, they're the least-cute of all the animals we treat here, yet I can't help but feel a tug in my heart to see the poor guy in such obvious pain.

The third photo shows what at first glance appears to be just a pile of litter on the beach—plastic bags and fishing nets. Only on closer inspection do I realize there's a sea turtle entangled, nearly buried, beneath it all. My hand squeezes as I stare at it, and I wish I could punish the person who threw their garbage into the ocean or left it behind on the shore. But the universe stays quiet. I don't feel the gentle swoop in the pit of my stomach, like I've felt when this bit of magic has worked before. After all, these animals were hurt a long time ago. That litter could have been thrown away weeks, months . . . even years before it did *this*.

Then an idea hits me. I gasp and spin to face Quint. He must see something in my face, because he drops his feet to the floor and sits up straight, ready to listen.

"A beach cleanup!" I say. "Let's host a beach cleanup."

TWENTY-THREE

Rather than being overcome with sudden inspiration like I am, Quint looks skeptical. "You want people to come pick up garbage?"

"Yes! Remember? People *want* to be a part of the solution, but first you have to show them an easy and convenient way to do it."

"How very generous of them," he deadpans.

"I'm serious." I smack Quint on the shoulder and drop into the chair beside him. Reaching across the table, I grab my notebook and pull it toward me. At the top of a blank page, I write "Beach Cleanup." "Most people have good intentions, they just lack initiative. If you make it seem fun and easy, and make sure there's something in it for them, you can get people to do pretty much anything."

Quint ticks off his fingers. "One: That's a really pessimistic view of humanity. Two: We have nothing to offer people because, again, no money. And three: How, exactly, is a beach cleanup supposed to generate money for the center? Because . . . see number two."

I ignore him. My mind is sprinting, racing a hundred miles per hour. I'm already jotting notes as ideas and possibilities rush through me. Quint leans forward, reading over my shoulder.

"We don't need to offer them something of *monetary* value," I say, once my initial burst of inspiration has waned. "If we make it seem like a big deal, like something everyone will be doing, then people will come for the peer pressure alone. After all, you don't want to be the only person in the community *not* showing up to help. A lot can be said for public shaming."

"Again: pessimistic view of humanity."

"But there are other ways to reward people, too. Maybe we can get sponsors from the local shops. Like . . . everyone who fills a trash bag will get a free ice cream cone from the Salty Cow, stuff like that."

Quint grunts, and though he doesn't say it out loud, I can tell he thinks this actually has potential.

"And as far as raising money for the center, we'll have a donation jar set out for people who want to donate, but that's not the primary goal here. This is community outreach. After all, I've lived here my whole life, but when you brought up the center, I thought it was something you were making up. So right now, we need to focus on getting the word out. Who we are, what we do . . . Maybe encourage people to come volunteer once in a while? We'll have a table with a sign-up sheet where people can get on the mailing list."

"We don't have a mailing list."

"Oh, but we will." I wink at him. He looks momentarily startled, but I've already returned my attention to the page. "But none of that makes any difference if we can't get people to show up. We're going to have to offer more than free ice cream if we want them to give up a few precious hours of their weekend."

"Agreed."

My excitement is boiling over so quickly I have to bite my lip. Quint gives me a curious look and a part of me wants to keep him in suspense, but the idea is so good, so brilliant.

I scoot my chair back so I can face him full-on. Sensing that I'm building up to something big, he turns his body toward me, too.

"How often are we releasing animals back into the ocean right now?"

He thinks about it and shrugs. "We had a release almost two weeks ago. We'll probably be ready to let Pepper and Tyrion go in another few days . . ." He trails off. His eyes widen. "Oh my god, Prudence. That's genius."

I'm beaming. "We tell people that they'll be able to come and witness the release of some of these adorable animals back to the ocean. We'll make it into a huge celebration. People will be lining up to see that."

"You're right," says Quint. "I've probably been to hundreds of releases since I was a kid, but they never get old."

I'm surprised that it gives me a happy shiver to think of being there when some of the animals from downstairs get to go back to the water.

Quint snaps his fingers. "The festival."

"What?"

"The Freedom Festival for Fourth of July. It's a week from Saturday, and the beach is always a wreck afterward, so we should do this on Sunday. There'll be tons of garbage to clean up, and we can sell it as, like, we have these animals that are ready to go back to the ocean, but we can't possibly set them free with all this garbage everywhere. So we all work together to clean up the beach, and when we're done, we celebrate with the big release."

I'm grinning at him. "It's perfect. We can advertise it at the festival. We could even make a play on the name. Something like, 'This Independence Day, don't just celebrate your freedom . . . celebrate theirs,' with a picture of the animals we'll be releasing. We can have flyers and posters and things made up for the festival."

"I love it." Quint holds up a hand for a high five, but when I slap my palm against his, he closes his fingers around mine and gives them a squeeze. My heart skips. "Good brainstorming session."

I laugh. "Go team."

His eyes crinkle at the corners, and I know he's thinking about all our failed lab assignments. I know, because I'm thinking about them, too, and wondering if it's possible I just didn't give us—the *team* us—a chance.

Quint releases my hand. "I can design the flyers and posters."

I shake my head. "No, that's okay. I can do it. And I'll call around to some local businesses. Maybe we can get a few sponsors for the cleanup. And I'll check with the festival, too, see if they have room for one more tent and if maybe they'll give us a discount on the rate, given our nonprofit status. And oh! I'll order up buttons to give out to all the vendors! They can say something like 'I support Fortuna Beach wildlife! Ask how you can, too!'" I start scrawling my thoughts on the notepad again. They're coming so fast, my wrist is starting to ache by the time I've jotted everything down.

"Okay," says Quint, slowly. "So what do you want me to do?"

"Nothing, for now. I've got this. You know what else? I'll make up some stickers. I wonder if we can get them shipped here in time. But we can put them on all the festival trash cans, with cute little encouraging—"

"Prudence."

I glance over at him. "Yeah?"

He opens his palms, a question in his eyes.

I blink. "What?"

"I'm perfectly capable of designing flyers and posters. And buttons and stickers, too."

I open my mouth to respond but hesitate. I try again. "It's okay. I'll do it tonight. Get everything ordered and then—"

"While I do what, exactly?"

He no longer sounds happy. If anything, he's starting to sound mad.

A little exasperated, I gesture toward the row of windows overlooking the yard behind the building, full of seals and sea lions. For the most part, their barking has become white noise, hardly noticeable, but every now and then something excites them down in the yard and sets them all off at once in a great noisy racket. "You have things to do here, don't you? Pools to clean or whatever?"

"Oh. So I'm just the manual-labor guy?"

My brow furrows. "What are you talking about? I'm just saying—"

"You're saying you don't trust me."

My jaw opens and closes again.

"You're saying that you can do a better job. On your own. Without my help."

I'm trapped. I know I'm trapped. He knows I'm trapped.

"Well . . . but that isn't—"

His chair legs screech as he pushes back from the table and launches to his feet. "I knew this was a bad idea. I knew I would regret this."

I gape at him. "Quint, stop it. This is what I do. I plan. I prepare. I'm a perfectionist. I like being in control of things. You know that! And seriously, what's the problem? You're off the hook! Go help your mom or . . . or do whatever else you do. I can handle this. Everybody wins."

"No!" He spins back toward me. "Don't you get it? This is the problem. *You* are the problem!"

The air leaves me as though I'd been kicked in the chest.

Quint drags a hand back through his hair. "Not . . . not *you*," he amends. Letting out a guttural sound, he steps closer again and grips the back of the chair he abandoned. "Okay. You like to be in control. You don't trust other people to help out, because you're afraid they're going to screw up. I get that . . . sort of. But I did not agree to work with you over this summer just to repeat biology class all over again. *This*"—he gestures between us—"isn't going to work."

This? What does he mean, *this?*

The biology project? The beach cleanup? Him and me?

"I'm sorry," I say slowly, with a knife-sharp edge to my voice, because, darn it, I'm still smarting from that *you*-are-the-problem comment. "But I don't understand what this is about. Two minutes ago, I thought we had a plan. We're finally getting somewhere. And suddenly . . . what? I'm too much of a control freak and you can't stand the idea of working with me or . . . ?"

"Kind of. Yeah. Actually, that's exactly what this is about."

I gape at him, dismayed. Heat climbs up my neck and I slam my mouth shut. We stare at each other, and I think maybe he's willing me to cave first, but this is too ridiculous. I'm offering to do all the work here. To make sure everything is perfect. So what if his pride is a little hurt? This is about what's best for the center, not him!

Turning away, I start to gather together the papers, shuffling them back into an orderly pile as quickly as I can. "Fine. I wasn't exactly thrilled to be working with you again, either."

"Prudence—"

"No. Whatever. I wish you and the center *all* the luck in the world."

Quint reaches forward and grabs the stack of paper out of my hands. "Would you stop messing with the papers and listen to me?"

"Why should I?" I yell, jumping to my feet. "So I can hear more about how difficult I am? How much you hated working with me? News flash, Quint! The last nine months weren't exactly a joyride for me, either!"

"That's not my fault!" he yells back.

"It is entirely your fault!" I make an angry sound and squeeze my fists tight. Please, Universe. Please bring your wrath down on him. For speaking to me this way. For making me feel like something's wrong with me. For rejecting my ideas, my help, *me*. "If you weren't so unreliable and irresponsible, then maybe I would be able to trust you! But how can I possibly know that you won't screw it up?" I stomp my foot, a little petulantly, but I don't care. "It's just better if I do it on my own!" I snatch the papers from his hands. An edge slices through one of my fingers. "Ow!"

I throw the papers back onto the table and inspect the wound. Sure, it's just a paper cut, but it's a gnarly one. I cast a disgruntled look up at the ceiling, the sky, the universe. "Seriously?" I shout.

Quint huffs and turns his back on me. I think he's going to storm away, which infuriates me more. *I'm* supposed to be the one storming away!

But he doesn't leave. Instead, he opens a drawer, riffles around for a minute, and then comes back. He's holding a box of bandages. He doesn't look at me as he tears open the box, takes out a Band-Aid, and rips off the paper. He holds it out to me.

I snatch it away and tape it around my finger. I'm still simmering. I can tell that he is, too. But our last brash words have started to dissipate in the silence, and when Quint finally speaks, his tone is even, if still frustrated.

"I wanted to help with our assignments. But within the first two weeks, you were convinced that I was a useless lab partner. I took notes—you took better ones. I drew graphs—you went home and made digital pie charts. I measured the salt for that . . . that saltwater experiment way back when? And you immediately started remeasuring. You double- and triple-checked everything I did. At some point it became clear that nothing I did was going to be good enough, so why keep trying?" He shrugs at me, but the gesture is anything but nonchalant. "I stopped helping you with the lab assignments because you didn't want help."

I stand there, not saying a word, my jaw clenched. It feels like there's a thundercloud brewing between us, preparing to let off a bolt of lightning, though I don't know which one of us it's going to strike.

"And yeah," he continues, "I know I suck at spelling and I'm not a great writer or whatever, but I'm not useless. I mean, design stuff? Things like flyers and posters? I'm actually pretty good at that. You saw the paper, didn't you?"

My shoulders loosen, just a little, as I think about his report. The columns, the footers, the fonts.

"Yeah, but I figured . . ."

He waits, daring me to finish that sentence.

I swallow. "I figured you just downloaded a free template or something."

"Of course that's what you figured." He shakes his head. Sighs deeply. And collapses back into a chair. Not the chair he was in before. He leaves that one empty—a wall between us.

I press down on the Band-Aid, feeling the sting of the cut underneath, and timidly lower myself back into my chair as well.

"It wasn't a template," he said. "I'm not completely incompetent."

"I didn't say you were incompetent."

He gives me a weary look. "Yeah. You did. Maybe not with words, but that's what you've been saying all year."

I swallow. Guilt is starting to scratch at my throat, and I'm finding it hard to hold on to my own anger when I can't fully deny what he's saying. The truth is, I did think he was incompetent. Or at least, not capable of working to *my* standards. And maybe I still feel that way.

"Look," I say, trying to keep my tone even, "I'm not trying to be difficult. I just know that when I do something myself, then I'll know exactly what I'm getting. I don't have to stress out about it, and whether or not it'll be done how I want it to be, or if it will be any good, or if it will be done on time. And yeah, I know my life would probably be a lot easier if I could just say, you know what? Who cares? They're just flyers and posters. It's not a big deal. Let someone else handle it. But I *can't*. I can't just accept . . ." I struggle to find the right words.

Quint finds them for me. "Crappy work?"

I flinch. "I was trying to find a nice way of saying it."

He shuts his eyes, clearly disappointed.

"For the record," I add, "the paper did look really nice. Nicer, probably, than even I would have done it."

His lips twitch humorlessly to one side. "Thanks for that," he mutters. "I'm sure it wasn't easy for you to admit." Then he sighs and looks at me again. "Prudence, I'm not asking you to accept crappy work. I'm asking you to accept that maybe, just maybe, I might be better at some things than you are. Like—that presentation board you'd made up? You definitely should have let me take care of that part."

I frown. "What was wrong with my presentation board?"

He gives me a look, like I shouldn't even have to ask. "For starters, you used the Papyrus font for the headers."

"So? What's wrong with Papyrus?"

He makes a gagging noise.

I cross my arms, offended. "That board was fine."

"I'm sorry, but I could have done better. And then we could have used my photos, too. Tied it in with the report. The whole project would have been so much better if you hadn't insisted on doing everything yourself. And if you can't see that . . ." He shakes his head, then throws up his hands in exasperation and gets out of his chair again. "Whatever. We're just going in circles now."

"*Your* photos?" I say, standing up, too. I glance up at the wall, those framed pictures again. Although those three pictures weren't in the report, they're similar to ones that were. "Quint. Did you take these?"

He turns toward the wall, as if needing to be reminded what's there. "I thought you knew that."

"And the ones in the paper, too?"

He doesn't answer, and he doesn't have to.

My gaze travels down the line of photos, each neatly framed. They're stunning, each one full of emotions that dig straight into the gut. They could be in an exhibit at an art gallery. They're definitely deserving of something better than this shoddy break room, at least.

"There! That!" says Quint, pointing at my face.

I jolt, surprised. "What?"

"That's what I'm asking for. Just a little bit of appreciation. Is that so hard?"

I laugh, but it sounds a little dazed. Because . . . maybe I am. I'm definitely impressed, which is almost just as weird.

"Quint, these are good. Really good."

He shrugs. "Naw. I mean, the subject matter is pretty intense, so . . ."

"No, it's more than that. I took a one-week photography class when I was in middle school and the teacher was always talking about light and shadow and angles and . . . I don't know. I didn't get most of it. I didn't really have an eye for it, you know? But these . . ."

"Aw shucks. You're making me blush."

I turn back to him, and though he'd sounded joking, he actually does look like I've made him uncomfortable.

"You're an artist," I say, a little bewildered.

He makes a hearty guffaw of a sound. "Um, no. It's just a hobby. I mean . . . I don't know. I've thought it could be cool to be a photographer, maybe, some-day. I'd really love to do underwater photography." He waves his hand. "But it'll probably never happen."

I slowly look up, meeting his eyes. The eyes of this boy who, it turns out, I hardly know at all. We sat next to each other for two whole semesters, and yet it feels like there's a complete stranger standing before me.

An artist. A volunteer. The sort of person who rescues sea otters in his spare time.

He has his hands tucked into his pockets, looking almost self-conscious as he studies his own photos. While I was left breathless by the pictures, I can see that he's critiquing them in his mind. Something tells me he has no idea how good they are.

And the truth is, I couldn't say with absolute certainty that they're any good, either. I don't have an artist's eye. I don't know about light and shadows, angles and dimension. All I know is that when I look at these photos, they bring a mixture of emotions storming through me. They make me *feel*.

"I'm sorry," I say. "I'm sorry I didn't trust you to help with our assignments."

It takes him a second, but when he responds, his voice is light, almost jovial. Good old laid-back Quint. "I forgive you," he says. Easy as that. "But first, can I grab my phone and record you saying that again? For future reference."

I glower, but there's no heat behind it. I look back at the photos. "You could sell these, you know."

He snorts.

"I'm serious. In fact . . ." I point at the image of the sea turtle caught up in all the garbage. "I think this is the image we should use on our posters for the beach cleanup. Although"—I shrug at him—"you're the designer, so I guess it's your call."

TWENTY-FOUR

Hi there! I'm with our local sea animal rescue center. We're hosting a beach cleanup party tomorrow, right here, where we'll be releasing four harbor seals back into the ocean. I hope you'll join us!"

I have said some version of this speech so many times, it's beginning to lose its meaning. Words slur together. Get jumbled in my mouth. But I keep smiling, keep moving. I have a bag full of blue flyers printed with the details of the beach cleanup, and—yeah, Quint kind of nailed it. That is, *we* nailed it, since I insisted he let me proofread them before he printed the whole batch, and I did end up catching two typos and one misspelling. I have to admit, though, that the finished product is far better than what I would have done had I made them myself.

The flyers are eye-catching. Simple but effective. On the back, Quint even included short biographies of the seals we'll be releasing—where and how they were found, what was wrong with them, and notes about their personalities. Plus, each one has a photo. Even in black and white and slightly grainy, the photos are fantastic, and people's reactions seem to be universal. A surprised gasp, followed by a soft *aww* that tapers into a bittersweet sigh. The reaction may not be original, but I can tell it's heartfelt. People are touched by these animals' stories. I hope that translates into attendance, and donations.

I pause to take a swig of water from the bottle in my bag. The festival started at nine this morning, but newcomers are still swarming the beach, and will continue to arrive until sundown with the promise of a fireworks show that will be set off from a barge out in the bay.

From where I stand, I can see the line of cars stretching down Main Street as people desperately search for parking that no longer exists. Homeowners as far as two miles away will be raking in some dough today, allowing people to park on their lawns for twenty bucks a vehicle.

A long row of tents is set up along the cliffs and boardwalk, selling everything from handmade bird feeders to spice packets. I'm inundated with the smell of sunblock and the sizzle of bratwurst from someone selling hot dogs off a tiny charcoal grill. A rope has been set up to keep a clear pathway for people to shop the vendors, but otherwise, the beach is packed full with blankets, towels, chairs, and umbrellas. It's the most crowded I've ever seen it.

I spy Jude farther up the shore and he catches my eye and waves. Ari is a little past him, talking to a woman selling tie-dyed sarongs and T-shirts. I've recruited them to help pass out flyers today, and even Ezra, Quint's best friend, showed up to help, though he claims it's only because Fourth of July weekend is when all the cute summer girls show up. I reminded him that he's representing the center today and to please not sexually harass the tourists. Then I armed them all with the blue slips of paper and explained as many details of tomorrow's cleanup as I could, trying to fill their heads with phrases like *community outreach* and *raising awareness* and *freedom for our local wildlife*. That is, until Jude silenced me with the look that he's perfected over the years. The one that lets me know I've gone from sharing helpful information to what he calls "Pru-splaining." Which, according to him, is almost as bad as mansplaining.

All in all, I'm feeling good. Even though Quint and I have had less than two weeks to pull this plan together, I'm excited that it's finally happening. I can feel that it's going to be a success.

Besides, I have the universe on my side.

I hand a few flyers to a large family who have created a palatial assemblage of towels and shade awnings. They're clearly hard-core beachgoers, having thought to bring everything from a portable Bluetooth speaker to mini tables and an ice bucket sporting a bottle of pink champagne, even though alcohol isn't supposed to be allowed on the beach. It's a rule that no one seems to care enough to enforce, though. The family sounds enthusiastic and they say they'd love to come to the cleanup.

I'm practically skipping as I walk away.

My attention falls on Quint, and only once I see him do I realize that a small part of me has been searching for him since . . . well, since I lost sight of him the last time. He's holding a camera. Not a phone, but an actual camera, with a big lens and little knobs on top that do things I don't understand. It's not the sort of thing a person would bring to school—I'm sure it weighs a ton and is probably really fragile—and yet it feels weird that I've never seen him with it before. Seeing him now, it's clear that he's in his element, adjusting the camera settings with ease and confidence. He crouches down to take a photo of something in the sand and I desperately want to know what it is. Then he stands up, looks around, and snaps a picture of the horizon. And a group of kids prodding a crab. He takes pictures of umbrellas, of empty towels and abandoned coolers, of a surfer standing with his board and staring out at the waves.

Quint pauses and turns in almost a full circle, peering around him with what I have to assume is an artist's eye. Maybe lining up angles or considering the lighting.

His attention lands on me.

I stiffen, embarrassed to be caught staring. But he just grins and raises the camera to his eye. I roll my eyes, but humor him, holding up a peace sign and smiling for the camera. Though it's too far away to be real, I imagine I hear the click of the shutter.

I stick my tongue out at him.

He beams. I can't hear him, but my memory supplies an easy, effortless laugh.

"You're right," says Ari, startling me. I hadn't seen her approach. She's watching Quint with a knowing smirk. "I thought you were just exaggerating all this time, but oh no. He's *repugnant*."

"I never said he was repugnant," I mutter.

"I'm pretty sure you did."

"Need more flyers?" I ask, seeing her empty hands.

She takes another stack from the bag on my hip and flounces away.

I make a point of *not* looking for Quint as I head the other direction.

Smiling. Chatting. Telling people all about the center and tomorrow's animal release celebration.

Until my attention snags on a kid, maybe ten years old, at the exact moment he stomps his foot through his baby sister's sandcastle.

I gasp. Indignation flares through me. Before I even realize I'm doing it, my hand has clenched into an angry fist.

A second later, the kid gets hit in the head with a beach ball. It knocks him over into the sand.

I flinch. I mean, I don't think it hit him *that hard,* but still. I feel especially bad for their poor mother, who now has *two* crying children to contend with.

I start to loosen my fist, but now that the surge of cosmic power has rushed through me, it's like my antenna has been recalibrated. I'm newly aware of the people around me and their less-than-exemplary behavior.

A few seconds later, a college-aged girl cuts in line at the shaved ice stand. Within seconds of taking her first bite, a swarm of black flies lands on the cone, attracted to the syrupy sweetness. When she tries to shake them off in disgust, she sends most of her treat toppling to the ground.

Then I see a middle-aged man taking one of the blue flyers from Jude. But as soon as my brother turns away, the man makes a face, scrunches up the paper, and tosses it over his shoulder. It gets caught in the breeze and bounces along the sand a few times before getting caught against someone's cooler.

Annoyance roars inside my chest. That paper is advertising for a *beach cleanup,* you inconsiderate jerk!

Both fists tighten this time.

From nowhere, a toddler appears, waddling toward the man in nothing but a diaper and a pink bow in her wispy hair. The child pauses and looks up at the man, a perplexed look on her face. He tries to step around her, at which point, she bends over at the waist and pukes on his sandaled feet.

He's wearing flip-flops, so there is a lot of barefoot contact.

He cries out in revulsion. The girl's mom appears, apologizing profusely . . . but the damage is done.

I'm laughing and wincing at the same time.

All the while, Jude remains oblivious, making his way through the crowd, his back to me and the litterbug. With a satisfied smirk, I start making my way toward the piece of crumpled paper that's been tossed away from the cooler and is bouncing around like a tumbleweed between the rows of beach towels.

There are people gathered all around, but if anyone's noticed the piece of garbage in their midst, none of them have bothered to pick it up. It's a little thing, maybe, but I can't help feeling exasperated at their laziness. It would take all of five seconds to pick it up. There are garbage cans positioned every thirty feet along the boardwalk!

I stomp after the paper, even though the wind keeps kicking it out farther and farther from me. I'm finally starting to close in on it when a long-armed grabber appears out of nowhere and clamps around the crumpled flyer.

I pause and meet the eye of a woman. She looks to be about my grandma's age—somewhere between seventy and a hundred. It's impossible to tell. She's holding a metal detector in her left hand, the grabber in the right. A belt is slung around her hips with implements of beachcombing and garbage collecting. Rubber gloves, a small trowel, a reusable water bottle, a large garbage sack.

She sees me and winks. "I've got this one," she says, depositing the crumpled blue paper into her garbage sack.

Then she turns and starts making her way down the beach, away from the crowd and the festival, her metal detector swinging meticulously from side to side. She stops every now and then to grab another piece of litter and stuff it into the bag.

I lean back on my heels, bewildered to realize how rare and unexpected a sight that was. To witness someone doing a good deed—not for glory, not for a reward—but just because it's the right thing to do.

And yeah, I know that picking up a bit of garbage is a small thing. Perhaps most people would even think of it as inconsequential.

But that one act leaves me feeling uplifted and encouraged, especially when it seems that lately all I've seen are strangers being rude and inconsiderate.

A thought occurs to me.

I look down at my hands, lips twisted in thought. *What if.*

I mean, Quint did find that twenty-dollar bill when I tried to punish him for being so late. I didn't know about the sea otter . . . but the universe did.

So maybe . . .

I look back up at the woman. She's picking up a beer can. She flips it over, emptying the last dregs of beer into the sand, before tossing it into the sack.

This time, instead of clenching my hand into an irritated fist, I inhale deeply and snap my fingers.

The second that I do, I hear a beep.

It's far away, but I know it came from the woman's metal detector.

She pauses and swings the detector back and forth over the spot. It beeps again and again as she homes in on the exact location of whatever treasure is buried there. My heart is racing, but she hardly even looks curious. I wonder how often a "treasure" turns out to be nothing more than a buried bottle cap, an aluminum can, a penny.

I inch closer, biting my lower lip. Because I know. I know it's not junk. I know it's not just a penny.

The woman crouches and unhooks a small hand shovel from her belt. She begins to dig.

It takes longer than I think it will. She's moving slowly, shuffling a bit of sand at a time, occasionally scanning the detector over the pile to make sure she hasn't missed whatever is buried there.

Then—she goes still.

Her fingers reach into the sand and pick up something. It's small and shiny and, for a second, disappointment surges through me. Maybe it *is* just a penny.

But then it glints in the sunshine and I gasp.

A smile stretches over my face.

I think it's an earring.

I think it has a diamond in it.

"Ever done metal detecting before?"

I scream. Literally, a complete and total over-reactionary *scream* comes out of my mouth as I spin around and whap Quint in the shoulder.

"Ow!" he says, stumbling back a step and rubbing where I hit him.

"You scared the daylights out of me!" I say, pressing my hand against my chest. "Why are you standing so close?"

He looks at me like I just asked him why fish swim in the sea. "I was coming to see how things are going. Sorry. I didn't mean to scare the *daylights* out of you."

He's teasing me, but my heart rate hasn't calmed down yet and I don't have the willpower to be annoyed. Or amused.

"Did you . . . see anything?" I say, suddenly self-conscious. What must it have looked like? The snap of my fingers, watching the beachcomber like some obsessed stalker. And then for her to find something so precious . . .

But Quint only looks confused. "I saw a gyro stand back there, and now I'm starving." He peers at me, but must be disappointed when I don't even crack a smile. "Why? What's going on?"

"Nothing! Nothing."

His eyebrows rise. Funny how his eyebrows almost seem to speak a language all their own—and I think I'm beginning to understand them. "Two nothings always means something."

"Oh, you're a psychologist now?" I glance over my shoulder. The beachcomber has started walking away, still swinging her detector back and forth with as much patience as before. I wonder if I'm imagining the extra bounce in her step.

"So?" Quint says.

"So, what?"

"So, have you ever been metal detecting before?"

"Oh. No." I tuck a stray hair behind my ear. I'm giddy with the new realization that my power works both ways. I probably should have figured it out sooner, with Quint and that money he found, but I was too irritated then.

But now—oh, the possibilities—I can punish *and* I can reward. It makes perfect sense. I'd just been so eager to right wrongs before that I hadn't considered how karma flows in two directions.

I realize that Quint is staring at me and a flush spreads down my neck. I turn my attention to him, trying to concentrate, trying to act normal. "What were we talking about?"

"Metal detecting," he deadpans.

"Right. Yeah. I don't know. It seems like it would take up a lot of time just to unearth a lot of junk."

He shrugs. "I have an uncle who used to be really into it. I went with him a few times. It was kind of fun. You never know what you'll find. It is mostly a lot of junk, but on one trip I found a watch. Got forty bucks for it at the pawnshop."

"Wow. Score."

"I'm not gonna lie. I felt like I'd dug up Blackbeard's treasure."

"Do you ever think that you might be too easy to please?"

His eyes spark with a challenge. "Do you ever think you might be too hard to please?"

I roll my eyes. "I don't like wasted time. You know that."

"One man's wasted time is another man's"—Quint seems to contemplate how to end this aphorism for a long time—"hobby, I guess."

I grin. "You could embroider that on a pillow."

"Har-har. I just think it's okay to be excited when something good and unexpected comes your way. Even if it is just a watch. Heck, even if it's just a penny. It's still, like . . . a good omen. Right?"

I want to make fun of him, and maybe in the past I would have. It sounds like something Ari's abuela, who I've learned is very superstitious, would say. Good omens, the language of the universe, the power of intuition.

Except, I sort of have to believe in that stuff now, don't I?

I wonder what the beachcomber thought when she dug up that earring. Does she believe it's nothing more than a happy coincidence, or does she know, on some deeper level, that it was a reward, a cosmic thank-you for helping keep this beach clean?

I shake my head. "I usually won't even bother to pick up a penny."

"A lucky penny? Really?"

"It's just a penny."

He looks for a second like this is the saddest thing he's ever heard. Like his disappointment in me cannot be properly expressed. But then his expression clears. "Probably for the best. Maybe the person who comes along after you really needed to find a lucky penny that day."

"So a stray penny is a gift from the universe, but choosing to not pick it up is like . . . paying it forward?"

"Who are we to question the powers that be?"

I have to bite the inside of my cheek to keep from laughing.

Ever since my fall at Encanto, I *am* the powers that be. It's a heady thought.

"Anyway." Quint reaches for the bag at my side and withdraws a large stack of flyers. "I was just coming to get more of these." He uses his fingers to fan through them, like thumbing through a flip book, then smacks the papers against his palm. I think he might be stalling, thinking of something else to say. "But let me know when you get hungry. Those gyros smelled amazing."

TWENTY-FIVE

I watch Quint walk away, weirdly mesmerized by the way the sun glints off his hair. My insides flutter.

Noooooo, my mind howls at me. Why is this happening? *How* is this happening?

I want to deny it. Oh, I desperately want to deny it.

But the evidence is right there in my traitorous little heart, which is still hiccuping from his presence.

Gosh darn it. I think I might be starting to like Quint Erickson.

I grimace. I am so annoyed with myself right now. To be crushing on lazy, irresponsible, goof-off Quint? It's unfathomable!

Except . . . how much of that is true? I've seen him working at the center. He's not lazy. He's not irresponsible. He's still relaxed and easygoing and fun. He's still charming, friendly to everyone. He's still quick to crack a joke.

But even if, by some bizarre twist of fate, it turns out that Quint *is* sort of my type . . . there is no way that I could possibly be his.

Do you ever think you might be too hard to please?

My stomach curdles. I don't think he was trying to be mean when he said that, but still, remembering the words makes me ache.

I'm startled from my thoughts by a commotion down the beach. I turn, squinting into the sun.

A log has washed up on the shore and some kids have abandoned their boogie boards to gather around it. I hear a mom yelling—*Don't touch it!* I frown. My feet carry me a few steps closer. A couple of adults are talking, pointing. Someone is cooing at the log, starry-eyed, like it's . . . like it's a . . .

An animal.

Like a helpless, frightened, friggin' adorable animal that just washed ashore.

I start to run. I don't know what I think I'm going to do, but Quint's photographs are flashing through my memory like a reel of tragedy and trauma. In the weeks I've been working at the rescue center I've heard countless stories of how animals were found. Some of the stories seem implausible—like the time a seal clopped in through the back door of a local pub and was found hanging out in one of the booths the next morning—but most of the time, the animals wash up onto the beach, just like now. If they're lucky, someone spots them and calls the rescue center. But sometimes people want to help. Sometimes they want to touch it.

Sometimes it doesn't end well—for the animal or for the people.

"Get back!" I yell, my heels kicking up sand. My cry startles everyone who has gathered around the animal. A sea lion, I can see now. My breaths are ragged, but my mind is suddenly full with the sight of the creature. It's just like Quint's photos, and now I can tell the difference between an animal that is healthy and strong, and one that's dehydrated and starving and probably on the brink of death. I think something might be wrong with its eyes. They seem cloudy and there's some thick yellowish liquid beneath one. Its body is quivering as I approach.

"Is it dead?" asks a little girl, getting ready to prod it with a stick.

I snatch the stick out of her hand and she makes an outraged sound, but I ignore her. "I'm with the sea animal rescue center," I say, pointing to the logo on my yellow shirt. Immediately, I have authority. I have the respect of everyone around. Suddenly, I'm the expert in this situation, and I can see relief in some of the parents' eyes when they realize that someone else has assumed responsibility.

At which point, I freeze.

Now what do I do?

Quint, my mind eagerly supplies. *Quint will know what to do.*

My arms are still outstretched, standing in front of the sea lion like a protective . . . mama . . . lioness? Egad, I don't even have the right vocabulary for this situation. Pureeing fish guts all day doesn't lend itself to a full bank of knowledge about these animals, after all.

"Don't touch him," I say to the crowd, all the while scanning the beach for signs of Quint. But it's so crowded. He could be anywhere.

"It's a boy?" someone asks, to which someone else replies, "How can you tell?"

"I can't—I don't know. But I do know that, while these aren't violent animals, they can lash out when they're scared. Please, just back up. Give him some space."

No one argues.

I spot a lifeguard stand, and I remember that part of the local lifeguard training involves knowing how to handle beached animals. Sometimes they even have kennels kept in their storage units for animals that need to be taken in for rehabilitation.

"You!" I point the stolen stick at the girl who had wanted to poke the sea lion with it. She jumps back a foot, her eyes wide. "You're in charge. Keep everyone back at least ten feet, okay?"

Her expression brightens, then floods with a sense of duty. It's the same expression Penny gets when she's charged with an important task. The girl gives me a determined nod.

I hand the stick back to her and turn to her mom. "I'm going to see if that lifeguard can help us. Can you call the rescue center? They can send a truck to come get it." I wait until she's started to dial the number that's printed on the back of my shirt before I take off running again. My legs are aching and my side starts to get a stitch, but soon I'm standing at the base of the lifeguard chair.

It's empty.

"What the heck?" I roar. Are they even allowed to leave their posts? It takes another few seconds of scanning the beach, seconds that feel like hours, before I notice the signature white tank top and bright red shorts. The lifeguard is near the surf, yelling at a couple kids who have swum out past the buoys. I race over to him. "I need help!"

He looks up, startled, and I'm surprised to recognize a senior from school, though I don't know his name. "There's a beached sea lion," I say, pointing. "It needs to be taken to the animal rescue center. Do you have a kennel?"

His eyes dart past me, but we can't see the animal from where we are. The crowd around it has gotten too thick. I really hope that kid is doing a good job of keeping everyone at bay.

He looks back to check that the kids in the water have started swimming back toward the shore, then nods at me. "I'll be right there. Don't let anyone touch it."

I scoff and point to the logo on my T-shirt again. "Don't worry. I know what I'm doing."

The first thing I notice when I get back to the sea lion is that its eyes are closed. Terror crashes into me. *Is it dead?*

"I didn't let anyone touch it," the little girl says, still gripping the stick like a warrior.

"Here!" her mom shouts, shoving her cell phone under my nose. "They want to talk to you."

I take the phone. Sweat is dripping down the back of my neck. I crouch down a couple of feet away from the sea lion, relieved when its eyes flicker open, still cloudy. It's probably my imagination, but it feels like the animal is happy to see me again.

"Hello?" I say into the phone, my voice strained.

"Prudence?" It's Rosa.

"Yeah. Hi. There's a sea lion washed up on the beach, just north of—"

"I know, I know," says Rosa. "Listen. There's no way a recovery vehicle can get in there. With the traffic going into downtown right now, it would take hours."

My heart squeezes. The sea lion has shut its eyes again.

I don't think we have hours.

"What do I do?" I say, panic gripping me. Suddenly, this feels like the most important thing in my life. This creature. This helpless, innocent, hurting animal. I remember Quint telling me, maybe my third day at the center, that not all the creatures they bring in survive. About 10 percent die within the first twenty-four hours, already too far gone to be rehabilitated, no matter what they do.

But that isn't an option. I have to save this one.

"If you can find something to transport it in," Rosa says, "maybe someone there has a vehicle you can use. It would be a lot easier for you to get a car out of downtown than it would be for us to get to you."

A commotion draws my attention upward and I see the lifeguard charging toward us, a large crate in hand.

"Prudence?" says Rosa.

"Okay," I say, a ferocious new conviction filling me. "We'll come to you."

"We'll be ready when you get here."

I end the call and toss the phone back to the woman. She scrambles, barely catching it before it drops into the sand.

"Pru!" Quint barges through the crowd, his face flushed like he's just run a mile. "I heard there's a—" He freezes in his tracks, his attention landing on the sea lion. It takes him all of two seconds to assess the situation and before I know it, he's taking charge, stealing my professional responsibilities with a few confident orders barked at the crowd. *You, see that bucket there? Go fill it with water.*

Yes, ocean water is fine.

And I need some wet towels. Can we borrow yours? Let's get that umbrella over here, give it some shade—we need to try to keep it from overheating as much as possible.

I experience a moment of irritation that he's stealing my authority, but it's smothered by a swell of relief. It's the opposite of biology class, where I was always the one giving orders, telling him what to do. It's a welcome change, especially in this situation, and . . . honestly, watching him take charge is kind of sexy.

I gulp, suddenly flustered.

"Quint?" says the lifeguard.

Quint glances at him and recognition fills his face. "Steven! Hey! How's your summer?"

"Busy," says Steven.

I gawk at them. "Excuse me!" I say, flabbergasted, and gesture to the sea lion. "Please focus."

Quint gives me a look, suggesting, *Hey, I can't help it if I'm friends with literally every person at our school.*

"What can we do?"

I look up to see Ari, Jude, and Ezra. A grin splits across my face. They're all wearing matching yellow shirts, and together we look like an official rescue party.

Seeing the stacks of blue papers in their hands, it occurs to me that I couldn't have planned for better publicity.

"Jude, help Quint and, uh, Steven," I say, taking his flyers and dividing them between Ari and Ezra. "Pass these out."

While Quint, Jude, and the lifeguard gently roll the sea lion onto a blanket so it can be hoisted into the waiting crate, I step away from their work and face the crowd. People all around us are snapping photos on their phones, watching with eager, worried eyes.

I inhale a deep breath. I don't have time to rehearse, but I also don't have time to get nervous.

"Folks, we're here from the Fortuna Beach Sea Animal Rescue Center," I say. "We obviously had no idea that this animal was going to wash ashore during our festival today, but this is a prime example of the sort of work we do. The rescue center works tirelessly to rescue injured and stranded sea animals—including sea lions like this little guy, but also elephant seals, harbor seals, fur seals, sea turtles, even otters."

"What about dolphins?" asks the girl with the stick.

I smile at her. "Unfortunately, our facility is too small to care for dolphins, but in the past, we have worked to rescue and transport dolphins to a larger center near San Francisco."

Her eyes go wide. "*Cool.*"

"When animals come into our care, we feed and rehydrate them. Our on-staff veterinarian cares for their wounds. Rehabilitation can take weeks or even months. But our goal, with every one of our patients, is to treat them until they are healthy and strong enough to be returned to their natural habitat." I swoop my hand toward the crashing waves.

With the sea lion secured onto the blankets, Quint and the others prepare to lift it into the crate. "Our hope is that *this* beautiful sea lion won't be with us at the center for long, but will very soon be brought back here, to his home. In fact, this time of year, we're releasing rehabilitated animals back into the ocean almost every week. And if you want to be a part of one of those releases, we're inviting all of you to join us—tomorrow afternoon, right here! We're hosting a community-wide beach cleanup beginning at ten a.m., and once this beach is clean and safe for our animal friends, we'll be releasing four seals that have recently been given a clean bill of health. I would love to see all of you here, helping to support our beach, our organization, and these gorgeous creatures." The sea lion watches me from inside the crate, its eyes fearful and confused. Quint crouches down in front of it to snap a few photos with his camera, before the lifeguard shuts the grate and latches it closed.

To my surprise, the crowd cheers.

I beam. "Grab a flyer if you don't have one yet, and you can learn more about tomorrow's cleanup-and-release celebration! And if you can't make it, we are accepting monetary donations! People, these animals eat a *lot* of fish, which doesn't come cheap."

There are a few chuckles, but with the sea lion no longer in sight, some of the less-interested members of the crowd are already meandering back to their blankets.

"Nice speech," says Quint, settling a hand on top of the crate. He swipes a sleeve over his damp brow. "How far out is the recovery vehicle?"

I blink at him, and he must see the horrible realization rush through me. His eyes fill with understanding. "They're not sending one."

"Traffic," I stammer. "Your mom said it would be easier if we had a vehicle that we could drive it out in . . ."

Quint turns to the lifeguard. "Do you have a car?"

"No, man. I rode my bike here." He points toward a packed bike rack up on the boardwalk.

"I have the wagon," says Ari. "It should fit."

I turn to her. Her eyes are wide and bright with concern, and I'm hit with a sudden, almost painful tug behind my heart. "Thank you, Ari. Where are you parked?"

She points, and I can see the turquoise car from here. She arrived early enough to get a premium spot, not half a block up the beach.

"Pull it around," says the lifeguard. "We'll have you back it up to here. I'll help direct you." He nods at Quint. "Keep the crowds back, all right?"

While we wait, I kneel down beside the crate. The sea lion is resting its head, its eyes closed again. I'm terrified for it. The fear that is surging through my veins is palpable.

"We're doing our best," I whisper. "Please don't die, okay?"

If it hears me, it shows no sign.

A hand brushes between my shoulder blades. Quint crouches beside me and I glance over at him, his face pinched with the same concern. I wonder how many times he's been through this. How many rescues he's seen. I wonder how many he's watched die, after trying so very hard to save them.

I don't think I could stand it.

"I've seen worse," he says, pulling his hand away from me and idly running it along the strap of his camera. "I think it'll be okay." His eyes slide over to me. "You'll get to name it, you know."

My heart lurches at the thought. I already feel a responsibility toward this creature, though it hasn't been more than twenty minutes since I first saw it. To name it seems like a privilege I'm unprepared for.

"Not yet," I whisper. "I need to know it's going to be okay first."

He nods, and I know he understands.

"Can you tell if it's a boy or a girl?"

He shakes his head. "Not when they're this young. When they get bigger, the males will develop a ridge on their head that females don't have. Plus, they're bigger and their fur tends to be darker. But it's too early to tell on this one." He looks at me. "Opal will give it an inspection at the center, though. She'll be able to tell us."

I'm digesting this information when I hear a series of short, almost polite honks. I look up to see the station wagon driving slowly along the beach. Jude and Ezra are holding back the crowd as Ari makes her way toward us. For someone who's barely comfortable driving on residential roads, I know she must be completely freaked out. But she has her brave face on, I can tell even with the windshield dividing us.

I think I might have my brave face on, too.

To my surprise, Quint grabs my hand and gives it a hasty squeeze. Then the touch is gone, as quick as it came. He doesn't look at me as he stands up. "Come on. Let's get your sea lion to the center."

TWENTY-SIX

I sit in the front passenger seat, giving Ari directions, while Quint, Ezra, and Jude cram into the bench behind us. Rosa was right. We pass hordes of vehicles trying to cram into downtown for the festival. For a long time, we're the only car heading the other direction.

"It's like running from the zombie apocalypse," muses Jude.

No one answers and, after a few seconds, Ezra leans forward, settling his chin on the bench between me and Ari. "I like your ride. '62 Falcon?"

Ari glances at him in the rearview mirror. "Uh. Yeah. That's right."

"Ever thought of putting a V8 in it? Get some more horsepower?"

"Uh." Ari's brow furrows as she tries to concentrate on driving. "No. Never thought about it." She shifts to a higher gear, but the movement is awkward, making the car jerk a couple times. I wince, feeling bad for the sea lion in the back.

"Let me know if you do." Ezra rubs his fingers along the cream-colored upholstery between me and Ari. "I moonlight at Marcus's Garage on weekends. Wouldn't mind spending some time under this hood."

I frown and glance at him over my shoulder, unable to tell if he's talking in euphemisms or not. "So what's your primary job?" I ask.

Ezra looks at me, surprised, as if he'd forgotten I was there, too. "What?"

"You said you moonlight at Marcus's Garage, which implies it's your second job. So what's your first job?"

He stares at me a second longer, before a slow smile spreads across his face. "Living the easy life, Prudence. It's a full-time gig."

I roll my eyes, and he turns his attention back to Ari. "Didn't I see you at the bonfire party? With the guitar?"

"Yeah, that was me," says Ari.

"You're pretty good. I didn't recognize the songs you were playing."

"Oh. I wrote most of them. I mean, some of them. Not all. I think I played some Janis Joplin that night and some Carole King, if I remember . . . Those definitely weren't written by me. Obviously." I glance over at Ari. She's blushing. My gaze skips back to Ezra, who seems oblivious to how nervous he's making her. I've never given much thought to Ezra Kent's looks, I guess like I'd never given much thought to Quint's, either . . . until recently. I guess Ezra could be called cute, in an unconventional way. He's thin, pale, and freckled, with red hair that's just a tinge too dark to be called ginger. He wears it long, to just beneath his ears. He has a troublemaker's smile.

This, I notice now for the first time.

I wonder when Ari started to notice—because I'm suddenly sure that she has.

I clear my throat. "EZ, are you wearing your seat belt?"

Ari gasps and swerves over to the shoulder before slamming on the brakes. Quint curses and immediately turns around to make sure the kennel in the back is okay.

"Sorry! I'm sorry!" says Ari, breathless and wild-eyed. "But you have to be wearing a seat belt!"

"Okay, okay. Calm down." Ezra sits back and pulls the seat belt around himself, clicking it in place. "There we are. Locked and loaded."

A new silence falls around us as Ari pulls back onto the road. "So, Quint," says Jude. "How long have you been volunteering at the center?"

I peer into the car's side mirror. When Quint leans the right way, I can catch glimpses of his mouth as he speaks.

"I pretty much grew up there," he says. "I wasn't allowed to start officially volunteering until I was fourteen. But I've been helping out since I was little."

"You work there during the school year, too?"

"Yep. Spring is our busy season, when we're taking in animals almost every day. We get shorthanded fast. For the most part the teachers have been pretty cool about it, though."

"They say that life is the best teacher," says Ari.

"And where do you go to school?" asks Ezra.

"St. Agnes," she answers.

Ezra gives a low whistle. "I've always liked a girl in uniform."

Ari's cheeks go crimson again.

I turn to glare to Ezra. "Do you have no filter?"

He looks back at me. "What do you mean?"

I shake my head.

The conversation circles back to the rescue center. Quint seems surprised when Jude and Ari start peppering him with questions about the animals and the care they receive and what we do as volunteers. I can feel him shooting amused looks at me, but I keep staring out the window, watching the palm trees flash by.

It's true that I've hardly told them about the center and my time volunteering. Honestly, there hasn't been much to tell. Planning the cleanup has by far been the most exciting thing I've done—and now, rescuing this sea lion, of course. Other than that, it's been almost four straight weeks of scrubbing and blending, blending and scrubbing.

But now I can feel them growing curious, just like those people on the beach. When you come face-to-face with one of these creatures, you become invested. You want to help.

I want to help. More than anything, I want to help this poor animal in the back of Ari's car.

Ari dares to drive five miles per hour over the speed limit, which is practically drag racing for her. The center isn't far, but it feels like it takes us a month to get there. My heart is in my throat. The sea lion is silent, and that silence is nerve-wracking.

Finally we pull into the gravel lot in front of the center. Rosa and Dr. Jindal are waiting, and the next few minutes are a blur of activity. My friends and I fade into the background as the kennel is lifted from the back of the car and rushed into the center. I know they'll take him straight to the exam room. We follow hesitantly, doing our best to stay out of the way, lingering in the narrow corridor as the sea lion—still alive, if barely—is administered fluids. As its eyes and wounds are inspected. As Quint prepares a formula of protein and electrolytes. The delicious fish smoothies will come later.

I notice Jude's nose wrinkling, and it takes me a moment to remember this is the first time he and Ari have been here. The first time they've been hit with the overwhelming stench of fish. Funny, over the past few weeks, I've almost gotten used to it. I never could have predicted *that* on my first day here.

When it's clear there's nothing I can do to help, I offer to give them a tour. We stand all together in the yard, admiring the harbor seals sunbathing on the warm concrete. The sea lions chasing one another in and out of the water. The elephant seals swishing their fins against their backs, throwing imaginary sand onto themselves, an instinctual mechanism for keeping themselves cool in the wild.

Everyone is smitten. Well, Ezra has been here before, but Jude and Ari are impressed. Ari coos in delight at how adorable they all are. But when she crouches down next to one of the closed gates to start talking to a harbor seal named Kelpie, I feel terrible that I have to put my hand on her shoulder and coax her away.

"We're not really supposed to interact with them," I say sadly, remembering when Quint explained this to me on one of my first days.

Ari gives me a baffled look. The same look, I'm sure, that I gave Quint at the time.

"They try to discourage us from bonding with the animals as much as possible," I explain. "And to keep them from bonding with us. We're not supposed to talk to them or play with them or interact with them at all, other than what we have to do to take care of them."

"But they're so *cute,*" says Ari, peering back down at Kelpie. "How can you stand it?"

Honestly, I hadn't much cared before now. Quint told me not to bond with them, so I didn't. No biggie. "It's easier if you think of them as wild animals," I say. "They aren't pets. The goal is to release them back to the ocean, and if they've been domesticated, it could be more difficult for them to survive out there. Plus, we don't want them to be too comfortable around people. If they approach a human out on the beach or something, who knows what could happen?"

I can see understanding in their faces, but they're still clouded with disappointment. I don't blame them. Why would anyone spend so much time here if they can't even interact with the animals?

I think of the sea lion back in that exam room, the one I'm already thinking of as *my* sea lion, and I can tell that it will be so much more difficult not to bond with it. Heck, I'm already attached.

But at the same time, I desperately want it to be okay. To get strong. To get to go back home.

"That's too bad," says Ari, stepping away from the enclosure where some of the sea lions have started to pile up on top of one another. "I guess I'd kind of been picturing you here . . . I don't know. Cuddling with them or something."

I laugh. "Not quite."

Then I remember—

"Actually," I say, my heart lifting, "let me introduce you to Luna."

I lead them back inside, to one of the enclosures. It's been set up specifically for Luna, the sea lion that had been brought in for the second time on the first day I came to the center. Unlike animals in other pens, she's been given a handful of toys. A couple of balls, a dog's squeaky toy, a length of rope. "This is Luna," I say. "She's super playful, and so smart. And unlike the others, we're encouraged to play with her. They want to get her used to the presence of people as much as possible."

"What for?" asks Ezra, leaning over the wall. He picks up the rope and tosses it toward Luna. It lands a few inches from her nose. But it seems like she's maybe just waking up from a nap, and she doesn't go for it. She just looks at the rope, yawns, then blinks at Ezra, unimpressed. "Playful, huh?"

"She's just tired," I say. "Luna has a cognitive disorder. She's never going to be able to feed herself out in the wild, so we can't send her back. She's going to be given to a zoo or something instead."

"Will she bite?" asks Ari.

"I haven't seen her bite anyone yet," I say, "but volunteers do get bitten here pretty regularly, so you never know." Opening the gate, I step inside and pick up the ball. I roll it toward Luna. She stares at it for a second, then rolls onto her tummy and takes the ball into her jaw. She chews on it for a second, before flicking it back toward me. I stop it with my toe, pick it up, and toss it again. This time she rears up on her flippers and bounces it right back to me.

I grin. I don't know if one of the other volunteers has been working with her to learn tricks, but it's the first time I've played catch with a sea lion, and the moment, as simple as it might seem, is magical.

"Prudence?"

I catch the ball on another rebound and turn. Quint has joined us, his eyes twinkling to see me in the pen with Luna. "Having a good time?"

"Yes, actually."

"We figured it out," says Ezra, draping his elbows casually over the wall. "The key to getting Prudence to loosen up is to be a seal."

I tense. "She's a sea lion," I say a little darkly.

Jude glances at me, then at Ezra. He opens his mouth, and I can sense him getting ready to come to my defense, but, to my surprise, Quint speaks first.

"Don't be an ass, EZ."

Ezra looks honestly confused. "Am I being an ass?"

"Sort of. Prudence is cool. Anyway, I came to give you guys an update."

Ezra looks from Quint to me. I happen to catch his eye as he's giving me a thoughtful, appraising look. I swallow and let myself out of Luna's enclosure. "Is it going to be okay?"

Quint knows immediately who I'm talking about. Before he can answer, Luna barks, annoyed that I'm abandoning our game.

"Sorry," I tell her, tossing her the ball. "I'll be back later, all right?" I face Quint, bracing myself for whatever news he has to give us. "Well?"

"It's a he," he says, "and we think he's going to be okay."

My heart lifts, and I know I'm not the only one. We're all committed to this animal now, and a surge of joy passes through our whole group. Even Ezra hisses excitedly, "Yes."

Quint's hands come up, a warning. "Nothing is guaranteed. There's usually a twenty-four-hour period when we consider them in critical condition. He could take a turn for the worse still. But Opal is optimistic."

I exhale what might be the first full exhale I've released in a long while.

"So," he continues, looking at me. "We need a name for his paperwork. Have you thought of one?"

"No," I say with a bit of a relieved laugh. "I've been trying not to think about it until I knew for sure." I bite my cheek. I know this isn't a big deal. They name so many animals at this place that by the end of the busy season they'll name them just about anything. Quint said he once called a sea turtle "Pickle" because he'd had a sandwich for lunch that day.

But it's a big deal to me.

I think about my sea lion and the way he'd looked up at me on the beach. Even though I know he was hurting, he'd peered at me with something almost like trust. And I hear John Lennon's voice in my head. *Why in the world are we here? Surely not to live in pain and fear . . .*

"How about Lennon?" I suggest. "Like, John Lennon?"

Quint considers it. His lips twitch at the corners. "I've heard far worse."

TWENTY-SEVEN

Since Jude and Ari helped me with the festival, it seems only fair that I get up early the next morning to help them open the record store before I have to go prep for the beach cleanup. Jude is not a morning person. He's been complaining all summer about how getting to the store by 8:00 a.m. so he can check the stock, organize the bins, and clean any fingerprints off the front glass windows might be Dad's way of punishing him for not keeping up with his guitar lessons years ago.

Dad, however, is chipper as ever as he unlocks the door and lets us in. Dad's first order of business, just like at home, is to pick a record to play over the sound system. "Any requests?"

Jude yawns and crams the last few bites of a toaster waffle into his mouth.

I consider asking for the Beatles, but I know that makes me sound like a broken record (*get it?*), so I just shrug and tell Dad to put on whatever he wants. A minute later, Jim Morrison's sultry voice croons from the speakers.

"All right, my little helper," says Dad, dancing through the store aisles. "You're on broom duty. And make sure you get the sidewalk out in front, too. People drag a shocking amount of sand up here from the beach. Jude, want to open up those boxes that came yesterday? Should be some new stock."

"Want to switch?" I ask. Jude grumbles, shakes his head, and disappears into the back room.

I find the broom and start sweeping. Ari arrives a few minutes later with a tray of mochas from Java Jive. She even brought one for Dad, who presses both hands to his heart when she goes to hand it to him.

"Hiring you was the best decision I have ever made," he says, taking the coffee. "Now get to work."

"Aye-aye," she chirps. She gets the glass cleaner and some paper towels from the supply closet and follows me outside onto the front stoop.

Dad's right. I hadn't really noticed before, but there is a ton of sand out here. We're more than a block off the beach. How does that even happen?

"How is our little sea lion friend?" Ari asks as she squirts some of the cleaner onto the glass-paneled door.

"Good, as far as I know. I'll go check on him later, but he seemed to be doing all right when I left yesterday. Plus, I called the *Chronicle* last night to give them the scoop on the sea animal that washed ashore during the big festival, with a nice tie-in to today's cleanup party and animal release, of course."

Ari laughs. "Of course you did."

"I'm not saying I'm glad that Lennon washed ashore, but I'll take all the publicity we can get."

Ari steps back to check the door for leftover smudges before moving on to the huge picture window. "Your plan to rescue the rescue center seems to be going pretty good."

"We're just getting started. But, yeah, things seem to be on track."

Ari hums thoughtfully. "Maybe you could use some of your magic to help out this place, too." She lowers her voice, even though I know we can't be heard inside, especially with the Doors reminiscing about Love Street. "Don't tell your dad I said this—I really do *love* working here—but we could use some good publicity. Or maybe a facelift, or something?"

I stop sweeping so I can take in the front of the store. I've been here so many times over the years, I no longer stop to look. But Ari is right. The yellow paint is chipping on the stucco wall, the neon VENTURES VINYL sign has had a couple of letters burned out for who knows how long, and from the outside, the store just looks . . . well, a little dated. But not in a cool vintage way. Just in an old, tired way.

The one saving grace is the window display that Jude made a week ago, with a bunch of red-white-and-blue-themed album covers set up for the holiday. Then he took some records that were scratched or broken, painted fireworks on them, and hung them from the ceiling with ribbon. I don't give my brother enough credit for this sort of thing, but he can actually be pretty creative. His artistry definitely expands beyond sketches of mythical monsters.

How would the store look with a fresh coat of sea-blue paint, I wonder. And maybe a bright orange door that welcomes you inside. Oooh, we could have a grand re-opening party!

I flinch, and do my best to stop the thoughts before I get carried away. I have my hands full saving one business right now. I can't handle two.

"Maybe you and Jude should talk to Dad," I say. "If you have ideas for ways to boost business, I'm sure he'd be open to hearing them."

Ari turns to me, suddenly looking a little shy, but also excited. "Actually, I did have a thought, but . . . I don't know. It might be weird. And I have no idea whether it's a good idea or not."

"I'm all ears."

"Well, I kind of got the idea from Carlos, doing the weekly karaoke thing. What if the store started holding weekly open-mic nights?"

My brow furrows as I glance through the windows. "Um . . ."

"Not *here*," says Ari, waving the wad of paper towels at the store. "I know there isn't space for it. But I thought we could team up with one of the restaurants on the boardwalk. We would, like, act as the sponsor. We could get some swag branded with the store's logo—maybe guitar picks or bumper stickers or something? And give out coupons for people to come in and get ten percent off their purchase?" She shrugs. "What do you think?"

I smile. "I think it's worth a shot. Would you be the host of these open mic nights?"

She cringes. "I don't know about hosting. But . . . *you* would be really great at that."

I smile, because it is a compliment, but inside I'm wondering how many times I would have to host a gig like that before I stopped panicking every time I went onstage. "For what it's worth, I think you'd be great, too." I finish sweeping the sidewalk. "You should bring it up to Dad, see what he thinks." I frown. "That reminds me. Remember how I said you could have my old keyboard?

I asked my parents, and it turns out they sold it, since it was just collecting dust. I'm sorry."

"Oh, that's okay," she says. "I'll check out Brass and Keys one of these days. If I decide to get one at all."

Brass and Keys is the local music store, another place that knows Ari by name. Something tells me that any keyboard she would buy there would be way nicer than the one my family picked up at the pawnshop all those years ago, anyway.

I check my watch. "I should probably get going. If I'm late, I'm sure Quint will never let me live it down."

I head back into the store and set the broom back into the storeroom. Jude is pulling brand-new vinyl albums from a cardboard box, each one still wrapped with cellophane.

I recognize the artist on the cover. Sadashiv, a British pop singer who's become super famous the last couple of years by modernizing old standards. His popularity probably isn't hurt by the fact that he's heart-stoppingly gorgeous. I think he was even voted *People* magazine's sexiest man alive last year, even though I'm pretty sure he's still a teenager.

Of course, I only know any of this because both Penny and Lucy are obsessed with him, as are a whole lot of girls in my school.

"Whoa," I say, staring over Jude's shoulder. "I didn't know contemporary artists still put out vinyl records."

"Oh yeah," says Jude, laying out the records so he can put price stickers on them. "It's the hip thing to do right now. These"—he taps the stack of Sadashiv records—"will be huge sellers." He drops his voice to a whisper. "When Ari and I told Dad that this guy had a new album coming out, his exact words: 'Sada-who?'" Jude rolls his eyes. "You'd think with five kids he'd have an easier time staying current."

"People like what they like. Hey, I have to get going. Thanks again for your help at the festival yesterday."

"See you later, Sis. Good luck today."

"Dad?" I call, stepping back into the main area of the store.

"Right here."

He's at the counter, wearing his reading glasses as he checks something off on a handwritten ledger.

"I need to go. Can I leave some flyers here?" I pull what's left of our blue flyers out of my bag and set them on the counter. "Maybe if anyone comes in this morning you can tell them about the cleanup?"

"Not only will I tell them about the cleanup," he says, pulling the glasses down to the tip of his nose, "I will threaten to sell them only Vanilla Ice records until they promise to go."

"Maybe nothing *quite* so dramatic?"

The bell on the door chimes, and I turn around, preparing to say goodbye to Ari.

But it isn't Ari coming inside.

I freeze.

It's *Maya*. Maya Livingstone. She's wearing an oversize UCLA sweatshirt that falls nearly to her knees, pale pink leggings, and flip-flops, and pulling it off like a model. I'm not sure if I'm jealous or impressed. Mostly, I'm bewildered. What is she doing here?

"Welcome in!" says Dad. "Take a look around. Let me know if I can help you find anything. And please"—he grabs the top flyer from the stack—"be sure to check out the beach cleanup happening—"

I put my hand over his. "It's okay, Dad." I force myself to smile. "Hi, Maya."

"Oh. Hi, Prudence," she says, blinking at me. "I didn't know you worked here."

"I don't, actually. I'm just helping out this morning. Uh . . . this is my dad."

"Welcome, friend of Prudence!"

She chuckles awkwardly as she makes her way through the rows of records. "Thanks. Um. I know it just came out, like, yesterday, but do you happen to carry the new Sadashiv record?"

Dad peers at her. "Sada-who?"

I roll my eyes.

Maya starts to repeat. "Sada—"

"Don't mind him," I say. Then, bracing myself for what's sure to be a really uncomfortable encounter, I cup my hands over my mouth and holler, "Hey, Jude! We have a customer who wants the new Sadashiv album."

There's rustling from the back and then Jude appears, record in hand. "See, Dad? I told you these would be——" He sees Maya and goes still. His eyes widen. "Uh. Hot . . . sellers. Maya! Hi!"

She smiles, but there's a bit of a cringe in the look, and I wonder if she's thinking about what she said about Jude at the bonfire party, and wondering what he may or may not have overheard.

I brace myself, flexing my fingers. If she says anything even *remotely* hurtful to Jude, I will call down the full force of the universe and squash her like a bug.

But then Maya's gaze falls on the record and she lights up. Rushing forward, she takes it from him, cradling the album in both hands and staring at Sadashiv's glorious face. Though he's a British artist, he's of Indian descent, with curly black hair and eyelashes so thick it looks like he's wearing perpetual eyeliner. And that's just the beginning. I've heard Penny and Lucy have entire dinnertime conversations about his lips, his cheekbones, even his *ears*. I mean, seriously? What's that about?

"I have been waiting for this for months!" says Maya, pressing the album to her chest. "I'm so happy you have it."

"See? Vinyl records!" says Dad, smacking his palm on the counter. "I knew they'd come back around, even with you young kids. I've been saying it for years."

I'm anxious to get going. I really don't want to be late for the cleanup. But Jude's cheeks have flushed and I'm hesitant to leave him. Does he need moral support right now? It's hard to tell when he can't take his eyes off Maya long enough to clue me in.

Jude clears his throat. "Is there, um . . . anything else I can help you with . . . ?"

She beams at him, and I can see Jude becoming more flustered by the moment. "Nope, this is all I came in for. Thanks, Jude. I had no idea you worked here. What a cool summer job!"

He chuckles, still blushing, and says a whole lot of nothing as he rings her up and takes her payment.

"Well, if anyone needs me," says Maya, backing away from the counter, still clutching the album to her chest, "I'll just be at home, listening to this on repeat."

"Wait! Take a flyer," says Dad, shaking one of the blue papers at her. "Beach cleanup party happening today!" He gives me an enthusiastic wink. "Prudence is in charge of it."

"Really?" Maya takes the flyer, a little wary. "I actually lost something on the beach, at the start of the summer."

I feign ignorance. "Oh?"

"Yeah. It's . . ." She hesitates and looks down at the flyer. "You know what? I might actually stop by for this."

"Well, don't be late. Don't want to miss out on the really good trash," I say, wholly unconvinced that she will be stopping by.

"It was fun to see you, Prudence. Jude." She waves.

Jude waves back, all dreamy-eyed, but she already has her back turned to him.

Ari comes in through the front door, passing Maya in the aisle. Maya pauses and snaps her fingers. "Oh, hey! Aren't you that girl who was at the bonfire party? With the guitar?"

Ari gets a surprised look in her eye. "Wow. You're the second person in two days who's recognized me from that."

Maya grins. "You were amazing! I overheard that song you did . . . something about . . . snowflakes on the shore . . ."

"'The Winter Beach Blues'!" says Ari, brightening. "That's one of my favorites."

"I'd never heard it before, but it was so beautiful! Who is it by?"

Ari immediately starts to shrink back into her shell, nervously toeing the wooden floorboards. "Um . . ."

"That one is an Araceli Escalante original," I pipe up.

Maya looks baffled. "Araceli Escalante?" She glances at Jude, then at Dad. "Do you carry any of *her* albums?"

We all laugh, and I take Ari's elbow. "This is Ari," I say. "She's a songwriter. That song was one of her own."

"Oh!" Maya claps a hand to her cheek. "That's so cool! I wish I could play an instrument. Or sing. Or write . . . anything. I'm so jealous."

And now she's officially flustered both of my best friends.

I peer at her, feeling a little disconcerted myself.

She's acting so normal. So *nice*.

Not that she usually acts like a supreme snob or anything, but I can't ignore the things she said about Jude. How she completely wrote him off. How she suggested that he was somehow beneath her. I struggle to recall her exact words from that evening, but it's all a blur. Still, I know I didn't just imagine it.

"Well, if you ever record anything," Maya adds, "I'd love to have a copy."

She waves at us all again, and then she leaves, creating a strange vacuum in her absence, like all the air is being sucked out of the store. The Maya Livingstone effect.

I stretch out my fingers, a little disappointed that I didn't get a chance to use my power against her this time. Which probably makes me a horrible, resentful person.

What did she say on the beach? I rack my brain to remember specifics, but all I can remember for sure is Katie making that inane comment about how D&D is some devil-worshipping game, and how Maya shot her down.

But there was more to it than that. There had to be.

Did she call him a nerd? Or was that Janine?

Someone said he was creepy. And oh! Obsessed. Someone definitely insinuated that Jude was obsessed with Maya. But was that her, or one of her friends?

But she definitely said that she wasn't interested in him, and she said it within earshot of Jude! That's not okay. That's downright heartless! And . . . and . . .

Honest.

I suppose.

She was being honest. And if she really didn't know that Jude was there and able to hear her . . .

"I like her," says Dad, interrupting my uncomfortable train of thought. He claps his hands as if he'd just completed a day's worth of work. "You kids sure do have nice friends."

I give myself a shake before my brain can charge down another bottomless rabbit hole. "I really, really need to get going," I say.

"Yes, go!" commands my dad. "Make this world a better place! And if you run into any tourists, send them our way, yeah? The crowds are starting to come in for the season, and we could use the business."

I nod, but I'm not really listening to him. My attention has darted to Jude. "Are you okay?"

He looks dazed and thoughtful as he leans back against the counter. "I don't look anything like Sadashiv."

I try not to laugh at this blatantly obvious statement, because Jude really does look weirdly upset by this piece of information. I give him a sympathetic look.

"Jude, he's supposedly the sexiest man alive. Maybe try not to be so hard on yourself."

TWENTY-EIGHT

Quint is giving me a sassy look as I race down the beach toward where he's already set up a couple of tables and carried down a bunch of boxes of supplies. He makes a big show of checking a nonexistent watch.

"Prudence Barnett, you are late," he says. "You know, my time is valuable, too. Whatever happened to believing in punctuality?"

I scowl at him. "Very cute. My *one* tardiness hardly excuses an entire year's worth of *yours*."

"Maybe. But it's a start."

I slap my hands together, scanning the stacks of boxes. "What do we need to do?"

"Help me set up the tent." He's brought a large white pop-up tent and stakes to help secure it in the sand. It takes us a few minutes to get it propped up. Quint even made a banner that he ties to the back posts of the tent, reading FREEDOM FOR US, FREEDOM FOR OUR WILDLIFE. Underneath, in smaller letters, it says: "Learn more about the Fortuna Beach Sea Animal Rescue Center!"

We finish setting up the supplies—reusable trash bags, grabbers, gloves—with minutes to spare. I look around, hoping to see a huge crowd of people heading our way, ready to kick off this epic beach-cleanup party.

Instead, what I notice when I finally take the time to scan the beach is slightly disturbing.

I see blue papers.

A lot of them.

"I'm noticing a flaw in our grand plan," I say, nudging Quint with my elbow. "Why does it seem like half the trash out here today is . . ."

"Our flyers." He nods, frowning at the irony. "I noticed that, too."

"People are jerks."

"At least we're out here cleaning it up, and we'll get a lot of plastics and junk off the beach, too. It's still a win."

I pull the zipper of my hoodie up to my neck. The wind is sort of brutal today. I hope we won't lose our workforce before the big release happens. Fortuna Beach is sunny and warm three hundred and twenty days out of the year, which means we're all wimps on the other forty-five days. People scurry for cover at the slightest hint of rain, and even an unexpected cold front can turn Main Street into a ghost town.

My nerves begin to ratchet up when five, ten minutes past the start time, it's still just me and Quint. We keep our conversation light. We busy ourselves tidying the stacks of tote bags.

But I know he's thinking it, too.

What if this is a gigantic flop? What if no one comes?

And then, at fifteen minutes past the hour . . . they come. At first, just a sprinkling of curious beachgoers. But then they keep coming. People I know, but also a lot that I don't.

Sure, the crowd is nothing compared with yesterday's festival, but it keeps growing. And, best of all, people actually seem kind of excited to be here helping out.

I breathe a sigh of relief.

People are here. They're learning about the center and its patients. They're *helping*.

With any luck, they'll be donating some cash, too.

Quint and I try to greet everyone, telling them about the center while we hand out bags and latex gloves. People begin to spread out across the shore, scouring the beach for garbage and debris left over from yesterday's festival. I'm pleased to see a lot of families there with children, who seem just as enthusiastic to pick up garbage as they are to collect shells and rocks.

We've set out a large donation jar on the table at the front of the tent, and as the minutes go by, I find myself constantly checking on it. I notice with glee that it's started to gather an assortment of green bills and change. I wish I could estimate how much money is inside, but it's impossible to tell. Are those singles or twenties? I'll have to wait in suspense to find out when we count it up after the event.

"All set for the big release celebration?" I ask Quint as I open another box of gloves.

"The patients are getting prepped back at the center as we speak," says Quint. "They're going to bring them down in an hour."

"Perfect."

"I have to admit it, Prudence, combining the cleanup with an animal release was brilliant. Everyone keeps asking when the release is going to happen. I guess they put a story in the paper about it this morning?"

I shrug. "I might have called the *Chronicle* to tell them about finding Lennon yesterday, and used the opportunity to promote this event."

He gives me a sidelong glance, beaming. "You do have a knack for this sort thing, don't you?"

I shrug again. "We have to work with our strengths, and I figure, no one can resist those cute little faces."

"I know I can't." His eyes crinkle at the corners, and it seems like he holds my gaze a second longer than necessary before turning away and pulling another stack of tote bags from a cardboard box.

Warmth spreads through my body. I bite down hard on the inside of my cheek to keep myself from grinning, because I know he didn't really mean anything by it.

I busy myself scanning the crowd, looking for people I know. Ari and Jude both said they would try to come down after their shifts, but I don't really think they'll make it. I do recognize a handful of people from school. Not friends, but acquaintances, or just people I've seen in the halls. I also spot my eighth-grade English teacher and one of the librarians from the public library and even Carlos, who I've never seen outside of Encanto before.

Around eleven o'clock there's what could almost be considered a rush. Quint and I hand out tote bags left and right, directing people where to throw their garbage and recyclables when their totes are full, and encouraging them to venture farther up the beach to where the earlier volunteers haven't gotten to yet.

"This is beyond a doubt the best beach party I have ever been to!"

I glance up, startled. My parents are walking toward the tent, grinning. Dad is holding Ellie's hand, and Penny is there, too, clutching something in both of her fists.

"Hey!" I say, going to greet them. Mom draws me into a hug. "What are you guys doing here? Dad, why aren't you at the store?"

"We wanted to surprise you," he says. "Besides, Jude and Ari can handle it. And I know, I know, you probably would have preferred that they come see you instead of your old man, but . . . what can I say? Your mom and I are dying to see what you've been working so hard on the last few weeks!"

"Look what I found!" says Penny, showing me the collection of broken shells she's holding.

"I found one of them!" Ellie pipes up, trying to peer into Penny's palms. She points at a broken shell. "That one."

"Yes, Ellie found that one," Penny concedes.

I smile at them both. Penny is the sort of kid who appreciates the simple things in life—things that I usually roll my eyes at—but today, I can almost understand what she sees in those broken, colorful bits.

And Ellie? Well, she'll take any excuse to dig through the sand. I notice that she's wearing her sparkly monkey dress again, and that there's still a faint tomato juice stain that will probably never come out.

The sight of it gives me an uncomfortable twinge of guilt.

"I'm glad you guys came," I say. "No Lucy?"

"Softball practice," says Dad, shrugging. "That girl."

That girl being a common refrain around our house, one that can refer to any one of us for just about any reason under the sun. In this case, I know Dad is commenting on Lucy's long list of social engagements and extracurricular activities, but he could just as easily use *that girl* to refer to the collages Penny likes to make from the pages of old dictionaries and encyclopedias (often leaving a huge mess in her wake), or Ellie screaming because she can't find the exact hair bow she wants to wear, or even my insistence that we organize our spice cabinet alphabetically because clearly that's the only logical way to do it.

That girl.

"Oh well," I say. "Are you guys here to help with the cleanup?"

"Of course!" bellows Mom. "This is such a great thing you're doing. We're so proud of you, Prudence."

"Looks like you're getting a great turnout, too," says Dad. "I'm impressed."

I turn toward the table to gather up some supplies for them and spy Quint watching us. He quickly turns away, busying himself by rearranging the boxes of gloves.

I hesitate, trying to recall whether or not I ever complained to Penny about my terrible lab partner. She would blab on me for sure if she put two and two together. But I can't *not* introduce them, right?

I clear my throat. "Um. Mom? Dad? This is Quint."

Quint's head snaps around, his smile already flush across his face. He greets them with uber-politeness. *Mr. Barnett, Mrs. Barnett, it's a pleasure to meet you.*

He admires Penny's shell collection.

He asks Ellie about the monkey dress and *oohs* with just the right of amount of wonder when she shows him how the sequins change color when you brush them up and down.

I watch the whole interaction, feeling supremely awkward, though I don't know why. This feels important somehow, but I don't know if I care whether or not my family likes Quint, or whether or not he likes *them*.

It shouldn't matter either way.

It doesn't matter.

Truly. Not in the least.

"So," says Dad, pretending to scowl, "you're the reason my daughter has been working so hard this summer and not having any fun. Don't you kids know that summer vacation is supposed to be spent goofing off? None of this"—he gestures around at the beach—"do-gooder nonsense!"

Mom rolls her eyes and grabs Dad's elbow. "He's just teasing. We think this is great."

Quint casts a sidelong glance at me. "Believe it or not, this actually *has* been fun. For me, at least."

My heart lifts as I realize, for the first time, this has actually been a lot of fun for me, too. The planning, the organizing—I thrive on that.

And Quint . . . well. His company hasn't been nearly as intolerable as it used to be.

Quint and I wave goodbye as the four of them take off with their bags. Ellie insists on using the grabber first, even though her hand-eye coordination isn't quite good enough to use it properly. I can hear my mom issuing a challenge—whoever collects the most garbage gets to choose what we have for dinner. Ellie screams *skabetti!* and races off down the beach.

"And you say you don't like having little siblings?"

I wince. "Sometimes they're not so bad."

"I thought they seemed great."

I can't look at him, otherwise he'd for sure see the way my heart is overflowing at this simple comment.

We've nearly filled up two giant garbage cans when someone else appears at the edges of the tent. "Hello, Quint. Prudence."

I turn around.

Maya is leaning over the table, holding the blue flyer that my dad handed her at the record store that morning.

My lips part in surprise. I cannot believe she actually came.

"Hey, Maya," says Quint, beaming. "Come to help out?" He holds an empty tote toward her.

A look of uncertainty flashes across her face, but she quickly conceals it with a smile . . . albeit it an unenthusiastic one. "I actually had a question."

"Shoot." Quint sets the bag down and steps closer to her. As if being drawn into her orbit.

I bristle, and then feel immediately annoyed with myself for it.

"I lost something a while back, at the bonfire party." She twists her hands. "I was wondering if maybe one of your volunteers picked it up."

"What was it?"

"An earring. A diamond earring."

I avert my attention to another cardboard box and start peeling off the tape.

Of course that's why she's here. Not to help out, but to see if we found her missing jewelry.

Odd how this comforts me, knowing that she isn't here to help with the cleanup. I know I shouldn't feel that way, but I'm still shaken from how nice she was to Jude and Ari this morning. It's difficult to reconcile with my hazy memories from the bonfire.

"Oh, bummer," says Quint. He knows—we all know—how unlikely something like that would be to turn up. The sand on the beach shifts every day. Something as small as an earring could be lost and gone within hours, swept out to sea or buried for the rest of time.

But . . . something tells me that didn't happen to Maya's earring. Though I can't know it for sure, I have a feeling that her earring was picked up by that beachcomber I saw yesterday. I didn't get a good look at the jewelry she found, but I do recall how it glinted in the sun.

I bunch up the tape and toss it toward one of the garbage cans outside the tent.

It ricochets off the side and lands in the sand.

I huff.

At least it's a good excuse to keep from looking at Maya. I know I have guilt written across my face, even if . . . I mean, I didn't actually *do* anything. It was all the universe. Punishments and rewards. *Karma.*

"I'm really sorry," says Quint. "I don't think anyone's turned in anything like that. Hey, Prudence?"

I freeze in the middle of picking up the tape.

"Has anyone turned in an earring?"

"Like this," Maya adds, forcing me to make eye contact with her. She has a small box in her hand and inside is a single drop earring. Delicate gold filigree surrounds a solitary diamond. A big diamond. Bigger than the stone on my mom's wedding ring.

The thing that strikes me about the earring, though, is its back. It's the sort of earring that has a levered back that snaps up against the hook, closing the loop to prevent the earring from falling out.

I have a pair of earrings like that, and I know that unless that lever piece breaks, they're practically impossible to lose.

Unless karma wills it so.

"Um, no," I stammer, with an apologetic smile. "I haven't seen anything like that."

"I can let the volunteers know to keep an eye out for it," says Quint. "Where were you when you lost it?"

"Right over there, by the cliffs," says Maya. "Please let me know if someone finds it. These earrings belonged to my grandma. They were . . ." She pauses, and my shoulders tense. Emotion is filling her voice when she continues. "She passed away last year, and they were the last thing she gave to me, and . . . I just . . . I've been out here almost every day since the party, searching . . ."

Raw guilt scratches at the inside of my throat.

But I didn't do anything wrong. Her losing that earring was her fault. It was retribution from the universe!

"I mean, I still have one. So that's something," says Maya with a weak smile. "But it's not the same."

"I'm really sorry," says Quint. "I'll let you know if anything turns up."

"Thanks, Quint." She pauses, looking from him to me. "Also . . . to see the two of you working together and, apparently, not contemplating murder is *really* bizarre. I feel like I just stepped into the Twilight Zone."

Quint chuckles as he glances at me. "Yeah. Us too."

"Well, it's inspirational," says Maya. Then, to my surprise, she takes one of the tote bags. "I guess I'll go do my part, then?"

She heads up the beach, in the direction of the cliffs. I stare after her just long enough to see her stoop and pick up a blue flyer and cram it into the bag.

"Man," says Quint. "That's gotta be awful, to lose something that sentimental. My grandpa gave me an old baseball, signed by the entire team of the LA Dodgers in 1965. If something ever happened to it, I'd be wrecked."

I take in a deep breath to try and clear the weight from my chest. "Yeah. Awful."

"Excuse me, are you Prudence Barnett?" I swivel around to see a man in jeans and a blue Fortuna Beach sweatshirt. A large camera hangs around his neck.

"Yes, that's me."

"Hi, I'm Jason Nguyen with the *Chronicle*. We spoke on the phone last night."

"Oh yes! Hi! Thank you for coming."

"Wouldn't miss it. This is a great event. I'd love to do a follow-up story to run in tomorrow's paper. Maybe also a longer piece about the center for next Sunday. Do you mind if I ask you a few questions?"

"Oh, wow. That's wonderful. Yes, of course, but—" I glance at Quint, who looks amazed that our little event has garnered the attention of an actual journalist. "It probably makes more sense for you to talk to Quint here. His mom founded the center and he's been volunteering there a lot longer than I have. Plus, if you need some supplementary photos for the pieces, he could show you some truly amazing ones."

Quint's awe fades, replaced with embarrassment.

"That would be perfect," says the journalist. He and Quint head out to the beach, and though I try not to stare, I can't help sneaking glances their way whenever I'm not busy answering questions from the day's volunteers. Quint speaks so passionately, his body language exuberant, his expressions running from distraught—I imagine he's telling stories of the sad states in which some of the animals have been found—to ecstatic as the conversation turns to more uplifting things. The patients' unique personalities and how it feels to return them to the ocean. While he talks, the journalist takes lots of notes and occasionally snaps a picture of the volunteers and the garbage we're collecting.

By noon, the beach is looking as spotless as if humanity had never set foot here to begin with. Quint and I help volunteers empty their totes into the bins, sorting the garbage from the recyclables. I'm surprised when some of the volunteers, who have really started to get into the swing of this altruism thing, even jump in to help us.

Finally, Quint makes a proclamation that everyone has done a great job, and thanks them for their help. While I give my prepared spiel about the center and its mission (which only take up six minutes of my life—I timed myself a few days ago), Quint calls his mom and tells her to bring the trailer around.

It's time to release some animals back to their homes.

TWENTY-NINE

A honk draws my attention toward the boardwalk. The van, emblazoned with the center's logo, pulls out onto the sand. A cheer goes up from the volunteers. I can hear the clicking of Jason's camera.

Quint helps guide his mom as she turns around so that the back of the van is facing the water. It seems like it would be a simple maneuver, but driving on the ever-shifting sands is tricky, and every summer there are stories of people losing their vehicles to the ocean because they were driving too close and their wheels got stuck in the wet sand. Rosa is cautious, though, and besides, she's probably done this hundreds of times.

As the van comes to a stop, the crowd moves in excitedly, phones and cameras readied. Quint and I have to remind everyone to stay back so that the seals have an open path to get out to the ocean. I've been told that most of the released animals waste no time once they see the crashing waves—they're excited to flipper their way down to the water and disappear into the welcoming bay. But every once in a while, according to Quint, there's an animal that is more curious about the volunteers and any people who just happen to be on the beach that day. The animals sometimes want to inspect bagged lunches or roll around in the sand like they're trying to entertain whoever's watching. Which is an adorable memory for everyone involved, but can also cause some difficulties for the release crew as they attempt to coerce the animal into going where it's supposed to.

Rosa and Shauna emerge from the van and Rosa greets the crowd with a wide, almost giddy smile.

"Wow," she breathes. "This is by far the most people we've ever had to witness one of our animal releases. I've been doing this job for almost twenty years, but this is the first time one of our release celebrations has been a public affair. I'm so happy you could all join us today, and I thank you from the bottom of my heart for helping to make our beach clean and safe for these amazing animals. I think, after you see how happy they are to be going back to their natural habitat, you'll be just as excited as I am to have been a part of this day." She gestures at me and Quint. "And I want to give an extra big thank-you to my son, Quint, and our newest volunteer, Prudence, who made this event happen."

I give an awkward wave to the crowd. People applaud graciously, if a little impatiently. I dare to glance at Quint and we share a proud look and then——he winks at me.

My heartbeat skitters.

"I'll be happy to stay and answer anyone's questions about the center after the release," says Rosa, "but for now, I know you aren't here to see me. You're here to see Pepper, Tyrion, Chip, and Navy, four harbor seals who are eager to get back to their home."

Rosa and Shauna open the back of the van, revealing four kennels. Dark eyes and furry, whiskered faces peer out through the bars, and a unanimous *aww* rises up from the onlookers.

We unload the crates, setting them into the sand. Rosa reminds everyone not to approach the animals and not to give them any food.

"But take as many pictures as you want," I add, "and please tag us if you post them on social media."

Behind the barred doors of the crates, I can see the harbor seals perking up, looking curiously out at the ocean. There's a near-overwhelming sense of anticipation.

The doors are opened.

Three of the four seals bolt from the crates as if they're in the Kentucky Derby. They belly flop their way down the shore, clustered together, their flippers smacking the sand. They dive face-first into the surf and within seconds they've disappeared beneath the waves.

The fourth harbor seal, Chip, is more hesitant. He takes his time poking his head out of the crate, taking in his surroundings. He inspects the crowd and shyly, uncertainly, plods out of the crate. And then he just sits there, looking around as if confused. Rosa and Quint have to get a couple of boards from the van and use them to nudge Chip toward the water, like one would herd a difficult pig toward its pen.

Finally, Chip seems to get the idea and takes off doing the inchworm down the beach. One of the other seals pops its head up from the water, as if he'd been waiting for his friend to join them.

Chip splashes into the ocean.

The crowd erupts with cheers.

For the next ten minutes, the seals can be seen off the coast, playing and diving together, enjoying their new freedom. We all watch, trying to capture as much as we can with our cameras and phones.

And then they're gone.

My heart has swollen to the size of a pineapple inside my chest. I inhale deeply, trying to stitch this memory into the folds of my mind. The smell of the ocean, the sting of the wind, the glint of sunlight. There are even tears gathered in the corners of my eyes, and a part of me wants to write it off as irritation from the wind, but then I see that I'm not the only one wiping tears away. In fact, as I glance around, I'm startled to see that Maya is still there and her eyes are shining, too.

She catches my eye and we share a smile, each of us embarrassed to be caught with our emotions on the surface, but also strangely bonded by this special thing we just witnessed.

My attention catches on another form toward the back of the crowd, someone I hadn't noticed before.

I gasp. It's the beachcomber. The same woman who found the earring.

She's loitering far enough away that she isn't quite a part of our little celebration, but I'm sure she got to see the release. The smile lingering on her wrinkled face says as much.

I swallow. My gaze darts toward Maya, but she's gone. I glance around and spot her up the beach, heading toward the boardwalk. Her shoulders are hunched and her hands tucked into the front pocket of that oversize sweatshirt.

I return my attention to the beachcomber. She's wearing the same belt with the hand shovel and her bottle of water and the little pouch to store her findings.

I remind myself of the mean things Maya said about Jude.

I remind myself that this sweet old woman was picking trash off our beach—not because she'd been promised anything in return—just because it's the right thing to do.

But then I think about the catch in Maya's throat when she explained that the earrings had been a gift from her grandmother.

The war in my heart is brief, but intense.

The crowd of volunteers start to disperse, many talking about going into town for a cup of coffee at the Java Jive. I squeeze through the crowd and dart after the beachcomber as she, too, starts to walk away.

She's adjusting a dial on her metal detector when I reach her.

"Excuse me?"

She looks up and I can tell it takes a moment for her to place me, but then she smiles warmly. "Hello, again."

"Hi. Uh . . . what did you think of the release?" I'm not sure why I say it, other than it seems like starting with small talk is better than jumping right into what I really want to ask her.

"Glorious," she says. "I love the center and what they do. You know, in all the years I've done this, I've found three beached seals and a sea otter. I like knowing we have a place nearby that can come help them."

"You have? Wow. That's amazing. You're like a hero."

She chuckles. "Just someone who really loves this town and its beaches."

"It's pretty great what you do. You know, helping keep it clean. This cleanup was awesome, but . . . you've probably gathered more garbage over the years than all of us combined."

She shrugs. "It keeps me out of trouble. And I like hunting for buried treasure." She pats the detector. "You'd be surprised the things you find."

It's my opening and I brace myself, trying not to seem too eager. "Speaking of that. There's this girl, someone I know from school. She lost something here a couple of weeks ago. An earring. A diamond earring."

The woman's eyebrows lift.

"It was really precious to her. The earrings belonged to her grandmother, who passed away, and . . . anyway. You wouldn't have happened to have found anything like that, would you?"

There's a second, the briefest second, when I expect her to lie. After all, a real diamond earring just might be the most valuable thing she's ever found. Finders keepers, right?

But then she takes a step closer to me, almost fervent. "Actually, yes. I did find a diamond earring. Right after I spoke with you. Over there." She points to the same spot where I saw her find the earring last night.

"Oh! Great," I say, relieved that she doesn't seem upset at all to know that her buried treasure belongs to someone else. "That's wonderful. She'll be so happy!"

"But I don't have it anymore."

I pause. "What?"

"I already sold it. That's what I do when I find anything that might have value. I take it over to the pawnshop on Seventh. I would offer to go give the money back for it, but . . ." She grimaces. "I don't have the money anymore, either."

"Really? But . . . that was just last night." I do the math in my head. If she sold the earring this morning, and then came out here . . . that only gives her an hour or two to spend the cash. What could she have done with it? I'm desperate to ask, even though I know it's none of my business.

"I know. Money doesn't usually slip through my fingers quite that quickly," the woman says with a mild chuckle. "But when I see a cause as worthy as the rescue center, I have a tough time saying no." She gestures toward the tent.

I follow the look. Rosa is talking to the journalist. Quint is putting the extra tote bags back into their cardboard boxes. Shauna is . . .

Shauna is screwing the lid onto the large glass jar, which is almost full to the brim with money.

"Oh, I see." I'm in awe as I look back at the woman. She finds a diamond earring—a total stroke of luck—sells it for cash. Then immediately gives that cash away to an animal rescue center?

Criminy. Should I be nominating her for sainthood or something?

Seeing my look, she shakes her head sheepishly. "I just don't need any more money. I'm retired with a good pension, my kids are grown and have families of their own. I have more than I could ever ask for in this life. When unexpected windfalls like that come by, it seems like the universe sent them my way so I could do something good with them. Seeing you passing out those flyers last night, and then being here to witness the release of those animals . . . well, that's just too many signs from the universe that I wasn't willing to ignore."

I nod understandingly. "I know exactly what you mean."

"But that still leaves your friend. I *am* sorry about that."

"It's . . . it's okay. I'll figure something out. Maybe if I talk to the pawnshop they'll . . . give it back. Or something." I hesitate. "I know it isn't any of my business, but, um . . . would you mind telling me how much money they gave you for it? Just so I have an idea of what they might be expecting to sell it for?"

"Well," she says, "Clark—that's the owner down there—he says it would have been worth more as a set, of course. Not too many people interested in just one earring. And he doesn't pay market value. Needs to make something for himself, naturally . . ."

I sense that she's stalling, and I think maybe she's embarrassed, but I'm not sure why.

Until—

"But, anyhow. He paid me twelve hundred for it."

It feels like I've just been shoved in the chest. I even take a step back.

A flurry of emotions cascades through me.

This woman just handed over one thousand two hundred dollars like it was nothing—and this, I'm certain now, is why she looked embarrassed. No doubt she'd intended that donation to be made anonymously.

And then . . . it hits me.

Twelve hundred. Our fundraiser made twelve hundred dollars today! And that's only from one person! Quint and I had felt like we'd be lucky to make half that much.

Except . . . is it really our money to keep?

My head is spinning. How did this all get so complicated so fast?

"I do hope it works out for your friend," the woman says, looking honestly concerned. "It would be terrible to lose a family heirloom like that. But Clark is a reasonable guy. Maybe you can work something out."

THIRTY

A purchaser of goods acquires only that which the seller has the power to transfer. The property still belongs to the legal owner.

This is what I've learned from a few quick Google searches. A piece of property still belongs to the legal owner, no matter who has bought or sold it since. Most of the articles I've found relate to stolen property that gets sold off to pawnshops. I know Maya's earring wasn't *stolen,* but the outcome is pretty much the same. She is still the legal owner of the earring. If she went to the pawnshop and asked for it back, they would be obligated to return it to her—especially if she presented evidence that it's *her* earring. I figure that showing the earring's mate would be evidence aplenty.

And this is what I've determined, regardless of the interference from the universe.

Maya's transgression—the hurtful things she said about my brother—was not deserving of the punishment she received. I'm convinced that she wasn't *trying* to be mean that day (though I can't say the same for her friends). And now she's lost a cherished family heirloom. Regardless of its monetary value, I know that earring will always be more precious to Maya, and perhaps someday her children or grandchildren, than to anyone who might buy it from the pawnshop. Especially because anyone who buys a single earring is probably planning to take out the diamond and have it reset into a different piece of jewelry entirely.

At which point, the heirloom would be gone forever.

So. Maya should have the earring.

But.

No one else who's become involved in this situation has done anything wrong.

The beachcomber didn't do anything wrong when she found the earring or when she decided to sell it.

Clark, the pawnshop owner, didn't do anything wrong when he paid twelve hundred dollars for it.

The rescue center didn't do anything wrong when they received that money as a donation.

If I ask Rosa to give me the money so I can buy back the earring—it hurts the center.

If I tell Clark that Maya is the rightful owner, he'd be forced to give it back and he'd be out all that money—it hurts him and his business.

I could just tell Maya that I saw her earring at the pawnshop and let *her* go get it back herself, but the only thing that solves is my avoiding an awkward interaction.

So what do I do?

Mulling it over has given me a headache, and for the first time since I realized the reality of this karmic power of mine, I'm mad at it. Why has the universe woven this complicated web and stuck me in the center?

It's a conundrum I've been deliberating all morning, my brain struggling to find a solution in which no one gets hurt, stretching and straining and running in circles, while my hands have been busy sorting and rinsing bucket after bucket of fish. I didn't realize until I'd arrived today that Quint wasn't on the schedule. He doesn't work until Wednesday, and *I* have Wednesday off, and I am extremely uncomfortable with how disappointed this has made me.

Quint Erickson.

Who's made my skin prickle with loathing for so many months. Who's been the source of fathomless irritation. Who's made my blood boil with anger. Who I have fantasized about strangling on more than one occasion.

Who isn't at all what I thought.

It's a problem, learning that I was wrong about him. Because if I don't hate him, then suddenly there's a big open spot where those feeling used to be and . . . well, that spot seems to be filling up with something else entirely.

Which is its own sort of terrifying. Despite the way we've grown comfortable in each other's presence and the way he's so quick to smile at me these days (although he smiles easily at everyone, I have to remind myself), despite all that, I don't think Quint likes me *that* way. I don't think he could. We've become friends, sort of, which makes me happy, in a way. But sad, too.

Fun-loving, easygoing, obnoxiously charming Quint Erickson—having a thing for Prudence the Prude?

Yeah. Right.

So, maybe it's a good thing I've had the moral ethics of a lost earring to consider all day to keep my mind occupied. To keep it from straying *too* often toward the topic of Quint. For down that path lies danger.

Finished with my food prep duties, I do a quick wipe-down of the kitchen before hanging up my apron. I start making my way down the corridor, peeking over the walls to check on the patients who haven't yet been moved out into the yard. Almost half the pens are empty now. The busy season for bringing in newly stranded sea animals has ended and I'm told the center will empty out almost entirely between now and the winter, before breeding season in the spring leads to a slew of new patients. Rosa told me after the release celebration that this is actually a great time of year to be refocusing their efforts on fundraising campaigns and community outreach, when they aren't quite as slammed.

Technically, with my work done for the day, I could go home. I haven't been trained to help with the hands-on care of the animals yet, so there isn't much else I can do. But I take my time, watching a harbor seal snooze on its blanket for a while and a volunteer clean an infected wound on one of the sea turtles. I see how many of the patients I can name without looking at their charts and am surprised to realize I recognize most of them. There are clear giveaways—such as wounds or scars left behind from various traumas and the geometrical markings we shave into their fur to help tell them apart. But there are other things, too. A unique collection of speckles on Junebug's brow. The tawny coloring of Clover's back. The way Galileo's bark sounds like an amused chortle.

Then I come across a sea lion and freeze.

I know him immediately. And—yes—the cloudiness in his eyes is probably a dead giveaway, but I think I'd know him either way.

I check the chart, and there's the name I gave him, right at the top. Lennon.

"Hey, buddy," I say, folding my arms on top of the wall that divides us. "How are you doing?"

Lennon lifts his head and then pushes himself up onto all four flippers and waddles closer to me. He looked so tiny on the beach, and I know he's still significantly underweight compared with a healthy sea lion, but even still, he seems much bigger today. His head, when he has himself pushed up to his full height like this, is nearly to my waist. He nudges his nose forward, right at me, his black whiskers twitch, and—

Oh, I can't help it. I break down and reach over the wall to give the top of his head a caress. He presses it into my hand.

"Holy schnikeys, you're soft," I muse. It's the first time I've touched one of the animals, and while I was aware that they used to be hunted for their fur and turned into luxurious coats, I hadn't understood why until now. Who wouldn't want to be wrapped up in something so silky soft? Of course, the thought makes me feel a little bit like Cruella de Vil, but I shrug it off. "Don't worry. I won't turn you into a jacket. It never gets cold enough around here anyway."

Lennon ducks back and, to my amazement, lifts one flipper and gives it a rapid shake.

"No way," I breathe. "Did you just wave at me?"

He sticks his nose at me again. Laughing, I pet him, with no reservation this time. I'm startled to find my eyes steaming with emotion. "I'm happy to see you, too. You seem to be doing a lot better than you were yesterday."

My heart feels like a balloon, expanding and swelling until my whole chest is full.

I've never really loved an animal. Not even that gerbil.

But wow. I am suddenly, inexplicably smitten with this little big pinniped.

I study him, which I didn't have the time to do on the beach. His front side has an almost golden hue, while his head and back are darker, like aged bronze. His whiskers are shorter than most of the others I've seen, and there's a collection of white freckles between his eyes. Like the others, he also now sports symbols shaved into his fur—two dashes and an upward pointing arrow. I don't know what number that is.

The wounds on his body don't look so bad now that they've been cleaned. He might be injured, but he looks worlds better than some of the animals I've seen in Quint's photos.

Plus, he's gorgeous. The best-looking sea lion I have ever, ever seen.

I make a show of glancing over at the harbor seal in the next enclosure, before leaning down toward Lennon and whispering, "Don't tell anyone, but you're my favorite."

His head bobs up and down a few times, as if this comes as no surprise. Then he starts to flipper his way around his little cubicle, inspecting the blanket in the corner, the drain, the small tub of water. He strikes me as extra precocious and I know he won't be in here for long. In no time, he'll be out in the yard, making friends with the other animals.

I sigh.

During my first days at the center, I was sure that the hardest part of working here would be dealing with the reek of dead fish that permeated the air, the walls, and—by the end of the day—my clothes and hair. But that's not the worst part at all.

Trying not to form bonds with the animals is far, far more difficult. At least, it is now. Funny how it didn't really strike me as anything too terrible when they were just a bunch of strangers from the ocean. It was kind of like going to the zoo every day. You might stop and watch your favorite animal for a few minutes, but pretty soon you get bored and head off to find a pretzel.

But this isn't like that at all. With Lennon, I'm attached.

Don't talk to the animals, they tell us. Don't play with them. Try to avoid even making eye contact with them if you can. They can't become reliant on people. They can't become dependent.

But despite knowing this, despite the importance that everyone puts on this rule, I feel a spark of defiance behind my sternum.

Stepping back from the wall, I glance up and down the corridor. It's lunchtime. Most of the volunteers have gone on their break. Rosa and Shauna are around somewhere, and probably Dr. Jindal, too, but I haven't seen any of them all day.

Sure that the floor is empty—of humans, at least—I reach down and unhook the latch on the gate. It squeaks a little as I pull it open.

Lennon barks excitedly when I step inside.

I shush him, holding my hands in what I hope might be a calming motion. He immediately waddles forward and tries to nip at one of my fingers.

"Hey, none of that," I say, pulling my hands away. "I don't have any fish for you."

Although he no doubt can smell it on my fingers.

"I'm sorry. I should have brought you a snack. Next time, okay?"

I close the gate behind me and latch it. The tiled floor has small puddles of water from Lennon's earlier washing, but I ignore them. Planting my back against the wall, I slide down to sit beside him.

He mimics me, turning so that his back end is against the wall. I laugh again. This guy could be in a circus. Maybe I should break him out of here and we could become a famous performance duo. I'll karaoke Beatles songs and teach him tricks. We'd be a hit!

"If only you were a walrus," I say, stroking the back of his neck. Then, amused with my own wit, I whisper, "Coo-coo-ca-choo."

With my hand resting on his back, I lean my head against the wall. Immediately my thoughts return to the two topics that have occupied my thoughts all day.

The earring.

And Quint.

I don't want to think of either of them.

"So, I'm meeting my friend Ari down at our favorite restaurant tomorrow night," I say. "Jude might join us, too. That's my brother. You met them both, remember? Anyway, we're going to this place we like called Encanto. They make a killer seafood stew. You'd dig it. Hey, I wonder if that karaoke lady will be there again?"

Lennon dips his head, nudging my leg.

"No, I can't take you to karaoke with me. I'm sorry. But you know what I should do?"

He lifts up his front flipper again and gives it a hasty shake like he did before.

"Exactly," I say. "I should go early and spend a few hours righting karmic wrongs. Rewarding people, punishing people . . . Maybe that would make me feel better. I mean, surely, all the justice I've doled out so far hasn't ended up being complicated. Most people deserve what they get. Right?"

In response, Lennon scoots closer to me and drops his head onto my thigh.

I inhale sharply and go very still. My heart was already going to burst when he waved at me, now I think it might have happened. It feels like warm gooey joy is flooding through my whole body.

"Okay, scratch the performance-duo idea," I mutter. "You can be my therapy sea lion. I'll get you a license, okay?"

I start petting the top of his head again and he rolls onto his side, almost like he's snuggling.

"Aw, man. This is the best thing that's ever happened to me." I shake my head a little sadly. "But I really hope this doesn't permanently mess you up for life in the ocean."

"So you *are* concerned?"

I startle, and only Lennon's head on my leg keeps me from lurching to my feet.

Dr. Jindal is standing outside Lennon's enclosure, watching us, her arms crossed over her chest.

THIRTY-ONE

anic jolts through me—could I get fired for this? Do they fire volunteers? "I'm sorry," I stammer. "I know we're not supposed to interact with them. But . . ." But I couldn't help it? But this cute little face was irresistible? But he is kind of *my* sea lion, so . . .

The words die on my tongue. I have no worthy excuse.

I should probably get up. Not just because sitting feels a bit disrespectful or because to stay motionless might suggest I'm not that sorry for breaking the rules—which I guess I'm not, really, even though I think I should be.

Plus, my backside is starting to hurt and there's dampness seeping in through my jeans. But Lennon still has his head on my lap, so I stay put.

"It's all right, Prudence," says Dr. Jindal. "I won't tell on you. I know how easy it is to get attached, especially to the ones you helped rescue."

Despite her kindness, I still feel chastised.

"Besides," she continues, "with Lennon here, it isn't going to make a difference."

I frown, petting Lennon's back again. I feel his muscles relax under my touch. "What do you mean?"

"You haven't read his chart?"

"No," I answer, glancing at the wall, though from here I can't see the clipboard that holds Lennon's medical information, from how much he weighs to the types of treatments he's received. The reports are pretty dry reading, so after the first couple of days at the center I stopped perusing them. "Why?"

Dr. Jindal sets down a stack of mail that I hadn't noticed her carrying. She unhooks Lennon's chart from the little peg, then unlatches the gate and lets herself in.

Lennon lifts his head. Probably hoping for a snack.

"He has an eye infection," says Dr. Jindal, crouching beside us.

I look into his eyes. Sweet, soft, intelligent eyes, still glazed, still cloudy. And now I can see a hint of yellowish goop in the inner corner of one eye.

"He's entirely blind in his left eye," says the vet, "and the infection has spread to the right eye now, too."

My heart convulses. "Is it painful?"

"Not at this stage. But there isn't much we can do. He's eventually going to go entirely blind."

"But if he's blind, how will he hunt? How will he survive?"

She gives me a sympathetic look. "He won't. Not out there."

Understanding spreads through me. Lennon can never go back to the ocean.

As if bored with our conversation, Lennon gets up suddenly, turns, and waddles back to his blanket.

Using the wall for purchase, I climb back to my feet. "What's going to happen to him?"

"We'll do our best to care for him and make him comfortable, like with any of our patients. And when the time is right, he'll be sent off to a new home."

"A zoo."

"Perhaps. There are also aquariums and sanctuaries. Rosa has a lot of good connections. She'll find the best place for him." She places a hand on my shoulder. "You still saved his life. It's just going to be a different life than he's known before."

I nod. "Thanks, Dr. Jindal. But saving him was kind of a group effort."

"They always are," she says, laughing. "And you've been here for a month now, Prudence. You can call me Opal."

Have I really been here for an entire month? It's gone by so fast.

I understand now why she wasn't upset with me. If Lennon is going to a zoo, he'll be surrounded by humans all the time, everything from zookeepers to rowdy children. The more acclimated he can become to the presence of humans, the better.

"Don't worry about him," she adds. "He's a fighter. I can tell." She gives me a look, and I have a feeling she feels this way about every animal that comes in here, no matter how bad off they are. "And this does all come with a silver lining."

"It's okay for me to visit with him," I say.

She pauses, and then chuckles. "Yes, actually. Two silver linings, then." She lets herself out of the gate.

I follow behind her, confused. "What's the other one?"

"Lennon isn't the only animal we have that can't be released. We're going to introduce him to Luna this evening. If they get along, we're hoping that we can find a permanent home that will take them both."

I brighten, immediately relieved to think of Lennon having a friend that will stay with him when he leaves the center. "Why wouldn't they get along?"

She shrugs. "Just like with humans, some animals just . . . rub each other the wrong way. But they can also grow on each other with time. If the sparks don't fly tonight, we'll keep trying. We'll have to see what happens."

I latch the gate and Lennon glances up briefly before flopping over onto his side. "Rest up, buddy," I whisper to him. "Sounds like you've got a hot date tonight."

Opal snickers. "You volunteers and your matchmaking."

"Don't tell me you haven't thought about it. Lennon and Luna . . . it has a nice ring to it."

"I confess, when they told me what you'd named him, that was the first thing I thought." She smiles, then gathers up the stack of bills and catalogs. "They're out prepping a pool that the two of them will hopefully be sharing soon. I know you're probably off the clock, but you could stay and watch the meeting if you wanted to."

"I wouldn't miss it."

With a nod, Dr. Jin—er, *Opal*—heads off toward the stairs. I turn back to the enclosure and watch Lennon for a few more minutes. I want to believe that he looks content, even in this tiny cubicle, which is nothing compared with the pool he'll be given wherever he ends up in. I know it will never be the same as the open ocean, but I have to believe he'll be okay.

I hope Rosa finds someplace that isn't too far away, so I can maybe go visit him from time to time. I wonder, when I do, whether he'll remember me.

"I'll always remember you," I whisper.

His back flipper kicks out a few times, and I hope he's having a good dream.

I'm about to turn away when a slip of yellow paper catches my eye. I crane my head. An envelope has fallen down into the pen.

I open the gate as quietly as I can so as not to disturb Lennon and grab the envelope. It must have fallen from the stack of mail that Opal was carrying.

I flip it over.

The card wasn't sent *to* us. Rather, the center is the return address. This card was supposed to be mailed to . . .

My heart leaps into my throat.

Grace Livingstone
612 Carousel Blvd.

The address, however, has been crossed out with a thin red marker. Beside it, someone at the postal service stamped the card: DECEASED: RETURN TO SENDER.

Livingstone. Could Grace Livingstone be Maya's grandmother? But if so, what connection does she have to the center?

I'm peeling open the envelope before I know what I'm doing. Inside is a white card with a watercolor print of a sea turtle on the front, and words in flourishing script: *Thank You.*

I open the card and recognize Rosa's handwriting, which I've seen plenty on the weekly schedules.

Dear Mrs. Livingstone,
   It's occurred to me that in all the years in which you've been a dedicated supporter of our center, I have never personally expressed my gratitude. We've

received your most recent donation, and I want to tell you how your monthly contributions have made an enormous impact on our ability to rescue and care for our patients.

Per your recent note, I am so saddened to hear about your declining health, just as I am incredibly honored to hear that you've thought to include our center in your will. I promise that you and your generosity will not be forgotten, and that we at the Fortuna Beach Sea Animal Rescue Center will do our best to honor your legacy by being careful stewards of such a gift.

Thank you, thank you—

Yours most sincerely,
Rosa Erickson

I read through the letter three times. Recent donation. Monthly contributions. Honor your legacy.

Deceased.

I tuck the card back into the envelope, dazed. Though I can't know it for sure, I have no doubt that Grace Livingstone *is*—or, was—Maya's grandmother. And the fact that she gave money to the center every month . . .

It's too coincidental.

It's a sign.

A sign from the universe.

Suddenly, I know what the right thing is.

That money that was donated at the cleanup doesn't belong to the center. It needs to go back to the pawn broker, and that earring needs to go back to Maya. Its rightful owner.

And it's okay—it's fair—because Grace Livingstone's legacy will live on. Her generous contributions to the center will continue.

I know what I have to do.

I check first to be sure that Shauna and Rosa are out in the yard. I wait until the last of the volunteers have finished with their lunch and gone back downstairs.

Even though I know I'm doing the right thing—that the universe has my back in this—my heart is still drumming as I open the door to Shauna's office.

The glass jar is sitting on the corner of her desk, still full of green bills and spare change. My palms are clammy as I shut the door, leaving it open just a crack so that I'll be able to hear if anyone is coming.

Okay. Let's make this quick.

I slip over to the desk and untwist the jar's lid. I reach inside and grab a fistful of cash. I drop it onto the desk and start sorting through the bills, but it's slow-going. Much slower than I thought it would be. People don't just throw money into these donation jars. No. They fold and roll them, like little origami trinkets. I have to unfold each one, smoothing it out and stacking like bills together.

On first glance, the amount in the jar had looked extremely promising, but the more money I pull out, the more skeptical I become. It's almost entirely one-dollar bills. A few fives, a handful of twenties. But mostly ones.

Probably the beachcomber would have dropped her donation in all at once, but there is no stack of hundreds or fifties. I keep digging. Keep unfolding. Keep sorting.

Sweat is beading on the back of my neck. Anxiety claws at my throat. Every time the animals start yelping down in the yard, it makes me jump out of my skin.

I'm not guilty. I'm not doing anything wrong. I'm not stealing. I'm just helping to return that earring to Maya, without hurting anyone. And this doesn't hurt the center, I tell myself. No one will even know that some of it has gone missing, and what they don't know can't hurt them.

At least, that's what I keep telling myself, all the while silently promising to work extra hard on the next fundraiser to make up for it.

I hear clomping, uneven footsteps. Someone is entering the break room.

I freeze.

I listen as whoever it is gets something from the fridge.

Water runs in the sink.

More footsteps. Someone else comes in—

"Oh, hey! You're back!"

My breath hitches. *Quint.*

"Yeah. Finally," says a female voice. "Still lugging this thing around, though."

There's a loud thud.

"I like that you went with the bright pink. Gutsy choice."

I dare to crane my head, peering through the gap in the door. I can't see Quint, but I catch a glimpse of the girl. It's Morgan, sporting a fluorescent-pink cast on her leg covered with doodles and words. Two crutches are propped up against the counter as she sips from an aluminum water bottle.

She glances my way.

I jerk back. I'm trying not to breathe, but the pressure from unspent breaths is building up inside my chest. I try to let the air out slowly, silently, but it only seems to make it worse.

"I feel like you've missed a lot," says Quint. "It's been exciting around here lately."

"Yeah, I heard there's some new girl who's been shaking things up."

"Prudence. Yeah. She's . . ." He pauses. I strain to hear what he's going to say, but whatever it is he's thinking, he must change his mind. "You've met her, actually. When we went to that place with the karaoke? She's the one that slipped and hit her head."

"Oh. Right. Is she doing okay?"

"I think so, yeah."

"Cool. That was a weird week. Hey—that reminds me. The petition I was working on that night? You know, to shut down that so-called farm? Sounds like we might be making progress. The USDA says they're going to investigate it."

"Nice," says Quint. "Congratulations?"

"Nothing's changed yet, but yeah, thanks. Anyway. I guess I'm on chart duty until I get this thing taken off. Still, it's good to be back. I missed all those little guys down there."

"They missed you, too."

More clomping as she and her crutches head back toward the stairs. I listen until Quint leaves, too, before finally releasing my breath, and just as quickly sucking in a new one. *Gah*, that was the longest two minutes of my life.

I turn my attention back to the stacks of money I've laid out. There's still plenty of change in the jar, but I ignore it. The beachcomber did not give us twelve hundred dollars in quarters.

But this doesn't look like enough.

I count through it, starting with the solitary fifty-dollar bill, then working my way through the twenties. The tens. The fives.

I know long before I start in on the ones that something is wrong.

This isn't going to add up to anything even close to twelve hundred dollars.

I pick up the tall stack of ones, but I don't bother. It's fifty dollars at most.

What the heck? Did that woman lie to me? Did she just say that she gave the money to the center so I wouldn't pester her about taking it back to the pawnshop?

But she seemed so sweet. So genuine.

It doesn't make sense.

And honestly, even without the twelve-hundred-dollar windfall I believed was in here, shouldn't there still be more than *this*? There had to be hundreds of people who put money into this jar.

But maybe I miscalculated. Or maybe I'd naively thought that most people would be handing over fives and tens, even the occasional twenty, when in reality, it was just the loose change at the bottom of their pockets.

Someone knocks at the door.

I gasp and look up as the door swings open—agonizingly slow.

Quint stands there, his hand still raised.

He blinks at me and looks from my face, which is already reddening, to the stack of dollar bills in my hands, to the near-empty donation jar.

THIRTY-TWO

rudence?" he says, brows furrowed. "What are you doing?"

"I'm sorry!" I spout, even though I haven't done anything. Haven't taken anything. Even though I have absolutely *nothing* to be sorry for.

I start shoving the money back into the jar.

"I was just dying to know what we made!" I laugh, and I know how nervous it sounds, how incriminating. My hands are shaking. "The suspense was killing me."

He chuckles, a little uncertainly. "Yeah, right. I asked Shauna earlier and she said she hasn't even gotten to it yet. That she'll let us know tomorrow."

"*Gah*, tomorrow! That's, like, ages away!" I'm laying it on too thick. I try to calm myself down as I twist the lid back onto the jar.

"I know. So?"

I stare at him. "So?"

His eyebrows lift and he gestures at the jar. "How did we do?"

"Oh! Uh . . ." I shrug helplessly. "I'd only just gotten everything sorted. I didn't have time to count yet."

"Oh." He still looks skeptical, even as he nods. "I guess we'll both be surprised, then?" A moment of awkward silence passes between us, before Quint's face starts to clear. "Regardless of how much it is, I know everyone is really happy with how the cleanup went. Mom said she's even had a few people call about volunteer opportunities."

"Really? That's great."

"Yeah." He presses his lips together and I can tell he wants to say something, but I'm still too agitated to guess what it is. Too freaked out that he's about to accuse me of stealing. Which . . . I didn't do. Which . . . it wasn't.

Was it?

No. *No.* I'm not a thief. Thieves are bad people. I am not a bad person.

I clear my throat and intercept whatever it is he's wanting to say. "What are you doing here?" Then, realizing that's a guilty-sounding question, I amend, "I didn't think you were on the schedule today."

"I'm not." He leans against the doorjamb. "Has anyone told you yet? About Lennon?"

"Oh! Yes. The blindness."

He nods and I can tell he's waiting to see how I'm doing. To see if I'm devastated at this news. But when I don't break down in sobs, he continues. "And they're going to try introducing him and Luna."

"That! Yes. Right. Of course you came for that."

He chuckles. His look is no longer accusatory, and so my thumping pulse is gradually returning to normal. "That's actually why I was looking for you. They're getting ready to move Lennon."

"Oh, great! Let's go!"

I start to brush past him, eager to get out of this office. But I'm only two steps into the break room when Quint catches my arm.

"Hey, can I ask you something?"

I look back, dread filling me. "Sure. Of course."

"How, um . . ." His hand falls away and hangs at his side for a second. Then he scratches behind his neck. "After Shauna counts up the donations, how would you like us to let you know? I can call you . . . or send a text? Or email?"

I stare at him. "Um. I mean, tomorrow's Tuesday. So . . . I'll be here. You can just . . . tell me?"

"Right, except. I counted, and . . . today is your sixteenth day volunteering. Which, according to our original agreement, means that today is your last day."

I lean back, startled. My mouth forms a surprised O, but no sound comes out.

Freedom, I think. I can have the rest of my summer to do whatever I want.

Why is it that I feel no joy whatsoever at the thought?

"And, in case you aren't sure, I'll definitely still help with the revised report. For Mr. Chavez. You held up your end of the deal, so I'll—"

"I'm not leaving."

Quint goes still. "Yeah?"

"I want to stay. I mean—Lennon needs me." I gesture in some vague direction toward the first floor. "And I still have so many more ideas for things we can do to raise more money and awareness. We're just getting started. Aren't we?"

His hesitation splits into a smile. "Yeah. We are. I just didn't know . . . I wasn't sure how you felt."

"Well. That's how I feel." I smack him on the shoulder in a way that might be considered flirtatious. "Come on, Quint. You know me. You know I can't leave a job half finished."

His perfect teeth flash in a perfect grin. "I was sort of counting on it."

I hold my breath.

Beside me, I sense that Quint might be holding his, too.

Rosa opens the door to Luna's kennel.

Luna—ever curious and energetic—wastes no time in scooting out through the open door. But she pauses when she spies Lennon lazing in the late-afternoon sun beside the small in-ground pool. The pool that will be theirs to share now, assuming they get along.

I can't believe how nervous I am. This is important. I want them to be friends. *Best* friends. There's even a silly little part of me that hopes they might be something more. Because if you were going to be shipped off to a zoo to live out the rest of your days surrounded by glass walls and zookeepers, wouldn't it be lovely to at least be stuck there with your soul mate?

Luna pushes herself up on her front flippers and waddles hesitantly in Lennon's direction. Suddenly, his head snaps up and he turns his face toward her. I wonder how well he can see. I don't think he's completely blind yet, but it's clear that he's already starting to rely on his other senses. He rolls over and pushes up onto his flippers, too.

261

There's a standoff, one facing the other, the pool between them.

Then Luna lets out a happy bark and pushes forward, sliding into the water. She does a few barrel rolls, before climbing out next to Lennon.

I press my hands to my mouth, waiting to see his reaction. He cocks his head to one side. He looks confused, maybe even annoyed to have his sanctuary invaded by this stranger.

But then he lifts one flipper and gives it a shake, just like he greeted me before.

Then he does a belly flop right on top of Luna.

I let out a laugh and grab Quint's arm. His other hand lands on top of mine and squeezes. We meet each other's eyes, sharing mutual dopey grins.

The meeting quickly dissolves into hijinks as Luna and Lennon start chasing each other around the pool deck, dipping in and out of the water. There are times when they start to look aggressive, but it never lasts long. They're playing, testing each other's limits. Getting to know each other.

While they may or may not be pinniped soul mates, they do seem to be fast friends. I wilt with relief, knowing that Lennon is going to be just fine. It all feels rather meant-to-be.

"All right," says Rosa, clapping her hands. "I'll call that a success. Now let's let them get acquainted, shall we?"

The volunteers scatter, but Quint and I linger behind.

Quint starts to shift away, and only then do I realize his hand is still on top of mine. And then it's gone.

I pull my hand away, too, because . . . well, it would be weird not to. No matter how much I might be wishing otherwise.

"You okay?" he asks.

"Yeah," I say. "I think that might have been the most beautiful thing I've ever seen."

"Even better than the release party?"

"Does it make me a bad person if I say yes?"

"Shauna! What are you wearing?"

Quint and I swivel our attention toward the next pool. Morgan's outburst was filled with such consternation, I half expect to see Shauna in a bedazzled leotard and fishnet stockings. But no—she's dressed the same as any of us, in her yellow T-shirt and faded blue jeans.

Oh, and cowboy boots.

Judging from Morgan's stare, it's the boots that led to the outburst.

Shauna tsks as she tosses a bucket of fish into a pool, to a chorus of happy barks from the seals. "Don't you start with your nonsense, Morgan."

Aghast, Morgan spreads her arms wide, balancing on the crutches beneath each arm. "They look real. Tell me they're not real." She hobbles forward a couple of steps, though she and Shauna are separated by a chain-link fence.

"I'll tell you what I choose to put on my feet is none of your business." Shauna hangs the empty bucket from the crook of her elbow and puts her hands on her hips. "I know you have big opinions on this stuff, Morgan, but you need to learn to respect other people's choices, too. These boots were a treat to myself, and I happen to like them."

"You work at an animal rescue center!" Morgan swings one crutch around, indicating the courtyard full of wildlife. Her voice has risen now, drawing the attention from other volunteers. I have that feeling like we should turn away from the drama, but find it impossible. Then Morgan points at one of the seals with the broom handle. "Would you wear one of *them*? How about a nice seal-fur coat, if you happened to 'like' it?"

Shauna makes a sound so full of disgust, I can tell she doesn't think this comment is even worthy of a response. But for me, the conversation is starting to make sense. I look at the boots again.

They're snakeskin. They probably weren't cheap, either.

Shauna turns her back on Morgan and starts to head toward the building.

"You either love animals or you don't!" Morgan shouts after her. "They're all deserving of life! You don't get to pick and choose!"

At the door, Shauna spins around, her wrinkled cheeks tinged red. "They're vintage," she says. "I bought them at Toni's Consignment." She counts off on her fingers. "That's recycling, supporting a local business, and making sure that the sacrifice of these animals has a purpose, rather than them ending up in a landfill."

"No, that's contributing to a culture that values fashion and vanity more than the sanctity of life."

Shauna throws her arms up in the air. "You know, you young people have mighty high opinions, but by the time you get to be my age, you'll have learned a thing or two about not being so quick to judge others." She lets out a frustrated harrumph and yells, "Back to work, people!" Then pivots and marches into the building. The screen door slams shut behind her.

"Hypocrite," Morgan mutters, sneering. She snatches a clipboard off a nearby table and though I can see she's trying to get work done, she's writing so hard I can hear the harsh scribbling of the pen across the paper, as if the paper had done something to offend her. I'm surprised she doesn't puncture a hole through it.

After a few seconds, without looking up, Morgan tosses one hand into the air. "You heard her. Back to work!"

Quint and I look at each other, our shoulders taut. After a few seconds, he seems to gather himself. He trudges toward Morgan as if approaching a wild animal.

I can see her cast more clearly now. The doodles are mostly sketches of farm animals interspersed with vegan slogans in all caps. Things like FRIENDS, NOT FOOD. And MAKE LOVE, NOT SAUSAGES. While I still barely know Morgan, somehow I'm not surprised that she's transformed this medical accessory into a wearable protest sign.

"You do always know how to make an entrance," Quint says. She frowns, then her gaze drops to his shoes.

And then over to mine.

I gulp.

Do my sneakers have leather in them? They might. I've honestly never thought of it before. But the last thing I want right now is to become the next target of Morgan's wrath.

But either I pass inspection or she can't tell or she just doesn't think it's worth starting another fight. Morgan flails a hand in the direction that Shauna went. "I hate that argument. Oh, it's *vintage*, so that makes it okay. It's such bullshit."

Quint nods, but I'm not sure if he agrees, or if this is just a tactic to try to soothe her.

I think I should probably play along, too, but . . . I can't.

"Shauna kind of has a point, though," I say, sidling up beside Quint. He shoots me a warning look, but I ignore him. "Would you rather they were thrown into the trash?"

"Yes!" Morgan says forcefully. I balk in surprise. "Because as long as people buy them and wear them, then the fashion industry will believe there's a market for it—because there *is* a market for it! Which means they'll keep making them. Keep slaughtering innocent animals, keep raising them in these awful, inhumane conditions, and for what? A pair of shoes? When we have plenty of other materials we could make boots out of? It's disgusting. I mean, would *you* wear them?"

I grimace. "I don't really like snakeskin that much."

Morgan rolls her eyes. "Oh, how saintly of you."

"Look," says Quint, "I don't know who's right or wrong here, but . . . people have different . . . you know, principles and stuff. Shauna's been working here for ages. She's helped save a lot of animals. Maybe it all balances out."

"Nice try," says Morgan. "But the truth is, if snakes were as adorable as these guys"—she gestures at Lennon and Luna—"then we'd be having a different conversation. But whatever. Fine. You just keep eating your pork tacos and wearing your leather shoes." She glances at my feet and for a second I feel about as big as a bug. "Because you volunteer at an animal rescue center, so that makes it all okay, right?" She tosses the clipboard back onto the table and storms off—as fast as she can, at least, limping along with her crutches and bright pink leg cast.

Once she's gone, Quint lets out a low whistle. "Sorry about that. You'd think she'd learn that it's easier to change people's minds if you're a little bit nicer, but . . ." He shrugs.

I'm barely listening. "Weird, isn't it?" I muse, as much to myself as to Quint. "That something like a pair of vintage boots can spark such completely different reactions in people? To Shauna, it's recycling and supporting a small business. To Morgan, it's animal cruelty."

Quint nods. "The world is complicated."

I realize it's the same with the billboard. What I saw as an unforgivable crime, Morgan saw as something completely different. To her, she was trying to give a voice to the helpless cows of this world that probably don't want to be turned into cheeseburgers.

But the universe punished her. The universe sided with *me*.

I want that to mean something, except the universe also stole Maya's earring, and I'm now thoroughly convinced that was a bad call.

I frown up at the sky. At nothing. At everything. What were you thinking, Universe? What's your endgame here?

And, a question I probably should have been asking all along . . .

Why involve me?

"Hey," says Quint, touching my elbow. "Don't let her get to you. She just feels strongly about these things. But we're all doing the best we can, right?"

I peer at him, not convinced that's true. Because if we were all doing the best we can, then there'd be no need for karmic justice in the first place.

THIRTY-THREE

Which brings the total donations to . . ." Shauna hums to herself as she punches a few numbers into a calculator. The money from the donation jar is spread across the table in the break room. Stacks of green bills and an entire bank vault's worth of quarters and dimes.

I *want* the number that's about to come out of her mouth to be spectacular. Mind-blowing. I want everyone to gasp and cheer and high-five each other.

But I know what the number is going to be. Or at least, I have an idea of what it's going to be.

My jaw is clenched as I brace myself to look surprised.

We're all in the staff room, me and Rosa and Shauna and Morgan and a whole bunch of volunteers . . . and Quint. Even though this is supposed to be his day off. His second day off in a row, and the second day on which he's shown up anyway. I keep telling myself not to make assumptions. He came yesterday to watch Lennon and Luna being introduced for the first time, and he's here now because he's curious to know how the fundraiser went. We're all curious.

It's not like he's here to see me.

Rosa beats her palms against the table, faking a drumroll. Quint and a couple others join in.

"Three hundred sixty-four dollars and eighteen cents!"

There's a moment of stillness in the room, and I know it's that space between high expectations and a disappointing reality. That moment in which expressions are dismayed, before everyone hastily tries to cover them up.

I glance at Quint. He's frowning at the piles of money, and I know he feels the same way. There should be more. Wasn't there more? He catches my eye, the corners of his mouth wrinkling with a frown. I return the look.

He doesn't know the half of it. There shouldn't just be more. There should be *a lot* more.

I want to go track down that beachcomber and demand an explanation. Why would she lie to me about selling that earring and donating the money to our cause?

My attention shifts to Rosa. She's smiling at me, but there's an apology behind it, like she feels bad for me. My gut wrenches.

"It's not terrible," she says. "It's on par with how our past fundraisers have gone. A little better than some of them, actually."

I force myself to smile. I know I'm doing a lousy job of concealing my own disappointment, despite how *chin-up* everyone around me looks.

"It's more money than we had last week, at least," I say.

"That's right," agrees Rosa. "It is."

But we're all smiling through our frustration. Especially Quint and I, who put hours and hours into that event. We tried so hard.

"But remember," says Rosa, "the purpose of the cleanup wasn't to raise money. It's far more important that we filled eleven huge trash bags with garbage that otherwise would have been going right out into our oceans."

I nod. "Plus, one of our big priorities right now is to raise awareness, and for a lot of people in our community, this was the first time they heard about us. And I like to think we made a pretty good first impression."

"Absolutely," says Rosa. "We should all be proud of what we accomplished this weekend."

A few volunteers start to clap and it's a struggle for me to swallow back my bitter disappointment and believe my own words. I still feel like I failed. *Three hundred and sixty-four dollars.* I don't even know if that's enough money to buy a day's worth of fish.

But wallowing about it won't fix anything.

"On that note." I take in a deep breath and clasp my hands together. "The beach cleanup and some of the outreach we've started doing, such as the website and social media pages that Quint has been building"—I gesture at Quint and he responds with an elaborate bow—"are all a part of the foundation on which we are going to build a thriving nonprofit."

So, fine. *One* event didn't save the center, but we all knew it wouldn't.

I'm not done yet.

"Plus, I've already started planning our next big fundraiser," I continue. "And I *know* it's going to be an enormous success."

I can sense Quint watching me, and I feel a twinge of guilt. I probably should have talked to him about this before bringing it up to the whole staff.

Rosa starts gathering up the money, tying rubber bands around the dollars to keep them organized. "I appreciate your enthusiasm, Prudence, but maybe we can celebrate one accomplishment before moving on to the next? We still have a lot of work to be doing around here, you know."

"No," I say fervently. Then I hesitate. "I mean, yes, of course, taking care of the animals is number one. Always. But now that we have people talking about us, we can't lose this momentum. Strike while the iron is hot! And I already have the perfect idea."

Rosa sighs and I can see her preparing to hit the pause button on whatever I'm about to say, so I rush forward, grinning excitedly, my hands flashing through the air as I look around at the other volunteers. "We are going to host an end-of-summer fundraising gala!"

There are a few raised eyebrows, a few confused frowns, plenty of curious smiles.

Beside me, Quint murmurs, "Gala? I thought we decided against that."

I glance at him. "I've had a change of heart."

One eyebrow shoots up, and that confirms it. I definitely should have discussed this with him first. But . . . too late now.

The idea came to me right after the beach cleanup and I've spent the last few evenings making plans. I wish I had a fancy report or presentation board that I could use to convey all my ideas, but for now I'll just have to get everyone on board through my persuasive exuberance.

"We'll find a nice venue to host us, with live music and a fancy cocktail

hour followed by a three-course dinner . . . The best part is that the opportunities to raise money are endless. We can have a raffle or a silent auction
or both! And we'll sell tickets to the event, plus I've been reading about this
fundraising tactic called a 'dessert dash' that I know will be a hit, and—"

"Okay, okay," says Rosa, raising her hands. "That all sounds great, of course.
But it also sounds expensive. Maybe it's something we can consider for next
year, when things aren't so tight."

"No, no, we can do it! That's the thing—if we do things right, we'll hardly
have to pay a dime. I'll get donations from local companies for the auction
items, and sponsorships from businesses and community leaders. I can make
it work."

I can see Rosa waffling, her face crinkled with hesitation.

"Trust me," I say more forcefully now. "I'll make it work." I hadn't planned
on this, exactly. I'd hoped that the money from the beach cleanup would allow
at least a small budget for pulling the gala together. But I'm too committed to
let a little thing like money stop me. I'll find a way.

Rosa sighs, her gaze lingering on the piles of money on the table. "All right,"
she says. "You know what? The cleanup was your idea, so . . . here. You want
to throw us a fancy gala? Here's your budget." She pushes the stacks toward me.
Some of the quarters tip over, fanning across the table with a magical clinking
noise.

"Are you sure?" I ask. "I mean, this belongs to the center now. Don't you
need it for food or new equipment?"

"Honestly, it wouldn't go far," says Rosa with a light laugh. "If you think you
can take this money and turn it into a whole bunch more, then you deserve a
chance to try." She shrugs. "And a gala *does* sound like fun."

My heart lightens. Determination wells up inside me as I reach forward to
take the money. It's hardly enough to throw a fancy party on, but it's better
than starting with nothing.

I know I can turn this three hundred and sixty-four dollars into a whole lot
more. Now it's time to prove it.

The staff disperses, off to their various tasks for the day. I'm on food prep,
again, and Quint offers to help, despite technically having the day off. I'm

more than happy to accept. We head down the stairs, and I'm bubbling over with excitement, with ideas, with potential.

"So. A gala, huh?"

I cringe and glance back at Quint over my shoulder. "I should have mentioned it to you first. I just—"

He waves a hand. "Hey, if you think you can pull it off, then I'm all in." He hesitates, before adding, "*Can* you pull it off?"

I grimace. "I think so?"

He laughs. "Well, then. What are you doing tonight?"

I stumble and nearly take a nosedive off the last step. I barely catch myself on the rail.

"Whoa!" says Quint, grabbing my elbow to steady me, a second too late. "You okay?"

"Yep!" I brush my hair back from my face. "Just . . . weirdly clumsy this summer for some reason."

"At least you didn't get a concussion that time."

"Thankfully. Not sure my head could handle another big lump."

He chuckles and lets go of my elbow. "So . . . tonight?"

"Tonight! Um. Tonight? Oh, I have plans, actually. Ari and I are meeting up at Encanto. And maybe Jude, if he doesn't have to work. But Ari really enjoyed that karaoke night and thought she'd give it another shot. I guess she has a couple of songs she's been practicing."

"Oh. That's cool."

I nod, already feeling like I just made a huge mistake, even if I was telling the truth.

Ari would understand if I canceled on her and . . . was he asking . . .

"Mind if I come?"

I stare at him. "You want to come to karaoke night?"

"Not to sing," he says quickly. "But we could start making plans for this gala of yours. You could fill me in on some of your ideas. I can start making up some posters or invitations or something." He shrugs, in a way that is perfectly nondescript. Not suspicious. Not nervous. Not awkward.

Ah. Not a date, then.

Of course not a date.

Obviously.

"Sure," I say. "I'll bring my binder."

"Binder?"

"For the gala."

"You already have a . . ." He pauses, then shakes his head, smiling lopsidedly. "Of course you do. All right, then. I'll see you there."

THIRTY-FOUR

So," says Jude, his head tilted to one side as he scans the notebook between him and Ari, the top page scrawled with my list of "Gala To-Dos." "Venue and rentals, catering, advertising, decorations, AV equipment, auction items, and . . . an orchestra?" He looks at me, his eyes full of speculation. "And you have how much to pay for all this?"

"Three hundred sixty-four dollars," I say, tapping the pen against my bottom lip. As an afterthought, I add, "And eighteen cents."

"Oh, good," says Jude with an exaggerated puff of his cheeks. "I was doubtful, but that eighteen cents makes all the difference."

"I think it's a lovely idea," says Ari. "So romantic. It will be like Cinderella's ball!"

"Yeah, sort of," I say. "Except you have to buy a ticket, and in the end, we save a bunch of seals."

"Even better." Her eyes have a glazed, dreamy look. "I want to go to a gala."

She mindlessly passes out the bundles of silverware wrapped in paper napkins. Me, Jude, herself. The fourth bundle she sets at the edge of the table, next to me.

"I'm sure I can snag you a ticket. I mean, I *am* the coordinator, so . . ." I toss my hair over my shoulder.

"It's a trap," says Jude. "She says she'll get you a ticket, but what she means is that she'll hand you an apron and put you to work passing out hors d'oeuvres."

Ari shrugs. "I would gladly help out if you need more people."

I point my pen at her. "I might take you up on that. Right now, I'm still figuring out how much help we need, and hoping that a lot of the center's regular volunteers can pitch in."

"What is it with girls and galas, anyway?" asks Jude.

"Funny, Quint asked me the same thing. The question is, what do boys have against them?"

"Tuxedos, for one."

"What's wrong with tuxedos?" asks Ari, as if this statement personally offended her. "They're so sexy!"

He makes a face. "Have you ever had to wear one?"

"Okay, first," I say, holding up a finger, "the only 'tuxedo' you've ever worn was for Cousin Johnny's wedding, and they didn't even make you wear the jacket. And second, there's no way tuxedos are half as uncomfortable as Spanx, so I don't want to hear any whining."

Jude opens his mouth, hesitates. Then shrugs, knowing I've spoken the truth. "Nevertheless, you still haven't explained how you're paying for all this. It sounds really expensive."

"That's the beauty of planning an event for a nonprofit. I've been researching the heck out of this, and if I play my cards right, we won't have to pay for hardly anything. Not if I can get some local businesses on board to act as sponsors. For example . . ." I swing my arm toward the bar, where Carlos is vigorously rattling a cocktail shaker. "Encanto! They cough up some money and are repaid with copious praise at the event. Free publicity for them! Plus, we'll put coupons for tostones in the goody bags, so it serves as advertising, too. Oh!" I click the pen and grab my notebook. I scrawl across the bottom of the list, *Goody bags.*

"And you've talked to Carlos about this?" asks Ari.

"Not yet, but I will. I have a whole list of potential community partners to approach." I flip a few pages and show them. "I'll be asking for donations for the silent auction, too. We'll handle the pickup and transportation of the goods, and I'll even put them in fancy gift baskets if necessary."

"Is someone donating the baskets?" asks Ari.

I consider this, then add "Sandy's Seaside Gifts" to the list of potential partners. "Sandy must sell baskets in her store, don't you think? I mean, she sells everything."

"Ventures is on that list," says Jude, frowning at the notebook. His eyes lift to meet mine. "I'm not sure . . ."

"I know," I say. "Not every business is going to be able to donate free merchandise. But I have to at least ask Mom and Dad, right? Maybe we can find a way that they can help sponsor the music or something."

Jude groans. "Please don't suggest that Dad bring a record player and act as the night's DJ. Because I guarantee he would say yes."

"Oh, that would be neat!" says Ari, pressing her hands to her cheeks.

Jude and I both grimace. "For now, I'm going to stick with my plan for the live orchestra."

"Hey, it's my little cadets!" says Carlos, approaching our booth with arms outspread. "Where've you been? I thought you were gonna be here every day this summer."

Ari looks truly regretful. "Sorry, Carlos. We've been busy."

"Oh yeah? What's kept you so busy you can't even stop in and say hi?"

"Well, Jude and I are working over at Ventures Vinyl, and Pru is volunteering with the sea animal rescue center."

Carlos brightens. "Oh yeah! I saw you at that cleanup party. Good for you. It's nice to see today's youth making contributions to society." He winks. "Not that I expect anything less from you three. So, you here for karaoke tonight?"

"Actually, yes," I tell him, nudging Ari with my toe. "Ari's been practicing."

Carlos hoots excitedly. "I knew this karaoke thing was a good idea. You know, it's actually been going really well. Definitely bringing in some of the tourists on these slow Tuesdays. And Trish is great, isn't she?" He glances over to where Trish Roxby is setting up her sound equipment. Her outfit is as eye-catching as the first time we saw her: heavy boots; neon-blue leggings; and an oversize black sweater that's fraying along her rib cage. Doesn't she know it's almost ninety degrees outside?

Honestly, I haven't seen enough of Trish to know whether she's great or not, but Ari obligingly responds that she's fantastic, while I'm distracted by the entry door opening, letting in a stream of sunlight.

I crane my head to see—

Nope. Just a couple of guys in board shorts, their hair still damp from the ocean.

I slump back down against the bench.

Carlos takes our order and moves on to chat up the newcomers.

"This does seem pretty packed for a Tuesday," says Jude, peering around the restaurant. "Karaoke. Who knew?"

"Everyone wants fifteen minutes of fame," I say. "Even if that fifteen minutes is really just three and a half minutes, and that fame is really just making a nuisance of yourself at a dive bar off Main Street."

"This isn't a dive bar." Ari scowls at me. "And singing isn't a nuisance!"

"It isn't when you do it," I amend. "But I can't say the same for everyone."

"So what song are you going to sing?" Jude asks.

"I thought I might do an Oasis song," Ari says. "I haven't been able to stop listening to it all week."

"Let me guess," says Jude. "It's obscure, haunting, and lyrical."

She laughs. "It's not *that* obscure." Then she gets a wicked look in her eye and leans toward me. "Did you know? Some people feel that Oasis is the best band to ever come out of England."

It takes me a second to realize her implication. That *some* people think Oasis is even better than the Beatles.

I gasp, horrified. "You take that back!"

"I didn't say *I* feel that way," she says, giggling. "Though I do love their music."

The front door opens again. I swivel my head.

A woman walks in wearing a floppy sun hat and huge sunglasses, scanning the room as if she were meeting someone.

I sigh.

"Worried he's not coming?" asks Jude.

I snap my attention back to him. Was I being that obvious?

"No," I say, checking my watch. We said we would meet at six. It's only five fifty-two. He's not even late yet. "I'm not worried."

And I realize it's true. I'm not worried. In the past I was always shocked on those few occasions when Quint didn't disappoint me. But now, I'd be more shocked if he did.

He'll be here. I'm sure of it.

And that is where my nerves are coming from. Quint and me. Outside of school, outside of volunteering, just hanging out at karaoke night. And yeah, we're supposed to be making plans for the gala, which is a totally legitimate reason to spend time together.

I know I shouldn't read into it, but I can't help it. Reading into things is what I *do*.

As a waiter stops by to deliver our drinks, I realize I've become fidgety with nerves.

Trish stops by and hands us a song binder plus a stack of paper slips for us to write down our song choices. "Happy to see you all came back," she says, grinning. "Your head doing all right, sweetie?"

"Just fine," I say, feeling the back of my scalp. The bump faded away weeks ago.

"Good, good. I hope you sing again. Your performance of 'Instant Karma!' was great." She leans forward, beaming at Ari. "And *you*. I've had Louis Armstrong stuck in my head all month thanks to you. You're singing again, right?"

"Planning on it," Ari squeaks.

"Glad to hear it. Remember, if something isn't in the binder, I might still be able to find it online. Y'all just let me know what you need."

She winks and walks off. Ari inhales a deep breath and grabs the top slip of paper. She immediately writes down her name and the song she wants to do. "Okay, I'd better give this to her before I talk myself out of it," she says, sliding out of the booth.

"Ari's gonna sing again?"

I jump, my head snapping around.

Quint, startled by my reaction, takes a surprised step back. Then laughs. "Sorry. Didn't mean to scare you."

"No! No. It's just . . ." I check my watch: 5:59 p.m. "I didn't expect . . ."

"Hey, I value punctuality," he says.

I raise an eyebrow at him.

He shrugs. "At least, I'm starting to."

Quint and Jude share a fist bump and some muttered boy-ish niceties. Ari has left a spot open on the other side of the booth, next to Jude, but Quint slides in next to me.

I swallow and scoot in a little farther to give him space.

Ari returns, bouncing nervously on her toes, and they all start talking about karaoke and Ari's song—neither Quint nor Jude has heard of it, either—and Ari sighs dramatically when she hears this.

"It's *so good*. I can't understand why it wasn't a single."

"I look forward to hearing it," says Quint—and I think he means it.

"Are you going to sing?" Ari asks him.

Quint guffaws. "Nope. There is zero chance of that happening."

"Come on," says Ari. "You can't be that bad."

"And even if you are," I add, "it isn't about being *good*, necessarily. It's about letting go of your inhibitions for a few minutes." I drop my arms to my side and give them a shake, a charade of "loosening up."

"Okay," says Quint, giving me a sidelong look. "Then what song are *you* singing?"

I wrinkle my nose. "Nothing."

"Aha."

"Anyway, this is a work meeting." I nudge my notebook toward him.

"Ah, the Prudence idea journal. I should have known I'd be seeing this again." He starts flipping through pages, but then Carlos arrives to take his drink order. "Oh, what was that thing you guys were drinking last time? With the cherries?"

"A Shirley Temple?" says Ari.

"Yeah." Quint snaps his fingers. "I'll have a Shirley Temple, please."

"You got it," says Carlos. He shoots a sly, semi-curious look at me, and I know he's wondering whether this is my *boyfriend*. But thankfully he doesn't say anything. I don't think I could keep from looking mortified if he did.

As Carlos walks away, Quint turns to Jude. "So you said you guys used to do karaoke as a family?"

"When we were kids," says Jude. "But it's been a while."

Quint's eyes twinkle. "Maybe you guys should do a duet or something. For old times' sake."

"Oh!" says Ari, clapping her hands. "How about 'Stop Draggin' My Heart Around' by Stevie Nicks and Tom Petty? I love that song. And you'd be so good!"

"Ew, gross," I say, at the same time Jude sticks his thumb at me. "Sister, remember?"

Ari deflates. "Oh. Well . . ." Her eyes light up again. "Maybe Pru and Quint should do it!"

"No, no, no," says Quint. "Count me out." He glances at me. "I wasn't kidding when I said that the idea of doing karaoke is pretty much my worst nightmare."

A waitress brings his beverage, all fizzy and pink.

I pull my own glass toward me, a soda, slick with condensation, and take a sip from the rim.

"There's nothing we can say to get you to go up there?" says Ari. "You might like it?"

"Nothing," says Quint. "I have many enviable talents, but singing is not one of them."

"Me, either," I say.

Quint gives me a look. "Maybe not, but you were pretty cute up there all the same."

I go still. In fact, we all go still. Except Quint, who picks up his spoon and starts trying to fish out one of the cherries from his glass. His tone was casual, but now he's staring at that cherry like it's made of solid gold.

"Thanks," I say. "That's nice of you to say. If also faintly condescending."

He spins toward me, horrified. "It was a compliment!"

"And I said thank you." I grin to let him know I'm teasing. I feel bright, like I've been lit up on the inside. *Cute.* He thinks I'm cute . . . at least when I sing. My heart is tap-dancing in my chest. Maybe I should do another song tonight after all. "Cute is nice. It's not *great.* I mean, you could have said that I was radiant. Or . . ." I search for another adjective. "*Fetching.* But cute is okay. Could be worse."

"'Fetching'?" he says slowly. "Honestly, Prudence, there are times when I wonder if you might be a time-traveler from a different century."

I laugh. "The old-fashioned name gave it away?"

"Maybe a little," says Quint.

Jude loudly clears his throat.

Quint and I both startle and look over at Jude and Ari. They're staring at us—Jude looks mildly embarrassed. Ari has a hand pressed over her mouth, but she can't conceal her impish smile.

Jude gestures at a table that just opened up across from our booth. "Should Ari and I give you some privacy or . . . ?"

I flush. Quint laughs, but it's tinged with discomfort.

"Welcome to Karaoke Tuesday at Encanto!" Trish howls into the microphone, and even though most of the restaurant patrons ignore her and continue on with their conversations, the four of us are more than happy to give her our full attention. Like last time, Trish explains how karaoke night works, then kicks things off by singing Shania Twain's "Man! I Feel Like a Woman."

She's good. Really good. Her voice is powerful and raw, her presence hypnotizing. At one point I glance toward the bar and see Carlos leaning over the counter, a dish towel forgotten in his hand. He's watching Trish with what could almost be categorized as a dreamy stare.

I reach across the table and nudge Ari, then point. When she sees Carlos, she claps her hands over her heart, swooning.

Always eager to see love, no matter where or when, or who. Even if Carlos has been *her* older-man crush for months, I can tell she'd be thrilled to see him find someone.

That's one thing I adore about Ari. She finds so much happiness in the joys of others.

Trish finishes the song to enthusiastic applause from the audience. She does do a good job of warming up the crowd, I have to give her that.

Next up is a guy who sings a hip-hop song I'm not familiar with, followed by a man and woman who perform a saucy duet. They're all pretty good. Not great, but not bad. The songs have been fun and they've all done their best to work the crowd.

Then Trish calls Ari to the stage, and suddenly, I'm nervous for her. Ari's voice might be beautiful, but her stage presence is . . . less impressive.

I hold my breath, silently rooting for her as she takes hold of the microphone.

The music opens with a melancholy guitar riff.

And Ari starts to sing.

The song is, indeed, haunting and lyrical, and Ari's voice is captivating. My heart swells with pride, to see her, to hear her. I can't wait until the day that it's *her* songs people are belting out through that microphone.

"She's really good," whispers Quint.

"I know," I say, wondering if the tiny twist in my stomach is envy. Except, thinking it only brings back Quint's earlier words . . . that I'm *cute*. Grinning, I lean closer to him. "Some would call her fetching."

He meets my eye. A shared smile. A shared joke.

I don't want to look away, but Ari's voice comes and goes in sweet but powerful eddies as she moves from the verse into a chorus. I devote my attention to her, and a strange contentment comes over me. An overwhelming sense of belonging, in this moment, in this place. To be here with my brother and my best friend, with Quint's elbow pressed lightly against mine, to have this unfamiliar yet beautiful song speaking to my soul.

And I guess I can understand why Ari longs to create music. It does have this uncanny way of bringing a moment into focus. Of making the world seem suddenly brilliant and magical and *right*.

I don't know if I'm the only one feeling it. But I do know that when Ari is finished, we all applaud our freaking hearts out.

THIRTY-FIVE

T here was a time when I was a regular visitor to the pawnshop on Seventh, though I was never on a first-name basis with the owner, Clark, like the beachcomber is. The shop is the sort of place that regularly takes in music memorabilia, so my parents used to stop in every few months, dragging us kids along, to see if they'd gotten new Beatles posters or merchandise, or if there were vinyl records they could get for cheap and sell at a higher price back at the store. Years ago my mom found a set of plastic Beatles picnic plates that we still use to this day.

The store is also a go-to stop for instruments. This is where we got Jude's guitar and Penny's violin, and even my keyboard.

But it's been years since I've been inside. So I'm surprised when I open the door and am immediately greeted with a slew of familiar smells—musk and lemon wood polish and cigar smoke. I'm even more surprised when the man behind the counter grins widely when he sees me. "Is that Prudence Barnett? Holy hell, you've gone off and turned into a teenager. Look at you!"

I freeze a couple steps into the doorway and smile awkwardly. "Um. Yep. Hi."

"Come in, come in." He waves his arms, like he's trying to drag me forward with the force of his gestures. He's a big guy. Like, Hagrid big. I'd remembered this, but thought that my young mind must have been exaggerating, because now that I think of it, I was a little afraid of him when I was a kid, even though he was always really nice to me and my siblings. But there's just something unsettling about being greeted by a guy well over six feet tall, who probably weighs twice as much as my dad. He has an unruly gray-peppered beard and is wearing a tweed newsboy hat. This, too, I remember from childhood.

"I expected your mom or dad to stop in any day now. Didn't think they'd be sending you in, but it sure is good to see you. All grown-up. I can't hardly believe it." He clicks his tongue, then lifts a finger, indicating I should wait. "I'll go get your money. Be right back."

I blink. Money?

But before I can say anything, he's slipped into a back room, a tiny office with a window covered in yellowed blinds. I approach the main counter, where he keeps the jewelry. There are so many little velvet boxes holding little diamond rings that it's dizzying. I move to the next case. Necklaces, watches, bracelets—earrings.

I inspect them all, but none of them is Maya's. He probably wouldn't keep a solitary earring with these sets anyway, I reason.

Maybe he has a missing-parts jewelry section?

I make a quick pass around the room. More glass cases hold antique cigar boxes, porcelain figurines, hand-painted teacups, pocketknives, collectible coins, baseball cards. One entire case is dedicated to used cell phones. The walls are covered in paintings. The shelves display everything from clarinets to laptops, bowling balls to table lamps.

There is a display of costume jewelry on one counter. I spend a minute digging through it, but there's nothing that resembles the earring, and if Clark really did pay more than a grand for it, I doubt it would be sitting out here unattended.

"Here we go," says Clark, emerging from the office with a white envelope. He lays down a handwritten receipt, then opens the envelope and takes out a handful of money. He starts to count it out, placing each bill down so I can double-check his math, but my attention is on the slip of yellow paper.

Guitar amp: $140.00
Tennis bracelet (diamond 1 ct): $375.00
Cordless drill: $20.00

DVD player: $22.00

Electronic keyboard w/stand: $80.00

At the bottom is my dad's signature and phone number.

My eyes linger on the last item. A keyboard. *The* keyboard, I'm sure, that I'd told Ari I would give to her, before I realized we didn't have it anymore.

Before my parents told me they sold it.

"Six hundred and thirty-seven." Clark finishes counting, then stacks up the bills again and slides them back into the envelope. He hands it to me, along with the receipt. My hand instinctively closes around it, feeling the heft of the money inside. "We've had some interest on that cutlery set, but no takers yet. Your pop mentioned he might be bringing in a guitar? Acoustic, I think? Those have been selling like hotcakes lately, if you want to let him know."

Cutlery? Guitar?

"Um. Okay. I'll mention it to him." I swallow. "Which cutlery set, exactly?"

"Ah, you know. This vintage one." He walks around the counter and ushers me toward another case, where he pulls out an old wooden box. When he opens it, I'm greeted with a set of silverware—lightly tarnished spoons and forks and a row of steak knives strapped to the bottom of the lid. There are some serving pieces, too—a ladle and one of those huge forks used for carving meat. I reach out and run my finger along the handle of one of the spoons, engraved with a motif of grapes.

I know this silverware.

"You okay?"

I snap my attention up to Clark. "Yeah. Yes. I just . . . didn't realize my parents were selling this off. This was my great-grandma's. We put it out every Thanksgiving."

I can't tell if his frown means he's worried for *me,* or that my sentimentality could keep *him* from making a sale. "You'd be surprised how many people are off-loading this sort of thing," he says, and I think he's trying to ease my mind. "Silverware like this? It's almost more valuable being melted down for the silver. Not a big market. It's pretty, but kind of a pain compared with stainless steel. People just don't know how to care for these things like they used to or they don't have the time or just don't feel like it. Can't hardly blame them."

I nod, but I'm barely listening.

My parents are selling off their stuff.

I know money has been tight. I know they've been worried about paying their rent at the record store. But I had no idea it had come to this—pawning their possessions to make ends meet.

Why didn't they tell us?

"Anything else I can do for you?" Clark asks.

I look down at the envelope in my hand. I consider giving it back to him. I really don't want to be walking around with hundreds of dollars in my bag all day. But I don't want Clark to know that my parents have been keeping this from me. I'm embarrassed to think how clueless I am about my own family's situation.

So instead, I smile graciously and tuck the envelope away. My bag feels fifty pounds heavier.

"There actually is one other thing," I say, clearing my throat. "I met a woman the other day. I don't know her name, but she spends a lot of time metal detecting out on the beach."

"Oh, you must mean Lila." Clark nods. "I'm amazed at the things she digs up out there. Once brought in an old sheriff pin—not a real one—but like they would have put in a cereal box, maybe from the thirties or forties? It was so neat. You just never know what's out there, waiting to be found. So what have you got to do with old Lila?"

"Well, she found something on the beach, and it turns out that it belongs to a friend of mine. A diamond earring? I asked her about it and she said she sold it here."

Recognition flashes over Clark's features, and is immediately followed by regret. "Aw, man. It belonged to a friend of yours?"

I nod. "Her grandmother gave the earrings to her before she passed away. She—my friend—still has one, but she lost the other on the beach at the start of summer."

Clark heaves a sigh and rubs the back of his neck. "That's tough, Prudence. I know exactly the earring you're talking about, and yeah, Lila did sell it to me, but . . . it already sold. I didn't have it in the case for more than a couple of hours before it was snatched up."

Disappointment sinks in.

"I was surprised, too—being just half the pair, you know? But the woman who bought it said she was gonna use it for a necklace pendant, I think. And it was a nice piece. Vintage. Quality diamond."

"Could you tell me who bought it?"

He frowns and strokes his beard. "I don't know her name. She comes in here every once in a while, but I've never had much of a conversation with her. I could maybe check back through our records, but . . . no, you know what? I remember now, she paid with cash, so I wouldn't have her name anyway."

"Cash? But it was pretty expensive, wasn't it?"

"It wasn't cheap. But our customers, you know, it's not that strange for someone to pay with cash. Either way, I'm really sorry. If she comes in again, I can see about getting her name and some contact info. Maybe your friend could work something out."

I'm tempted to tell him that, legally, she'd be obligated to give the earring back, but . . . that doesn't really matter right now. I may never find the woman. I may never find the earring.

I feel like I've failed Maya, and despite how much I've tried to justify what happened, I can't help but feel partially to blame for the loss in the first place. This feels like cosmic injustice, the exact opposite of what I wanted. Jude may not have deserved Maya's saying mean things behind his back, but Maya didn't deserve losing her beloved heirloom forever, either.

At least, that's how I feel.

And if the universe feels differently, well, I'm beginning to wonder whose side it's on.

THIRTY-SIX

uccess!" Quint hollers, charging toward me, a sheet of paper in his waving hand.

We've been buzzing around downtown Fortuna Beach all afternoon, since Quint finished up with his morning shift at the center. I'm waiting for him on a bench just off the boardwalk, checking businesses I've spoken to off my list. It's been a busy day, going door to door along Main Street, telling people about the rescue center and the gala and asking for donations and sponsorships. Or—if nothing else—asking if they'll let us put up an advertising poster in their window once we get them printed.

For the most part, business owners have been eager to join our cause. Sure, there were some who were quick to declare that they couldn't afford to give any handouts, and some were downright rude about it, too, but by and large, the local businesses have been happy to help. People want to be involved, especially given the publicity the beach cleanup and seal release garnered. I'm convinced that, money conundrums aside, this is the perfect time to be hosting the gala and capitalizing on the progress we've already made.

This has been just the distraction I needed after my trip to the pawnshop. Every time I find myself with a quiet, idle moment, my mind goes straight back to the envelope of money in my bag, and the family silverware that will never again be placed on our Thanksgiving table.

I've always known we aren't rich. I know there have been financial concerns with the store since Jude and I were kids. But this feels like a desperate act. After all, what happens when they run out of things to sell? They'll still have bills to pay, and a record store that isn't making enough money. This is only a Band-Aid solution. They must see that.

But then . . . what's the real solution?

I can't think of it right now. I have the center and the gala to worry about, and that's plenty to keep my mind occupied.

Quint reaches me and, to my surprise, starts dancing. An over-the-top victory dance, right there on the boardwalk, that paper flashing in and out of the sun. He might have just scored a winning touchdown for all his enthusiasm. "Blue's Burgers is donating not one, not two, but *three* gift baskets for the silent auction, including gift cards, branded T-shirts, and travel mugs. Plus they will be supplying coupons for the goody bags, *and*—wait for it . . ."

He stops dancing and holds the paper out so I can see, even though it's the same sponsorship contract we've been using for all the businesses. He taps his finger against a line at the bottom, where he's handwritten an extra note.

I shrug. "I can't read your handwriting."

He whips the paper out of view. "They've agreed to cater the meal! Cheeseburger sliders, baby! *BOOM.*" He starts to dance again, then to my surprise, he grabs my hand and pulls me off the bench. I yelp as he spins me once beneath his arm. "We are so good at this!"

Laughing, I allow myself to be spun around a couple of times before dropping my hands on Quint's shoulders and forcing him to hold still. "Okay, calm down. That's excellent work, but there's still a lot to do."

His face is positively glowing. His hands, I realize suddenly, are on my waist.

Something passes between us. An electric current. A snagged breath.

I quickly pull away and turn my back on him. Tucking a strand of hair behind my ear, I turn back to the bench and gather up my notes, pretending like that moment, whatever it was, didn't happen.

I'm sure it was mostly in my imagination, anyway.

Quint hops up onto the bench in one graceful bound—*gah*, he makes that look easy—and sits down on the backrest, his elbows settled on his knees. "Okay. What's my next mission? I'm on a roll."

It's a beautiful sunny day, with a salty breeze coming in off the ocean and fluffy clouds speckled along the horizon. Weather reports have been saying we're in for a big storm this week, but there's no sign of it now——just sunbathers on the beach and roller skaters on the boardwalk, ice cream sundaes and the cry of seagulls and everything that makes Fortuna Beach a paradise this time of year.

I scan the list of businesses and put a smiley face next to Blue's Burgers. "That was a really generous offer from them. They're not charging us anything?"

"Not a dime. I think they've been hit hard lately with all that animal-cruelty stuff that's going around, and they think this could help them start to recover their reputation."

"You mean those rumors that they were getting their meat from some factory farm?" I step up onto the bench and sit beside him, the notebook on my lap.

"Turns out, not just rumors," he says. "They were importing their meat from some factory farm, despite their whole advertising schtick——grass-fed, pasture-raised, free-range . . . whatever. But it's more than that. That farm was just fined for some pretty big health-code violations." He shudders.

I'm staring at Quint, but all I'm seeing is that billboard and the spray-painted X.

LIES.

"Morgan actually helped draw attention to the story," Quint adds. "Remember that petition thing I was telling you about? I guess activists have been trying to get these farms shut down for years, and it's finally paid off. Pretty cool, right? It's like all that social-studies-in-action stuff that Mrs. Brickel is always talking about."

I tap my pen against my lip, staring out at the ocean. "So, don't be mad. I appreciate your hard work with Blue's Burgers, and this is an awesome donation they've agreed to. But . . . do you think it will look bad for us to partner with them so soon after they've been involved with this huge scandal? I mean . . . animal cruelty, health violations . . . and we're an animal rescue center."

"I know, there's an irony here," says Quint. I look at him. His eyes are on my pen, on . . . my mouth. They shift immediately out to the ocean. "But we weren't planning to do a vegetarian menu, other than for guests who request it, and Blue's assured me that they've already established some new relationships with local farms. Farms that have been certified humane this time. They want to move on from this as quickly as possible." He shrugs. "They're a landmark business. They've been here since the sixties. They deserve a second chance, right?"

His gaze returns to mine. I smile. "Everyone does."

He shifts an inch closer and looks down at the notebook. "So, how are we doing?"

"Great, actually. Kwikee's Print Shop agreed to print all our flyers and posters pro bono, I've got tons of people giving us stuff for the silent auction, and the folks at Main Street Bakery are already dreaming up dolphin-shaped cookies and starfish-topped cakes for our dessert."

"Sweet."

I roll my eyes at the pun, though I'm not entirely sure he was trying to make one. "That pretty much takes care of the auction and catering. Which leaves only entertainment, rentals, decorations, AV equipment, and . . . the big one." I look up from the binder. "A venue. Oh! And we still need to decide how we're going to handle ticket sales, and how much we're going to charge for them."

"I know there are websites that handle tickets for things like this, and I think you can set it up to deposit straight into your bank account," says Quint. "I'll talk to Shauna about it and see about getting something linked up on the website."

"How much should we charge?"

He looks at me. I look at him. We're both clueless. What's the going rate for a ticket to a fundraising gala? The sort of fancy, but not super pretentious kind? The sort being planned by two teenagers who've never done anything like this before?

"I'll look into it," I say, making a note.

"What if we keep the ticket prices low," says Quint, "but include an option for people to make additional donations when they buy their tickets? Kind of like an honor system. You pay us what you think this ticket is worth."

I consider this. It's a little risky—what if no one pays anything extra? But it could also swing the other direction. People could end up paying way more than we would dare charge them.

"I like it," I say. "Takes the pressure off us to figure out what it's worth, at least. And what do we have to lose?" I turn to the "Tickets page" of my notebook and jot down Quint's idea. "Also," I say, flipping back to the fundraising section, "I thought, in addition to doing the silent auction, maybe we could also do a raffle? Like for a *big* prize. Something really cool. People could buy as many tickets as they want, but everyone would have a chance of winning, so it wouldn't just be for the richest person in the room."

He drags a hand through his hair, thinking. A lock of hair tumbles back over his forehead in a way that makes my stomach clench. "A big prize. It should be something unique, that they can't just go out and buy. Like, maybe a private tour of the center?"

"That could work . . . ," I say. "Or we could name the next rescue after them?"

Our heads are bobbing, but neither idea feels quite . . . *right.*

"Well, let's keep brainstorming on it," I say, putting a star next to that item.

"I was thinking," says Quint, "if this goes well, this gala could become an annual thing we do for the center."

"Yeah, that crossed my mind, too. Every year could be bigger and better than the last."

He crosses his ankles. "Do you ever think things might not go according to your master plan?"

"Well, the beach cleanup wasn't quite the financial success I'd hoped it would be. And there was our biology project that completely tanked."

"Yeah, but both times you assumed they'd go great, right? And here you are, sure that the gala will go great. You don't give up."

I doodle a starfish in the corner of the paper, filling in around it with swirls of seaweed. I'm not a great artist, but I read somewhere years ago that doodling while taking notes helps with knowledge retention, and the habit has stuck. "What would be the point of giving up?" I ask. "You keep trying enough things and something's bound to work, eventually."

"I don't think that's how most people would see it, but I like that you do."

I press my lips tight to keep them from turning up in a bashful smile. "Well, this gala is definitely *not* going to be great if we don't figure out a venue, and soon."

"And why can't we just have it at the center again?"

"The center smells like dead fish."

He grunts. "Your standards are almost impossibly high sometimes, you know that?"

I glare at him, but there isn't much heart to it.

"Okay," he says, scanning the boardwalk as if in search of inspiration. "Can we have it here on the beach? Can hardly beat that view. And we could rent one of those giant tents they use for weddings."

"Not a terrible idea," I muse, "but what would we do for restrooms? Port-a-potties?"

We both grimace.

"Let's keep it on the maybe list," I say, writing it down. "We'd probably need to get permits, but . . . it *does* fit the theme."

"Hold on. There's a theme?"

I frown at him. "Saving the lives of helpless sea animals?"

"That's a mission, not a theme."

"Close enough."

He shakes his head. "No, no. We *should* have a theme. A real one. Like prom. 'Under the Sea' or whatever." He snaps his fingers. "I vote pirates."

"Pirates?"

"Picture it. We can give out those chocolate gold coins in the gift bags, and all the staff will wear eye patches."

I wait until I'm sure he's joking before I allow myself to laugh. "I don't know. A theme seems sort of cheesy."

He raspberries his lips. "Please. People love a party theme. You know how kids always have themes, like—My Little Pony or Batman or whatever? It's like that, but a grown-up version."

This argument does nothing to convince me.

"I mean," says Quint more forcefully, because he can see I'm not getting it, "that it brings everything together. The invitations, the posters, the decorations, even the food! Plus it can make it easier to make decisions, too. Should we go with the starfish cookies or the submarine cookies? Well, which one is more in line with the theme?"

"Submarine?" I gasp and smack Quint with the back of my hand. "That's it! That's our theme! We'll base it on 'Yellow Submarine' by the Beatles. My parents have tons of memorabilia we can use for decorations. Our ads can say something like . . . 'Come aboard our Yellow Submarine, and learn about . . . sea animals . . . oft unseen'?"

He snorts. "Okay, Shakespeare."

"It's a rough draft."

His lips twist to one side and I can tell he's thinking about it, before he slowly nods. "All right, I can get behind that. But next year . . . pirates!"

I laugh and write "Yellow Submarine" across the top of my notebook, before scanning my lists, again—pages and pages of lists. We've made great progress this week, but it feels like every time I cross something off, I think of two more things to add. "Once we have the venue figured out, we can set up the ticket sales and then get serious about advertising. And I'm going to talk to some local media, too. I bet I can get the *Chronicle* to run a story about it, and there's a radio station out of Pomona College that might be interested in interviewing your mom. Do you think she'd be up for it?"

"I don't see why not."

"Great." I jot down a few notes. My thoughts are spinning in a thousand directions and I feel like I can't capture them fast enough. I need to get organized. Make a plan.

"What about the theater?"

"Hm?"

"For a venue. How about having it at the Offshore Movie Theater?" Quint pulls his feet back up on the bench. His legs are restless, his knees jogging in place. I've seen him like this before, this excited energy burning through him. I'm beginning to think that *movement* might be his version of list-making.

"We could have the presentation in the auditorium," he goes on, "and they have that huge lobby we could use for the dinner tables. I know they have weddings there sometimes. And we had our eighth-grade dance there. Remember?"

"I didn't go."

"Oh. Well. It was nice. Plus, we wouldn't have to worry about AV equipment. I'm sure they have everything we'd need."

I chew the tip of the pen. "It's not a terrible idea."

"Which I know translates to 'Wow, Quint, you're a genius!'" He leans toward me. "I'm beginning to speak Prudence."

I laugh, then close my notebook and hook the pen over the cover. "Should we go check it out?"

"The theater? Naw, let's wait for tonight."

"Tonight? It's just two blocks away. Why not go now?"

"Because we'd be early. The movie doesn't start until seven."

I frown at him. "What movie?"

"The special screening of *Jaws*."

I freeze. Gawk at him. Picture a sharp dorsal fin and blood in the water and that iconic music thumping through my chest. *Bu-dum, bu-dum, bu-dum.*

"No," I say.

"Yes," Quint counters.

"I'm not watching it."

"Yes, you are. I already got tickets."

"Well—" I hesitate. "You did?"

I can feel heat climbing up my chest, my throat, spreading across my cheeks, and think maybe if I blush deeply enough he'll start to think it's a sunburn.

"I did. These special showings always sell out early and I didn't want to miss out. Come on. It's a classic. And you need to meet my namesake."

"You mean, Captain Quint? The shark hunter?"

"The one and only."

"Quint—I'm already afraid of sharks!"

He scoffs and nudges me with his shoulder. "It's an animatronic shark from the seventies. I think you can handle it. And we'll be scoping out the theater for a potential venue. It'll be productive."

I groan. "Oh no. You've discovered the magic word."

"Told you. I'll be fluent in Prudence-speak soon enough."

I have no desire whatsoever to see *Jaws*. Having lived here my whole life, I've spent years scanning these waves for shark fins, sure that—despite all the statistics telling us how sharks really aren't that dangerous to humans and how you're more likely to die in a plane crash or get struck by lightning than ever get bit by a shark—I was certain that if there was ever a shark attack at Fortuna Beach, it would be me getting devoured.

I know myself well enough to know that seeing the most famous shark-attack movie ever made is a terrible idea. I know I'm going to regret it.

But somehow, I hear the words coming faintly from my mouth. I, too, am trying to sound nonchalant. "Fine. You win. I'll go."

He thrusts both fists into the air. "*Yes.* Music to my ears." Bringing his hands back down, he claps once and then rubs his palms together. "Okay. Let's consider the venue problem solved for now. Man, I am full of answers today. Give me something else. I'll have this gala planned in time for popcorn."

THIRTY-SEVEN

Under any other circumstances, I would be extremely nervous. It's the first time I've ever been to a movie with a boy, at least, one that I'm not related to. But I'm not thinking about Quint and the way my heart trips when he looks at me. I'm not even thinking about the movie we're about to see, one that I've done my best to avoid.

As we walk past the ticket booth and step into the theater lobby, I have thoughts only for the gala. I'm scanning the paneled walls, the concessions counter, the light fixtures. It's a cool old theater, dating back to the late 1920s and the era of silent, black-and-white films. Just like Quint suggested, the lobby would definitely be big enough for dinner service, and according to their website, which has a page that gives details about renting the theater for special events, they can seat up to three hundred people. There's a neat art deco vibe to the crown moldings and chandeliers. The parquet flooring is dated, the wall paint is a little dingy, and the smell of buttered popcorn is overwhelming—but I can probably overlook all that.

"This could work," I whisper, leaning in to Quint, who is standing in the concessions line. "We could set up the auction table along that wall, and use this counter for the desserts." I tap my finger against my lower lip, nodding. "I like it."

Quint hums to himself. "Butter, yes or no?"

I glance at him, and it takes me a second to realize he's the next person in line. "Yes. Of course."

"Oh, good. If you'd said no, I was going to make you get your own."

We're among the first people to arrive, so once we enter the theater, we're able to claim a couple of seats nearly dead center, but I don't sit down. I'm turning in circles, considering the small upper balcony, where we could seat former donors as a VIP perk. And the stage upfront, where Rosa could give a speech. Given that this is a theater, we could even put together a video that shows footage of the center and the animals. We could show some of our recent rescues, and some of our releases.

Beaming, I drop into my seat. "I have a job for you."

He looks tentatively curious, but once I explain the idea of having a video to show at the gala, he's 100 percent on board. As the theater slowly fills up and the same slideshow of paid local advertisements rotates on the screen for the billionth time, Quint and I talk about whether or not we should try to have live music (I haven't had any success in finding an orchestra that would play for free) or if putting together a playlist is good enough. We go over the list of auction items that businesses have already pledged, and who we might still try to approach. I go over my plans for selling raffle tickets, even though we're still not sure what prize to raffle off.

I'm surprised how many people fill the theater by the time the lights dim. There's a different atmosphere here than any movie I've ever been to, and it's clear that a lot of people in the audience come to this special showing every year. There's an excited energy in the air as the opening credits begin to play. The music strikes me—the classic *bu-dum, bu-dum, bu-dum* that has become synonymous with shark attacks. I gulp and lean closer to Quint. I feel him peering at me, but I don't return the look. I'm already thinking, once again, that this is a horrible idea. Why did it have to be *Jaws*? But I'm stuck now, and . . . well, it doesn't seem so awful once I feel the warmth of Quint's shoulder pressed against mine.

Aaaaand . . . now I'm nervous.

All the questions I've been ignoring arise unbidden in my thoughts. Is this a date? Why didn't he ask anyone else to come with us? Why *didn't* he make me get my own popcorn? The enormous bucket balancing on the armrest between us feels momentous.

But a quick glance at Quint suggests that I'm the only one thinking about any of this. He's tuned in to the movie, mindlessly tossing popcorn into his mouth.

I sink into my chair and try not to overthink. For once, Prudence, *don't overthink.*

The audience, it turns out, is into this film. *Really* into it. Within the first few minutes, people are shouting at the screen—*Don't do it, Chrissie! Stay out of the water!* I gulp, gooseflesh crawling down my arms when it becomes clear what's about to happen to the girl skinny-dipping on the screen. I turn my head, ready to bury it in Quint's shoulder if I need to, and he scoots closer to me, as if encouraging me to use his shoulder at will.

Which I do.

The movie is terrifying . . . and also not. The idea of it is the worst part, the suspense of knowing that the shark is nearby whenever that ominous music begins to play. It isn't long before I'm gripping Quint's arm, my fingers digging into his sleeve. He doesn't pull away.

On the screen, a shark has been caught—a tiger shark. The townspeople have it hanging from a hook on the dock as the mayor of Amity Island tells the media that the predator responsible for the recent attacks is dead. The audience around us shouts at the mayor: *It's not the right shark! Boo!*

"Poor shark," I find myself muttering.

Quint gives me a knowing nod. "Terrible, right?"

Terrible—because it actually happens.

The movie goes on. Tourists flock to the beaches. Chief Brody's young sons go out into the water—

A small blue screen catches my eye. I frown, distracted. Someone in the next row is looking at their phone.

I tilt forward. They're . . . scrolling through Instagram? What the heck?

Someone behind me notices it, too, and yells, "Hey, turn off your phone!"

The phone clicks off.

My attention returns to the screen. The music is building again. Chief Brody is running. The children have no idea—

The blue screen blinks on again. Though I can't see the person's face, I can see their phone crystal clear. They're typing a text message to someone named Courtney. *Busy tomorrow? Swim Source is having a big sale.*

I'm not the only one getting annoyed. People are starting to shout at the phone user now, not the screen. "So inconsiderate." "What's wrong with you?" "Watch the movie!"

Quint shakes his head—I only know because he's been leaning his brow against my hair as I've clutched ever tighter to his arm. "Some people."

"Yeah," I mutter, one hand settling into my lap. "Some people."

My fingers curl into a fist.

A song starts to blare from the screen. The girl jumps, dropping the phone. The song keeps playing, a peppy pop song I remember being really popular when I was a kid.

Quint snorts. "I think the name of this song is 'Rude,'" he says, giving me an amused look. "Fitting."

The girl scrambles to find the phone on the floor, while more people join the chorus yelling at her. "Turn it off!" "What are you doing?" "Quiet down!"

She manages to pick up the phone, and I have to cover my mouth to keep from laughing as she hits every button she can, swiping the screen left and right, toggling the switch on the side. Nothing works. If anything, the music just gets louder. *Why you gotta be so rude?*

Finally, an employee of the theater arrives and insists that she leave the theater.

As she's led out of the auditorium, head hung with embarrassment, the whole crowd cheers.

The shark is dead. The sun is setting. The ending credits begin to roll. The theater lights come back up, and the audience enthusiastically applauds.

I release a long, traumatized breath. I'm clinging to Quint like a barnacle. I've probably left permanent impressions where my fingers have been digging into his arms, but if he's bothered by it, he hasn't given any indication.

I slowly turn my head and see him grinning at me.

"So?" he asks. "What'd you think?"

I'm not entirely sure how to respond. Despite being absolutely horrified, I actually did like the movie. The writing was good, as were the characters. The shark was . . . well, an animatronic shark from the seventies, but the idea of the shark was chilling.

"I have a question." I retract my hands from his arm and turn to face him more fully. He shifts toward me, waiting.

"Quint?" I say.

"Yeah?"

"No, that's my question. *Quint?* Your mom—your sea-animal-loving mom—named you after *that* guy? Not just a shark hunter, but some surly, cranky, reclusive shark hunter?"

Quint is laughing. "He's a war hero!"

"He's a jerk. He does nothing but mock and bully that poor . . . what was the other guy's name?"

"Hooper."

"That poor Hooper the whole movie, and then he gets devoured by a shark! Honestly, were your parents trying to traumatize you? Why couldn't they name you after the main guy? Chief . . ."

"Brody."

"Brody! They should have named you Brody. That's not a bad name."

"It is a fine name. Unfortunately, it was already taken."

"By who?"

"Our dog."

"You have a dog?"

"We did when I was little. Brody the golden retriever. My parents worried that if they named me Brody, too, people wouldn't get the reference and they'd think I was named after the dog. So . . . Quint it was."

I almost can't comprehend this. Shaking my head, I swing my arm toward the rolling credits. "He. Hunts. Sharks! It's like the embodiment of everything your mom is against!"

"I know, I know. But believe it or not, she really likes this movie. And she was a big fan of Peter Benchley, the guy who wrote the book, because he ended up becoming a huge advocate for the protection of sharks." He lowers his voice to a secretive whisper. "I think he had a lot of guilt to work through. Oh, and also, my parents' first date was to see *Jaws.* An anniversary showing, right here at the Offshore Theater. So . . . there was that." He shrugs. "I've come to terms with it." His eyes are shining. The theater is quickly emptying out. Some of the employees have begun making their way through the front rows, sweeping up popcorn and stray candy wrappers. We should probably go, but I don't want to.

"So what happened to Brody?" I ask, hoping it isn't a touchy subject. "The dog, I mean."

"He went with my dad after the divorce," says Quint, munching on another handful of popcorn. We've barely made it halfway through the bucket. "He passed away a few years ago, and my stepmom replaced him with"—he pauses for dramatic effect—"a *pug.*"

"Oh?" My eyebrows rise at his dramatic tone, but I have no idea why. "And that's a bad thing?"

"It's hilarious," he says. "My dad hates lapdogs. At least, he used to. I'm pretty sure if you asked him now he'd say they're the best thing ever, because what's he gonna do? She loves that dog! He was a rescue from Guadalajara, which she brings up every time I visit. I think it might her way of bonding with me. Like—hey, you rescue animals? Me too!" He shrugs. "I mean, she's trying."

"Do you like your stepmom?"

"She's not bad." He chomps through another handful of popcorn. "I can tell they really love each other, her and my dad, so I'm happy for them." He pauses to side-eye me. "You're fishing for that childhood trauma story, aren't you?"

I squeeze one eye shut, feeling like he caught me. "You were just so adamant before that you're totally cool with your dad being remarried, living in San Francisco . . . It just seems like maybe you're hiding something."

"Well, maybe you can meet them someday, and then you can decide for yourself."

My heart jumps, and Quint, as if realizing what he just said, immediately looks away. "My dad is actually kind of unhappy with me right now."

"Oh? What for?"

"I usually spend the last two weeks of summer vacation with him. But I called him yesterday and told him I didn't think it was going to work out this year."

It takes me a second to realize . . . "Because of the gala?"

He nods. "I want to be here to help you with it. It didn't feel right to leave."

"Oh, Quint! I didn't know. Nothing is decided yet. We could postpone it until—"

"No." He shakes his head. "It's fine, really. My dad will get over it. We're already planning some long weekends during the school year, and he'll get me for pretty much all winter break." His face softens and he looks almost uncomfortable as he adds, "I don't want to go to San Francisco right now."

The way he says it, there's something else implied there.

Don't overthink, Prudence.

He clears his throat and looks around. "We should probably go," he says, and I realize we're the last two people in the theater. We gather our things and stand up. "So, other than your distaste for my namesake," he says as we slip between the rows of chairs, "you liked the movie?"

"Ha! Speaking of being traumatized!" I joke. "I'm glad you took me snorkeling already, because that's probably the last time I will ever go into the water."

"Give it a few weeks. The fear will pass."

"Nope. Never. I do look like a seal, you know. From underwater? I'd be the first to go."

His smile fades slightly as he peers at me. "We all look like seals from underwater. At least, to a shark we do."

"And thank you for confirming why I am never swimming in the ocean ever again."

"We'll see about that. I can be pretty persuasive."

I grunt, unconvinced, though a part of me can't keep from imagining what he could do to lure me back into the waves. I shiver as a number of possibilities float unbidden through my mind.

"Speaking of snorkeling," says Quint as we leave the auditorium. "I have something for you." He reaches into his back pocket and produces a glossy photograph. It's a little warped from being in his pocket all day, and the printing quality isn't the best, but my heart still leaps when I recognize the sea turtle.

My sea turtle. The one I spotted when we went snorkeling. He captured it with its head raised, looking directly at the camera, waves of light flickering over the sand below. It's beautiful.

"Sorry it got a little bent," Quint says, uncreasing one of the corners. "I can print another copy if you want."

"I will cherish it always," I say, cradling the photo in my hands. I mean for it to sound like a joke, but I'm not sure that it is.

"I'm holding you to that. When you die, I want you to be buried with that picture."

I laugh and tuck the photo into my notebook. "Thank you. Truly. I love it. And . . . okay, *maybe* someday I'll go snorkeling again. Maybe. We'll see."

His grin widens. "See? Persuasive." He starts heading for the doors, but I stop him and make a beeline for the concessions stand instead.

"What are you doing?" he asks.

"I'm going to ask to speak to the manager. See about getting this place booked for the gala."

"Now? We can't do it tomorrow?"

"No time like the present!" I chirp.

But when I start to talk about event space rentals and community events, the boy behind the concessions stand gives me a perplexed look and tells me the manager isn't in, and I should maybe try calling or something?

"Told you so," says Quint as we head to the exit doors.

"Psh. It was a worth a try."

Though it was daylight when we got here, the sun has set now and Main Street is glowing with twinkling lights that have been strung through the trees and along the roof lines of the iconic hundred-year-old buildings. A wind has kicked in, tossing the boughs of palm trees overhead. A thick cover of clouds obscures the stars. It feels like a storm is moving in, after all.

I cross my arms over my chest. It hadn't occurred to me to bring a jacket.

Quint's brow creases as he takes in the wind. "Did you ride your bike?"

"Yeah, it's down this way."

"Mine too."

As we hurry along the sidewalk, the first spattering of raindrops strike our heads.

"So, when is our next"—Quint pauses—"gala planning meeting?"

I wonder if he'd meant to say *date*.

"Tomorrow?" I say. "I'll call the theater in the morning, and if we can get it booked, then we should start working on our advertising plan."

"Sounds good."

He barely gets the words out before the rain begins in earnest. It's so sudden, the change from fat but sparse raindrops to a torrential downpour. I cry out in surprise and duck under the nearest overhang. Quint crowds in beside me and we stand in silence, watching as the rain fills up the street gutters, puddles on the sidewalks, floods the storm drains. The few cars on the street slow down, their headlights barely cutting through the storm.

I'm so amazed at the power of the rain that I don't realize I'm hugging myself for warmth until Quint puts his arm around me and starts briskly rubbing my shoulder. I tense. My brain nearly short-circuits.

"Hey," he says, drawing my gaze upward. My breath catches. I've never been this close to him before. Never been this close to any boy before. But I know instantly that his mind isn't on the same topic as mine. His expression is worried, his brow taut. "I'm going to go to the center."

"What?" I say. Even this close, we almost have to yell to be heard over the downpour.

"We're probably closer than any of the volunteers and . . . I want to check on the animals. We've had issues with flooding before, during bad storms like this. I'm sure it'll be fine, but, anyway, I just think I should go. But I want to make sure you get home okay first. Should we make a run for the bikes?"

My eyes widen as I think of the outdoor pools. I imagine the yard flooding, and all the animals trapped and afraid.

"Yes," I yell. "But I'm coming with you."

THIRTY-EIGHT

I've ridden my bike in the rain before, but never rain like this. Downpours like this are rare in Fortuna Beach, and I'm not sure I've ever seen it this bad. Dodging puddles is like dodging land mines, and the water that courses through the gutters threatens to knock my wheels out from under me more than once. Luckily, it's a short trip. Even with the storm, it takes us less than fifteen minutes to get to the center—our time aided by the weather's clearing the roads of most vehicles.

We drop our bikes in the parking lot and rush to the door. Quint has a key and soon we're inside, breathing heavy, tearing off our helmets.

We're soaked through. I feel more drenched now than I did when we went swimming. I'm soon shivering inside the air-conditioned building.

No point getting dry though. Quint and I tromp straight through to the yard, where the animals all look like huddled dark mounds in their enclosures.

Because of the way the center is situated, with sloping hills behind it, I can immediately see why Quint was anxious to get here. Already, the back corner of the yard is swelling with water that has nowhere to go.

As for the animals, some of them are squeezed together in what appear to be frightened piles. Or maybe they're sleeping through this torrent—it's impossible to tell.

Others, however, seem to think this is the best thing ever. A group of sea lions are playing and splashing around in the water like they've just gotten passes to the world's best water park.

"What do we do?" I ask. "Do we need to get them inside?"

"Luna and Lennon need to be put inside," Quint says. "I don't think they've built up enough of a blubber layer to stay warm in this. The rest should be okay, but we'll have to clear those pools." I assume it isn't the water he's worried about—they are marine animals, after all—but there are tree branches and debris in the water, swept in by the rain, and they could easily get hurt.

I nod, and we get to work.

I prepare one of the inside pens before going back to get Luna and Lennon. They seem happy to follow me out of the storm when I herd them through the door, using a large strip of plastic to coax them in the right direction. Quint stays outside, working to relocate the animals from the flooded pools to some of the enclosures that are closer to the building.

I get some blankets for Lennon and Luna to help them stay warm. The rain wasn't that cold, but now that they're inside, I want them to get dry as quickly as possible. I find a couple of their toys, too, thinking it might help them feel more at home, but the toys I toss into the enclosure go ignored. Luna piles herself on top of Lennon, tucking her head against his neck. I can't tell if she's afraid or just tired.

At least they're safe. I lock their gate and am halfway to the back door when an odd burbling noise catches my ear. I turn in a full circle, trying to figure out where it's coming from, when I look over the nearest wall into an enclosure that's currently empty.

The drain in the middle of the floor is overflowing.

Water is coming up from the ground.

My eyes widen. "Quint!" I yell. Turning, I sprint down the hallway and burst out into the yard just in time to see Quint latching the fence behind the last of the relocated animals. "Quint, the drains! They're . . . water is coming up and . . . what do we do?"

He frowns at me for a second, then runs past me to see for himself. A second later, he's on the phone to his mom. He's breathless as he tries to explain to her that we're here at the center, we moved the animals, but the drains are flooding. I can hear her steady voice on the other side of the call, coaching him in what to do.

We find flood gates for the doors and plugs for the drains exactly where Rosa said they would be. The next few minutes are chaos as Quint and I run around the building, plugging the drains. I find one of our newer patients, an elephant seal, sleeping on top of one, and I have a long internal debate about whether we could just leave him there to keep the water at bay, but eventually Quint and I decide to wake him up and get him to move so we can plug the drain for real.

I'm exhausted by the time we have the center secured and the animals taken care of. I feel like I've just run a marathon. A very wet marathon.

"I'm going to call my mom again," says Quint, sounding equally breathless. "See what else we should be doing."

I nod. "I'll make the rounds one more time, make sure everyone's doing okay."

My shoes slip and squelch on the linoleum floor as I check on the animals in their pens. Most are sleeping, oblivious to the storm, but Lennon and Luna are awake. Luna is still draped over Lennon like a rag doll, her flippers covering her eyes.

I open the gate. They both startle. Lennon presses his flippers against the tile, trying to scoot farther into the corner, but he can barely shift with Luna's weight on top of him. It's the first time I've seen either of them act afraid. Usually they perk up when one of the volunteers shows up, expecting food. I regret not bringing a couple of fish with me.

"Hey, guys," I murmur, stepping closer. It's a constant battle to remind myself that they're still wild animals. They could be dangerous, especially when they're frightened.

But they don't move as I slide down to sit on the tiled floor. I grab a slightly deflated beach ball and roll it toward them. It bounces off Lennon's nose. He shakes his head in surprise. It's dark in here, but not so dark that he shouldn't have seen that. I wonder if his eyes have gotten worse in the last couple of days.

Luna rolls off him and then they're both plodding toward me. Luna's head nudges my thigh and I spend a few minutes stroking their fur. "That's some intense rain out there, isn't it?" I say, trying to keep my voice soothing. "But it's okay. You're safe in here. And I'm glad to see you've been taking care of each other."

The rain continues to pound on the rooftop overhead, but it seems to have eased from the initial torrents.

"Prudence?" Quint's voice echoes down the long corridor.

"Back here." I stand up and the sea lions immediately return to snuggling each other.

When Quint reaches us, he looks concerned—but his face softens as soon as he spies the animals. "I wish the lighting was better in here," he says. "That'd make a great picture."

"It's probably decent enough for a social media post anyway? People might be wondering how we're faring with this storm."

He nods and takes out his phone. When the flash sparks, Luna covers her head with her flippers again, but Lennon just peers up at Quint, confused.

"What did your mom say?"

"We should be good. Not much more we can do until the storm lets up. She's happy we're here. She wanted to come herself, but I guess there are flash floods happening all over the place and she didn't think it would be safe to drive. And she said we might be better off staying here until the storm passes?"

I let myself out of Luna and Lennon's pen. "I should probably call my parents, too," I say, heading toward the lobby, where I'd dropped my phone and backpack as soon as we got here.

The phone rings twice before my mom answers, sounding frantic. I assume she's been worried about me—but no. Ellie, who they keep trying to put to bed by eight o'clock, is still wide-awake, fighting her nightly sleepy-time routine with gusto. I can hear her wailing in the background. As for me, Mom had assumed that I was still on Main Street, probably hunkered down in Encanto. I tell her Quint and I came to the center to make sure the animals were okay, and after a moment's hesitation, she offers to drive down and pick me up.

The offer is comforting, even though I can hear the exhaustion in her voice.

"No," I say. "It's all right. I'll just stay here until the storm is over."

"All right, sweetheart. That's probably for the best. Be safe, okay?"

"Okay, Mom. I'll call you if anything changes."

I hang up and turn around to see—

Quint.

Quint is standing in the doorway, just a few feet away from me.

Quint is shirtless.

Quint is wearing a faded blue towel around his waist, and using a second towel to dry his hair.

I yelp. "Holy—! What—! Why are you—?" I spin back around, my face aflame. My elbow knocks my backpack off the reception desk and it lands with a splat on the floor, scattering my pens and a couple of slightly damp notebooks.

Even though I'm not facing Quint anymore, I squeeze my eyes shut. "Where did your clothes go?"

There's a moment of silence, and then—Quint loses it. His laughter comes on strong, and it doesn't stop. I frown, listening to his guffaws, his howls, his gasps for air.

After a while, my surprise and embarrassment start to give way to annoyance.

Bracing myself, I turn just enough so I can glare at him over my shoulder. Quint doesn't seem to notice. He's fallen against the wall and is struggling to breathe. He has tears on his face. Honest-to-goodness tears.

"Sorry," he gasps, once he's managed to bring his hysteria under control. "Just—your face! Oh my god, Pru." He wipes the tears away. "I'm sorry. I didn't mean to freak you out. But . . . I mean, you've seen guys without shirts before, right? You've been to the beach?"

"That's different!" I stomp my foot. Petulantly. Immaturely. I don't care. *Why is he almost naked?*

There's still a distant amusement lingering on Quint's face, but at least he seems to be done laughing at me. "How is it different?" he says, clearly teasing me.

Because it just is, I want to say.

Because they're not *you.*

I clear my throat. "You just surprised me. It's fine. I'm fine."

"You're not scarred for life?"

"Remains to be seen."

I turn back to him, but can't bring myself to meet his eye. I find myself staring at the satirical *Jaws* poster instead. "So, where did your clothes go, exactly?"

"The dryer. I was just heading upstairs to grab some volunteer shirts for us."

Oooh. The dryer. I wilt with relief to hear such a practical explanation. We use the washer and dryer daily for the animals' blankets and towels, but it didn't occur to me to use it for *us*.

"Right. Okay. Good idea."

Quint hands me a towel and I start drying my hair.

"I'll go get those shirts," he says. I can still hear the occasional chuckle as he heads up the stairs.

I make my way to the small utility room with the washer and dryer and close the door behind me. Peeling off my wet shirt and jeans is like peeling off a second skin. My bra and underwear are damp, too, but I can live with that. I toss my things into the dryer. They land on top of Quint's shirt and pants. Criminy, this is weird. I start blushing all over again.

I grab a new towel from the shelf and wrap it around my body sarong-style. Then I start the dryer and stand there, listening to it rumble and thud, wondering what to do now. I am not going to go strutting around Quint in nothing but a towel, but it will be at least half an hour before our clothes are dry.

The second I have this thought, the lights flicker.

I glance up.

They flicker again—then go out.

I'm plunged into darkness so thick, it feels like I've been sucked into a black hole. The dryer whines to a stop. Our heavy, damp clothes thud down one last time. An eerie silence falls over the center, broken only by the torrential rains that continue to pound against the side of the building and the occasional unhappy barks of the animals.

"Prudence?"

Gripping the towel, I open the door and peek my head out into the corridor. Quint is moving toward me, illuminated by the flashlight feature on his cell phone. He's put on a shirt, thankfully, but still has the towel around his waist.

"You okay?" he asks.

"Yeah. The power . . ."

"I know. Here." He hands me a yellow T-shirt.

"Is there a generator?"

"I don't think so."

I duck back into the room and turn on the flashlight on my phone, too. It casts the small room in a faint white glow as I pull on the T-shirt and tie the towel skirtlike around my waist.

I grimace. I can secure the towel around my hips, but it leaves a gap across one thigh. I cannot go out there like this.

Then I remember that there's a stack of blankets next to the washer. I take off the towel and grab a blanket instead. I feel better immediately, with the fabric more than covering my hips and falling all the way past my ankles. It smells like fish and seawater, given that it usually lives in the pens with the animals. Not all that long ago I would have been completely grossed out by this, but now I'm just grateful. Besides, I'm often the person doing the laundry at the end of the day, so I know the towels and blankets are regularly washed.

I grab my phone and open the door.

"Now what?" I ask, before realizing that Quint is holding my backpack.

He holds it out, gripping the handles. "You dropped this in the lobby," he says. "I didn't know if you needed it."

"Thanks." I take it from him, but he looks troubled.

"What's wrong?"

He clears his throat and holds out something else. Two things, actually. A pale yellow envelope that's been ripped open, and a white envelope, thick with dollar bills. "These spilled out."

"Oh." I swallow. "The money is for my parents . . ." I feel like I should say more. It's weird to be carrying around all that money. But—I don't want to tell him about the pawnshop. I don't want him to know that my parents have resorted to selling off our possessions. I've done a good job not thinking about it all day today, but whenever it does crop up in my thoughts, my stomach twists. With worry. With guilt. I've spent my whole summer so focused on trying to help the center. Should I have been trying to help my own family instead?

In the end, I don't tell Quint anything, just tuck the money back into my bag and zip it into one of the side pockets, which I probably should have done from the beginning. It's really none of his business, anyway.

But I'm still holding the yellow envelope, and his eyes are on it, his brow tense. "My mom wrote a bunch of thank-you notes to some of our donors last month," he says, "just like you suggested. I helped her put stamps on them . . ."

I know he's telling me this to clue me in that *he* knows what this is. Almost like he's trying to get a confession out of me.

And maybe that's reasonable. This wasn't my mail to open, and it certainly wasn't mine to keep.

I sigh. "Dr. Jindal dropped it the other day when she was bringing in the mail. I picked it up, and when I saw who it was addressed to . . ."

I flip it over so Quint can see Grace Livingstone's name, and the post office stamp: DECEASED.

Understanding flickers across his features. "Maya's grandma."

"I know I shouldn't have opened it, but . . ." I hesitate. But what, exactly? It seemed like the *universe* was trying to tell me something? I shake my head. "I shouldn't have opened it. I'm sorry."

Quint takes the card, and for a moment, he looks torn. But then a wisp of a smile crosses his face. "I would have been curious, too. I'll tell Mom that I was the one who opened it, that I go to school with her granddaughter. I think she'll understand."

My heart expands. I wasn't expecting that.

"Thanks," I whisper.

A beat of silence passes between us, and then the energy shifts again. Quint smiles, easy and relaxed. "Are you hungry?" He juts his thumb toward the staircase. "I've got quarters for the vending machine. We could have Pringles by candlelight."

"How romantic," I say. "Except, I don't think vending machines work during a power outage."

He winces. "Damn. I bet you're right. I don't actually know if there are any candles, either."

I shrug. "Let's go find out."

THIRTY-NINE

In the staff break room, we spend some time digging through the drawers jumbled with silverware, offices supplies, and random takeout menus that have probably been buried in here for the past decade. Ultimately, we find two boxes of birthday candles and a book of matches. Quint settles the candles into a decorative bowl full of sand and seashells and lights them. I've never seen birthday candles lit for longer than it takes to sing "Happy Birthday," and I suspect they won't last long, but for now, their glow is comforting and strangely joyful as the wind and rain rage outside. Plus, both of our phones are getting low on battery life, so we figure it's best to conserve them as much as possible.

After digging through the cabinets, we pull together something like a picnic. An open bag of stale potato chips, some saltine crackers and peanut butter, a box of Cheerios, some marshmallows.

Even though I'd been joking before, as we settle in at the long conference table, it actually *does* feel romantic. The storm rattling against the windows. The glow of the candles.

And that we're pretty much trapped here . . . together.

"Do you think we'll be stuck here all night?" I ask, trying not to sound hopeful when I say it. Because it would be awful, right? Who wants to sleep on a cold, hard floor, when they could be safe at home in a cozy, warm bed?

And yet, I'm in no hurry to leave.

"I don't know. At this rate . . ." Quint glances at the window. "It's not looking good. Were your parents worried?"

"I think they're okay. They said to stay here until the storm passes."

He nods. "I guess we can use the blankets from downstairs to make a bed of sorts. It may not be the most comfortable thing in the world, but . . ."

"It could be worse."

Which is true. We have shelter and food. It's warm enough. There's light for the time being, though the candles are burning awfully fast.

"At least we have cereal." I pop a handful into my mouth.

The first candle flickers out, leaving a trail of dark smoke curling up through the shadows. We both look at our little collection of candles stuck into the sand. They've already nearly burned down to nubs.

"Maybe we should have rationed those," says Quint.

"Isn't there a flashlight around here somewhere?"

He considers this. "You'd think so."

We go on a hunt again, risking the battery life of our phones to dig through every cabinet, closet, and cupboard we can find. Finally—success. We find five flashlights stashed away with some of the rescue nets and other supplies, although only three of them have batteries that work. While we're downstairs, we fill our arms with as many blankets as we can carry before retreating back to the break room. We push the table against one bank of cabinets, clearing out a space large enough that we can spread out the blankets, building them up into something like a mattress. It occurs to me that maybe we should be making two separate beds, but . . . I don't say anything, and neither does he.

"What would you be doing right now if you weren't here?" Quint asks.

"Sleeping?"

"Really? It's not even midnight."

"I'm more of a morning person."

"That does not surprise me." Quint sits down on the makeshift bed and rolls up a couple of towels to use as a cushion behind his back. I hesitate for a few seconds before sitting down on the opposite side, facing him. We're close enough that it feels intimate, especially with the dim lighting of the flashlight reflected off the ceiling, but far enough that I can pretend it isn't totally awkward. "Okay," he says, "if you weren't sleeping, then what would you be doing?"

"I don't know. Planning the gala? Making sure everything will be perfect?"

Quint clicks his tongue, as if chastising me. "Do you ever think you might be too much of an overachiever?"

My nose wrinkles. "Jude keeps me aware of that, yes. I can't help it though. There's always more to do, and I don't want to settle for less than perfect, you know? Why be mediocre? But it can be hard to know when enough is enough, or how to prioritize my time. Like this summer. I've been thinking so much about the center that I've done hardly any work on our biology project at all."

"I've been wondering about that," Quint says, his eyes twinkling. "I was sort of hoping you'd forgotten about it."

"I definitely have not forgotten about it. I still want to do something extraordinary. I actually thought that maybe we could use the gala as a real-world example of how ecotourism can function to help the environment. But I still need to bring more science into it, and that's got me stumped. So then I set it aside and focus on the center and fundraising . . . even though I know that by putting it off I'm just creating more stress for myself."

"What? You? Hold on." Quint leans toward me conspiratorially. "Are you saying that you, Prudence Barnett . . . have been . . . *procrastinating?*" He says it like it's a bad word, his face drawn with disbelief.

I can't help but laugh at the overdramatization, even though it does give me a hiccup of anxiety when I realize the revised project is due in only a few weeks. "Absolutely not," I say emphatically. "I've just been . . . conducting copious amounts of research."

"Uh-huh, sure." He winks at me, sending my heartbeat on another erratic drum solo. "Just so long as you know that when *I'm* procrastinating, research is my go-to excuse, too."

"I am not procrastinating. That word is not in my vocabulary. But I will admit that it's hard to spend my time writing a report about saving wildlife when I could be . . . you know. Helping to save actual wildlife."

His teeth flash in a gigantic grin. "I couldn't agree more."

As he says this, a thought occurs to me. One I can't believe hasn't crossed my mind until now.

I think of the times I tried to cast karmic justice on Quint at the start of the summer. When he refused to help with the biology project because he "had other things to do," or when he was late to meet me on Main Street. I was so mad at him. So sure he was being selfish and lazy. But he wasn't. He really did have other things to do. Seals to feed. Sea otters to rescue.

That's why my attempts kept backfiring. Instead of punishing him, the universe was rewarding him. The extra credit from Mr. Chavez. The twenty-dollar bill.

All that time, I couldn't see what was right in front of me. But the universe could. The universe knew.

"What?" says Quint, and I realize I've been staring at him.

I flush, and shake my head. "Nothing. Just spacing out." It takes me a second to remember what we were talking about. "Anyway, don't get the wrong idea. I do still think that revising the report and improving our grade is important. If I'm going to get into one of my top college choices, I can't let my GPA slip."

"Where do you want to go?"

"Stanford," I say, with no hesitation. "Or Berkeley. They both have really good business schools."

He makes a face. "Business? What, did you look up the most boring majors possible and that one ranked just above political science?"

"Excuse me. Business is fascinating. The psychology of why and how people spend their money, the reasons why some businesses fail and others keep going strong . . . And I figure, a business degree can be applied to almost every field out there, so no matter what I'm drawn to later, I'll be able to make it work." I hum thoughtfully. "Sometimes I think, if either of my parents had any business sense, their lives would be so much easier. I never want to worry about money like they do."

My thoughts go back to that wad of cash in my backpack. The box of silver-ware in the pawnshop. I swallow.

"That, I can understand," says Quint. "I know Mom doesn't want me to worry, but it's impossible not to. This center is her passion, but it's also her livelihood. If it fails . . ." He doesn't finish the thought. I wonder what Rosa would do if she couldn't run the center anymore. "But money isn't everything. She works really hard here and it's always a struggle to keep things going, but I don't think she'd want to do anything else."

I don't respond. Sure, money may not be everything . . . but it is *something*. I can't imagine working as hard as Rosa, or my parents for that matter, and still having so little to show for it, no matter how much I love my work.

"Let me guess," I say, cocking my head speculatively. "You've given precisely zero thought to where you want to go to college, or what you want to study."

"Not zero thought," he says a little defensively. "I may not be working off a five-year plan like *some* people . . ."

"Ten, actually."

"My mistake." He rolls his eyes. "But right now, I'm pretty sure I'll be taking a gap year."

My gasp is so horrified that Quint looks legitimately concerned for a second.

"A *gap* year? Oh, come on. That's just a fancy way of saying you're either too lazy to go to college or too indecisive to pick one."

"Whoa. Uh-uh." He points a finger at me. "Just because it isn't *your* plan doesn't make it a bad one."

"It just delays the inevitable! If you're going to go to college, then go to college! Why mess around, wasting a whole year of your life . . . backpacking Europe or whatever cliché thing you think will make you 'well-rounded.'" I make air quotes.

Quint crosses his arms over his chest. "For your information, studies have shown that people who take gap years regularly perform better in college once they get there."

I narrow my eyes, unconvinced.

"Look it up," he says mildly.

"I don't want to drain my phone battery," I grumble.

"You don't want to admit that I could be right. Again."

"We'll see." I huff. "So what do you plan on doing during your year of slackery? Please tell me you won't actually be backpacking through Europe."

"Australia, actually. I want to dive the Great Barrier Reef before it's too late."

My eyes widen in surprise. I spend a moment mulling this over. "Okay, that's actually kind of a neat goal."

"Translation from Prudence to English: That's a brilliant idea, Quint. You should totally do that."

I shake my head. "Not so fast. You don't need a whole year to do that. Why not just go on summer vacation?"

He starts to fidget, adjusting the towel behind his back. Crossing and uncrossing his ankles. "I don't want to just rent some gear, spend a day at the reef, and check it off my bucket list. I want . . ." He hesitates, his expression becoming almost serious. "So . . . my ultimate plan, if you must know, is that I want to get my scuba-diving license and spend the year building up my portfolio. My . . . photography portfolio." He picks at some lint on the blanket. "When I do go to college, I'd like to study art and design. Maybe minor in photography. I'd love to do underwater photography eventually, but the equipment is expensive, and my best chance is to get a really great scholarship. And for that . . ."

He doesn't finish, but I've already connected the dots. "You need a great portfolio."

"It's one thing to take photos of the animals here at the center, but if I could have more underwater experience when I apply, I really think it would help."

I stare at him, even though, for some reason, he's stopped meeting my eye. My opinion of Quint does another flip. "You could be in *National Geographic* someday."

He grins, his eyes crinkling at the corners as he finally looks up at me. "One can dream, but that's . . . I mean, their photographers are top-notch. I don't know that I could ever . . ."

"You could. You will," I say, with surprising conviction. "You're so talented."

He drags a hand through his hair. "Naw. Average at best. But I do love it, so . . . we'll see."

"I can't believe you were teasing me about my ten-year-plan when you've been keeping all that a secret this whole time."

He still looks uncomfortable as he rolls out his shoulders a few times. "It's weird to talk about. I mean . . . you tell people you want to dive the Great Barrier Reef and become an underwater photographer? It's kind of far-fetched, as dreams go."

"It's not. I mean, someone has to do it, otherwise we wouldn't have all those cool documentaries about bizarre sea life that Mr. Chavez made us watch."

"True. That's a good point." His eyes are glinting, almost gratefully.

"That's one thing I like about you, Prudence. No one can say you aren't an optimist."

"I like to think I'm more of a realist who's willing to work hard."

He grins. "Even better."

My cheeks warm. It's my turn to look away, my fingers digging into the plush blankets. I curl my knees up toward my chest, draping my arms around them. "I have to believe that, with enough diligence and effort, you can make anything happen. And I do get that I'm a ridiculous perfectionist and, yes, probably too much of an overachiever. But it's all I have, so . . . I figure, better make the best of it."

"What do you mean, it's all you have?"

I wince. I shouldn't have said anything. A part of me wants to backtrack, to say, *never mind, I was just rambling,* but . . . there's something about the dim lighting, the rain that's turned from a torrent to a melodious pattering, the way Quint just confessed this close-held dream, that makes me brave. Or, if not brave, I at least feel like maybe it's okay to be a little vulnerable.

"It's like, Jude, for example," I say, quietly, careful with my words. "He's so nice. Everybody likes him. He just gets along with people, everywhere he goes. I know I'm not *that.* And Ari, she's so talented, and so passionate about music, but I'm not really passionate about anything, other than wanting to succeed. To do my best. But I can make plans, and I can stay organized, and if a teacher assigns a report, I'm going to write the best darn report they've ever seen. If I'm throwing a gala, I'm going to throw a party that no one will ever forget. I can do that. And if I can impress people, then maybe they won't notice that I'm not witty or beautiful or . . . *fun.*"

I stop talking and tuck the lower half of my face behind my arms. I can't believe I just said all that. But at the same time, it feels good to admit that all the confidence I show the world is a diversionary tactic. A cover for the fear that lies underneath.

"I mean," says Quint, finally, as if *he* were the one who'd been saying too much, "you're not . . . *not* beautiful."

A sound, part laugh and part cough, bursts out of me. I dare to look up at him, but quickly have to look away again. "First of all, double negatives are not grammatically acceptable."

He groans. "I can't win with you."

"Second of all," I say, ignoring him, "I wasn't fishing for a compliment. But . . . thanks? I think?"

"I know you weren't." He clears his throat, and I sense that he might be as uncomfortable with this conversation as I've become. "But I had to say something. I've never seen you self-conscious about anything before. And I mean it. You're . . ." He trails off.

I viciously shake my head. "You don't have to say it. Don't get the wrong idea. It's not that I think I'm hideous or anything, but . . . being surrounded by girls who wear nothing but cutoff shorts and string bikinis all summer long? I mean, I know I don't look like *that*."

Quint makes a humming noise, and I can't tell whether he's agreeing with me or not. When he speaks again, I expect a refrain of the same semi-compliment: *You're not* not *beautiful.* And yeah, my whole body is still flushed from those words. But instead, he says something that is somehow a hundred times better. Something that I don't think anyone has *ever* said to me before. "For what it's worth, I think you're pretty fun. At least, when you're not criticizing everything I say or do." His cheeks dimple. "Actually, I've had a lot of fun with you this summer."

We stare at each other in the flashlight's glow, the rain drizzling against the windows. My throat tightens. I'm startled to find that my eyes are misting, and I hope it's too dark for Quint to see. He can't know—he can't possibly know—how good it feels to hear those words. To know he means them.

"Also . . ." Quint loudly clears his throat and adjusts his legs, crossing one ankle over the other. "I have enormous eyebrows."

I snort and clap one hand over my mouth. "What?"

"I do. In case you hadn't noticed." He leans toward me and points at one eyebrow. "You can come closer if you need to verify."

"Um. I've seen them, thanks."

"Yeah, exactly. Everyone's seen them. Aliens on Mars can see them."

I laugh. "Quint—"

"No, don't try to tell me they're not that bad. I own a mirror. I know the truth." He sighs dramatically and leans back against the cabinet. "When I was a kid, I once asked my mom to help me pluck them."

"You didn't."

"I did. She refused. Gave me some you're-perfect-just-the-way-you-are mom nonsense. So I sneaked into her bathroom and got ahold of her tweezers and pulled out one hair—just one. It hurt so bad *I cried*. Seriously, why do girls put themselves through that?"

"I often wonder the same thing."

"Anyway, I couldn't bring myself to pull any more, which made me cry even *harder*, and then my mom found me and was like, what the heck is wrong with you? They're just eyebrows! But the thing is—they make me look so mean. I was worried everyone would think I was some bully and no one would be my friend."

Sympathy squeezes my chest.

"And when I told my mom that, she said . . . all I have to do is smile. Because you can't look mean when you're smiling." His lips turn up, but there's a sadness, recalling this story. "Anyway, I took those words to heart. Ever since then, I've tried to be, you know. The guy that smiles. It's better than being the guy with the mean eyebrows, anyway." He chuckles, a little self-deprecatingly.

While I sit there feeling like the biggest jerk, remembering how I mocked his eyebrows when he came to karaoke all those weeks ago.

And now I can't even remember what made me say such awful things. I *like* his eyebrows. I like how expressive they are. The way they quirk up when he's teasing. The way they furrow when he's annoyed. Though I like them less when he's annoyed at me.

I want to tell him this, but the words are stuck. My throat is dry.

"Anyway," says Quint, "I guess we're all self-conscious about something."

"I guess so." My words are barely a croak.

He meets my eye and there's a second—an hour—an eternity—in which neither of us looks away. He has that crooked half smile on his face. My brain falters, leaving me suspended, breathless, trapped.

His attention dips, ever briefly, to my mouth. My insides clench. The distance between us feels like a mile.

Quint inhales and I can't move, waiting for him to speak, to say my name, to say *anything*—

But when he does speak, his tone is clipped and brash. Nervous. "Should we talk about something else? The gala? Or biology? Or—school field trips, or something?"

I lick my lips. That *does* sound safer, and it seems clear neither of us will be falling asleep anytime soon.

"We still need to figure out our raffle prize?" I suggest.

"Good. Right. Something priceless, but that we can actually afford."

We spend a few minutes pondering. Quint throws out a few ideas—Ari could write them a personalized song? Or the winner could invite some of their closest friends to the next animal-release celebration, like a private party? They're all good ideas, all possibilities, but nothing seems *quite* right . . .

I'm looking around the break room, hoping inspiration will strike, when my attention lands on the photo of the sea turtle caught in the netting and debris.

I gasp. "Quint!"

"What?"

I jump to my feet, tightening the blanket around my waist as I cross the room. "These! Your photos!"

He stands up too, but less enthusiastically. "My photos?"

"Yes! What if we made a series of limited-edition prints showing some of the center's patients? You could sign each one and number them. They're so beautiful, and they do such a great job of capturing what the center is all about. People would go nuts for them!"

"Shucks, Pru. That's mighty kind of you to say." Despite his joking tone, I can tell he's embarrassed by the praise. "But come on. They're too sad. No one would want them."

I consider this. "Yes, they are sad. But lots of great art is sad. And these pictures, they make you feel something, you know? You capture these moments, these emotions . . ." I press a hand over my heart, remembering the way my throat had closed tight the first time I'd seen the animals in the photographs. "The pictures are heartbreaking, but they're also honest, and they explain in the most visceral way why the rescue center is important. I know you didn't take the pictures so you could sell them, but for a raffle . . . What do you think?"

He's frowning at the photos on the wall. "I don't know. I mean, I'm glad you think they're good, but . . . they're just . . ." He shrugs. "Depressing. Besides, I'm not some great artist. No one will pay money for these."

"I think you're wrong. I *know* you're wrong." I grab his arm, pleading. He tenses. "And they have just the right amount of personal touch. They're perfect!"

His lips twist to one side. I think I might be wearing him down, but I can also see he's not convinced. "I guess we can put it on the maybe list."

I pout. "Fine. It's your art. I shouldn't tell you what to do with it." My hands fall to my hips and I look back at the framed photos, shaking my head in disappointment. "You can do whatever you want to do."

Quint doesn't respond.

I wait, fully expecting him to give in. To throw up his hands and proclaim— fine, Prudence, *you win.* Use the darn photos if it's that important to you!

But his silence stretches on and on.

Finally, I glance at him.

He's watching me, his eyes glinting with the faint glow of the flashlight.

"What?" I ask.

His mouth opens, but hesitates. Two seconds. Five. Before—"I can do whatever I want to do?"

I'm immediately wary. My eyes narrow. "Within reason."

He exhales sharply. "It might be too late for that."

I'm about to ask what he's talking about, when he lowers his head and touches his lips against mine.

I freeze.

All thoughts evacuate my brain, leaving me with nothing but mental static.

My lips tingle. It's a brief touch. Hesitant. Unsure. And then it's gone. His eyes are hooded as he peers at me, waiting for my reaction.

And I—I can't react. I can barely breathe.

Quint Erickson just kissed me.

He starts to look concerned. He gulps so loud I can hear it.

"I've . . . wanted to do that for a while . . . ," he says, which might be an explanation? Or an excuse? And then he's pulling away even farther, and those eyebrows, those glorious eyebrows are knitting together, and I can tell he's embarrassed and hurt and—*why can't I move?*

"But if I shouldn't have . . . I maybe misread . . . um." His shoulders rise defensively. "Should I say I'm sorry?"

"No!" The word is all I can manage. Anything to get him to stop talking, to stop backpedaling, to stop looking like he might have just made a mistake. "I just . . . you surprised me. Is all."

His head slowly lifts, slowly falls, in something like a robotic nod. "Okay. Good surprised, or . . . ?"

I laugh, the hilarity hitting me all at once.

Quint. Quint kissed me.

He kissed *me.*

"Pru—"

I don't let him finish. I grab his shoulders and kiss him back.

FORTY

"The second-to-last day of school."

"Second-to-last day of school?" I say, baffled, trying to remember what, if anything, was so special about the second-to-last day of school. But then I shake my head. "No, no. I know you're lying, because the *last* day of school is when we got our grades from Mr. Chavez, and you implied that only a masochist would willingly work on that biology project with me over the summer."

"Oh yeah. I'm not saying it was the first time I realized I *liked* you. I was still thoroughly convinced that you were a terrible person. I'm just saying, the second-to-last day of school is when you became a terrible person that I sort of wanted to make out with."

I blanch. "Quint!" I say, hiding my face behind my hands. "Honestly!"

He shrugs. "You asked."

I stutter a laugh, even as heat burns across my cheeks. We're sitting on the pile of blankets. The power is still out, though the storm has dulled to a steady drizzle. Quint's arm is draped around my shoulders, as comfortably as if we did this all the time.

I don't know how many hours we've been sitting here. We've gone past that period of late-night delirium when everything becomes hysterically funny, through the point when everything seems impossibly profound, and now we're both sleepy and yawning and refusing to close our eyes. I never want this night to end.

"So what was it? My extremely detailed miniature model of Main Street, or . . ."

"Karaoke, obviously."

I gasp. "Oh! That was karaoke night, wasn't it? When I . . ." I touch the back of my head, remembering my fall. Then I look at him, dubious. "You have a thing for girls with concussions?"

"I honestly don't know what I have a thing for." His fingers mindlessly trace circles around my upper arm. "But there was just something . . . I don't know. At one point you did that little shoulder-shimmy thing . . ." He wiggles his shoulders in imitation. "Plus, that lipstick of yours . . ." He brings his free hand to my face, pressing his thumb lightly against my lips, even though there's no way I have any lipstick left after this night. I shiver. "I usually don't get the whole makeup thing, but that lipstick. I've had dreams in that exact shade of red lately."

"You're kidding."

"Is that weird?" His eyes crinkle in the corners, and I want to tell him that every word out of his mouth for the past I-don't-know-how-many-hours has been weird.

"It might be a little weird," I say. "But I'm not complaining."

He grins and his eyes dip to my mouth. I'm coming to recognize this look, right before he kisses me. His hand moves to cup the side of my face. He leans down and I tilt my head up to meet him. My lips are swollen. Twenty-four hours ago I'd never been kissed. Now I've been kissed into oblivion.

"Your turn," says Quint, pulling away and settling his forehead against mine. "When did you first want to kiss me?"

I close my eyes and try to remember. Right now it's hard to imagine a time when I *didn't* want to kiss him.

"Snorkeling."

"Yes!" Quint pumps his elbow. "I knew you were totally into me that day. I could sense it." He snaps his fingers. "Was that also the day that I helped rescue that sea otter? It was, wasn't it? Man, that was a good day for me." He sighs wistfully, as if he's an old man feeling nostalgic for his youthful prime, rather than something that just happened a few weeks ago. "It was kind of magical watching you snorkel for the first time. I don't think I'd ever seen you that happy before."

I consider this. "I wasn't happy so much as amazed."

"No, you were happy. I can tell, you know."

"Oh? How?"

"I could see your dimples." His eyes glint, almost teasingly, though he's trying to keep his expression stoic and wise. "They don't show up as much when you have one of your snarky smiles on."

My heart thumps, and I can't help but grin. Flustered, but happy.

"See?" he says, knocking his shoulder against mine. "Like that."

I bump him back. Then my eyes catch on the windows and I blink. "Hey, Quint. Do you see what I'm seeing?"

He turns his head and it takes him a minute to realize what I'm talking about. *Daylight.* Just a faint hint of it illuminating the windows. Not sunshine, but the promise of sunshine. A dim greenish-gray light cutting through the drizzle.

"What time is it?" He grabs for his phone reflexively, before remembering that our batteries both died eons ago.

I glance at my watch. "Almost six." We look at each other, realizing that we've been awake all night. Not only that, but the storm seems to have passed.

We're free to go.

"I'd suggest we go get pancakes," says Quint, "but most diners probably require pants."

I break into giggles and collapse into him, burying my face into his shoulder. If we'd been thinking last night, we would have hung our clothes up. They'd probably be dry by now, or close to it. But they're still in the dryer, lying in a sopping-wet clump.

"Pancakes sound *so good,* too," I say.

His arms encircle me. His lips press against my neck, right below my ear.

Pancakes are forgotten, along with everything else.

Until a few seconds later, when a door slams downstairs.

We both jump.

The sound must have awoken some of the animals downstairs, because there's a short round of barks from the seals, squeaks from the otters.

Then we hear Rosa, yelling. "Quint?"

Quint and I exchange looks. A brief but deep disappointment passes between us before we disentangle our arms from each other.

"Up here, Mom," Quint calls back as we both stand up and straighten our T-shirts and check the knots on our towel-kilt and blanket-gown, as we dubbed our makeshift clothing around three o'clock in the morning.

We hear Rosa jogging up the stairs. A bouncing white light precedes her, and when she arrives in the break room, she swings her cell phone so fast in our direction, it blinds us both. Quint and I throw up our arms, shrieking. We could be vampires faced with a sudden deluge of sunlight.

Rosa lowers her phone. "A tree took down some power lines up the road. I saw crews working to get it fixed. Has the power been out all night?"

"Yeah," says Quint. "Went out not long after we got here."

Rosa makes a sympathetic noise in her throat. "You poor kids! If I'd known . . ." She trails off, because, what would she have done differently? Sent out a search party for us?

"We're okay." Quint rubs his eyes. "Though we didn't get a whole lot of sleep."

"No sleep," I amend. "We got exactly negative amounts of sleep."

Quint snickers at this, which makes me giggle, too. Our sleepy minds finding something hilarious in this sentence.

Rosa looks between us, a little concerned.

"We're fine," Quint says emphatically this time.

"We're great," I say. And then I blush, wondering how much the word *great* implies about the night we spent together. Does *great* automatically suggest seven straight hours of confessions and truths and kisses? So. Many. Kisses.

And yet, somehow . . .

Not.

Enough.

Kisses.

"Have you been to check on the animals?" asks Quint, even though we both just heard her come in.

"No. I thought I'd better make sure you were both okay first."

"Do you have a portable phone charger?" I ask, holding up my dead phone. "I should call my parents."

"Afraid not. But you can use the phone downstairs."

I frown. "The power is out."

Rosa looks like she's trying not to laugh at me. "Yes, honey. Landline phones still work, even when the power goes out."

"*What?* How?" My mouth drops open and I turn to Quint. "Did you know that?"

He shakes his head, looking as bewildered as I am. "I had no idea. It seems like—"

"Sorcery!"

He throws his arms into the air, howling, "Sorcery!"

I burst into giggles again.

Rosa clears her throat. "All right. Prudence, you go call your parents. Quint . . . why are you wearing a towel?"

"Our clothes were drenched from the storm. They're down in the dryer, but it's not working."

"Unless!" I gasp. "Can dryers work without power, too?"

"No," says Rosa.

I snap my fingers, bummed.

I go down to the lobby and call my parents to let them know I'm all right and will be heading home soon, and that my phone is dead. Mom reminds me to be careful riding my bike—there's standing water all over the roads—but beyond that, they don't sound too concerned. I sometimes think this is the plight of the oldest child, or children, in the case of twins like me and Jude. There's no babying, no helicopter parenting, no late-night pacing after curfew. We're the ones who can take care of ourselves. I'm extra grateful for that autonomy now. If Mom had insisted that she come get me last night, when the storm was raging, I would have missed out on the most amazing night of my life.

As I hang up the phone, I hear clumsy footsteps on the stairs. Quint is hauling our massive pile of blankets back to the laundry room. He pauses when he sees me. His hair mussed, his face a little puffy from our sleepless night.

I smile at him, suddenly bashful. He smiles back, just as shy, just as eager.

It takes everything in me not to grab one of those blankets, throw it over both our heads, and . . .

His eyes darken, like maybe he knows what I'm thinking. Like maybe he'd be okay with it.

But then I hear Rosa coming down the steps behind him and we both shrink away from each other.

"Want help?" I ask.

"There were a couple more blankets up there still."

I'm passing Rosa on the stairs when the lights suddenly flicker on above us, and the perpetual hum of technology returns to the walls, the air conditioner, the refrigerator in the break room.

"Ah," says Rosa, smiling brightly. "That's better."

No, I want to tell her. *This isn't better at all.*

But I just return her smile and go to collect the blankets. When I catch up with Quint in the laundry room, the dryer is running again, and he's busying his hands by folding all the blankets we used. They're not really dirty, so there's no need to wash them. I drop my blankets into a pile on the floor and start helping him, all while our eyes perform a complicated tango I didn't know they knew. I look up, he looks away. He looks up. Our eyes meet. We both scurry back.

He swallows. "So. Any plans for today?"

I want to say: *I plan to spend the rest of my day going over last night with a fine-tooth comb, analyzing every word you said, remembering every touch, swooning over every kiss, until I've melted into a pile of Prudence-shaped goo.*

What I actually say is "Go home and take a shower, then probably try to get a few hours of sleep."

"Good plan," he replies, even though he's looking at me like he knows the truth. I don't want to sleep. I never want to sleep again. What if sleep washes away every blissful thing that's happened between us?

Once we've put the blankets away, we head out to the yard to see how the animals fared last night. It's still early enough that none of the volunteers have started to arrive for their shifts, so it's just us and Rosa. She's already hard at work, using a push broom to shove puddles of water into the in-ground pools.

The yard is a mess, especially where the concrete flooded. The seals could be swimming laps in all this water, if it wasn't for the debris floating around. Sticks and tree branches and leaves and palm fronds, and even some trash from one of the garbage cans that got blown over by the wind. One section of the chain-link fence has been squashed by a particularly huge branch.

"This will take a few days to clean up," says Rosa, pausing to lean against the broom handle. "And that fence . . . hopefully insurance will pay to have it fixed."

"Is there any other damage?" asks Quint.

"Not that I've found so far. And no one seems hurt, which is the most important thing." She turns to us, taking us in with a worried-mom look. "You're both exhausted. I'll call around to some of the volunteers and see who can come in today. You should go home, get some rest."

"I'm fine," says Quint, flopping his arms as if the ability to move his limbs proved his ability to work.

"Me too." I copy the movement.

Rosa is unimpressed. "Go home," she says sternly. Then her eyes drop down to our legs. "Put on some pants, first."

We both start to giggle. It's almost uncontrollable. Rosa rolls her eyes and waves us away.

We're just turning to head back inside when Quint grabs my hand. "Look."

I follow his look. A group of sea lions have discovered a new game— paddling full-speed toward an enormous puddle, sliding across it on their bellies, and landing in their pool with a massive splash. They've created their own Slip 'n Slide.

We all start to laugh. The game is so *human* it catches me off-guard.

"Well," says Quint, "at least they're having a good time. I guess the storm was good for something."

I glance his way, startled to find him grinning at me. My stomach flutters.

"I guess it was," I say, squeezing his hand.

We stumble back to the laundry room. Our pants are still a little damp, but I figure I can suffer for one bike ride. Quint takes his clothes to the bathroom to change.

The sun has peeked over the horizon by the time I'm dressed and strapping on my bike helmet. I linger in the parking lot. I can't leave without saying goodbye. Without, perhaps, just *one* more kiss before I go.

A second later, Quint comes charging out, carrying my backpack. "You almost forgot this."

My eyes widen as I remember that it has not only my Very Important Gala notebook . . . but also my parents' money from the pawnshop. I'm momentarily ashamed to have been so careless with it, but with everything that's happened, I'm not sure I'm entirely to blame.

"Thanks," I say, taking the bag and threading my arms through the straps.

Our bikes are wet and splattered with mud, having been dropped unceremoniously the night before. Quint uses the hem of his shirt to dry off my bike seat, despite my wet pants.

"What a gentleman," I say.

Grinning, he hands the bike to me. I put up the kickstand. He picks up his bike and does the same.

We're going opposite directions, which means . . . neither of us moves.

"So," Quint says.

"So."

The moment stretches out between us, each smiling our goofy, sleepy-eyed grin.

My fingers tighten around the handlebars. "Thanks for the movie. And . . . everything else."

His smile widens at the mention of *everything else*. "We should do it again sometime."

I hum thoughtfully. "We should get stuck at an animal rescue center in the middle of the year's worst storm with no food and no power?"

"Exactly."

I lean toward him. "I'll be there."

His hand scoops the hair from the back of my neck as he kisses me. For a few brief seconds, we are nothing but lips and fingers and heartbeats—

And then I lose my balance. My bike tips over, crashing against Quint's. I nearly go down with it, but he catches me by the shoulders. We haven't even caught our breath before we're laughing.

"Okay, we should probably go," he says. He gives me one more kiss, quick, chaste, but promising more to come. Soon. I hope. Then he stands me back up and swings one leg over his bike before he can change his mind.

I do the same. "See you tomorrow?"

"Tomorrow."

I wink at him. "Sweet dreams."

Then I kick off and start pedaling, my heart soaring in my chest, my brain addled and fogged, but my whole body humming with energy. I'm delirious, but happy. I laugh all the way home.

FORTY-ONE

I fall asleep immediately, barely taking the time to greet my family and throw my damp, gross clothes into the laundry and put on some pajamas, before collapsing onto my bed. I wake up to Jude shaking my shoulder.

"Pru, Mom says you should get up."

I groan and toss my arm over my eyes. "What for?"

"Because if you keep sleeping, you'll never go to bed tonight, and your sleep schedule will be screwed up for all eternity."

I wrinkle my nose.

"Or at least, like, a week. Come on, you've been napping for four hours."

"Still sleepy."

"You'll survive. Want some lunch?"

Ooooh, lunch. My stomach rumbles, answering for me.

Jude nods knowingly. "I'll set out some sandwich stuff." He starts to walk backward toward the door, before giving me the I'm-watching-you gesture, fingers to his eyes, then back at me. "Don't go back to sleep."

"I won't. I'm up. I'm getting up. Fine."

It still takes me a few minutes to pull myself from the cozy blankets. I grab my phone, which I dropped on my desk when I got home, but the battery is still dead. Oops. I plug it in, and check my watch. It's almost noon.

I stretch my back. Rub my eyes. Throw my bathrobe on over my pajamas.

I'm tying the robe's belt when last night crashes into me with the force of a bulldozer.

Quint.

And Quint's kisses.

And Quint's words.

And Quint's smiles.

And Quint's arms.

And . . . am I dating Quint Erickson?

We didn't talk about *dating* or *boyfriend-girlfriend* or anything official like that. But how could we not be official? We even had our first date. Because, in hindsight, *Jaws* was definitely a date.

I wonder what he's doing right now. Sleeping? Dreaming? About me and my red lipstick? My heart jolts to think of it.

I can't wait to see him again. I want to call him, but we've never exchanged numbers, and I'm not about to call the center and ask Rosa for it.

We're both working tomorrow. I'll have to suffer until then.

By the time I get downstairs, Jude has set out an array of deli meats and condiments. He even took the time to slice a tomato *and* an avocado, because he is an awesome human being.

"Thanks," I say, squirting mustard onto a slice of bread. "I barely ate anything yesterday."

Ellie runs in from the living room. "Pru's awake!" she says, grabbing me and pressing her face into my hip. "You were gone all night! And there was so much rain!"

"I know," I say, rubbing the top of her head. "Was that the biggest storm you ever saw, or what?"

She looks up at me with huge eyes. "I thought you were going to drown!"

"Nope. I didn't drown. Besides, I know how to swim."

"Not very good."

"Hey! How do you know that?" I unwind her arms from my waist. "Are you hungry?"

"No." She bounces on her toes. "Will you play with me?"

I cringe. "Not right now, okay? I need to eat something."

She pouts in disappointment.

"Let's play checkers after lunch," says Jude. "Go get the game set up."

She nods excitedly and dashes off.

Jude finishes making up his own sandwich and sits down at the table. "How was it spending the night at the center? Are there even beds there?"

"No, we just spread out a bunch of blankets on the floor."

"We?"

I glance up at him. Did he think I was there alone all night? Did my parents?

"Uh. Quint was there, too."

One eyebrow shoots up, amused. "Anyone else?"

I gulp and focus on alternating slices of turkey and ham, making sure they overlap in perfect increments. In other words—doing my best to avoid Jude's gaze. "Sure. The animals were all there, too. Some of them were pretty freaked out by the storm. We even lost power."

"Wow. Sounds traumatic."

Traumatic isn't the word I would use to describe it. Should I tell Jude what happened? I mean, normally I tell him everything, but . . . there's never really been *boy* stuff to talk about before, and suddenly I feel weird about it. He might be one of my best friends, but he's still my brother. Plus, he knows Quint. He witnessed our mutual dislike of each other firsthand. How am I supposed to explain how quickly and completely things have changed?

"It was an adventure," I say.

I'm saved from giving further details when Mom comes into the kitchen with a cardboard box tucked against her hip. "You kids don't have any interest in golf, do you?"

We both look at her.

"Golf?" I say, not sure I heard correctly.

Jude, equally dumbfounded, adds, "As in, the sport?"

"I'll take that as a no. We have those old golf clubs that were your grandfather's, but . . . I think I'm going to get rid of them. Your dad and I are trying to clean house a little bit, so if you guys have anything else you're not using anymore . . ." She pats the side of the box, smiles at us, then walks back out.

I gulp, remembering the receipt for our belongings at the pawnshop. "I'll be right back," I tell Jude, abandoning my half-finished sandwich on the counter.

The envelope of money is still tucked into my backpack, which I'd haphazardly thrown onto the entryway bench when I came. Seeing it reminds me of my visit to the pawnshop and everything that preceded it. The lost earring, the beachcomber, the missing money from the donation jar.

I clutch the envelope in both hands and go in search of Mom. She's in the garage, using a damp towel to dust off a bag of old golf clubs.

"Hey, Mom? This is yours."

She glances up, surprised. "What is it?" she asks, taking the envelope. Her eyes widen when she sees the money inside.

"I stopped by the pawnshop yesterday morning, looking for something, for a friend . . . but Clark thought I'd come in to pick up your money. So he gave me this. There's the receipt, too, so you know what sold and for how much . . ." I hesitate, before adding, "The silverware hasn't sold yet, but someone did buy the keyboard."

She closes the envelope and looks at me, concerned for a moment, before her face softens. "It's all just old stuff that we're not using. Stuff we don't need anymore. You know that, right?"

"Yeah. I know." I tighten the belt on my robe. "But we also need the money, don't we?"

She sighs and drapes the rag over one of the clubs. "We're not desperate, if that's what you're wondering. Business has started to pick up at the store, thank heavens for tourist season. We can pay our bills. We're fine."

"But?"

She presses her lips together. "You know, things sure do get harder to hide from you kids when you guys get older."

"Mom."

She nods, wiping her palms on her jeans. "Lucy wants to sign up for soccer and basketball again this year, but she'll need new jerseys, new shoes. Penny's bike isn't going to last another summer, and of course, there are still music lessons to consider. And Ellie's preschool teachers mentioned a science-based summer camp coming up next month that she's of course dying to do . . ." She looks away. "Your dad and I have always wanted to give you kids every opportunity, every experience we could. But life is expensive. Families are expensive. And as much as we love the store . . . it is never going to make us rich."

I bite my lower lip. I know I shouldn't ask, but . . . "Mom. Do you ever wish . . ." I can't bring myself to say it.

"What?" she asks. "That we didn't have you kids?"

"That you didn't have so many of us."

She laughs. "Easy for the oldest to say, isn't it?" She tucks the envelope of money into her back pocket, then takes my face into her hands. "Never, Prudence. You and Jude and your sisters bring us more joy than any amount of money ever could. And . . ." She releases me and glances at the golf clubs. "If I can trade some of our old junk in order to make your childhoods a little brighter, I will in a heartbeat. This is just stuff. But you only get to live your life one time."

She cocks her head, studying me as if to see if I believe her.

And I think I might.

"I'll go through my room today," I tell her. "I'm sure I have some things I can contribute to the cause."

"Only if you want to," she says. "I don't expect you to start giving up all your worldly possessions."

"I do want to. You're right. It's just stuff." I hesitate, considering. "Also, Mom? I should tell you. I'm planning this gala for the center. Kind of a fancy shindig thing, to raise money. And I've been asking local businesses if they can contribute gift baskets to the silent auction. I'd love to have something from Ventures Vinyl, especially because our theme is Yellow Submarine. But I get it if you guys can't contribute anything."

Mom's grin spreads across her face. "Listen to you. I always knew you were going to be my little entrepreneur."

I roll my eyes. "Mom."

"I can't help it, honey. Watching you kids grow up . . ." She sighs. "Well, maybe you'll understand someday. Anyway. I don't know about a gift basket. I'll have to discuss it with your father. Could be a good opportunity to let more people know about the store. But you're right. Money is tight, and I don't know if we're in a great position to be making charitable contributions."

"I know. Totally no pressure. *But* . . ." I lift my finger. "While we're on the topic, I've actually had some ideas about the store, and Ari has, too. Some things we can do to drum up new business or at least make the store feel more current. Maybe someday we could sit down and talk about it?"

She fixes me with a thoughtful look, the corners of her lips barely lifted. "I think your dad and I would like that very much."

I nod. "I'll start putting together a business proposal."

She laughs and goes back to cleaning the golf clubs. "You do that."

My eye catches on a box on a shelf, where Grandma's old china tea set is settled into a bed of packing peanuts. "Are you getting rid of those teacups?"

Mom follows my look. "I was thinking about it."

"Okay . . . but not today." I grab the box. Mom doesn't stop me and doesn't ask what I'm doing as I carry it into the house.

Eleanor is in the living room, making a tower of alternating red and black checker chips.

"Hey, Ellie. While Jude and I are eating our lunch . . . do you want to come play tea party with us?"

The smile she gives me is all the reward I need.

FORTY-TWO

I'm twenty minutes early the next day, in part because my sleep schedule is indeed completely wonky. After yesterday's long nap and an early bedtime, I woke up at four this morning, which is ridiculously early, even for me.

No matter. I had plenty of pleasant memories to keep my mind occupied before I managed to pull myself out of bed. I used my morning hours semi-productively . . . when I wasn't caught up in unhelpful fantasies, at least. I'm giddy as I swing my bike into the parking lot, eager to tell Quint and Rosa and the other volunteers about my new ideas for the gala.

That—and I can't wait to see Quint again. It's been an entire day, and there's a small part of me that thinks it might have been a fluke. Maybe we were just caught up in the romance of the storm. Maybe he'll take one look at me this morning and regret everything.

But every time these doubts start to creep in, I think about his words, right after he kissed me the first time. *I've wanted to do that for a while.*

It wasn't a fluke. It wasn't a mistake. And I cannot go another minute without seeing him and kissing him and confirming that it was real. That he still likes me as much as I like him.

There's only one car in the parking lot—Rosa's, I think. None of the other volunteers have arrived yet. I tear off my helmet and practically skip to the door.

No one is in the lobby, so I make a quick pass around the yard and lower levels. No one in the kitchen, or the laundry room, or with any of the animals. I do stop to greet Lennon and Luna, but I can tell that they're only interested in me because it's almost breakfast time.

"I'll be back soon," I whisper. "First, I need to see Quint before I explode." I squeal in the same way Penny squeals whenever she sees a photo of Sadashiv on one of those celebrity magazines they keep at the checkout line at the grocery store. I feel faintly embarrassed for myself, but it doesn't keep me from practically jogging back down the hall.

"Hello? Anyone here?" I call, even as I'm ascending the steps to the second floor.

I'm passing the break room when Rosa sticks her head out of her office and blinks at me. She looks bewildered. "Prudence."

"Hi!" I beam. "I know, I'm early. Is Quint here yet?"

She doesn't speak for a minute. Doesn't move. Then she clears her throat and glances over her shoulder, back into her office. "Yes," she says slowly. Her jaw is set when she faces me again. "Actually, I'm glad you're here, before the others. Can I . . . can we talk to you?"

"Of course! I want to talk to you, too." I clap my hands excitedly. "I secured us a venue for the gala! I mean—it was Quint's idea, so I can't take all the credit, but it's perfect!" I follow Rosa into her office.

And there's Quint, his hands gripping the edge of a low bookshelf, his ankles crossed in front of him.

My heart leaps at the sight of him.

His head is lowered slightly as his eyes dart toward me, and there's a second—just a second—when I remember his story about his eyebrows, and how he was afraid they made him look mean, and I can kind of understand why he would have thought that. But the moment passes, and no, he doesn't look mean. He looks *nervous*.

He probably hasn't told his mom about us yet.

I can't be hurt. I haven't told anyone, either, not even Jude or Ari.

I smile at him.

He looks away.

Ooooo-kay. Not quite the reception I've been dreaming about all morning, but . . . maybe his mom doesn't want him dating anyone yet? Not that we're dating. Officially. Or anything. But it *has* to be heading in that direction. You don't kiss someone for seven straight hours without wanting it to become a regular thing.

At least, I know I want it to become a regular thing.

"So!" I chirp, trying to dispel the weird tension in the air. "I called the Offshore Theater yesterday and told them all about the center and what we're planning for the gala, and they are totally on board. They'll let us use it free of charge, as long as we don't do it on a weekend, so I went ahead and booked it for the eighteenth, which is a Tuesday. It's going to be perfect. They have a kitchen for the caterers to use, plenty of tables and chairs we can set out, and just like you thought, they should have everything we need for the AV equipment, too. The manager I spoke with seemed really excited to be a part of the event. I told them we're hoping it will become an annual thing, and . . ." I swallow. Rosa is rubbing the back of her neck, looking concerned. "They love the 'Yellow Submarine' theme. They do a Beatles movie marathon every couple of years, so they said they can put out some of the posters from that." Quint's jaw twitches. His eyes are still glued to the floor. My chest feels like it's starting to cave in, and the only way to prevent it is to keep talking, so I do. "Plus they're also going to supply a date-night-themed gift basket for the auction, complete with movie tickets and a free bucket of popcorn! Isn't that . . . so . . . generous?"

My shoulders fall. I can't keep going. No amount of enthusiasm could hide the fact that I feel like I'm talking to a brick wall. Two brick walls. Why isn't Quint looking at me? Why isn't Rosa smiling and saying how great this is?

"Okay, *what?*" I say. "Is it one of the animals? Is Lennon okay? Luna?"

"The animals are fine," says Rosa. She glances at Quint, her brow furrowed. His knuckles whiten where he's gripping the bookshelf.

"Then what's going on? Is the insurance not going to cover the damages from the storm?"

"No, Prudence . . ."

"Then why do you both look so miserable?"

Rosa inhales deeply. She looks again at Quint, and I think she's maybe waiting to see if he wants to say something, but his mouth is shut so tight a muscle has started to twitch in his cheek. "Prudence," Rosa says again, clasping her hands together in front of her. "Is there, perhaps, something you'd like to tell us?"

I stare at her. Then my attention darts to Quint. He shifts his shoulders, hunching forward, and still does not look up. I look back at Rosa again.

"Other than how the gala is really coming together?"

Quint makes a disgusted sound in his throat—the first thing he's almost said since I got here. I feel my hackles rise. I've heard that sound. I used to hear it all the time.

Rosa massages her brow. "I think you know that isn't what I'm referring to."

"I have no idea what you're referring to. Quint, what is going on?"

He releases the bookshelf, but only so he can cross his arms over his chest. At least he manages to look me in the eye, and I take back what I thought before. He *does* look mean.

I can feel panic starting to claw at my throat. Have I just stumbled into some alternate universe where this summer never happened and Quint still despises me? What did he say the other night—that he used to think I was a terrible person? I'd given him a pass on that comment, because he'd made it quite clear that he no longer felt that way. And I couldn't entirely blame him, either, after how awful I'd been toward him all year.

But that was then. So why is he looking at me like this *now*?

"A woman came to the center yesterday," says Rosa. "She had an interesting story to tell, involving a lost earring and a large cash donation made during the beach cleanup." She pauses, waiting to see my reaction. I don't know what she thinks she sees on my face, but Rosa looks disappointed. "I can see that I don't need to tell you the whole story. The short of it is, she felt bad about selling off this earring that didn't belong to her—though of course she had no way of knowing at the time who it did belong to. She came here trying to make amends. To get back the money she donated so she could repurchase the earring and give it back to its rightful owner. But as you and I both know, that money isn't here. So, tell me, Prudence . . . where could twelve hundred dollars have disappeared to?"

And there it is. That's what this is about.

They think I stole it.

"I don't know." My voice is strained, and somehow I feel like I've already incriminated myself. Because I did know about the earring and the money. I knew there was money missing.

"This is your opportunity to tell us the truth," says Rosa. I can tell she's trying to be gentle about this, but at the same time, there's anger simmering under her calm exterior. "The woman said she talked to you, so I believe you were the only person who knew there was such a large donation made that day."

I shake my head. "She did tell me about the money, but I don't know what happened to it. I didn't take it."

"I saw you!" Quint snaps. His voice is so loud, so harsh, I jump from the sound of it. Unlike his mom, he's making no show of trying to disguise his fury. "I saw you in Shauna's office, pawing through that jar! And all that money you had in your backpack! You're honestly going to try to say it wasn't you?"

"It wasn't!" I'm yelling now, too. Desperation hums through my veins. He can't think I did this—this thing I absolutely did not do!

Although, whispers an irritating little voice. *Although, I had* intended *to take it that day* . . .

I swallow. That isn't the point. I'm innocent.

Quint pushes himself away from the bookshelf and takes a couple steps toward me, his arms flailing aggressively as he talks. "You stood right in front of me, a wad of cash in your hand, and lied to my face. How could you do this?"

"I didn't do anything! I . . . yes, I knew about the donation, and I wanted to count it and see how much the total was, but when I did, there wasn't nearly as much there. Only . . . three hundred and whatever. Whatever Shauna told us the next day."

Quint's glare turns sharp. His words are sharper. "You told me you didn't have time to count it."

My stomach twists. "I . . ."

He lifts one eyebrow, waiting. But I can't look at him, not when he's looking at me like that. I close my eyes. "I did count it. But I was . . . the money wasn't there. The twelve hundred dollars was already gone. I didn't take it."

"Right," says Quint. "And what else have you been lying about?"

"Nothing!" I open my eyes, determined to face him, to make him see he has this all wrong.

"What about going through our mail? What have you been looking for, exactly? More donations? More money? More things you can take without anyone realizing it?"

"Stop yelling at me!"

"Stop lying to me!"

"Quint, that's enough," says Rosa, putting a hand on his shoulder.

He shakes her off and takes a step back away from me until he's half-sitting against Rosa's desk, arms tightly crossed again. "I get that your family is having money problems. I know you want to help your parents. But . . . really, Prudence? Stealing from an animal rescue shelter? And from my mom, from *me*?"

The first tears spill out, sliding down my cheeks. I hastily brush them away, but they keep coming. "I didn't. Take. That. Money."

"Then who did?" he asks.

"I don't know! Maybe nobody. Maybe it got lost."

He snorts, the sound so derisive and disbelieving it makes me wants to throttle him. "Please. You had the opportunity, you had a motive. It's crime scene 101."

I glower. "Innocent until proven guilty. It's justice 101."

He rolls his eyes. "You could just admit it, you know. Give the money back?"

"I didn't do it!" I yell, tossing my hands toward the ceiling.

His nostrils flare and I see a tiny crack in his armor. A doubt, perhaps. A desire to believe me, if nothing else.

Then he looks away, and his face hardens again. "You are a lot of things, but I never thought you'd stoop as low as this."

"Oh?" I say, a dare in my tone. "And what things am I, exactly?"

It's a mistake, this question. I know he will rise to the bait, and I know I will never be able to unhear whatever comes out of his mouth, and I know I will regret for the rest of my life that I asked for it.

But I don't back down. Maybe I want him to hurt me. Maybe, on some level, it will be easier to believe we never would have worked out anyway.

He holds my gaze, but I see him hesitate. The goodness in him, warring with his anger. I take a step forward, goading him on. I don't even care that his mom is here. Let her hear it all—the worst of him. The worst of me. What does it matter?

"Go on," I say through my teeth. "Not two days ago, I was pretty and confident and fun. But what do you really think?"

"Well, you're clearly a liar," he says, his eyes flaring. "You're self-absorbed. Critical. Judgmental. A hypocrite. Selfish. And honestly, trusting you was the biggest mistake I've ever made in my life."

"*Quint,*" says Rosa. A warning, but too late.

He's done.

We're done.

Hurt makes my insides boil. I want to scream at her, at both of them. I want karma to reel up from the ethers of the universe and punish him for daring to judge me like this.

I squeeze both fists tight. As tight as I can. It's never worked on Quint before. This horrible, backstabbing power has always failed me when I tried to do something to Quint. But this time, he's being downright cruel.

This time, he's breaking my heart.

This time, he actually deserves it.

My fingernails dig into my palms.

Tears blur my eyes.

To my surprise, Quint winces in sudden pain. He turns his face away from me, his jaw clenched, his face contorted. A hand comes briefly to his chest, like something has hurt him there, but he just as quickly drops it. He does not meet my eye again.

And maybe it's trite, and maybe it's naive, but I hope—oh, I hope with all my being that his heart might just have shattered, too.

"Prudence," says Rosa, stepping between us, maybe afraid that I'm about to start throwing things. "You should go."

My breath catches. That's it. I'm being fired. I don't even get paid, and somehow, I'm being fired.

Jaw tight, I reach into my bag and pull out the notebooks and folders I'd been keeping for the gala. I throw them on Rosa's desk and turn on my heels.

I leave, practically running down the stairs and through the small lobby.

I crash into a woman on the doorstep. Shauna startles and catches me. "Whoa, calm down there, sweetie pie. Are you all right?"

I swipe the tears from my eyes. I can't look at her. I just want to get away.

Then my attention catches on her necklace, a sparkling pendant worn against her chest.

My breath snags.

It's Maya's earring.

Shauna cranes her head, worry etched across her elderly face. "Prudence?"

Shaking my head, I back away from her. Stumble off the stoop and grab my bike. I swing my leg over the seat and pedal away as fast as I can, trying to drown out the memory of Quint's harsh words.

I'm a good person.

Selfish. Critical.

I am a good person.

Judgmental. Self-absorbed.

I. Am. A. Good. Person.

A liar. A hypocrite. A mistake.

My vision is blurred. I can't keep going. I pull over onto the sidewalk and drop my bike against a palm tree before collapsing beside it. The sobs overtake me.

"I'm a good person," I cry to myself, to no one. Maybe to the universe, if it's listening.

But a question digs at me. Quint's words, barbed and hateful. His accusations. My own insecurities.

I believe I'm a good person.

But what if I'm not?

FORTY-THREE

You're donating a basket," I say, my jaw unhinged. "You've got to be kidding me."

My dad gives me a sympathetic look, even as he's tucking a gift certificate for Ventures Vinyl into an envelope. "I understand that things didn't end well between you and the animal rescue, but that's hardly the animals' fault."

"They accused me of stealing!"

He tucks the card into the basket, along with a John Lennon bobblehead doll and a guitar-shaped Christmas ornament, among the other musical tchotchkes. "Okay. You tell me. In all honesty. Are they doing good work there? Are they deserving of people's donations or not?"

I press my lips together. It feels like a betrayal. My own parents—who can barely support themselves—opting to donate a gift basket to the gala's auction? It's bad enough they put one of the posters in the store window. That they have flyers promoting the gala next to the cash register. Whose side are they on, anyway?

But I can't tell him that the center doesn't need the money or that they won't do something worthwhile with their donations. I think of Lennon, *my* sea lion, that I haven't seen for almost three weeks, and that I hope with my whole heart is doing well, and I know Dad is right. Just because Rosa and Quint accused me of stealing money doesn't mean the animals should be punished. They've suffered enough.

I groan. "Fine. Whatever. Do what you want."

"I usually do." Dad hums along to the record playing over the store speakers as he puts the finishing touches on the basket. "I'm going to run home in a bit, grab some lunch. You need anything?"

"No. I'm fine."

Fine, fine, fine. I'm always fine these days.

Grumbling, I stomp back behind the counter. Jude is standing in front of a box of records that were brought in yesterday. Dad has started letting him price the new stock, teaching him how to evaluate the condition and look up the market value. He's holding a Motown record in his hands, but he's watching me, concerned.

He's been concerned ever since the Incident. He knows, more than anyone, how crushed I was. I still haven't told anyone about me and Quint—what would be the point? But while my parents think I'm upset over being wrongly accused of something I didn't do and then fired for it, Jude can tell there's more to the story. I've walked in on him and Ari in the store's back room a couple of times, talking in worried, hushed tones, and I know they were talking about me. I've done my best to ignore them.

At least they believed me when I told them I didn't steal the money. Ari perhaps said it best—"You may be ambitious, Pru, but you're not steal-money-from-a-struggling-nonprofit type of ambitious. Anyone can see that."

Her words made me feel a tiny bit better. But it also made me wonder. If anyone could see that, then why couldn't Quint?

Quint, who had been there the whole time. The beach festival, the cleanup party, the gala planning, the rescue center the night of that storm . . . He, more than anyone, should have seen how hard I was working to help those animals. He, of all people, should have known that I didn't steal that money. That I wouldn't.

But he hadn't stood up for me. He hadn't believed me. And not only that— he'd been mean, in the most ruthless way.

My eyes still sting when I remember the things he said. The words were intended to cut deep, and they did.

In less than two days, I'd experienced the best and worst moments of my life. Their memories are intertwined so tight I have trouble remembering one without the other.

"Want to do the stickers?" Jude asks, holding up the label maker.

"Nope." I sit on the stool behind the cash machine. It's been slow, even for a Tuesday, so I'm not too worried that a customer is going to ask me to ring up their purchase. Dad keeps trying to train me to work the register, but I'm not interested. I'm counting down the days until summer ends, when I can be free of the store. When I can immerse myself in homework and college planning and as many extra-credit assignments as I can sink my teeth into. I will distract myself like my life depends on it.

Until then—it's just day after tedious day.

Dad gives Jude a hundred reminders about running the store before he leaves, even though he's only going to be gone for half an hour. I ignore them both and boot up the laptop. The report is open, waiting for me. I read over the last sentence I wrote. Or tried to write.

Ecotourism can benefit many ocean habitats by

By . . . what? My brain is mush, as it has been every time I've tried to work on this awful paper. The thought of researching, taking notes, drawing conclusions, and implementing my findings makes me dizzy. It all feels like an insurmountable amount of work. The deadline for resubmitting our projects is only a few days away, but I've made painfully little progress. Every time I get stuck, I imagine talking to Quint about it and how we would come up with some brilliant solution together, and it would be easy and fun and—

And then I catch myself mid-daydream and plummet back to earth.

I don't even know why I'm wasting my time. Without Quint's participation, Mr. Chavez probably won't even accept the revised report.

The worst part is I don't even know if I care. About biology. About this report. About my grades. Any of it.

I procrastinate—again—by grabbing my phone and checking the rescue center's Facebook page. It's a form of self-torture I've become adept at lately. Quint has been doing a great job of keeping it updated and incorporating a lot of the strategies we talked about. Videos showing the sea lions at play. Photos of former patients, with captions describing their unique personalities and interesting stories about them. Interviews with the volunteers explaining why they're passionate about working with sea animals.

Most of the photos on the page are taken by Quint—at least, I assume so—because he's hardly ever in the pictures himself. But every now and then there will be one where I can see him in the background. Hosing down a pool or feeding a bucket of fish to the seals, and the yearning that tugs at me upon seeing these grainy candid shots is overwhelming.

I know I should stop looking, but I can't. No matter how much it hurts.

And, oh, it does hurt.

And then the hurt makes me angry.

And the anger makes me sad.

Wash. Rinse. Repeat.

How can the universe allow this? How can I sit here, betrayed and devastated, while Quint goes on with life as usual? Karma has abandoned me. There is no justice. There is no universal reprieve.

An update about Luna and Lennon catches my eye. I smile to see a short video of the two of them passing a ball back and forth with their noses. The caption spells Lennon's name "Lenin," like the dictator, which is how I know Quint wrote it. My heart twists.

Update: Lenin and Luna have been offered a permanent home at a respected zoo! We're excited that they will be placed together, and be able to enjoy many more years of friendship (or something more?). We will post more info as their transfer date and details are confirmed.

I don't know if I'm happy or sad at the news. What if I never see Lennon again?

The bell jingles on the front door.

"Hey, Ari," says Jude.

"Hey, Jude. Pru."

I turn off my phone and look up to see Ari strolling through the aisles, her fingers skimming over the tops of the records in their bins. "What are you doing here?" I ask. "You're off today."

"Yeah, but I thought I'd check on you. See if you needed some moral support."

Ah—because the gala is tonight. I'm doing my best to forget, though the universe keeps throwing it back in my face.

I was shocked at first to learn that they planned to continue with the gala at all. How could they do it without me? It was my idea. These were my plans. It was practically *my* gala!

But they are continuing with it, and—to my endless annoyance—they seem to be doing a pretty good job of promoting it, too. I see the posters everywhere I go, not just in our own store window, but plastered all over town. And, *gah,* I hate to admit it, but they're great posters, with artwork and typography reminiscent of the Beatles' *Yellow Submarine* movie poster, and not a single word misspelled.

They've been talking to the media, too. Not just the *Chronicle,* but also local magazines and radio stations. Rosa even appeared on a feel-good regional lifestyle TV show, promoting the center and their mission.

A vengeful part of me wants to see them fail. I want the gala to be a disaster. I want Quint to come crawling back, begging me for help.

But from what I can tell, that's never going to happen. Maybe I'm not as irreplaceable as I thought.

"So," says Ari, drumming her hands on the counter. "It's Tuesday. Which means . . . who's up for some tacos and karaoke?"

Jude makes a sound like he's *very interested,* but I know he's just doing it to encourage me. Another attempt to pull me out of my slump.

"Nice try," I say, "but there is no karaoke tonight."

Ari frowns. "What do you mean? Carlos isn't doing it anymore?"

"No, he is. But tonight, Trish Roxby will be setting up her karaoke equipment at the Offshore Theater, as the entertainment at the first annual rescue center gala." I add, grumbling, "I saw it on their Facebook page."

"Karaoke? At a gala?" says Jude. He shakes his head. "That'll be a complete bust."

I force myself to smile at him, because I can tell he's trying. "Thanks, Jude. But I actually think it's kind of genius."

He knocks his fist against the counter. "I know. I do, too, but I was hoping I wouldn't have to admit it. Karaoke will be so much better than some boring symphony."

I wince, but I don't think Jude notices. I have a feeling karaoke was Quint's idea. And it is a good idea. It'll easily take what could be a stuffy, tedious event, and make it fun, memorable, unique.

I hate that he thought of it and I didn't.

I hate that I'm not going.

Jude clears his throat. "We could play D and D? I could call the gang over, make some popcorn, finally get you two set up with your own characters . . ."

Ari and I exchange looks.

"Just an idea," says Jude. "I don't want you to mope around all evening, Pru."

"I do not mope."

Ari's lips twist to one side.

"The last few weeks notwithstanding."

"And justifiably so," says Ari. "But not tonight. Let's go see a movie—oh. Never mind."

The Offshore Theater is the only movie theater in town, and Ari hates driving to the big cinema off the interstate. Mostly because she hates driving anywhere outside Fortuna Beach.

"How about we go toilet paper the rescue center while they're all at the party?" suggests Jude.

A smile twitches at the corners of my lips. "Thanks, guys. I appreciate you trying to cheer me up. But I don't want to go to the center, and I don't want to be anywhere near Main Street tonight."

"So you're just going to wallow in self-pity instead?" asks Ari. "Because I simply am not going to allow that. I know! How about a chick-flick marathon?"

Jude and I both groan.

Normally, I wouldn't be opposed to this suggestion, but right now, the idea of watching beautiful people fall deeply in love makes me want to gag.

"Oh, come *on*. It'll help take your mind off . . . things."

I'm saved from having to respond by the little bell jingling again.

Jude puts on his customer-service face. "Welcome to Ventures Vi—oh."

I glance toward the door, and can't keep in the groan that escapes me. I knew this day was going to get worse.

FORTY-FOUR

Morgan casts a curious look over the racks of albums as she makes her way to the counter. Without the cast, without the crutches.

Then she sees me and freezes.

Her eyes narrow.

My jaw tightens.

Ari shifts uncomfortably to the side so she isn't standing in the icy gale between us.

"Er . . . can I help you?" says Jude.

Inhaling sharply, Morgan turns her attention to him. She's wearing the yellow volunteer shirt from the center, and I can't help but feel like she's mocking me with it.

"I'm here to pick up a gift basket," she says.

"Right. It's over here." Jude walks around the counter to where Dad left the basket. Morgan gives it a once-over, then nods and picks it up. "Thank you for your generosity." Then her gaze shifts back to me. "But then, I guess you do owe us."

My mouth dries. I'd been hoping that maybe Quint and Rosa wouldn't spread gossip about me and the missing money, but clearly that was too much to ask.

"Excuse *you,*" says Ari. "Prudence worked her butt off trying to help that center! You all owe *her.*"

Morgan scoffs. "Yeah. Sure. Just, a piece of advice? Keep a close eye on that cash register."

Snarling, Jude grabs the gift basket out of her hands. She makes a startled noise.

"You know what?" he says. "We've changed our mind. Good luck with the auction."

Morgan blinks—at him, at the basket—before shrugging. "Fine. It's not that great of a prize, anyway."

"No, hold on," I say. "Jude, give it back to her. Like Dad said, the animals shouldn't be punished just because I was blamed for something I didn't do."

Morgan faces me, her hands on her hips. "Oh yeah, I heard how you tried to deny it. Nice try, when you were literally caught *holding the money.*"

"I didn't take anything," I say, working hard to keep my tone even. "I don't know what happened to that money, but I don't have it and I never did."

"Uh-huh. You know what's really sad about all this?" Morgan approaches the counter that divides us. "All the things you were doing, they were actually working. If you hadn't stolen that money, the beach cleanup would have been one of the most successful one-day fundraisers we've ever had. You were actually making a difference for those animals. Too bad you had to go all 'selfish human' and ruin it."

I have to bite back my words. I know nothing I can say will convince her of my innocence.

Seeing that I have no response, Morgan snatches the gift basket from Jude and starts to head back to the door.

"Hold on," I call.

She pauses. Sighs. Slowly turns back, scowling.

But I don't care what she thinks. Something she said is resonating with me, reminding me of something Rosa said months ago.

They've had fundraisers, but they're never successful. They never bring in enough money to be worthwhile.

"Why is that?" I say out loud.

Morgan's glare deepens. "What?"

"The center has had fundraisers before. They've been trying to find ways to raise money for years. But . . . I show up, plan one little beach cleanup event, and suddenly it's the most successful one-day fundraiser you've ever had?"

"No, it wasn't," says Morgan, with a harsh laugh. "Because the money mysteriously vanished, remember?"

"That's what I'm saying!" Suddenly jittery, I hop off the stool and come around the counter. "Maybe this has happened before. In fact . . . I bet this has happened a lot. What if every time the center has hosted a fundraiser, some of the money's gone missing? That's why the campaigns are never successful." I press my hands back through my hair. "That's it. That's how I can prove it wasn't me. This has happened before, over and over again . . . long before I ever became a volunteer!"

Morgan looks at me like I've just grown a tail. "Are you really trying to convince me that—"

"I'm not trying to convince you of anything!" I snap. "I know it wasn't me. I figured it got lost or misplaced or maybe that beachcomber made a mistake and didn't donate the money after all. Because what sort of person would steal from an animal rescue?"

Morgan gives me a seething look, but I ignore her.

The question rings in my head, like it should have been ringing all month. The signs. The clues.

Has this happened before?

It doesn't make sense that all their fundraisers have been so disappointing in the past. Clearly, people want to help the center. They care about the work.

But if money was coming in, it was also going out.

Who would do it?

And *why*?

I think about what Quint said. Crime scene 101. Opportunity and motive.

It has to be someone who's been there awhile. Long enough for Rosa to give up on fundraising efforts altogether. Someone who had access to the money they were bringing in.

I don't realize I've started pacing until I stop cold.

"Shauna," I whisper.

Morgan laughs. "Shauna? The sweet little old grandma who volunteers her time to animals in need?"

"She doesn't volunteer. She's a paid employee."

"Oh! Well, then she must be a criminal."

"Look. I don't know if it was her. But I know it wasn't *me*. And she's been there for years! Plus, she does all the bookkeeping, handles all the money. She could easily be skimming some off the top. And—" I gasp. "At the beach. I saw her holding the jar. She was the one who brought it back to the center. She could have taken some out anytime, and no one would ever have known."

Morgan rolls her eyes. "I've heard enough. Guess I can't blame you for trying, but wouldn't it be easier to just confess, rather than trying to stick the blame on someone else? On *Shauna* of all people?"

"And the boots! It wasn't two days after the cleanup that she wore those brand-new boots. Or—brand-new . . . vintage boots. Whatever. Those can't be cheap. And right after I got fired, I saw her with the earring, the one that was lost? And it's a real diamond."

Morgan guffaws. "So now you're going to tell me she stole the earring, too?"

"No! I think she bought it from the pawnshop, and I know it wasn't cheap. I always thought that jewelry she wears was costume jewelry, but if not . . . then how is she paying for it all? Rosa can't be paying her that much."

Morgan shrugs. "Social security? A pension? She retired, like, twenty years ago. She must have done pretty well for herself."

My brow crinkles. Morgan is right. Shauna could have retired wealthy. Maybe working at the center isn't about the money at all, just something to keep her busy, to feel like she's doing something worthwhile.

I swallow, knowing that I could have this all wrong. I could be grasping for anything to help clear my name, and obviously, I have no real evidence that Shauna has done anything. I can't go accusing her without proof.

I know how that feels, and I refuse to do it to someone else.

"What's her last name?" asks Jude.

I turn to him. I'd forgotten he and Ari were there, but they're both staring at me and Morgan like we're on *CSI*, Fortuna Beach edition.

I have no idea what Shauna's last name is, but Morgan says, "Crandon, I think."

Jude types something into his phone.

Morgan crosses her arms, looking from him to me, to Ari.

"Yes!" Jude yelps, startling us. His grin is stretched wide, but as he looks up, he quickly schools it into a disturbed frown. "I mean, actually, this is kind of awful. But——Pru, this should be enough to at least have her looked into."

He hands me his phone. He's found a news article from a Los Angeles newspaper. There's a picture of Shauna at the top, wearing a slick business suit. She's quite a bit younger, with her hair just beginning to gray.

The headline: ORANGE COUNTY NONPROFIT DROPS CHARGES AGAINST BOOKKEEPER ACCUSED OF EMBEZZLING MORE THAN $200,000.

"No way," says Morgan, grabbing the phone from my hand.

"Hey!" I try to grab it back, but she turns her back on me and starts scrolling through the article. I huff and read over her shoulder.

According to the article, Shauna worked at another nonprofit, one that helped provide services to the homeless, for six years before she was suspected of embezzling money in order to make personal purchases, and even to pay her bills. She was fired, but the charges were ultimately dropped.

"Why would they drop the charges?" asks Ari, crowding in beside us.

"It doesn't say." Morgan hands the phone back to me, looking dazed. "Legal battles are expensive and time-consuming. Maybe they just didn't want to be bothered with it."

"Or maybe they didn't have enough evidence?" I suggest.

Morgan shakes her head. "You'd think, once they knew about it, evidence would be pretty easy to find. She was probably using money from the business account to buy things online and write . . . checks . . . for . . ." Her eyes go distant. Her jaw falls. "*No.* The gala donations!"

I pass the phone back to Jude, who is preening like he's just solved the biggest mystery of the year.

"What gala donations?" I ask.

"We set the ticket cost for the gala really low, but when people buy their tickets, they can also make an extra donation, completely optional."

"And?"

"And no one donated extra money. It's been a complete bust. Tons of ticket sales——we might even sell out the event by tonight——but extra donations? Not happening. It's been driving Quint crazy. You should hear him rant about what a terrible idea it was to keep the price low, how much money we've missed out on doing it this way."

"I bet people *are* donating extra!" Ari says, suddenly excited. "But the money is going to *her*."

Morgan nods. "She's the one who set up the online sales. I bet she's having all the bonus donations routed straight to her own account, bypassing the center entirely."

I slap a hand over my mouth, disgusted. "Who would do something like that?"

Morgan gestures at Jude's phone. "Her, evidently. She's done it before." Then a shadow comes over Morgan's face as she looks at me. Not with scorn, but . . . guilt? She curses lowly to herself, shaking her head. "I guess I owe you an apology."

"You're not the one who fired me," I say, grabbing one of the flyers off the counter. I've looked at it a thousand times. The illustrated yellow submarine. The bright retro-style text.

Spend an evening aboard the Yellow Submarine, in support of the Fortuna Beach Sea Animal Rescue Center. Good food, good friends, and good karma!

"Ari, can you cover the rest of my shift?" I fold up the flyer and shove it into my pocket. "I need to get ready for a gala."

FORTY-FIVE

Morgan agrees to meet me outside the theater. She's not dressed up in the traditional sense. While gala guests are passing us by in cocktail dresses and suits, Morgan is wearing sleek black pants and a sweater with a sequined cow on the front. The only indication that she's going to a semiformal event is the swipe of thick, sparkly black eyeliner on her eyes and the way she's braided her hair into an intricate crown that frames her face.

I'm wearing a red-and-white polka dot dress that I wore to an uncle's second wedding last fall, along with a red cardigan and red ballet flats. It was the best I could pull together on short notice, and . . . well, I feel bolstered because it makes my red lipstick pop.

Dream about *this,* Quint Erickson.

Morgan gives me the once-over when I approach, before nodding. I'm not sure what she approves of. Maybe that there isn't a speck of leather to be seen.

"I like your lipstick," she says, before adding, "I hope it wasn't tested on animals."

I laugh, grateful for the icebreaker. "Me too," I say, because I am starting to care about that sort of thing, and I'll be devastated if I have to give up my favorite brand over this new set of principles that have elbowed their way into my life.

"Ready?" Morgan doesn't wait for me to answer, and before I can catch my breath, we're joining the steady stream of smiling, excited guests and making our way into the theater.

"Ticket?" asks a volunteer as we pass through the doors.

"She's with me," says Morgan, drawing the girl's attention to her.

"Oh, hi, Morgan," the girl says. "Volunteers are all meeting in the kitchen to get their assignments." Then she frowns at me, and I can see a flicker of recognition. "Prudence?"

I've seen the girl around the center before, but we've never been formally introduced. It's unnerving that she knows my name and I don't know hers.

Am I infamous now?

Morgan grabs my elbow and pulls me into the lobby without another word.

It looks . . . nice. Really nice, actually. Round tables are draped with white tablecloths and bright yellow table runners. Yellow Submarine bath toys act as centerpieces, along with a framed photograph of one of the animals currently being cared for at the center.

There aren't a lot of decorations, but the theater feels festive. I'd suggested yellow balloons when Quint and I were first starting to plan the event, and had received a decisive no. Evidently, latex balloons are extremely harmful to sea animals, and now I'm certain I'll never be able to enjoy the simple pleasure of a birthday balloon again. But in place of the balloons, yellow paper streamers twirl around the ceiling and hang from doorways. There's also an assortment of cardboard cutouts of sea animals dangling from the overhead beams, and a painted octopus taking up the entire back wall. Each of its arms is holding a sign thanking the event's various sponsors.

And then there are the photographs. Quint's photographs. Professionally framed and matted and set out on easels around the room. I know they're his immediately, except these are not the photographs I've seen. My heart swells to see that Quint didn't take my suggestion after all, not exactly. The raffle prizes aren't pictures of seals being strangled by fishing line and sea lions punctured with dozens of fishhooks.

Instead, they are pictures of the animals after they've been rehabilitated. When they're healthy, splashing and playing in the outdoor pools or being released on the beach, their flippers paddling against the sand as they flop toward the ocean.

My heart twists when I spy one photo of a sea turtle swimming languidly in the open sea.

My sea turtle.

Guests are already clustered around the photos, discussing them, grinning, pointing out various details. The eyes of those animals follow me as I pass through the room.

I spot Trish Roxby adjusting her sound equipment on a small platform, but I avoid making eye contact with her. The last thing I need is to get swept up in small talk about karaoke and head injuries. In fact, I'm pretty much avoiding eye contact with everyone. I recognize most of the guests here. Small-town syndrome and all that.

I've been going over what I'll say to Quint when I see him, but I still don't know if I'm dying to see him or dreading it.

More volunteers are handing out bags of popcorn as guests are ushered into the auditorium for the night's presentation. Even though Morgan is supposed to help work the event, she takes two bags of popcorn and we move along with the crowd.

As soon as I step into the theater, I see him. He's standing onstage in front of the red-velvet curtains that frame the large screen, talking with Rosa, Dr. Jindal . . . and Shauna.

I stop so suddenly someone bumps into me from behind. I hear them apologize, but I can't take my gaze off Quint.

He's wearing dark-washed jeans, a crisp button-up shirt, and a tie.

And goodness gracious, he looks . . .

I don't finish that thought.

Morgan pulls me off to the side so we aren't taking up the aisle. The seats are filling up fast. There are a ton of people here. I realize, a little bewildered, that it actually worked. My idea, all my plans. They *worked*.

A slideshow is playing on the screen, showing photographs of sea animals from when they were first brought into the center, injured and malnourished, to shots of them being fed and bathed or playing together in the pools. There are a lot of images of seals sprawled out leisurely on the concrete, and little sea lion heads popping out of the water. Stacks of sea otters piled on top of one another. Every time one of these images shows up on the screen, the entire audience melts with a unanimous *aww*.

There are advertisements, too, promoting all the businesses that helped make the gala possible, and, occasionally, a slide thanking the volunteers who helped organize the event. Quint is at the top of the list, while my name is nowhere to be seen. It feels like one more betrayal.

I feel eyes on me and shift my attention back to Quint. He's staring at me, his lips parted in surprise.

I lift my chin, refusing to look away. Whether or not he believes it, I deserve to be here every bit as much as he does.

He closes his mouth and I see his jaw tense. A shadow comes over his eyes and he turns away.

My palms have gone sweaty and I try to distract myself by shoveling a few handfuls of popcorn into my mouth, but despite the butter and salt left behind on my fingers, I don't taste a thing. I need a better distraction.

Rosa takes a microphone from one of the theater staff members. They must be getting ready to start.

Quint leaves the stage and walks up the aisle. Toward me. But he makes a point of not looking at me as he passes by.

I swallow. Shauna starts to make her way off the stage, too. My eyes follow her, scowling. On instinct, I squeeze my fist shut.

I wait.

Three seconds. Five.

Nothing happens.

The projector clicks off, leaving the screen black. The houselights dim, leaving the stage illuminated. Rosa walks to the center and begins by thanking everyone for coming. She thanks the sponsors, the donors, the volunteers. Then she begins to talk about the center and their purpose, giving statistics of how many animals they've helped over the years, and how they continue to need the community's support.

I turn and push through the doors, back into the lobby. Rosa's voice fades behind me.

Quint is standing by the concessions stand, helping another volunteer arrange napkins in front of a stack of champagne glasses.

"Quint?"

His spine straightens. He sets down the stack of napkins, exhales loudly, and slowly turns to face me. "If you're not here to return that money, then I hope you at least bothered to purchase a ticket."

I grind my teeth. Is he really going to make a scene here, in front of a stranger? But then I look at the volunteer at the counter and see it isn't a stranger at all. It's Ezra.

He gives me a casual smile and a playful salute. "Looking good, Prudence."

His comment almost doesn't filter past my irritation with Quint, but . . . it is something to be said for Ezra Kent. He's good at diffusing tense emotions. I feel the knots in my shoulder unwind, just a tiny bit. "Quint, I need to talk to you."

"Oh? Why do I get the feeling you didn't come here to apologize?"

My shoulders tighten right back up. "Maybe because I have nothing to apologize for?"

He starts to roll his eyes.

"Listen to her," says a voice from behind me. Morgan appears at my side, her hands on her hips. "There have been developments."

He looks at Morgan, surprised. "What are . . ." He doesn't finish, his attention darting between the two of us, growing more curious by the second. "What's going on?"

I glance around. Volunteers are starting to set the tables for dinner. It's too crowded, and I don't want any eavesdroppers.

"Can we go somewhere else to talk? I think I might know who took that money, but if I'm wrong . . . well. I know how terrible it is to be wrongfully accused of something."

"But we're pretty sure we're right," adds Morgan.

Quint's frown deepens. I can see him contemplating. Not believing me, but . . . *wanting* to.

"Okay," he says finally. "I'll bite."

"Oh, thank god," says Ezra. "The suspense was killing me."

Quint glances at him, then at the array of champagne flutes. "Could you—"

"On it," says Ezra, taking the napkins. "Just bring me juicy details when you're done."

Quint leads me and Morgan through an Employees Only door, past a break room where chefs from Blue's Burgers are piling cheeseburgers on top of large platters—Morgan makes a face, but refrains from saying anything. We end up in the small corridor beside the theater's back exit. A bag of trash is sitting in the corner, waiting to be taken out to the alley. A corkboard holds an array of required government materials, outlining discrimination and sexual harassment policies. The papers look like they haven't been updated in thirty years.

"Well?" says Quint, crossing his arms over his chest. "Go ahead. If you didn't steal that money, who did?"

FORTY-SIX

Quint looks pale as he finishes reading the article that Jude found online. "How could we not have known about this?"

"I'm sure she didn't mention it on her résumé," I say. "If your mom didn't go out of her way to look her up, she wouldn't have known."

"And who's going to bother to cyberstalk a cute little old lady like Shauna?" says Morgan. "Plus, I mean, your mom is great at a lot of things, but she's not really a businesswoman. She wants to save animals, not worry about bookkeeping. She was probably so happy to have someone to hand those responsibilities off to, she might not have bothered to check out her credentials."

Quint nods slowly, like this makes sense to him. He hands Morgan back her phone, then his arms fall to his sides. He looks dazed. "She's been here since I was a little kid. She could have stolen . . ." He doesn't finish. Who knows how much money she could have embezzled in that time period.

"Now, we don't know for sure that she's been stealing money," I say. "We need to find a way to prove it."

"But," adds Morgan, "if she is doing it, there's a good chance she's taking money tonight, from the fundraiser."

Quint blinks at us. "What do you mean?"

"You know how people could opt to give an extra donation when they bought their tickets?" I ask.

"Yeah, but . . . it didn't work. Nobody . . ." His eyes widen and he pushes himself off the wall. "No. She's the one who told us that. She's the one who's been tracking the sales. She's the one who linked the sales to our bank account."

"So she could have linked the donations portion to *her* account," I say.

He makes a frustrated sound, dragging his hands through his hair. "I can't believe this. How could she? We trusted her!"

"This is all still speculation," says Morgan. "But it seems like a good guess."

Quint waves this comment away, and I don't blame him. But still, I want proof. I want my name to be cleared for good.

"Is there any way for us to see how the ticket sales were linked up? If she really is having the money siphoned straight into her personal account . . ."

He nods, rubbing his jaw. "Yeah. Maybe. I think so. Um. Give me a minute." He takes out his phone and walks away, not out of sight, but far enough that I can't tell what he's doing. Morgan and I exchange glances. This corridor shares a wall with the theater, and though the soundproofing is decent, every now and then I can catch bits of Rosa's speech. Not what she's saying, but the passion in her tone.

Quint holds the phone to his ear, making a call. I frown. Is he calling the police?

The crowd in the theater erupts in cheers. Morgan inhales a long breath. "Dinnertime."

I nod. Nothing will be resolved tonight. We should let Rosa enjoy the gala. We don't need to make a scene.

But I want to enjoy the gala, too. I want to be here, to be a part of this. I don't want people to look at me and see the selfish girl that took money from animals in need.

And, if Shauna is guilty, I really don't want her to get away with this for a minute longer.

It seems like Quint's conversation goes on forever. He keeps his voice low. There's a lot of uh-huhing, a lot of okaying, and a lot of numbers, which doesn't make any sense to me.

Finally, he pulls the phone away from his ear and hangs up. And then he just stands there, facing away from us, his shoulder against the wall, his head low.

I gulp and dare to approach him. "Quint? What did you find out?"

He shifts his face farther away from me and raises a fist to his mouth. I hear him release a shaky breath. "Um. Yep." His head is still lowered as he turns and presses his back against the wall. He scratches one of his eyebrows. "That was the third-party company that runs the ticket sales for us. They checked, and, uh, sure enough, there are two bank accounts linked to tonight's sales. The Fortuna Beach Sea Animal Rescue Center . . . and Shauna Crandon."

I close my eyes. Relief hits me hard. Relief and satisfaction. It may not prove that Shauna took the money from the beach cleanup, but as far as I'm concerned, it's close enough.

But all those thoughts are swept away when I open my eyes and find Quint staring at me, his eyes awash with more emotions than I can name. He looks miserable.

"Prudence," he whispers, his voice strained. Which is when I realize that what I'm looking at is remorse. "I—"

"Later," I say, cutting him off. Though I've imagined Quint begging me for forgiveness plenty of times these past few weeks, now that we're here, I don't know what to do with the ragged feelings in my chest. *Self-absorbed. Judgmental. Hypocrite.*

He flinches, and I know my tone was harsh, but so was his when he said those awful things.

"All right!" says Morgan, clapping her hands. "Now what do we do?"

"We have to tell my mom," says Quint. "After that, I don't know. I guess we call the police?"

Silence descends on us as we consider that. How serious that seems. But this *is* serious. I thought twelve hundred dollars missing from a big glass jar was a big deal, but if this really has been going on for years, then we could be talking thousands of dollars. Tens of thousands of dollars. Maybe more. This isn't a petty crime.

"Do you think she could go to jail?" I ask, and I can tell as soon as the words leave me that Quint and Morgan were thinking the same thing. It's hard to imagine Shauna in a jumpsuit and prison cell.

"Probably," says Morgan. "If Rosa decides to press charges."

"I guess that's up to her." Quint draws himself up, squaring his shoulders. "All right. Let's go find Mom."

The theater lobby is full of excited chatter. Trish is currently acting as DJ and "With a Little Help from My Friends" by the Beatles is playing. The three of us pause, scanning the crowded room. Though lots of guests have taken their seats and started on their cheeseburgers, plenty of people are loitering by the silent auction table and around Quint's photos. A few others are chatting with Trish and flipping through her karaoke songbook, maybe gearing up to perform once dinner is over.

Rather than pay the exorbitant amount it would have cost for professional servers, food is being passed by more volunteers, including a fair amount of students I recognize from our high school, all wearing matching yellow volunteer shirts as they carry plates of cheeseburgers, clear tables, and refill water glasses. Something tells me this, too, was Quint's doing. Popular Quint, pulling people into his sphere, asking for their help, and actually getting it.

This would have been the highlight of the evening, at least for me. The food smells delicious. The auction prizes look great. Wallets are opening, and the snippets of conversation I can hear suggest that Rosa's speech was well received. Everyone is having a good time. The Fortuna Beach Sea Animal Rescue Center's inaugural gala is, by all measures, an enormous success.

I might feel pride in knowing that I had a part in making this happen, but it's overshadowed by my resentment at not being able to see it through to the end.

"Dude," says Ezra, walking toward us with half a cheeseburger slider in his hand. He's wearing a yellow volunteer shirt, but something tells me he hasn't been taking his server duties very seriously. "These are the best sliders I've ever had. Have you tried one yet?"

"I'm good," says Quint, waving off his friend. "Hey, EZ, have you seen my mom?"

"She was over there a minute ago," Ezra says, pointing with the burger before taking another bite. "So, is there a whodunnit story or what? Wait! Don't tell me. Let me guess." He lifts one pointed eyebrow. "It was the lifeguard, in the pool, with a fishhook!"

Quint stares at him blankly.

"What, not even a smile?" says Ezra, throwing his head back in dismay. "Come on! I've been working on that joke for, like, ten minutes."

"Really?" drawls Morgan. "And *that's* the best you could come up with?"

"Look, I'll fill you in later, okay?" says Quint. He starts to pass him, but Ezra stops him with a hand on his arm.

"Hold on, dude." He reaches over and grabs a glass of wine off the bar. "You look like you need a drink." Then he adds, whispering, "And they're totally not carding anyone."

"Uh. No, thanks," says Quint, ignoring Ezra as he searches for his mom.

"Prudence? Snarky girl whose name I don't know?" says Ezra, holding the glass toward me and Morgan.

"I'm fine," I say.

Morgan just gives him a look of contempt.

"Suit yourself." Ezra tips the glass up, downing half of it in one gulp.

"There, I see her," says Quint.

I follow his gesture and spot Rosa near one of the easels. She's holding a glass of wine and gesturing at the photo as she talks with a guest.

Shauna is with her. She looks completely at ease, her gray hair neatly curled, a bright-colored silk scarf around her neck. She's wearing big rhinestone earrings that catch my eye even from the other side of the room.

Just for the heck of it, I try squeezing my fist again. Come on, Universe. If you could just take care of this mess for us, this evening would go so much smoother . . .

But, like in the theater, nothing happens.

Quint inhales slowly and makes his way across the room. Morgan and I follow close behind. We are a united front.

Quint interrupts the conversation. "Mom? Can I talk to you?"

Rosa startles, turning so fast she bumps into Quint's arm. The wine splashes out of her glass, spilling across the parquet floor. "Oh gosh, I'm so sorry," she says, looking around for a napkin.

"It's fine," says Quint. "Mom—"

"I've been wondering where you ran off to." Rosa is still beaming. "I was just telling this gentleman all about your interest in photography and how you want to get your diving certification after . . ." Her attention lands on me and her smile falls. Surprise and confusion war across her features. "Oh. Hello, Prudence," she says, her politeness tinged with frost. "I didn't expect to see you tonight."

"I'm glad she's here," Quint says forcefully. "Actually, Mom, I'd like to talk to you and Shauna, if I could." He glances at Shauna. "In private."

Bewildered, Rosa looks around at all of us. The man she was speaking with clears his throat and excuses himself to get a refill on his drink.

Shauna looks bewildered, but a second later I see the wheels turning as she looks between me and Quint.

"This seems like a rather inconvenient time," says Shauna, chuckling, though her smile has an edge. "We are in the middle of throwing a party. Why don't the three of you kids grab some food and go relax. Quint, I know how hard you worked to pull this off. And, I suppose, so did you, Prudence. Despite . . . everything." Derision coats her words, and I glare at her.

"Shauna is right," Rosa says. "I need to keep mingling with our guests—"

"This will only take a minute," says Quint. "And it can't wait."

"It will have to," says Shauna. "Rosa, I see Grace Livingstone's family over at table nine. I think you should probably offer your condolences."

I turn around and spy not just Maya's parents, but Maya herself, wearing a royal-blue shift dress and looking beyond bored.

"Oh, you're right." Rosa puts a hand over her heart. "Grace was such a good supporter." Then she pauses, her tone going cold again. "But I suppose you already know that, don't you?" She gives me a look, and I bristle.

She goes to walk past us, Shauna on her heels, but Quint blocks their path. "I don't want to make a scene," he says. "But this is important. Please."

Shauna's cheeks take on a reddish hue, and her eyes spark. Suddenly, she looks like a different person. An angry person. A defensive person. A person suddenly, unexpectedly backed into a corner.

"You don't want to make a scene?" she says, and unlike Quint's, her voice goes higher. We're beginning to draw attention, which I suspect is exactly what she wants. She tosses her arm in my direction. "Then what is she doing here, Quint? And why are you with her? She is a liar and a thief. She has no business being here and I think she should leave."

"Shauna," Rosa hisses, even while trying to smile at the nearest guests. "Okay, Quint. Fine. Let's step back into the auditorium and you can say what you need to say."

"No," says Shauna. "This is typical adolescent peer pressure, Rosa. And while I know he is your son, you do not need to tolerate this. For him to bring in this drama on our big night—the center's big night. You should know better, Quint." She clucks her tongue in a way that vaguely reminds me of my grandmother. "Now, if you'll excuse me."

She tries to step around Quint, but this time I step forward, my arms crossed. I'm shaking with adrenaline and anger. And unlike Quint, I'm not so worried about making a scene.

After all, I know there are reporters here, planning to do a big write-up about the event in this week's papers. Quint may not agree with this, but as far as I'm concerned, no publicity is bad publicity. Make a big enough scene and we might even make the front page.

"I'm not the one causing all the drama," I say, my voice loud enough that all the people who are pretending not to eavesdrop can hear me plainly. "You are, Shauna. You stole that money, just like you stole money from your last job, just like you've stolen the donations from tonight's ticket sales." I look at Rosa, who looks appalled and embarrassed, but also the tiniest bit curious. "That's why there's never as much money in the account as you think there should be. Shauna has been embezzling it. She's done it before."

Rosa is shaking her head. "What are you . . . okay. That's enough. Let's go. Into the theater. Come on."

"I'm not going anywhere," says Shauna. "And I will not stand here and listen to these unfounded accusations!"

"I checked tonight's ticket sales," says Quint. "I know you're having funds routed directly to your own bank account."

There's a gasp around us, and I realize we've become the center of attention. Everyone has gone silent. Everyone is watching. Even the music has stopped.

"But . . . Shauna has been with us for more than a decade," says Rosa. "I would have . . ." She trails off, and I know she's wondering whether she would have noticed if Shauna was stealing from her. She's always so busy, but her roles at the center are managing the people and caring for the animals, not the finances. When it comes to money, all she does is sign where she's told to sign.

Where Shauna tells her to sign.

She looks at Shauna, dismayed. "Is this true?"

"Of course not," Shauna spits, and it's easily the worst lie she's ever told. Her face has gone red, her breathing short, her eyes ablaze. "This girl"—she points a finger at me—"this girl has been nothing but trouble since day one." She takes a step closer. I hold my ground, relatively certain that she wouldn't try to hit me, not surrounded by this many people. Even so, I see Quint tense out of the corner of my eye, and I brace myself for whatever horrible thing she'll say next, knowing that this time, at least, I'm in the right. I haven't done anything wrong, but *she* has, and her lies are piling up, mounting by the second. She deserves to be punished. "And now she's spreading these awful rumors, trying to turn you against me to save her own—"

I clench my fist.

Her heel hits the puddle of spilled wine and she yelps. Her arms flail. One of her hands catches my arm, yanking me forward.

Then we're both falling.

She doesn't let go.

I can't brace for the fall.

My head strikes the corner of the auction table and, for the second time this summer, my world goes black.

FORTY-SEVEN

I open my eyes to twinkling lights and yellow streamers. Quint is hovering over me, one hand cradling my head. His lips curl in relief when my eyes meet his.

"Déjà vu," he mutters.

I respond with a groan. The throbbing in my head is every bit as terrible as it was when I fell at Encanto, and the worried chatter around me isn't helping.

"Give her space," says Quint, gesturing for everyone to move back.

I slowly sit up, pressing my fingers to my temple in an effort to stop the pounding.

"There, see?" says a shrill voice. Shauna is sitting in a chair nearby, holding a bottle of cold water to her shoulder. "She's fine. And for the record, I did not assault her. It was an accident. You all saw."

"That's enough, Shauna," says Rosa, her voice sharp. "Besides, this isn't the lawsuit you should be worried about."

Shauna gapes at her, astounded. "You wouldn't . . . after all I've done for this organization?"

Rosa's chest puffs out and I know it's taking all her willpower not to scream some mighty harsh things at Shauna right now, but she manages to hold her tongue in front of so many guests. "I'm not making any decisions tonight, but I will be meeting with an attorney. In the meantime, just in case there was any confusion . . . you're fired."

Shauna holds her glare for a heartbeat, before snorting. She drops the water bottle on the counter and grabs one of the champagne glasses that's been left there, half-drunk. "Fine. See how long your precious charity stays open without me."

"Oh, I think we'll do okay," says Rosa. "We might finally be able to flourish, without you draining the funds every chance you get."

Shauna ignores her, downs the champagne, then stands up and storms off through the crowd.

I try one more time before she goes, squeezing my fist.

Nothing happens.

Not only does nothing happen, but my grip feels weak. My chest feels strangely hollow.

I look down at my hand, dread whirling through my thoughts. Could it be . . . ?

"Here," says Morgan, throwing a white linen napkin onto the spilled drink and mopping it up. "Don't need anyone else getting hurt."

It's a simple act, but a selfless one. A good deed.

Please, oh please . . .

I snap my finger and hold my breath.

"Either you're really clumsy," Morgan says, picking up the napkin, "or really unlucky." She drops it onto a serving tray cluttered with empty dishes and abandoned wineglasses.

And . . . that's it.

No kismet befalls her. No unexpected windfall. No reward.

Maybe cleaning up a spill isn't a big-enough deed to warrant the universe's attention. I peer around the room and spy a man dropping some cash into the donation box on the stage.

I try again. Snap. Snap. *Snap.*

The man returns to his table. If he's received good karma as a result of his donation, there's no sight of it.

"No," I whisper. "Please."

"Pru?" Quint is frowning at me. His hand is still supporting me, pressed between my shoulder blades. "What's wrong?"

I pout at him. I can't help it. "I think it's gone."

"What's gone?"

I sniff, even though I know I'm being melodramatic. I don't care. There were times when I thought my karmic ability was a curse, but . . . for the most part, it was a fun curse.

"The universe," I mutter.

Quint's frown deepens. He watches me for a long moment, before turning toward his mom. "Maybe we should call an ambulance."

"No," I say. "I'm fine. Could you help me up?"

"I'm not sure you should—"

Ignoring him, I grasp Quint's arm and use it to pull myself up. He stumbles once but we both manage to make it to our feet without crashing back to the floor.

"Prudence?" says Rosa, grasping my elbow. "You should see a doctor, especially if this is the second head injury you've had this summer."

"Ugh, fine," I say. I don't have the strength to argue anymore. Not with anyone. Not tonight. "I'll go tomorrow. Just . . . please don't call an ambulance. This night has been weird enough."

Rosa frowns. I can see her waffling, so to prove that I'm all right, I smile at her. "I'm okay. I promise."

She sighs heavily. "Quint, why don't you get her some water?"

Quint glances around. "Ezra," he says, pointing at his friend in the crowd. "Water?"

"Gin and tonic, coming right up," says Ezra, scurrying off to the bar.

"He's joking." Quint smiles sheepishly at his mom. "I think."

Rosa takes my hands into hers. "You were very brave to come here tonight, especially after everything that happened. I'm so sorry to have put you through this. I'm sorry for the way we treated you. I'm not sure you'll want to come back after everything that's happened, but please know that you are always welcome at the center."

I pretend to consider this. "Don't suppose you're in need of an event coordinator?"

She laughs. "I don't think I'm in a position to be hiring full-time staff yet, but you'll be the first person I contact if I do."

"Prudence would probably make an exceptional office manager," says Quint, grinning. "And I hear that position just opened up."

Rosa groans. "I will have to replace Shauna. Forgive me if I try to find someone with a bit more experience."

"Just as long as you Google them first," I say. "Maybe check for a criminal record?"

She nods. "Lesson learned."

"As for me . . ." I smile. "I definitely want to come back. I need to spend as much time with Lennon as I can before he goes to his new home."

Rosa's eyes crinkle in the corners and before I know what's happening, she's pulled me into an embrace. "Thank you, Prudence." She sighs as she pulls away and looks around at the crowd watching us. She laughs. "Well. This has certainly turned into a memorable evening, hasn't it?" Then she waves her hand at the crowd. "Everyone, please, let's sit and enjoy our meal."

After that, the night begins to blur from moment to moment, and I'm not sure if it's the dull thrum in my head that's causing it, or simply that there's so much going on. Dinner is followed by dessert. The winners of the silent auction are announced, and I'm ecstatic to learn that the record store's basket went for a lot more money than I expected it to. Then raffle tickets are drawn for Quint's photos. I'm not surprised at how many tickets have been purchased, and the people who win them appear genuinely ecstatic to be taking one of the masterpieces home with them. When one woman's ticket number is called, she literally screams with delight.

I glance at Quint. His expression is priceless. Bewildered and proud at the same time.

As dishes and chairs are cleared away, the karaoke begins—Trish and a couple of volunteers sing "Yellow Submarine" to get people in the mood, and practically the whole room joins in for the chorus.

And just like that, the ambiance of the evening changes from serious and charitable to energetic and fun. This is an event that people will be talking—and joking—about for weeks.

Not only did Quint have the brilliant idea to have Trish host karaoke, but he even thought to incorporate another fundraising portion. Guests have to pay five dollars to sing, with all proceeds, of course, going to the center. I never would have thought it would work, and I would have been wrong. People are lining up to write down their names and song choices on those little slips of paper.

I hear nearby tables coercing one another, even bribing and cajoling one another to go up on that stage. I hear debates over which songs to sing and whose voices are truly terrible. Rather than the required donation keeping people away, asking them to pay seems to have encouraged them.

As a lovely white-haired lady with a walking cane gets up to sing "Stardust," one of my favorite old standards, I feel a twist of envy. I know, with my head still throbbing, I'm in no form to get up there and sing. I couldn't give it my all, and without giving it my all, there's really no point.

I scan the crowd, again, as I have every few minutes. It's like I have a radar attuned to Quint, and I keep hoping that maybe he'll seek *me* out. Despite having done what I came here to do, the evening feels unfinished. Anticlimactic. I know there's a lot left unsaid between me and Quint, but every time I see him, he's busy talking to someone new, grinning and gesturing at one of his photos. He's in his element, and I want to be happy for him, but . . . I also can't help but wonder whether he's avoiding me.

Despite how much he hurt me, in all my fantasies over the past few weeks, one thing has stayed constant. Yes, I want his apology. Yes, I want him to plead for forgiveness. Yes, I want to hear him say how wrong he was not to trust me.

But more than any of that, I want him to still *like* me.

As much as I still like him.

But what if that isn't the case? What if in these last weeks he's realized he never wanted me to begin with. That it was all a huge mistake—just like he said.

I need to get out of here.

I stand up. I'll slip out while no one is watching. I won't have to say goodbye to Morgan or Rosa or anyone. As I make my way to the exit, I don't look back at Quint, just in case he notices me trying to leave. Because I couldn't stand it if he saw and didn't try to stop me.

I'll have to face him eventually. If I'm going to continue volunteering at the center, I'll have to confront the way he hurt me. And school is starting again soon, and there's a good chance we'll have some classes together. I'll have to accept that whatever happened between us is really and truly over.

As I pass the now-empty auction table, something catches my eye.

I nearly trip over my feet. There's something glinting up at me, tucked just behind one of the table legs, almost hidden by the tablecloth.

I crouch and pick it up.

It's a vintage diamond earring hooked onto a chain necklace. The clasp must have broken when Shauna and I fell.

The diamond winks at me.

I chuckle to myself. "Nice one, Universe."

I turn and spot Maya sitting at the same table where I noticed her before, staring at her phone. I could go give it to her, but I don't really want the credit for finding this earring any more than I want the blame for it first having been lost.

"Excuse me?" I say to a passing volunteer. "Could you give this to that girl over there? I think she lost it."

"Oh, sure." The volunteer takes the earring with some uncertainty, but doesn't ask any questions.

I stick around just long enough to see the earring delivered. To see Maya's shock, her disbelief—her utter joy. She actually starts crying as she clutches it to her heart, then stands up and gives the stunned volunteer a tight hug.

Too bad that isn't Jude, I think. Then I would have just made two people's nights.

Onstage, the sweet old lady finishes her song, and I clap with as much enthusiasm as I can—but my heart isn't in it. The theater might be overflowing with good vibes, good music, and more generosity than I could have imagined, but my heart is still broken.

I start to turn away.

"Next up," Trish says into the microphone, "one of the rescue center's most beloved and longtime volunteers. Please welcome to the stage . . . Quint Erickson!"

I spin around so fast I nearly lose my balance.

Surely she didn't just say . . .

And there he is, walking up onto the stage. He smiles nervously at Trish as he takes the microphone from her. He looks positively terrified.

He clears his throat, nodding gratefully at the applause that's followed him to the platform. "Sorry," he says, giving an awkward wave to the audience. "You all don't deserve the torture I'm about to put you through, but . . . it's for a good cause, right? So . . . here goes."

There's some mild laughter. Some encouraging whoops.

The music begins.

My stomach drops.

"*Dear Prudence . . . won't you come out to play?*"

I hear a few gasps and feel people searching me out and, when they find me, pointing and whispering.

Quint, too, is scanning the room. But once he finds me, his eyes stay locked on mine.

My mouth goes dry as I listen, and a small part of me thinks I should be mortified by the attention, but I'm not.

I'm awestruck.

I'm delirious.

I'm . . . a little worried that this might not mean what I want it to mean.

"*The sun is up, the sky is blue. It's beautiful, and so are you, dear Prudence . . .*"

My heart is beating so hard it might pound right out of my chest.

His singing voice is . . . not great, I'll admit. But the way he's looking at me, and the way he's blushing, and how he goofs up on the second verse and has to check the lyrics on the monitor and how he looks so flustered and so scared, how he still somehow manages to find me in the crowd again . . .

I. Am. Mesmerized.

The song ends, and I dare to breathe. It might be the first breath I've taken since he went up there.

Quint clears his throat and puts the mic on the stand. He backs up like he can't get away from it fast enough.

The theater fills with applause, as it has after every song. Quint waves nonchalantly, an aw-shucks-but-please-stop wave, charming as ever, and steps off the stage.

I'm moving before I realize it, making my way through the tables.

His lips quirk when he sees me. He looks painfully insecure, but also hopeful. "I tried your trick," he says, once we're close enough. "I thought, it's only four minutes of your life, Quint. You can get through this. But is it just me, or is that song, like, two hours long?"

"Songs always seem longer when you're up there. I call it the karaoke time-warp."

"Now you tell me." His lashes dip briefly. His voice lowers. "So. How'd I do?"

I don't know what to say. I can barely think, much less form coherent words.

And so, I start to laugh. Embarrassed, I clap a hand over my mouth.

Quint grimaces. "That bad?"

"No," I say, daring to take one more step. He shoves his hands into his pockets and takes a step toward me, too. "I mean, you're no John Lennon. But I've heard worse."

"I'll accept that." He squeezes one eye shut. "Can we talk? Um . . . somewhere else?"

I take in a long breath, and nod.

The auditorium is empty and eerily quiet once Quint shuts the door. I walk a little ways down the aisle, needing distance, needing space to calm my thundering heart, before I turn to face him.

He's leaning against the door. His expression is positively tortured.

"I was awful," he says, before I can say anything. "I was mean. I was trying to hurt you, and I said all those things, and . . ." He inhales deeply. "I'm so sorry, Prudence. I didn't mean them."

I look away. The apology is so sudden, so fast on the heels of his song, that my emotions have tangled together. I'm nothing but a ball of feelings. I want this apology, I do, but it doesn't feel earned. Not exactly. Not yet.

"Are you sure about that?" I ask.

"Prudence . . ."

"No, really. You can't tell me you hadn't thought those things about me, probably a thousand times before you actually said them. Critical, judgmental, selfish . . ."

He winces and his head falls. "I . . . yes, I used to . . . but I don't . . ."

"The thing is, Quint." I brace myself. "I'm not sure you said anything that wasn't true."

He shakes his head.

"Except the thief thing. I didn't take that money. But . . . I did think about it."

His gaze snaps back to me, surprised.

"Not for me or for my parents. I thought I would use it to buy Maya's earring back for her. And honestly, I still don't know whether that would have been the right thing to do or not."

His brow furrows thoughtfully. "Well, the right thing probably would have been to talk to my mom about it. She would have helped get the earring back."

I stare at him, momentarily dumbfounded. How does he do that? This ethical dilemma that had me tied in knots . . . how can he solve it so simply, so easily?

"Huh," I say. "It probably should have been given to you."

Quint frowns. "The money?"

"No. Never mind." I squeeze my eyes shut. It doesn't matter if the power of cosmic justice was given to me, and it doesn't matter that I very well might have been the wrong person to wield it. I'm fairly certain it's gone now. "I was just thinking that your moral compass might be a bit more finely tuned than mine."

Quint waits for me to look at him again before responding, "That's a weird thing to say."

"I know."

"But, thanks?"

"Look, my point is, those things you said about me before . . . I don't want them to be true." My voice squeaks, and I know I could start crying any minute. "I want to be someone who's kind and forgiving. The sort of person who sees the good in other people, rather than . . . casting judgment all the time." I smile sadly. "And when I'm around you, I become more like that person."

I swipe at my eyes before any tears can fall. Take in a deep breath. Then wave my hand at Quint. "Okay. Now that I said all that . . . you can go back to telling me how sorry you are. I probably shouldn't have interrupted."

His expression starts to relax. "You do make it hard to give you compliments, you know that?"

I raise my eyes toward the ceiling. "So I'm difficult, too?"

"*Yes,*" he says, with so much feeling I can't help but feel a little defensive. "Yes, Prudence. You are easily one of the most difficult people I've ever known." He opens his palms, looking helpless. "And yet . . . I still really want to make out with you."

I snort, then immediately cover my face with both hands. "Quint!"

He's laughing at me when I dare to peek through my fingers. He hasn't moved away from the door, almost like he's guarding the exit in case I decide to make a run for it. But there's nowhere I would rather be than right here, blushing and awkward and hopeful.

I slowly lower my hands. He's still smiling, but it's taken on a serious note.

"Honestly?" he says. "I like you, Prudence. I like you a lot. And I know I hurt you, and I am so sorry."

I nod slowly. "I forgive you."

He hesitates. "I don't think it should be that easy."

I gesture toward the lobby beyond the door. "You just serenaded me in front of all those people. How much harder would you like me to make it?"

He looks thoughtful, as if he'd almost forgotten about this tidbit. "You're right. That was the hardest thing I've ever done. And also, like, really romantic of me."

I chuckle. "Besides, I'm sorry, too. For all those times I was so difficult."

We stare at each other, the aisle spanning an entire ocean between us. I so badly want to take a step toward him, but my feet are glued to the red carpet, and he hasn't made any move toward me, either. So we're stuck. I feel like we've been stuck here, hopelessly divided, all year.

"You know what, Prudence?" he says. "If you're going to apologize to me for something . . . it should be that lipstick."

I start, and reach my fingers to my lips.

He shakes his head, forlorn. "I mean, come on. That's just cruel."

I bite down on my lower lip, and he groans quietly. I flush and can't keep from smiling. "Morgan thinks it might be tested on animals, so . . ."

"I think it's been tested on me plenty."

My pulse dances.

"Quint?"

"Prudence?"

I take a step toward him, at the same moment he finally pushes away from the door.

We meet in the middle.

FORTY-EIGHT

Prudence: A
Quint: A
Overall: A+

Thoughtful presentation, concise writing, and a number of convincing arguments, all well-researched and well-executed. I'm impressed! I particularly enjoyed hearing how you've been working together to implement your ideas at the sea animal rescue center. You've proposed a truly ingenious plan for bringing ecotourism to our area in a way that benefits our community and our local wildlife and habitats. This report is a great example of what can be accomplished when two people overcome their differences and work together.

I'm exceptionally proud of you both. Nicely done.

"Satisfied?" asks Quint. We're in our booth at Encanto, reading Mr. Chavez's email on his phone.

I screw my lips to one side, considering. "How come we got an A+ overall, but I only got an A? What's up with that?"

"Because," he says, sliding an arm around my shoulders, "you're pretty great on your own, but you're even better with me."

I grumble, even though . . . I can't deny it.

He reaches over and closes the email. The screen switches to his home screen. The wallpaper beneath his apps is a picture of me—the photo he took on the beach during the Freedom Festival. When he showed it to me, he said it might be his favorite picture he's ever taken. In part because the lighting was just so good that day, but mostly because my dimples are on full display.

I told him that would be really flattering if I wasn't mostly competing with injured, malnourished pinnipeds.

"You two are making me uncomfortable," says Jude, sandwiched between me and Ari. He has his sketchbook in his lap, trying to come up with a fearsome new creature to use in his D&D campaign. The only part of it he seems happy with is a pair of vicious-looking horns on the creature's head. Everything else has already been erased and redrawn a hundred times.

I reach out and smack him on the shoulder. "Admit it. You think we're super cute."

Jude raises an eyebrow at me. "I think Ewoks are super cute. I think you two are a made-for-TV movie."

"*I* think made-for-TV movies are super cute," Ari points out.

"Got it!" yells Ezra, jamming his finger down on the songbook. "'Too Sexy.' That's my song. All the way."

"As in, 'I'm Too Sexy'?" asks Morgan.

"No," says Ezra. "As in, *I'm* too sexy." He taps his chest. "Though you're not half-bad."

Morgan looks briefly disgusted, but then she gets a wicked look in her eye and leans toward him. "Do you know what's *really* hot?"

He leans toward her.

"Maturity."

A devious grin spreads over Ezra's lips. "Oh my god, you are so right. For example, Quint's mom is a total babe."

Quint groans and hides his face behind one hand.

Ari casts me a look, but I can only shrug. I'm not entirely sure what to do with EZ, either, but he and Quint have been best friends since elementary school, so I think it's a package deal.

"Hand me one of those slips, would you, Jude? Jude the Dude?" asks Ezra.

Jude looks up from his sketchbook, but Ari has already beat him to it. She hands Ezra a karaoke slip with a look of resignation, before taking the song-book for herself. "I have an idea for you and me, Pru," she says, flipping through the pages. "Here. What do you think?" She holds the book up. "Of Monsters and Men duet?"

I shrug. "I don't know who that is."

"Prudence!" She throws her head back. "I don't know how much longer I can be friends with you if you don't start expanding your musical knowledge."

Jude nods. "Even I know Of Monsters and Men."

I look at Quint. He shrugs. "Yep. They're pretty good."

Morgan and Ezra nod at me, too.

I turn back to Ari. "Sorry?"

She sighs and starts flipping through the book again. "I'm going to find something you can't say no to. And *not* John Lennon and Yoko Ono. There has to be something else in here."

"Hey," I say, turning my attention back to Quint, "did you get your class schedule yet?"

"Not yet. Why?"

"Just wondering whether we're going to be in the same chemistry class. I thought maybe we could be lab partners, if they aren't preassigned."

He raises an eyebrow. "Only a masochist would volunteer to be *your* lab partner."

"I'll be your lab partner," says Ezra.

I cringe, then look pleadingly at Quint. He hums to himself, as if this were a big decision and he really has to think it over.

I kiss him. He melts against me, his arm tightening, drawing me closer.

Beside me, Jude mutters, "I would literally rather be thrown into the fires of Mount Doom than be stuck in this booth right now."

I pull away and kick my brother under the table, but he just starts to chuckle. I know he has to play the grossed-out-brother card, but I also know he likes Quint and he's really happy for us.

Someday, I hope to see him this happy. And Ari, too, for that matter.

"So?" I ask, refocusing on Quint. "What do you say, *partner?*"

"Hey, did you not see my kickass presentation on shark fin soup? Evidently, that stuff is delicious."

Morgan gasps audibly. "You are barbaric."

I meet Quint's eye again. "Please rescue me."

He grins. "I guess someone has to be your partner, so I might as well take one for the team."

"How very generous of you."

"Just trying to build up my good karma points."

"I'm sure the universe will reward you greatly."

"You know what?" says Quint. "I think it already has."

We kiss again, and I can't help but smile against him—blissfully, cosmically happy.

I swear I can feel the universe smiling back.

Acknowledgments

So. Much. Gratitude.

To begin, I am exceptionally indebted to the incredible volunteers and staff at the Pacific Marine Mammal Center in Laguna Beach, California, for giving me a behind-the-scenes peek into their facility and for allowing me to pester them for hours with questions about their center and the animals they care for. I came away from this visit with a heart full of love for these beautiful creatures and with a head full of amazing real-life stories, many that went on to inspire the stories of various animals in this book. I am particularly grateful to Amanda Walters, the education instructor at PMMC, for answering my questions about rainstorms and flooding protocol, among other things, and helping to fact-check the final book. If the stories of sea animals in this book have touched your heart, I highly recommend following the Pacific Marine Mammal Center on Instagram, @pacificmmc, or visiting them at pacificmmc.org.

Similarly, I am so grateful for the staff at the Point Defiance Zoo & Aquarium in Tacoma, Washington, for answering yet more of my endless questions about sea animals and their habitats, care, and rehabilitation. (As a sidenote, any factual errors related to the animals or the care they receive are entirely my fault or a result of creative license.)

Thank you also to Alexander Atwood for his musical expertise, particularly with his help writing the chapter in which Ari nerds out over "Daniel" by Elton John. (Alex is also a great ukulele instructor—thanks, Alex!—and has a YouTube channel for anyone interested in learning how to play bass guitar. Find him at youtube.com/stepbystepbass.)

I am so grateful to all my Spanish-speaking readers on Twitter who helped me figure out what on earth to name Carlos's restaurant. (I will always be a little sad that ¡Vamos Plátanos! or Let's Go Bananas! didn't work out, but I'll probably get over it.) Many thanks as well to Alejandra for her focused sensitivity read.

As always, I send all the gratitude in the world to my excellent team at Macmillan Children's Publishing Group. Liz! Jean! Jon! Mary! Jo! Morgan! Rich! Brittany! Allison! Mariel! Everybody else! You guys are the best, and I am so proud and honored to call Macmillan my publishing home. I also owe many thanks to my copyeditor, Anne Heausler, who always keeps me from making truly embarrassing mistakes. And to my audiobook narrator, Rebecca Soler, for using her talent to bring so much fantastic life to my stories and characters.

Speaking of homes—an enormous thank-you goes to my agent, Jill Grinberg, and her whole crew: Sam Farkas, Denise Page, Katelyn Detweiler, and Sophia Seidner. Your support and diligence are unparalleled, and I am so delighted to get to work with you.

And of course, to the best beta-reader any author could ever ask for, Tamara Moss (@writermoss). I truly don't know what I would do without you and the years of feedback, encouragement, and writerly wisdom you've given me. I send you all the hugs.

Last, but never, ever least—to my husband, Jesse (whose favorite movie is *Jaws*), and my shark-obsessed daughter, Delaney (whose favorite movie is now also *Jaws*), and my non-shark-obsessed daughter, Sloane, both of whom provided so much delightful fodder for Pru's little sister. I guess I must have done something right because the universe was definitely smiling on me when it brought you three into my life.

Thank you for reading this FEIWEL & FRIENDS book.
The friends who made

possible are

Jean Feiwel, PUBLISHER

Liz Szabla, ASSOCIATE PUBLISHER

Rich Deas, SENIOR CREATIVE DIRECTOR

Holly West, SENIOR EDITOR

Anna Roberto, SENIOR EDITOR

Kat Brzozowski, SENIOR EDITOR

Dawn Ryan, SENIOR MANAGING EDITOR

Kim Waymer, SENIOR PRODUCTION MANAGER

Erin Siu, ASSOCIATE EDITOR

Emily Settle, ASSOCIATE EDITOR

Rachel Diebel, ASSISTANT EDITOR

Foyinsi Adegbonmire, EDITORIAL ASSISTANT

Ilana Worrell, SENIOR PRODUCTION EDITOR

Follow us on Facebook or visit us online at mackids.com.

Our books are friends for life.